THE SEVEN SISTERS

Frederic Prokosch

THE
SEVEN
SISTERS

New York
Farrar, Straus and Cudahy

THE SEVEN SISTERS

Part One

The mist in the morning that covers the cool, unruffled coves,
the autumn leaves burning and the lapping among the reeds,
the musk of rotting woods and the coppery rush of the pheasant:
these are the ghosts that haunt the Chesapeake and they haunt it
still today just as they haunted it a hundred or a thousand years
ago.

The green of Bishop's Neck was even greener than the rest of
the shore. The mists at Bishop's Neck were tart with myrtle
and sassafras. The buzzing of bees hung over the fields in the
summertime. The dusk-light was striped with tigerish shadows
down in the rushes and the dawn-light was veiled with a lurking
uneasiness. The hills in the distance were as blue and sleek as a
catfish; the echoes came wandering out of nowhere into nowhere. And there were times when Bishop's Neck didn't seem

to be a place at all, it was merely the spectre-like peace of the unrememberable.

Peter lived with his grandmother in a cottage above an inlet, with a path leading through the orchard down to the road to Pendleton's Landing. He picked strawberries in the spring when the air was fresh and cool and the irises were flowering in the swamp in Burpee's Hollow. Then the foliage grew rich; black-eyed Susans bloomed in the field; he picked raspberries from the bushes and blood-red cherries from the cherry-trees. There were crabapples and peaches and quinces and blackberries, and all of these were turned into jams and jellies in granny's kitchen. She would pour them into jars and neatly seal them with paraffin, and these beautiful glowing jars were set on a stand by the roadside, with the shapes of the fruits still faintly visible through the glass, their tiny seeds floating in the crimson and amber gelatine. Sometimes he sold only a single jar all afternoon, and sometimes he sold as many as five or six of them; the price was a quarter apiece.

Granny also raised chickens as well as vegetables, but everything she raised grew somehow wrinkled and gnarled and leathery. Her old-woman smell clung to the plums and tomatoes, and her radishes had a sour, fermented taste, almost like vinegar. Sometimes Peter stole silently into the chicken-coop behind the kitchen and watched the hens in their nests, looking stupid and tense and purposeful, and he'd pick up an egg, still warm and aromatic. He'd hold it against the light and marvel at the smooth warm perfection, always the same flawless shape and the clean, delicate texture.

He used to sit in the kitchen and watch his granny peel potatoes, and he watched her with the same clandestine wonder that he felt for the egg. He looked at her face with the slate-blue blotches on the cheeks and the network of fine mustard wrinkles under the eyes. He looked at the wisps of hair on her chin and the keen, shrewd shape of her ears, and the most mysterious part of her was the quick-darting eyes, not pale like his mother's but a deep inky black in which wisdom and slyness and lunacy all melted together. There were times when she looked like a witch, crouching low as she stirred the kettle; there were times when she looked like destiny, knitting away in front of the fire; and there were times when she looked like a ghost, so terribly thin, almost like smoke, almost invisible among her multitude of petticoats and shawls. As he watched her sinewy hands and the quivering of her Adam's apple he sensed that she was no longer a woman, no longer a mere individual, and instead of seeming old and wrinkled and a little bit crazy she grew mysterious and supernatural, she grew inhuman as the wind in the cedars.

When he had a wart she dipped a needle in the blood of a chicken and pierced the wart with it. When he suffered from hiccoughs she tucked a peanut behind his ear. When he had a cold she boiled some hornets in a mixture of vinegar and cowpiss and wrapped the hot poultice around his throat. And all of these cures were marvelously effective, he was healed almost instantly, and he knew that there was a power in his grandmother which was deeper than mere wisdom. She was in tune with all the hidden communications of nature; she was like the brook gurgling in the hollows or like the whispering among the cat-tails.

Sometimes at night she sat by the stove and started to sing one of her songs—"Down the Street the Storm is Blowing," or "Beneath Thy Window I Walk Alone." They were songs that dated back to her childhood in Poland, and as she sang small blue tears shone on the pouches under her eyes.

She told him about Cleopatra, who was swallowed by a dragon, and Boadicea, who turned into a wolf; she told him about Catherine of Russia who dined on roasted peacocks, and Catherine de Medici who swallowed the blood of her victims. She told him about Queen Christina, who gave birth to a softshelled turtle, and the Dowager Empress of China, who turned her lovers into eunuchs. And as she told him about these queens, with the firelight flickering in her eyes, she seemed to absorb all their passions and embody all their wickedness; they found a tremulous reincarnation in his wrinkled old granny.

Sometimes he said, "Will you tell me the story about the wood-elf, please, Granny?" and she answered in Polish, "All right, you little canary, just listen quietly . . ."

She folded her arms and muttered softly, "The moon was shining, I still remember, it was as bright as a silver dollar. I was walking in the woods down by Selenovice. I was bringing home a barley-cake from my cousin Wanda's. I stopped by the river for a moment, looking down into the water, and the carp were floating in the stream, so still and shiny, like silver knives. I almost thought I could pick one up and cut a slice of cake with it. But then I heard someone calling my name in the bushes. It was a sprite, a little wood-elf, no bigger than my middle-finger. His hair was green as moss and his eyes were shining like pearls. 'Help me!' he croaked, 'help me, darling!' And I said, 'What's wrong? What's happened to you?' 'I'm bewitched, that's what!' squeaked the wood-elf in a voice no louder than a mouse's. 'What can I do?' I said gently. 'Grieve for me, darling!' cried the wood-elf. 'Every tear that drops from your cheeks will bring me closer to freedom!' 'I can't grieve for you,' I said, 'I hardly know you, it isn't natural.' 'Try, try!' said the wood-elf. 'Just one tear, just one little tear!' And so I wept, out of pity or maybe it was only nervousness, and the elf started growing in front of my eyes. He grew into a child and then a boy and then a beautiful golden youth, and then he gradually grew older and started to shrivel like a prune. He turned yellow and green and then purple and black and finally he crumbled into dust, right in front of my eyes."

"Did he die?" said Peter.

"Yes, he died," said his granny. "But it's better to crumble and die than never grow up at all. And it's only through pity and love that people grow up, and if they crumble and finally die, it can't be helped, that's how things are . . ."

The only visitors that came to the house were Miss Malachi, who lived at the mansion, and Mrs. Lochwitzky, an elderly widow from Frenchman's Creek. Mrs. Lochwitzky would sit at the table with her face against the window, ruggèd and bruised and pock-marked, the face of an ancient gladiator. "Och," she said, "the whole world is going to the dogs, *kochanie!* It's heading for misery! And why? Because of ingratitude, that's why, ingratitude! I gave birth to three sons. As strong as gorillas, all three of them. One went to Warsaw and made a fortune and I never heard from him again. One went to Lodz and visited the brothels and I never heard from him again. The third brought me to America and one fine morning he went to Mexico and that was the end of it and I never heard from him again. From whose womb did they spring? Who brought them into the world? Ingratitude, just plain ingratitude! It's bringing the world to destruction!"

Peter was frightened of Mrs. Lochwitzky. There was something dark and primeval about her. Whenever she entered the kitchen he felt the breath of dank caverns, he detected a whiff of old, bloodthirsty ceremonies. He watched her butcher-like hands hammering away at the table and her poisonous gray eyes staring fiercely through the window.

Miss Malachi was a lean, towering spinster with coal-black hair. She taught music and painting to the Nightingale sisters, and dropped in on Saturday mornings for a cup of coffee with granny. She too, like Mrs. Lochwitzky, carried an aura of things unmentionable. Not savage and paleolithic, like Mrs. Lochwitzky, but caustic and sybilline; her voice was the voice of a prophetess.

"Daphne," she'd say, "is down with chicken-pox. I have a feeling about Daphne. She's a tom-boy. She's heading for trouble. Her head's in a turmoil . . ."

Or she'd say, "Poor Elizabeth. She twisted her ankle again. I don't know what it is, there is something doomed about Elizabeth . . ."

Or: "You should have heard our little Grace playing the *Grande Valse Brillante*. There is genius in the girl, if I can only bring it out of her . . ."

Or: "I am terrified for Augusta. Those bitter black eyes of hers! She struck Barbara across the face today. She is capable of murder . . ."

And Peter kept wondering about these seven strange sisters, whom he saw now and again through the iron-grilled gateway, poised motionless in the sunlight, like shapes in a frieze.

II

Armies crumbled and whole cities went up in flames, but nothing penetrated the sun-dazed stillness of Bishop's Neck. There were rumors of bloodshed in Crete and Tripolitania, but the spiders still dangled from their threads out in the garden. Finally one day, it happened to be the day after his fourteenth birthday, Peter saw Mrs. Lochwitzky come striding up the path.

She stormed into the kitchen and threw her hat on the table. "Well, at last, thank the Lord! We've joined the battle! We'll kill the villains! . . ."

And after that he did detect a slight darkening of the atmosphere, nothing tangible or dramatic, merely a lingering malaise. The dusk over the Chesapeake seemed a little darker than usual, tinged with long wispy clouds that looked like the smoke of distant battleships. And the cry of the loon that drifted over the water had a deep, deathly resonance: there was menace in the air.

But even so, since wars are usually a matter of men more than women, the change at Bishop's Neck was almost imperceptible. His granny still kept baking her apple strudel and Miss Malachi still came for her Saturday morning coffee. And when summer returned he went roving in the woods again, sometimes alone and sometimes with Cleophas, who lived in a shack on the road to Euphoria. He learned from Cleophas how to hit a sparrow in flight with a pebble, and he learned not to mind if a bee stung him in the cheek. He learned how to kill a copperhead with a whack behind the head; he even learned how to catch a cat-fish in the shallows barehanded. Cleophas was the handsomest man he had ever seen, with a voice so low that it was like a vibration in the air. He was young but his life in the woods had aged him prematurely. He was so shaggy and so enormous that he seemed a bit inhuman, more like a bullock than a man, more like an oak-tree than a human being. He wore a lumberjack shirt and corduroy pants and he usually carried a gun as well as a sack for birds or rabbits. In his belt he carried a small leather bag filled with bullets and a knife with an ivory handle which was carved like the head of a ram. His trousers were flecked with stains—the blood of beasts, birds and fish— and his hands were all gnarled with little bulges and calluses. From time to time they went fishing in the creek together, and when Cleophas caught a trout he deftly loosened the hook and took the wriggling fish and gave a twist to its head. And then the fish lay still as a stone in his big wet palm.

"Why doesn't it wriggle any more?" said Peter.

"Dead," said Cleophas in his purring voice.

"Dead," said Peter, staring at the fish.

Cleophas grinned. "Dead and done for . . ."

Cleophas had a little brown bitch whose name was Sappho, and occasionally they went hunting for pheasants with Sappho. As they moved through the trees Sappho suddenly came to a halt and up on a bough, tucked in the leaves, sat a beautiful cock-pheasant. There was a single loud burst from Cleophas's gun and the bird fell through the air, with a few red feathers drifting behind it. And a little later Cleophas put the gun in Peter's hand, pointing up at a bough, and Peter carefully took aim: and the darkish female pheasant came fluttering through the air, limp and bleeding and much sadder in her death than the tawny cock-pheasant. But when they walked back through the cedars the feeling of sadness wore away, the thought of blood was forgotten and the thought of death was forgotten, and when the stars peeped through the branches and he caught the musk of Cleophas's body a feeling of deep, trusting happiness rose in his heart. Sometimes they walked down to the hollow where Cleophas had set a trap, and once an unusually fine cock-pheasant was caught in the trap. Cleophas knelt down and took the bird from the trap and lovingly stroked his metal-bright head. The bird blinked his eyes and opened his beak in terror and Cleophas ran his gnarled ruddy hand over his back. Then he took out his knife and struck at the bird, quick as lightning. The bird gave a shudder and seemed to wilt like a broken flower, and only a single drop of blood trickled down on Cleophas's palm.

"Beasts and birds," said Cleophas thoughtfully, "are just born to keep on living, and so they live as long as they can and finally they stop living. Don't listen to all that talk, Peter, that they talk in the churches. Beasts are born, they live, they die. See that squirrel? He lives and dies."

"And after they die?"

"Well, that's the puzzle. That's what nobody's figured out yet. Whether they turn into air or whether they turn into ghosts, or whether they turn after a while into some other kind of animal, that's the puzzle and nobody knows but my own opinion is that it's over. They live and die like you and me, and when they're dead the whole thing's over, and it's sad but it's natural and there's no point in worrying about it . . ."

And at that moment, with the smell of the myrtle and grapevines all around them, and the gnats in the air and the mist settling in the underbrush, it seemed that Cleophas must be right. Whatever was natural was inevitable and in the end, however sad, was somehow bearable and even beautiful.

Once he fell over a twig and his knee started to bleed and Cleophas muttered: "Here, Pete. Get on my shoulders. I'll carry you home." And as he sat on Cleophas's shoulders with his hands resting on his head, he felt his hair under his palms and the powerful neck against his thighs, and he suddenly experienced a blinding love for Cleophas, a love that was partly gratitude and partly hero-worship but also something buried in the mists of an ancient memory. And after that he adored Cleophas and the heat and power that were in Cleophas, and this adoration was intensified when Cleophas made him a present of his ram-headed knife. There was a simplicity about Cleophas that made him seem like a part of the forest. He resembled everything that he touched, he became a part of everything he touched, and the earth and the trees grew close and intimate in Cleophas's presence.

And yet, in spite of his love for Cleophas, there was something about Cleophas that frightened him a little. Not only the ruthlessness and rawness but something sultry, impenetrable, as though some nameless malignancy were lurking in that shaggy body. Once the boy watched him bathing in the creek below the waterfall and he was fascinated by the look of smouldering power in his body. The sleek coat of soap shone on his chest muscles and belly muscles; the bubbles of lather clung to his armpits and thighs. He smiled at Peter and there was a sly sensuality in his smile, which was mirrored in the smile of his belly. And once Cleophas wandered into the bushes with the idiot girl Proserpinny and he beckoned to Peter to come and watch them through the foliage. Flecks of sunlight drifted down on the two half-naked bodies, she with her skirt drawn up to the waist and her dusky breasts uncovered, he crouching above her, bare from the navel down to the calves. It looked like the paroxysm of a two-headed monster, grunting and writhing in anguish. And after this Peter's love for him was tainted with disgust, he avoided Cleophas and stopped roving through the woods with him.

III

Now and again on one of his rambles he caught sight of Mrs. Nightingale carrying her paint-box down the path toward Burpee's Hollow. She was a small wispy woman, frail in an exotic sort of way, with bold expressive eyes and a smiling cynical mouth. She wore sandals of cowhide and a green linen smock and an enormous peaked hat of lemon-colored straw. He peeped through the trees and watched her squatting among the azaleas, squinting at the clouds and daintily sketching in the canvas. The creek lay calm and glassy; a fish jumped for a gnat; a leaf went spiraling across the dusty sunlight. And the water, the fish, the leaf took on a ritualistic significance, as though they were a part of Mrs. Nightingale's creative processes. Once she saw him lurking in the shadows and beckoned with her paint-brush.

"What is your name, dear?" she said in a broad melodious accent.

"Peter Kosowsky," said Peter.

"Where do you live?"

"Down the road a ways."

"With your family?"

"With my grandmother," said Peter fastidiously.

"And your parents?" said Mrs. Nightingale.

"They're dead," whispered Peter.

Mrs. Nightingale regarded him thoughtfully, with a kind of sly, searching tenderness. "I see. You like painting? You must tell your grandmother to buy some paints for you. You can start off with watercolors. Then you'll graduate into oils. All it needs is an eye for color and a feeling for mystery." She cocked her head sideways and measured the distance with her brush-handle.

"People think it's all brush-strokes and color and composition but the only thing that matters is a feeling for mystery."

He watched her squeeze the tubes onto the paint-speckled palette and dip her narrow brush in a tiny keg of oil. She mixed the blue and the yellow to produce a brilliant green, not quite blended but with the streaks of blue and yellow still visible. All of her colors, as she casually mingled them and thrust them on the canvas, had this queer streaky texture, half one thing and half another, so that the effect on the canvas was a chaos of rioting colors and the shapes of the trees melted into thick, gaudy whirlpools.

"You must learn not merely to *see* things," declared Mrs. Nightingale. She planted a daub of crimson across the horizon. "You must feel them. You must identify with them. You must look into the core of things. You must learn to see the mysteries that nobody else has seen there . . ."

And there were days, usually sunny ones, when he watched Mr. Nightingale as he strode through the meadow with his net on his shoulder. Mr. Nightingale was a tall, thin, absent-minded man with misty gray eyes and an iron-gray mustache. Once Peter found him kneeling in the path with a large blue butterfly in his trembling fingers.

"*Argynnis diana,*" he murmured, glancing solemnly at Peter. "They're very rare around here. This is the second one I've seen . . ."

That same evening Peter built himself a net with a sawed-off broom-handle and after that he used to stroll with Mr. Nightingale on his excursions. He quickly learned the Latin names of the various genera and species and he listened with care to Mr. Nightingale's commentaries.

"Life, my boy, is a struggle for existence. The ones that survive are the sly and crafty ones. Or it's the fast ones, or the nasty ones, or the persistent and plodding ones. Look at *Grapta interrogationis.* It is beautifully camouflaged; no one can see it. Look at *Danaus plexippus.* The flavor is so foul that no one will eat it. Look at *Samia cecropia.* It looks so frightening that no one will touch it. So it is with human beings. The frail and the beautiful perish. The ones that survive are the tough, the unpalatable, the camouflaged. And yet in the end, when you stop to think about it, the others keep surviving, *Papilio phile-nor* seems to survive just as capably as *Xylophanes tersa,* and maybe the frail and the beautiful have their own secret strength. Maybe there are times when it is a handicap to be too powerful or clever . . ."

And now and again, in the course of his wanderings, Peter caught sight of one of the sisters and he came to know their different faces and even their different names. Augusta was the oldest and darkest and most formidable, the one who went riding up in the woods at Blue Hills. Barbara was the blondest, the most beautiful; she floated through the sunlight like a creature from a fairy-tale. Consuelo was the third one; small and wispy like her mother, with the same look of mischief and astuteness and boldness. Daphne was the ugliest of the seven, with a face full of freckles and a blurred little nose and a blunt, clumsy body. Elizabeth was the fifth: he never managed to see Elizabeth clearly, her slender elusive shape seemed to melt into the foliage. Then came Freya, the happy-go-lucky one, perpetually roving and exploring: he'd see her darting through the trees in a breathless pursuit, though what she was pursuing was always something of a mystery. And finally there was Grace, who was born with a shrunken leg: the small one, the pitiable one, with the night-dwelling eyes. He would pause at the gateway or peer through the cedars, and as he watched them he was reminded of Mr. Nightingale's ruminations. The girls were like butterflies, black or yellow, obscure or speckled, one was swift and one was halting, one was luminous and one was furtive, and it was impossible to guess which of them would survive and which would perish. They all carried a shimmer of the unpredictable about them. They dissolved into whorls of color like the trees of Mrs. Nightingale.

One evening in the middle of August he was sauntering home with his net. He crossed the bridge at Frenchman's Creek and climbed the slope toward the waterfall. Suddenly he heard a voice singing very softly among the birches. He peeped through the leaves: a young girl was standing on the edge of the pool. She dove lightly into the water, then climbed out and crouched on the rock. The sunlight flashed on her body and her coppery hair streamed over her shoulders. She was naked and it was the nakedness which veiled her identity. For a moment it looked like Daphne and then he was sure it was Consuelo. But then she rose, ready to dive again: it was neither Daphne nor Consuelo. She had thin boyish legs and tiny flat breasts and a faint pubic shadow darkened the pit of her belly. She looked up and saw the boy standing motionless among the elderberries. Her face darkened suddenly; she glanced away and sank to her knees.

Peter stood there and stared at her through the leaf-dappled sunlight and after a while he said politely:

"I'm sorry. Excuse me, please."

"That's all right," said the girl.

"Who are you?" said Peter.

"Nobody special," said the girl with gravity.

"What are you doing here?" said Peter.

"I live here," said the girl.

"Here in the woods?" said Peter, startled.

The girl nodded calmly. "I pretend I live in the house. But it's only pretending and I really live in the woods here."

"What's your name?"

"I don't have a name. Most of the time I pretend I'm Elizabeth and the people in the house all think that I'm Elizabeth. But I'm really somebody else, I'm a person without a name, and there's something rather silly about them calling me Elizabeth."

"But," said Peter, "if they call you Elizabeth and everybody thinks that you're Elizabeth, well, that's who you are, isn't it? There's nobody else who is Elizabeth!"

The girl smiled craftily. Her face grew speculative in the sunlight.

"Who knows? Maybe there's another girl who's turned into Elizabeth. Else why do I keep thinking that I'm not really Elizabeth? At home I try to be cozy and pretend I'm Elizabeth but here in the woods I know that I'm not really Elizabeth . . ."

"But," said Peter, frowning slightly, "why do you worry about a word? Elizabeth is only a word and if they call you Elizabeth, it's only to make things simpler, like calling it Chesapeake Bay. After all, the bay was here long before they called it the Chesapeake but now to make things simpler they call it the Chesapeake."

"But things aren't so simple!" cried Elizabeth, waving at a gnat. "A bay is only a bay, there's no soul in a bay, but a person has a soul and it's her own and nobody else's. And it's queer but when I hear someone talking about Elizabeth or when I see the name written down, Elizabeth Nightingale, I know that it isn't me and it's never been me, and I feel that I might as well be a nymph in the woods!"

And she sprang to her feet and ran off into the shadows and Peter could hear her laughing as she scampered through the trees.

IV

He walked back by the edge of the water toward Cleghorn's Inlet. The day was dry and windless and the bay lay sleek as glass. Now and again the glass was broken by a fish leaping for a fly. A flock of starlings came suddenly wheeling over the estuary. He kept thinking about the strangeness of having a name and the feeling of separateness which came from having a name, and also about the strange awareness in people of their separateness and the mystery of that awareness and the whole complexity of that mystery. And after a while it grew so intricate that everything blended together; the birds and the fish shared in the awareness as well as the mystery, and it no longer seemed absurd that a girl should turn into a nymph.

Dusk fell. He sat down by the inlet and stared into the water. The face that stared back at him was pale and thin and timorous, with ash-blond bangs dangling over a broad, troubled forehead and huge, astonished eyes peering into the murky green depths. He whispered the word "Peter" and it had a strange, fluttering sound to it: as though it weren't his own name but the name of a bird or an insect. Then he whispered the word "orphan" and it had a sad, cool sound to it: like the name of cloud or a small white flower or a musical instrument.

The stars were beginning to twinkle by the time he reached the house. All was still and for a moment he thought that his grandmother was sleeping. But she called out his name and he tiptoed into her bedroom, which was dark except for the bottle-blue light that flowed through the window.

"Come," she said, in Polish as usual, "sit down, *kochanie*. I want to look at you."

He walked over to the bedside and looked down at the sick old woman. Her face was unnaturally purple and her nose looked sharp as a knife.

"Bring me some water," she muttered, and he hurried into the kitchen and came back with a glass of water which he held while she drank from it.

Her throat quivered strangely as she gulped down the water. Then she reached out her hand and took hold of his wrist.

"My darling," she whispered. "I think I'm going to die now."

He said nothing; he sat quietly on the chair beside the bed. He detected a curious odor, like the smell of rotting turnips. The old woman looked at the ceiling with a knowing expression and then her eyes rolled in their sockets and stared at Peter with a black intensity.

"You poor lobster," she whispered. "What will ever become of you?"

And she kept on staring for a very long time, until it suddenly dawned on him that the glow had gone from her eyes. He no longer felt love, he no longer felt pain, all he felt was a sickening loneliness as he looked at her prune-like face, with the eyes staring emptily and the lips drawn back in a snarl.

V

Life was dirty and sad and cruel at the Chicapasco orphanage. Sometimes at night Peter woke up and it was like falling into a pit. The dull haze of night fell on the long row of beds. Sometimes a bat came flitting through the window and zig-zagged crazily and flew out again. The air stank of dirty feet and wet dreams and stale urine, and now and again one of the boys would start screaming out of a nightmare.

There were forty boys in the orphanage and they slept in an enormous attic. In the winter it was icy and in the summer it was like an oven. The cots were narrow and creaking, side by side, almost touching, and at the head of each bed stood a wooden box for "personal property"—maybe a comb or a greasy necktie or a picture postcard from Baltimore.

The asylum was an old plantation house fallen into decay. Balls of mistletoe hung in the elms; beards of moss drooped from the beeches. A long, bare table covered with oil-cloth stood in a once-majestical dining-room. In the parlor the brocade curtains were stained with mildew and ripped into shreds. The whole atmosphere was that of a fetid mid-Victorian daydream through which its inhabitants groped their way in a slow, trance-like misery.

There was Mr. Quigley, who ran the orphanage, a puckered man in his middle fifties, who wore dingy red tweeds and a curly black wig. There was Miss Kempff, the nurse and the housekeeper, a big broad woman with a face like a bulldog's. There was Mr. Delbanco, who taught them to write, swarthy and damp and cadaverous. And there were the boys. Forty desolate and superfluous little souls whom nobody loved and nobody wanted. There was Jock the albino, who collected the corpses of katydids. There was Higgins the tattle-tale, perpetually whispering and spying. There was Fiddle the little masturbator, whose bed kept trembling with his secret paroxysms. There was Gus the somnambulist and there was Scipio the idiot. And there was Malcolm, the strong one, who looked like the David of Michelangelo.

The wintry days and wintry nights passed in a haze of dull obscenity. Pornographic drawings were scrawled on the blackboard. Furtive orgies took place in the lavatory. Jock's box was filled with horse-dung and a mouse-trap was tucked in Fiddle's trousers. There were grim little contests in the chilly twilight: wily tortures and humiliations, bird-like noises and beast-like postures, eerie battles which plastered the beds with feathers and excrement. One night as he crept into bed Peter felt something peculiar: a cool, scaly rope gliding slowly across his thighs. He flung off the blanket and listened to Scipio's crazy laughter as a long black bull-snake crawled lazily over the pillow.

"You're all sinners," Mr. Quigley would scream at them across the supper table. "That's all you are! Just sinners! Born of sin and headed for sin! Filth! Scum of the earth! You're lucky to be alive at all, do you hear me? Nobody else would dream of having you. But we're charitable in Chicapasco. We try to teach you. We try to help you. We've got humanity. So be grateful for what we're giving you. Stop whining and complaining. And if I catch one of you bastards cheating or lying or dirtying the sheets again, you'll get your lousy guts whipped out of you! Just don't forget it, that's all I'm telling you!"

Now and again, amid this misery, he thought of the house at Bishop's Neck, and the miraculous seven sisters poised in the deep windless sunlight. They all blended together in his memory, the blonde and the dark, the strong and the delicate, and he wasn't quite sure which was Freya and which was Barbara. They were the inhabitants of a world which was the opposite of Chicapasco: serene and impregnable, immaculate and golden. It was a world much less real, much less desperate than Chicapasco, and yet in the glaze of his memory it took on a deeper reality, a deeper passion, a deeper intricacy than he had ever seen elsewhere.

When the warm weather came they were marched down to the quarry and Mr. Delbanco sat on a stone while the boys were floundering in the shallows. The fresh April sun shone on their skinny, scab-marked bodies. Little patches of soap-lather lay floating on the rusty water. They kept splashing each other with thin, bleating cries and every so often the big one, Malcolm, would dive from the top of a rock. Now and again Mr. Delbanco would leave them for a while and the boys would flock around Scipio and whisper, "Come on, Scipio, show it to us!" And Scipio, grinning affably, would display his sexual precocity and the boys would all titter, "Come on, Fiddle, pretend you're a girl now!"

One morning Peter discovered that his ivory knife was missing and that same evening he found it hidden in Higgins's wooden box.

"It's mine," he said reproachfully.

"Polish rat!" shouted Higgins.

"It's mine," said Peter sullenly, "and I'm not a rat and you stole it."

"He's a liar! He's crazy! I'll knock the guts out of his belly!"

Higgins sprang out of his bed and hurled his body on top of Peter and started to kick viciously at his groin and abdomen. And while Peter, who was much the smaller, lay groaning beside the bedstead he saw Malcolm, the big one, come striding down the aisle. He saw Malcolm lift Higgins as one lifts a cat, by the scruff of the neck, and deal him a single powerful blow in the solar plexus. And then Malcolm strolled casually back to his bed again while Higgins lay gasping and vomiting on the floor.

After that something new entered Peter's existence. Little flashes of brightness shone through the dirt and desolation. There were moments in all that misery when he felt a sudden surge of happiness; there were inklings of hope, of a half-suspected freedom. The sky over the hills turned to a warm fiery blue and the smell of the clover lay fresh over the meadows.

VI

Summer came: the heat was hovering like a mania over the orphanage. The bull-frogs croaked in the marshes; the mosquitoes swarmed in the attic. One night Peter awoke and saw Malcolm leaning over him.

"Come," he whispered, "let's go for a dip in the quarry. How about it?"

So they tiptoed down the stairway and along the main corridor and crept through the pantry into the littered back yard. They climbed over the wall, clinging to the ropes of withered ivy, and soon they were out on the road to the quarry. All around them hung the dead waxy smell of rhododendron. The road branched into a path that wound past an old cemetery. Then it dipped through the pines toward the old deserted quarry where the water lay gleaming in the night, dark as ink. In the daytime the rocks were a bright ruddy color but in the dark they looked clotted and grim, the color of blood. Rusty pulleys and chains lay scattered among the stones and at the edge of the water there was a broken pair of rails. Down below them the water looked evil and bottomless. The dead, dampish air carried a whiff of potassium.

They stopped and sat on a ledge and stared down at the wicked water.

"Looks dangerous," said Peter.

"Nothing to be scared of," said Malcolm.

"You're never scared? There's nothing in the world you're ever scared of?" said Peter.

"Nothing much. Nothing living. Maybe a bomb," murmured Malcolm.

"How old are you, Malcolm?"

"Sixteen, maybe," said Malcolm.

"You'll be leaving Chicapasco?"

"Any day now," said Malcolm.

"Where will you go?"

"Anywheres. I'll just go bumming. It don't much matter."

"Down to Baltimore?"

"Or maybe Florida. I'll bum along. It's nothing to worry about."

"Tell me, Malcolm. What happens to the boys when they leave Chicapasco?"

"Nothing special. They get jobs. Waiting in restaurants or washing dishes."

"That's not much fun. What do you think?"

"That's why I'm heading for Florida. Anything can happen down in Florida."

"What, for instance?"

"Somebody rich. A rich old woman. Or a rich old man."

"You mean, maybe they'll adopt you?"

"Call it adopt. It don't much matter."

"And what would you do? Just live in Florida?"

"Just live in Florida till something happens."

"Look," said Peter. "A firefly!"

"Feel like a dip?" whispered Malcolm.

And suddenly, for no particular reason, a feeling of terror took hold of Peter. The water had a deathly look to it, the night was still and oppressive, the pulleys and chains looked like instruments of torture. Malcolm rose and stood on the ledge, spreading his arms in the darkness. His body looked cold and unnaturally pale, like a marble statue.

He looked down and smiled at Peter with a cool, white intensity.

"Do you dare me?" he said.

"No," said Peter, "why should I dare you?"

"Think I'm scared?" whispered Malcolm.

"No," said Peter. "There's nothing you're scared of . . ."

Malcolm rose on his toes and flexed his knees lightly. His body swung through the darkness in a white easy arc. The water splashed over him and a moment later he emerged again, all spluttering and streaming, and stroked his way back to the rock.

"That was fine," said Peter, tremorous.

"Nothing to it," growled Malcolm.

"I'd be scared," said Peter guiltily.

"Wait. You'll see," murmured Malcolm.

He climbed over the ledge to the top of the cliff. None of the boys had ever dared to dive from the top of the cliff. And now especially, in the looming darkness, it looked eerie and dangerous. Malcolm stood there for a while, glossy white against the blackness, and already in all that stillness there was a ghostly look about him.

"Don't!" cried Peter. "You'll get hurt!"

"Think I'm scared?" called back Malcolm.

"Look!" cried Peter. "How dark it is!"

"Now! Watch me!" cried Malcolm.

He stood motionless for what seemed like a very long time. The drops shone like beads on his powerful young body. He rose on his toes, spread his arms and measured the distance; and then slowly, as though he were floating on the wings of a gull, swung down into the emptiness. He fell more and more swiftly, until his body looked like an arrow. He struck the water, which exploded like a great black mirror.

Peter stared into the darkness. The water closed and grew

glossy again. Ever so faintly he saw a few tiny bubbles rise to the surface. He waited. Nothing happened. He screamed "Malcolm! Where are you?" But his voice echoed feebly in the emptiness of the quarry.

He climbed to the water's edge and stared desperately into the water. Way below it seemed that a thin white shape was stirring faintly. He kept calling, "Malcolm! Malcolm!" But only the echo called back: "Malcolm . . ." He slid clumsily into the water and swam around in a panicky circle, but then his terror got the better of him and he paddled back to the rocks again.

He sat crouching in the darkness, waiting for a miracle to happen. Maybe it was all only a joke. Maybe Malcolm was hiding in the rocks. He waited. Time passed. Great clouds covered the stars and the water below him looked even blacker than before. A strange feeling came over him: that this place wasn't one particular place, and this moment wasn't one particular moment any longer, but that the rock where he was crouching rose up into an arctic immensity and that the chasm below him dipped into the very heart of the universe. A peculiar calm, a gentle peacefulness gradually came over him, and after a while in all that darkness things seemed as they had to be: huge, impersonal and incomprehensible, tinged with the grandeur of catastrophe.

VII

"Do you realize," said Mr. Quigley, "what it is you have done?"

Peter lowered his head. Nothing that Mr. Quigley said could possibly matter to him.

"Do you realize," snarled Mr. Delbanco, "your responsibility in this tragedy?"

Peter stared through the window. Nothing that Mr. Delbanco said had any meaning to him.

"What you did," said Mr. Quigley, "was vicious and disobedient."

"You egged him on," said Mr. Delbanco. "You caused his death. In a way, you murdered him."

But the words "death" and "murder" were quite meaningless to Peter. He merely stared through the window and longed to dissolve into the thin gray dawn outside.

"No remorse," said Mr. Quigley. "That's the worst of it all."

"There's more than meets the eye," said Mr. Delbanco, with a probing expression.

"A final verdict on the matter is none of our business," snapped Mr. Quigley.

"I will have to make a report to Mr. Blakeslee," said Mr. Delbanco.

That night, as he lay in the darkness, he held Cleophas's knife in his hand. He drew the cold blade of steel along the veins in his wrist. How terribly easy, he kept thinking; no more fear, no more misery. He dug the blade into the base of his palm very delicately. An ice-cold pang shot through his body. And suddenly he felt liberated, almost gay. It was as though he had already sliced through the thread of existence.

Higgins's eyes shone like a lizard's. He whispered across the darkness: "It was all your fault. You kept on teasing him . . ."

"No, no!" pleaded Peter. "I couldn't help it! I tried to stop him!"

Silence fell. A lonely bat came flitting in through the open window. A frog started to bellow; the mosquitoes kept whining. A half-strangled groan rose from a bed in the far-off corner. Then silence again. The poor wretches were all asleep now.

Peter slid from the bed and picked up his sneakers. He tiptoed toward the door, where he paused for just a moment. He looked back into the dormitory, where forty miserable little bodies lay panting and sweating in the labyrinth of their dreams. Then he stole down the stairway and slipped through the pantry and crept through the yard and started scrambling over the wall.

Just as he reached the top of the wall he heard a voice from the attic window. It was Higgins, waving his flabby white arms in the darkness.

"Quick! Stop him!" he screamed. "He's running away!"

Peter leapt and raced wildly through the thicket of rhododendron. He ran down the path until he came to the edge of the barley field. A thick hedge of brambles skirted the edge of the field and he ducked for a moment and looked back at the asylum house. A light was shining in the attic dormitory and suddenly three more lights went on—one in the stairway, one in the hall, one in the garage that adjoined the kitchen. He heard voices in the distance. Mr. Delbanco was shouting, "Hurry up, Agatha!" A door slammed; two dark figures were racing across the driveway. There was the blaze of automobile headlights and the growl of a motor.

He darted across the field and made for the woods behind the cemetery. He stumbled and fell headlong; his face struck a stone. For a moment he lay stunned. Great white flashes danced in the air. Then he rose to his knees and crawled into a nest of black bushes. Blood was pouring down his chin but he hardly was aware of the pain, which seemed to exist outside his being, like a pebble in his pocket. He crouched without stirring. Suddenly he felt a terrible itching, and when he touched his naked calves he realized that his flesh was swarming with ants. He jumped up in a frenzy, ripping his clothes off as he ran, and when he reached the shade of the woods he hurled his pants on the ground and hysterically whisked off the insects from his flesh. His whole body was on fire with a hideous, multitudinous itching. He could hardly keep from screaming; he stifled his voice into a low, dull cackle. He kept staggering around in a half-crazed circle, waiting for the itching to grow less and for his sense to come back to him.

A sickly half-moon oozed up out of the valley. He could see the blistered stones shining faintly in the graveyard. He stood motionless and fixed his eyes on the moonlit cemetery, and with a fierce concentration he started to count the little stones— some of them leaning over sideways, most of them spotted with lichen, all of them watching him quietly with a kind of mild, gray aloofness.

The itching grew less and soon it was gone altogether and all that was left was a feverish flush that filled his body. "Sixteen, seventeen, eighteen . . ." But now the pain no longer mattered; he picked up his clothes, swirled them violently through the air, then tucked them under his elbow and headed for the railway track, which followed the narrow valley in the direction of Euphoria.

He passed a farm. Two horses were standing motionless in a meadow, and at the edge of the field stood a coal-black pony. Peter paused by the fence and the pony strolled up to him. It craned its neck over the fence and gazed imploringly at Peter. He stroked its nose and scratched the back of its furry black ear, and then he hurried across the field toward the thistles that lined the railway.

He saw the lights of a car sweeping along the distant turn-pike, and he knew it was Miss Kempff and Mr. Delbanco in the Chevrolet. He squatted under a juniper and waited for the car to vanish. He knew he would never lay his eyes on Mr. Delbanco or Miss Kempff again.

He dug his way through the thistles and followed the tar-smelling railway tracks. Suddenly he realized that he was naked; he slipped on his clothes again. The night was still and sultry and he walked in a kind of daze, feeling the fever of the ant-bites swirling around him like the smoke from an oven. Something crackled in the underbrush; a deer, or maybe a wood-chuck. An owl flew over the tracks, its great dark wings beating like velvet. A stream dipped out of the woods and he squatted by the water and washed the dirt-clotted blood from his swollen cheeks. He lay down by the stream and fell asleep for a while and the next thing he knew was a violent explosion, like a bolt of thunder. The air seethed, the earth trembled, the express train roared past him, leaving in its wake a shower of sparks and a stench of burning metal.

He rubbed his eyes and looked around. Wisps of fog covered the tracks. Way in the distance a cock was crowing and a second cock crowed back at him. The sky was pale gray with a tinge of violet in the distance, and the stars were very faint, like little pin-pricks in the grayness. There was a wonderfully sweet and spicy smell in the air, the smell of dew-wet tar and dew-drenched thistles and oozing resin, the smell of peppermint and pine-needles and the awakening of the woods. All the smells blended together into a great winging freshness, which was the smell of a miraculous and unimagined freedom.

He got up, feeling a deep shuddering ache run through his limbs, but sharper than the ache was the dizzy joy that filled his body. The leaves in the wind started to ripple with a dewy brightness and a big, blurry sun shone through the lemon-edged mist. He knelt by the creek and lapped at the mushroom-tasting water; then he washed his skinny legs, which were criss-crossed with scratches. Finally he got up and spread his arms, sniffed expectantly at the air and then headed along the tracks toward Pendleton's Landing.

VIII

It was late afternoon when Mr. Nightingale with his net came strolling along the path toward the empty cottage at Cleghorn's Inlet. He saw Peter sitting on the step with his head in his arms, fast asleep.

"Well, young fellow. Back again?"

Peter blinked his eyes wearily.

"Come, child," said Mr. Nightingale. "You'd better be coming along with me."

Peter rose and walked obediently down the path toward the big red mansion.

And there he stayed, in the big red mansion, for four untroubled years. He became "one of the family," as Mrs. Nightingale kept gently reminding him.

"You must think of them as your sisters," said Mrs Nightingale delicately.

"I'll try," said Peter, blushing.

"You must learn to love them," said Mrs. Nightingale.

"I'll try, ma'am," said Peter.

"And keep them," said Mrs. Nightingale, "from doing silly things. Seven girls in one family, it's a bit of a strain, with one thing and another."

The house stood on a small grassy knoll above the inlet. On windless days the Georgian columns hung reflected in the murky water and fronds of sea-weed trailed over the reflected columns like streaks of cloud. Now and then a small ripple set the mirrored majesty of the house atremble and it looked as though the house itself were crumbling and disintegrating. Stillness, absolute stillness: that was the climate of Bishop's Neck, a stillness so intense that the wind seemed less than the windlessness, and the noise less real than silence, and the awakening less real than the sleep. The cry of the thin white waterbirds sounded less like the crying of birds than like a distillation, a culmination of all that floating stillness.

In his youth Mr. Nightingale had been in the diplomatic service, and he had served as an attaché in Tokyo and Sofia and Copenhagen. It was in Tokyo that he met a Brazilian girl named Maria Pinto-Coelho; they married and had a child and then Maria died of cholera on a trip to the Philippines. In Sofia he met an Italian girl named Luisa Avarelli and he proposed and she accepted but a week before the wedding she fled to Naples. And in Copenhagen he met a Russian woman named Olga Ibarra who had married twice before but still was beautiful as well as witty and he fell profoundly in love with her and they married in Elsinore. Not long after Mr. Nightingale was stricken with diabetes and he resigned from the foreign service and went to live in Bishop's Neck where he wrote exhaustive articles on the rhapalocera of the Eastern seaboard. It was a rambling sort of place which had belonged to the family since 1820, and the aroma of the previous century still lingered about the rooms, lightly spiced with mementoes from the Balkans and Polynesia.

There was a garden below the house where chrysanthemums grew in the autumn and delphinium in the spring and great red roses all summer. At one end of the garden stood a solitary chestnut tree, and under the tree hung a swing where Daphne and Grace would sit swinging. At the other end stood a summer-house, a kind of vine-draped gazebo, and here Barbara and Consuelo would sit reading their Maupassant. Below the veranda lay a lawn where Elizabeth and Freya played croquet, and beyond the lawn was a narrow field where Augusta practiced her archery.

The house itself was a little ramshackle. Things were falling into decay. The paint was cracking on the columns; the rafters squeaked and the shutters rattled. In the drawing room stood a grand piano on which Miss Malachi taught her music lessons, though only Grace of all the seven had a feeling for music. Behind the drawing room was a kind of "studio" where Miss Malachi gave her painting lessons, but of the seven only Freya revealed a talent which was comparable to her mother's. And across the hall from the "studio" was the library, where Mr. Nightingale kept his collection of butterflies and where Miss Malachi gave her lessons in French and arithmetic: but only Consuelo displayed a penchant for literature and only Barbara had a flair for numbers, and even they began to lose interest when it came to Zola and trigonometry. And they were all a little startled after Peter joined the family, since he loved Mr. Nightingale's butterflies as well as Mrs. Nightingale's landscapes, he even enjoyed Miss Malachi's Scarlatti and listened carefully as she read *Tartuffe*. He hurried to fetch the mallets for Freya and Elizabeth and watched with admiration as Augusta shot her arrows.

Little by little he grew to know each of the seven sisters separately, and he developed a different humor for each of them. It was adventurous with Freya, grave with Augusta, aloof with Barbara, rebellious with Daphne. It was Grace, who was the youngest, whom he first grew to love. He felt sorry at first for Grace, with her enormous eyes and shrunken leg and her swarthy, almost octoroon-like complexion. Then he came to detect the mysterious "inwardness" of Grace, which gave her such a precocious self-confidence and cunning.

"Have you ever seen a ghost?" said Grace.

"No," said Peter, "not an honest-to-God one."

"There's a ghost," said Grace gravely, "that creeps into the library from time to time. She keeps trying to tell me something but I don't know what it is. She has curly blond hair and wears a faded blue dress, and she's carrying a rusty old box in her hands."

"Is she a real, authentic ghost?"

"Don't be ironical, please," warned Grace. "She has a message. All ghosts have messages. Maybe they're happy and maybe they're sad, but they always have a meaning and we'd be silly to ignore the meaning . . ."

"Yes," said Barbara one day. "I've heard about that little box. Mrs. Bontecue told me about it and so did Miss Malachi. It's a treasure; a buried treasure; hundreds and thousands of lovely gold pieces. Way back in the Civil War Theodoric Nightingale took the family gold. The Yankees were coming and he buried the gold down in the garden. And ever since, year after year, the impoverished Nightingales have been looking for the gold. They've dug in the rose-beds, they've dug in the orchard, they've dug in the asparagus patch and down in the rock-garden. But they've never found the gold, maybe there wasn't any gold, and it's a pity, a terrible pity, we could use those beautiful gold-pieces . . ."

Peter felt troubled whenever he looked at Barbara's blue-eyed beauty, it was so radiant and crystal-clear, like the sun-light on the waterfall. But under the radiance he detected a hint of vengefulness, of calculation, and he wondered whether such beauty was always accompanied by scorn and vanity. And yet, as he looked at Barbara playing with her beads in the sun-lit garden, he felt that vanity and scorn, when joined to such loveliness, were almost lovable, and his infatuation for Barbara was even intensified by his distrust of her.

It was Augusta he was afraid of. "I loathe men," muttered Augusta. "Men are dull and disgusting and I have no intention of ever marrying." And when Mrs. Nightingale murmured, "Just wait and see, you'll know better," Augusta picked up her racquet and strode off toward the tennis court. Augusta was very tall and powerfully built and very sombre. She never smiled; she was never frivolous; she never tried to look beau-tiful. There was a grand and faintly sinister kind of handsome-ness about her but she seemed to be deliberately trying to look coarse and uncouth. Only at the sight of an animal, a horse or maybe a dog, did her eyes melt a little and her face soften with tenderness. When she stood in the archery range with her bow and arrows Peter was struck with the fervor with which she shot off her arrows and with the venom in her expres-sion when she hit the bull's eye.

Augusta was the oldest. She was the daughter of her father's first wife, the Brazilian lady whom he had met at the Embassy in Tokyo. Barbara was the second; she was the daughter of Mrs. Nightingale's first husband, a sculptor named Palmgren, but her mother had changed her name to Nightingale. Consuelo was the third, the daughter of her mother's second husband, a Spanish poet named Ibarra, and she had likewise changed her name to Nightingale. Consuelo was also a brunette but in a different way from Augusta: not grim and sardonic but supple and tzigane-like, with a feverish glow in her eyes and a perpetually dancing body. Once Peter late at night, after the rest of the family were in bed, happened to notice the flickering of candles that were burning in the dining room. He peeped through the door and saw Consuelo poised in front of the mirror, both arms raised, slowly stretching her leg in an arabesque. She was wearing one of her mother's black shawls over her head; the rest of her body was nude, rose-colored in the flamelight, and she stared with defiance at Peter's reflection in the mirror. He could see the trace of a belt still imprinted on her waist and the faint, dusky triangle of hair on her abdomen.

"I hate Maryland," she whispered, swinging around on her toes. "I hate father. I hate mother. I hate the whole silly family. I'm going to leave Bishop's Neck and live in Paris, or maybe Spain. I hate all this stuffiness and pompousness and sterility . . ."

"And what will you do when you get there?"

"In Paris? I'll be a dancer."

"And you'll never come back to America?"

"Not till I'm married," said Consuelo.

"You'll get married?" said Peter.

Consuelo glared at him scornfully. "I'm going to marry a famous artist. Not just a dauber. A genius! Full of vision and passion and idealism!"

Daphne was the fourth, and the first of the daughters born of Mr. and Mrs. Nightingale. She was a homely imp-like creature with a freckled, turned-up nose and a square angry chin and troubled eyes set far apart. She spent most of her time in the woods or down on the shore. She avoided the rest of the sisters, all but Grace, whom she loved, and Augusta, with whom she had shared some shadowy affinity. She gradually developed a kind of gruff camaraderie toward Peter, not really intimate, not wholly natural, but tinged by a secret necessity, and together they strolled through the woods by Frenchman's Creek, watching the chipmunks and squirrels and skipping pebbles across the water.

"What," said Peter, "will you do when you're older, do you think, Daphne?"

"I'll be an explorer. Or an archaeologist," said Daphne somewhat gloomily.

"Isn't it sad," hinted Peter, "to think of all of us growing older?"

"I'm going to die," whispered Daphne, "before I'm twenty. Wait and see!"

Elizabeth was the mystery. All of the sisters were a little odd, but Elizabeth's oddity was of an almost wraith-like quality. She was blond like Barbara. She had freckles like Daphne. She loved animals, like Augusta. She had visions, like Grace. Like Freya she was perpetually loitering down by the water and like Consuelo she'd go dancing at dusk through the corridors. But a very special feeling of fate hung over Elizabeth, as though she were aware of a uniqueness in her destiny. She had a collection of properties which she kept on a shelf in the studio: Japanese flowers, which expanded into blossom when they fell in the water; a box of tiny eggs that turned into snakes when they were lit; Roman candles and Catherine Wheels; puzzles made out of metal and ivory; crystal elephants and ebony crocodiles as well as a whole set of dolls. Russian dolls and Chinese dolls, Haitian puppets and Peruvian marionettes, dolls of wax, dolls of plaster, dolls with patterned chintz bodies, every conceivable kind of doll except those vulgar dolls that looked like babies, all cast in a tangled heap on the studio shelf like a pile of corpses.

She especially loved snakes. The rest of the sisters all looked horrified when Elizabeth came through the garden with a snake curled around her arm.

"It's repulsive," said Augusta.

"It's evil," said Barbara.

"You'd better be careful," said Consuelo, "or you'll get bitten by a rattlesnake."

But Elizabeth, who rarely spoke, passed through the garden in a kind of trance, fondling the serpent's head gently and gazing at the sky with a rapt expression.

And that left Freya, who was the youngest of the seven except Grace. She was the one who loved the water, just as Peter loved the water, and together they went rowing across the inlet in the afternoon, pausing now and again at one of the tiny reed-fringed islands. She was neither beautiful nor ugly, neither blonde nor brunette, neither clever nor stupid, neither ordinary nor odd. Indeed, the queer thing about Freya was that she fell into no category, she had no special traits, she seemed to change like a chameleon. She reflected the passing moods of each of her six sisters, she might be gnome-like, like Daphne, or tzigane-like, like Consuelo, and the only thing that was different was a perpetual inner gayety, so that even when she was sombre, in imitation of Augusta, there still was a certain zest lurking about her.

"I'm going to spend my life on islands, nothing but islands," she said thoughtfully.

"What kind of islands?" asked Peter, trailing his oars in the water.

"Tropical islands like Tahiti. Desolate islands like the Galapagos. Haunted islands like Delos. Windy islands like the Orkneys. If I ever live in a city it will be an island, like Venice. If I ever live in America it will be in Manhattan, or Nantucket."

"There are other islands, too."

"Snow-white islands and coal-black islands! Islands with sheep and islands with penguins! Islands with temples, islands with cocoanuts!"

"How do you know so much about islands?"

"I've made a specialty of islands. I've been studying them for years. I know everything about islands."

"But in the end," murmured Peter, "it's not quite real to live on an island, is it?"

"Not quite real maybe but free! That's what I want. Eternal freedom!"

Four years slowly elapsed, and they were years of a dream-like monotony. He gradually learned to love the sisters, as Mrs. Nightingale had recommended, and at fleeting moments he thought of them as his sisters, as she had likewise recommended, but most of the time they seemed too odd and impenetrable to be his sisters and his feeling was too speculative and furtive for brotherly love.

The chrysanthemums bloomed and shriveled, the chestnuts flowered and fell, the war came to an end and the sisters grew taller and older. Mrs. Bontecue still baked her pies and Miss Malachi played her Scarlatti, but the shadows of impermanence grew deeper and longer. Spells of homesickness for Europe were taking hold of Mrs. Nightingale, and Mr. Nightingale's face was beginning to twitch with queer little spasms. And the time finally arrived when a malaise crept into the household and the sisters one by one developed a new, puzzling restlessness. First it was one and then it was another and then it was a third who drifted away, each of the three in her fashion and with her own particular sadness. It was as though the end of the war had also brought an end to peacefulness, and the life at Bishop's Neck was beginning to disintegrate.

Part Two

I

Twice a week, on Tuesdays and Thursdays, Augusta went strolling to Blue Hills. And there she spoke to old Mr. Aspinwall and doddering Miss Aspinwall and nodded politely to Cyrus Aspinwall. Then she walked down to the stables where Antonio was waiting for her and he held up the stirrup while she mounted the horse, which was always the big chestnut gelding whose name was Hannibal.

She was especially fond of Hannibal. He stepped daintily through the grasses and when the road was muddy he carefully avoided the puddles. She could see that he liked the smell of the woods and the meadows and he liked the glow of the warm bright sunlight on his back. She sat Hannibal with grace and an easy self-confidence and she knew that she looked her best on a horse. And as for Hannibal, it was clear that he was fond of

Augusta but there was something tense about him, he was restless and over-sensitive, there was always something or other that suddenly made him nervous.

In March there still were pools in the rutted black road and chilly gusts swirled in from the Chesapeake. In April the wind swept over the grass in silky waves and in May the mares started to neigh in the pastures.

June arrived; the dusk crept in from Pendleton's Landing and the swallows swooped past and the smell of nettles hung over the road, and then came July with the heat-waves sizzling in the underbrush and the butterflies waltzing as she rode through the maples.

It was a warm autumn day. The sky blended with the horizon and both sky and horizon were the color of muddy water. Here and there a bluish mist settled slowly among the trunks. Now and again there was a flurry of raindrops and the leafy earth was swollen and spongy. She wore a thin tweed coat but no gloves and no hat and her wet black hair was streaming over her shoulders.

As she entered the woods the rain stopped again and the glow of the evening seeped through the trees. The drops shone brightly as they dripped from the branches. The horse was black from the rain and his neck was drenched and scrawny, and the saddle and bridle were sticky with moisture.

There was a tumble down hunting-shack at the edge of the woods. Here she halted for a rest, as she sometimes did in the afternoon. She sat down on the wooden steps, which the overhanging branches had kept dry, and the horse lowered his head and started to graze in a patch of sunlight. There was something trance-like about the place, something frozen and unalterable, and the calm was the calm that had lived here for centuries. Maybe it was this very peacefulness, this haunted stillness which suddenly alarmed her. The drops fell from the trees in a ceaseless clock-like rhythm and the smell of dead leaves carried a dark little warning.

She ripped a splinter from the edge of the steps and started to gnaw at it.

"So this is what it's like. Just on and on and nothing happening? Just on and on while the leaves keep rotting and something in myself keeps rotting too? Just on and on, nothing changing in the big dark stillness and only the small separate things gradually rotting away? Good God," she suddenly thought, "is this what I was born for? Just to rot away in this horrible stillness?" And then she thought, not quite in words but with a lucidity as clear as words: "Why is it that I despise myself? Why do I feel such a disgust for myself? Could it be because I am ugly? No, I'm not really ugly. I'm too tall and too dark but I'm not really ugly. Is it because I am stupid? No, I'm not really stupid, I feel sluggish and bored but Miss Malachi has told me that I'm far from stupid. Is it because I am weak? Yes, I often feel terribly weak, all flabby and stagnant, unable to move almost, but sometimes I feel a great strength welling up in me, something powerful and violent that's lurking in my blood. Is it something I've done? No, I've done so very little, nothing to hurt, nothing wicked, nothing out of the ordinary. No, it's something deep inside me, curled up in the darkness, something that hasn't got a face and that nobody has a name for, something curled up and waiting, nibbling away at my nerves. I'm sick of my own body and yet I have to love it because it's mine, and I'm sick of my own personality yet I have to bear with it because it's a part of me. Here I am, the oldest of the seven and the only one without a purpose, without a talent, without a passion, without anyone to love or anyone to be loved by. I used to love Daphne but then that ugly thing happened and now there's a wall between Daphne and me. And even Daphne is loved by Grace and even Grace is loved by Miss Malachi and Freya loves Peter and Peter loves Barbara. And even Consuelo loves my father and my father still loves my stepmother, and as for my stepmother, yes, there is someone whom she loves though I don't know who. What is wrong? Is it something in the way we've been living or is it something in life itself? Or is it something only in me, something rotten that I was born with? Everyone around me is capable of love and is capable of being loved and only I am squatting in the darkness, rotting away, like something cursed . . ."

II

At that moment she saw a tall dark shadow among the trees. It paused, then retreated and half-hid behind a trunk. She sat quietly and folded her arms and stared intently into the woods. Then she reached down and picked up her riding stock and held it in front of her. The shadow moved closer. Now she could see who it was: the hunched, half-crippled shoulders and the tentative sloping gait.

"You're surprised to see me?" said Cyrus.

"Not especially," said Augusta curtly.

"You look surprised. You even look angry, just a little," said Cyrus, stammering.

"I've never seen you out of doors, now that I think of it," said Augusta.

Cyrus was thin and abnormally tall, even taller than Augusta. There was something crane-like about his posture and his whole appearance. His nose jutted hungrily, his chin shot back with alarm, his eyes had a glassy and mesmerized mournfulness. He wore tweeds, russet and peppery, with leather patches under the elbows. He smoked a pipe and carried a cane. A bright red handkerchief glowed in his pocket.

"I detest the out-of-doors," he said, half-glumly, half-defiantly. "I loathe the birds and the insects. Trees depress me. Flowers bore me. I've always had a grudge against what people call nature. Maybe it's partly because nature was never particularly kind to me." He was speaking more quickly now, with a kind of pleading intensity. "You've never liked me, have you, Augusta?"

"What makes you think so?" said Augusta.

"Because I'm a freak, that's why," said Cyrus. "I'm a freak, and I know it. They told me so when I was at Woodbury and they told me so at Charlottesville. At first I hated being a freak and I hated even more being called a freak but then I didn't mind and finally I almost started to enjoy it. I used to stare at myself in the mirror. I thought I looked like Abraham Lincoln but there was something about me that was somehow different from Abraham Lincoln."

"You've been hurt, that's the reason. You've been wounded," said Augusta gravely.

"Oh yes," said Cyrus, carefully leaning his cane against the wall, "we all get hurt but some of us are strong enough to get over the hurt, some of us build a kind of carapace and learn to ignore what people think of us. I've been trying to grow a carapace, I've been trying for years but then you wonder whether it's worth it, and maybe the carapace is worse than the misery."

"Isn't there something wrong with a world where we keep on worrying about what people think of us?"

"Don't you worry about what people think of you?"

"No, I don't," said Augusta sullenly.

"Then you're lucky," whispered Cyrus, looking down at her with a glowering tenderness. "You're strong, that's the point. You're strong and self-sufficient. There's nothing feminine about you. You don't look for admiration. You're like a man, you do what you do and you think what you think and that's the end of it."

"Well, I wish it were so. I really do," said Augusta wryly.

"Oh, don't worry," said Cyrus rapidly, "I've been studying you, Augusta, I've been analyzing you in my mind and I've arrived at certain conclusions." He crouched on the steps beside her and glared at her with a wasp-like urgency. "I'm an eccentric, yes, I know it, I'm a bit of a crackpot by your standards, you love nature and animals and I'm the opposite of nature and animals. I can't help it, it's in my glands, the family blood's been running thin I suppose and sometimes even my mind feels all brittle and combustible. I don't pretend to be an Adonis, I don't expect to be desired, I've worried about it enough and I know it won't happen. I'm resigned to doing without sex, if you'll excuse my being blunt about it, and I've even gotten so that I don't especially want it." He kept stroking his pipe with his thickly knuckled fingers. His great myopic eyes shone beseechingly behind their glasses. "Tell me, Augusta," he whispered, "I don't expect you ever to love me but do you think you might get so that you started to like me a little?"

"Silly questions," said Augusta sternly, "deserve silly answers. What earthly difference does it make whether I like you or not?"

Cyrus's lips were twitching nervously. "You're inhuman, Augusta, that's the trouble with you! You love horses and dogs, you love the woods and the water, but you have no feelings for people, that's what's wrong with you, Augusta!"

"You're being childish," said Augusta, "and I don't like people who are childish."

"It's you who are treating me like a child! Like an idiot child!" bleated Cyrus.

"If you stopped," said Augusta grimly, "thinking about yourself all the time, you might learn to grow up. You might learn to be a character. That's what one has to be: a character. And nobody will love you until you are a character."

Cyrus lowered his head and gazed at her with a sloping expression; a delicate smile shone on his face; his voice grew almost loving.

"Yes, I knew it, you've been trying to figure me out, haven't you, Augusta? You're perfectly right, I know I'm weird but I'm not as weird as all that. I'm a human being. I'm struggling and groping, just like everybody else." He took off his glasses and tucked them hurriedly into his breast-pocket. He buried his face in his hands for a moment, then looked up with a radiant expression. "Augusta, listen! I know I'm crazy but there are times when you have to be crazy. Don't laugh at me, please! Will you marry me, Augusta?"

Augusta felt very calm, very wise all of a sudden. A feeling of detachment swept through her, rather incongruous to the occasion yet somehow appropriate and even inevitable and profoundly soothing. An uncontrollable little smile distorted her lips for a moment; a smile of power freshly discovered, wily and musing, faintly demoniac.

"Listen, Augusta!" cried Cyrus desolately. "I know what you're thinking! You're thinking how horrible it would be to have to go to bed with me, aren't you? But I promise you I'll never make you go to bed with me, Augusta. It's not that kind of love, I assure you. It won't be that kind of marriage. Your strength, that's what I need—your marvelous strength and self-confidence!"

Augusta rose to her feet and touched him lightly on the head. His hair felt dry and frail, like the wings of a dragon-fly. "Come, Cyrus, pull yourself together. You're in a state," she said gently. "You're all worked up about nothing at all. It's after six. I'll have to be going . . ."

When she arrived at the house she found her stepmother in the garden, squatting down in one of the beds, snipping away at the chrysanthemums. Her hair hung over her brow and her cat-eyes glittered with enthusiasm. Little droplets of sweat hung from her broad, sun-tanned cheeks.

"You've been riding?"

"Yes," said Augusta.

"Nice, was it?"

"Moderately," said Augusta.

"Look at the color of this chrysanthemum. Isn't it amazing?" said her stepmother.

"I have something to tell you," said Augusta in measured tones.

"Poor child. You're all flushed. Hurry with your bath. It's time for dinner."

"I've just decided . . ."

"Watch out, Augusta! Don't step on the calendulas!"

"Listen to me, mother."

"I am listening, dear. Don't be so agitated. It doesn't become you."

"I am getting married," said Augusta quietly.

"How very nice," said Mrs. Nightingale. "Your father will be delighted to hear it, I'm sure." She finished snipping a large blossom and dropped it into the basket. She whirled about all of a sudden. "What did you say? You're getting married! Good God, Augusta, you're out of your mind! Who is the gentleman, may I ask?"

"Cyrus Aspinwall," said Augusta, motionless.

"Cyrus Aspinwall," said Mrs. Nightingale.

"In December," said Augusta.

"Oh. I see," said Mrs. Nightingale.

III

The house at Blue Hills was built of rose-coloured bricks which were tinged with weathery patches of écru and lavender. Two bow-windows bulged out on each side of the door. A formal garden spread from the terrace with a long stone wall on the left of it. On the right the lawn sloped down toward a thick hedge of privet which was neatly clipped into a row of urns and obelisks. Beyond the hedge a winding path led through the dogwood down to the inlet, which was narrower than at Bishop's Neck and much more shady and secluded.

Augusta and Cyrus both agreed not to bother about a honeymoon and after the wedding festivities their life subsided into a placid monotony. Old Mr. Aspinwall sat erect in his mahogany chair in the morning, peering at the stamps in his album through a magnifying glass. He wore a white batiste neckcloth, usually a little bit stained, and his bushy white sideburns were tinged with a rusty yellow.

"Do you realise," he said to Augusta, picking up a stamp with his tweezers, "how much one learns from being a philatelist? What is the currency of Siam, for instance? Who was the King of Montenegro? What is the capital of Borneo? Have you ever heard of Thurn and Taxis? Just think, this little stamp was probably licked by a beautiful lady who was sending a love-letter from Luxembourg to Cairo! Every stamp was once the agent of a forgotten little drama, bringing messages from Padua to Venice, or from Bangkok to Lima . . ."

"It is fascinating," said Augusta.

"Memories, memories," said Mr. Aspinwall. "Thousands of separate little dramas, forgotten by the world but tucked in my album. It is staggering just to think of all those dramas tucked in my album. Here we are, waiting for lunch with the fire burning in the fireplace, and all those little dramas tucked away in my album!"

Miss Aspinwall entered the room with a book under her arm. "Rain," she muttered. "Just as I predicted. There. Twelve-thirty. Late as usual . . . You've been reading about Korea? Incredible, isn't it? . . . And the soufflé yesterday. I'll speak to Bridget . . . There's a chapter on Caligula. Simply appalling . . . That's southern weather for you. Shocking, isn't it? . . . Savages, that's what they are, just bloodthirsty savages . . ."

Mr. Aspinwall winked at Augusta. "There, you see. Nothing but dramas. Life is a perpetual series of crises, even here in Blue Hills!"

She went prowling around the house in the long wintry mornings. Into the drawing room with its Piranesis and its dowdy Chippendale mirrors; into the dining-room with its fluted can-

dlesticks and its Alma Tadema; into the library with its barometers and first editions of Kipling, and the conservatory,
where tropical vines hung in festoons over the faded card-table;
and even occasionally into the chilly guest-rooms, with their
Lowestoft ginger-barrels and their andirons shaped like Hessian
mercenaries.

And then she walked down to the kennels where the bloodhounds were yelping. The little bitch whose name was Toffie
had given birth to a litter of puppies, and what with the worm-
ing and feeding and the injections and innoculations there was
always something to keep her busy on the drizzly afternoons.

And now and again when the sun was out she took the gelding into the woods again and rode along the creek toward Pendleton's Landing. But these rides had lost their flavor, they had
lost their casualness and airiness, and when she arrived back at
the house she felt mysteriously disconcerted, and she sensed
something black and oppressive hovering in the atmosphere.

IV

On New Year's Eve they waited for midnight and opened a bottle of champagne and then the four of them sat by the fire listening to a recording of *Turandot*.

"Memories, memories," said Mr. Aspinwall. "More and more
we live on our memories."

"Pangs, pangs," echoed Miss Aspinwall. "Listen! The thunder! And those terrible Chinamen . . ."

Midnight tolled, they drained their glasses and climbed up to
their bedrooms. The wind snapped at the shutters; down in the
kennels a dog was wailing.

Augusta was sitting in the bathroom when she heard a knock

on the bedroom door. She glanced quickly into the mirror and threw a robe over her broad, thick shoulders.

She called hoarsely: "Who is it?"

Cyrus's voice: "May I come in?"

"Certainly," said Augusta after a moment.

The door swung open and Cyrus entered.

There was a flush on his cheeks. His eyes looked swollen, a little blurred. He was wearing a black kimono and a pair of red morrocco bedroom slippers.

"Am I bothering you?" he said.

"Not in the least," said Augusta.

"Do you mind if I sit on the bed?"

"No, why should I?" said Augusta, shrugging.

Cyrus lowered his head and stared at the floor with intensity.

"We've been married a month now," he said, somewhat hoarsely.

"Yes, a month," said Augusta warily. "Do you feel you're getting to know me?"

"Know you!" cried Cyrus, clutching at the pillow. "How can I ever get to know you? You've been treating me like an insect! That's what! Just like an insect! Oh God, Augusta, if you only knew all the thoughts that go through my head—thoughts about closeness and happiness and mutual trust and understanding."

"Platitudes," said Augusta, tightening her robe. "You've been reading cheap novels."

"Not a bit of it," snapped Cyrus. "I've been reading Pirandello, and there's a lot in Pirandello about loneliness and misunderstanding. Do you remember what you told me once? About growing into a character? That's what we need—we need to be characters and we'll never become characters unless we learn to have relationships with other persons."

"Well," said Augusta. "And what about it?"

"You're like a statue! You're like a corpse! I see you at lunch and what do you do? You sit and stare into space and then you go into the woods or hang around the kennels, and then I see you at cocktails and you're staring into space again and then I see you at the dinner table, still staring into space. God knows I'm no Apollo, I have no illusions on the matter, but why do you refuse to look at me? Why won't you let me draw closer to you?"

"I married you," said Augusta, "because we're both of us lonely and there's nothing we can do to change the loneliness. Nothing whatever."

"Oh, yes, there is!" said Cyrus bitterly. "If you'd only shed that mask of yours! If you'd only let me touch you! If you'd only put your arms around me! Yes, I know, I promised that I wouldn't insist on having sex with you, but all the same we're husband and wife. Good God, I'm in love with you, Augusta!"

Augusta rose and stood in front of him. "You've been drinking," she said.

Cyrus's lips started twitching. He closed his eyes with a little moan.

"We made an agreement before we married. We shall keep that agreement," said Augusta.

Cyrus sprang to his feet. "I just won't have it, do you hear? I'm your husband and you're treating me like a worm under your feet!" He snatched at her arm. "It's been a month now! It's time you treated me like a man!"

Augusta swung back her arm and slapped him violently across the cheek. "You idiot! Let me go! Can't you see that you revolt me? I married you out of pity and pity is all that I felt, but when you act like a drunken fool what I feel is revulsion. That's what I feel for you, do you hear? Revulsion and nausea! Leave me alone, that's all I ask! I'll sit at your table and I'll listen to your chatter but if you ever dare to touch me again, I'll pack my bags! That's what I'll do!"

Cyrus's chest started to shake with heavy sobs as he looked at her. He kept clasping and unclasping his long bony hands. Finally he grunted: "I see. So that's how it is. Yes. I see." He flung open the door and lunged grotesquely into the corridor.

Augusta locked the door and sat down in front of the dressing table. Her blood-red dressing gown sagged from her shoulders, like a discarded skin. She stared into the black impenetrable eyes in the mirror.

"Why do I do these things?" she whispered. "I'm detestable. Detestable . . ." A single huge tear started to roll down her cheek.

v

In early May Consuelo went for a weekend to Blue Hills. It was the first time since her wedding that Augusta had a guest. The chestnut trees were blossoming and Antonio had mowed the lawn and the parakeets were preening their gaudy wings in the aviary.

"How lovely," said Consuelo. "You've put new curtains into the guest rooms, haven't you?"

"The place needs cheering up," said Augusta, drawing the blinds.

"You've been putting on weight, dear."

"Have I really?" said Augusta.

"Tell me, Augusta," purred Consuelo. "What's it like to be married?"

"I wouldn't know," said Augusta, staring grimly into space.

Consuelo looked at her thoughtfully. "But, after all," she began.

"Cyrus and I," said Augusta, "have nothing to do with each other. To put it crudely, we've never slept together. If that's what you're wondering about."

"But he's in love with you, isn't he? We all decided he must be in love with you."

"I'd rather," said Augusta, "not go into details. If you don't mind."

They had cocktails out on the lawn. The evening light flowed over the tennis court and the smell of chestnut blossoms hung in the air, tart, suggestive. After dinner they had coffee and brandy out on the terrace. The Chinese lanterns were lit, a loon was crying in the distance, and a firefly clung to the snout of the silver coffee pot.

"When I consider," said Mr. Aspinwall, "what is happening all over the world, in places like Asia and Africa, in those sizzling jungles and boiling deserts, I come to realize that a whole way of life is coming to an end."

"Misery, misery," said Miss Aspinwall, "that's what we're heading for, just misery."

"I'm not so sure," said Mr. Aspinwall. "When I contemplate that way of life and when I meditate on its various distinctions and achievements, I begin to realize that it was only a ritualistic ceremony at the best of times and a murderous hallucination at the worst of times, and whatever is coming, and let's assume that something *is* coming, at least the rituals will be done away with and the bloody illusions will be done away with. It will be charmless and bleak but at least it will be clean."

"You are speaking like a rebel," said Miss Aspinwall, somewhat absently.

"I am sick of all these shabby old memories," said Mr. Aspinwall.

Two hours later, when they had finished *The Marriage of Figaro* and the lights were put out and they'd all gone to their bedrooms, Augusta crept downstairs and walked into the garden. The lines on the red clay tennis court shone faintly in the starlight. The dew shone on the racquets that were leaning against the net. Beyond the gate in the wall there was a half-deserted arbor. Fronds of myrtle and jasmine were drooping over the trellises. She stepped through the weeds and sat down on the iron bench. Down below her lay the inlet, smooth and black behind the willows, and beyond shone the lights of Pendleton's Landing.

Suddenly she noticed a rowboat moving silently across the water. Two figures were sitting in the boat and as it slowly moved closer she could hear the splash of the oars and the low taut murmur of voices. Then it slid behind the foliage of the over-hanging willows. She heard the clink of the chain and then the rustle of footsteps as they climbed up the serpentine path through the dogwood.

"She is an enigma," Consuelo was saying. "She's the puzzle of the family."

"She's unhappy. She broods. I can see it in her eyes," muttered Cyrus.

"You really loved her? You're sure?"

"Yes," said Cyrus. "I was really in love with her."

"And now?"

"I don't know. I still love her. But I'm afraid of her."

"She'll never love you. I know Augusta. She is doomed. There's a curse on Augusta."

"You're afraid of her too, aren't you?"

"Yes, I'm terrified of Augusta. And at the same time, you know it's funny but I can't help adoring her. She is selfish and cruel and sometimes she is utterly horrible, but there is something about Augusta. There is a splendor about Augusta . . ."

Augusta kept sitting on the bench for a very long time. She watched the water so intently that it gradually lost its blackness, it grew brilliant and hard, like a sheet of ice under an arc-light. She somehow felt that if she kept looking at it long enough and intently enough, something would rise out of the water, some emanation or exhalation, something to throw a beam of light on the anarchy inside her. She vaguely realized that the feelings of rot and revulsion were really masks which hid the face of a darker and more dangerous emotion.

VI

It was a warm, windless day. Barbara was dozing in the summer-house and Consuelo was lying on the lawn, playing with the Persian cat Semiramis. Mrs. Nightingale was down by the pier, sketching a pattern of lily-pads, and from the drawing room came the tinkle of a Haydn duet from Grace and Miss Malachi.

Elizabeth was out in the orchard playing a game called diabolo. She took the spool, which was shaped like an hour-glass, and started spinning it on a string which was fastened between two rods. It wobbled uneasily as it spun but she managed to keep it balanced, and then she jerked the string tight and the spool shot high in the air and she caught it on the string again, still spinning briskly as she beat the rods. She caught it twice, thrice, four times, but then she suddenly lost control and the fifth time that she tossed it the spool shot into the cornflowers.

She laughed and tucked the spool and the rods under an apple tree and skipped through the grass toward the sun-soaked cedar grove. Down below, through the web of the cedars, shone the silver-blue bay. She crossed the field and climbed nimbly over the weathered wooden fence. She paused to stare at a cow's skull which lay nuzzling under a berry-bush; it was bleached to a peppery white, like fly-specked old vellum.

She hurried on. The ground rose into a thicket of twisted oaks. This was her own private territory. Only the bees and crickets lived here. Barbara stayed in the garden, Daphne roamed through the birches, Freya clung to the water and Grace loitered by the creek, but this insect-ridden copse was Elizabeth's own kingdom and none of the others ever bothered to walk here.

The weeds stirred faintly in a patch of sunlight. There was a dry, leafy rustle, which was followed by a sinuous, almost imperceptible heightening of tension. She stepped closer. She could see the beautiful embroidery of scales, a row of green lozenges that looked like a delicate mosaic. The snake craned its neck, then moved on again leisurely. She tiptoed stealthily after it through the crisp high grasses. It moved faster, straightening the rope of its powerful body. She started to run. She couldn't bear to lose sight of the inscrutable creature. The snake shot over a rock and rolled swiftly into a coil. It raised its head several inches and glared fixedly at Elizabeth. She crept toward the rock and leaned over, enthralled. It was like gliding into a whirlpool. Her nerves were stretched with excitement. Neither she nor the snake was stirring. Then the head started throbbing and the rope suddenly uncoiled and the snake shot up with the speed of a lizard's tongue.

It was like a blow from a twig, sharp and quick, not yet painful. She drew back and watched the snake flow casually into the underbrush. All was still. Nothing stirred. The day was balanced on a hair-fine pivot. And then gradually, half-dreamily, she grew aware of the pain—a faintly burning sensation that spread upward from the wound and burrowed through her flesh like a thin, boiling artery.

She lay down beside the rock. "Quiet," she thought. "Be brave. Be brave now." But then she realized that to be brave would never be enough again. She stared with awe at the two pinkish dots in her ankle, then leaned forward and tried to suck out the poison from the dots. But the poison had fled from the wound. She felt it racing up her thighs—a dull, clutching heat that stung like a powerful liniment. The heat subsided and instead of the heat there was something else now—a slow, grinding cold that dug at her bones like an icicle. She called softly: "Help me, Peter!" But Peter was nowhere around. She called: "Father! Help me, Father!" But her father couldn't hear her. Her voice had a throttled sound, as though it were crushed in cotton wool. Great tears started to trickle over her mouth and down her chin. A crazy jab of pain suddenly shot through her abdomen; it sprang through her belly into her chest and up her ribs and down her spine. She screamed softly and rolled over on the gravelly ground, clutching at a large round pebble which she pressed to her cheek. She closed her eyes. For several minutes the pain went away again. She panted with relief and opened her eyes and stared at the sky, which glowed with a supernatural vividness through the claws of the little oaktrees. A bird flew overhead, brilliant red; a Kentucky Cardinal. Time passed. The light darkened, then sharpened, then darkened again. She fell asleep and in her sleep she felt the earth swiftly revolving, grinding away on its axis with a cool, scaly majesty.

It was twilight when she awoke again. She was sweating with fever. She saw the clouds spilling over the branches, coiling and uncoiling, faster and faster. She was hardly aware of the pain, it possessed her so utterly. It was no longer merely pain. It was the earth. It was the air. It was the trembling in the leaves; it was the scream of the cricket. It was the whole world around her, which had suddenly splintered into thousands of glassy chips, and each of the chips was a piece of this strange, inhuman pain.

She raised her head but the strain of it was more than she could stand. She tried to scream. But all that issued was a muffled growl, like a puppy's.

The ground sank below her. She slid into the bottom of a gully and the heat in the gully turned into a shrill wintry cold. All around her fangs of ice dripped from the overhanging stones. Deep in the heart of the gully sounded a roar like galloping horses. Then the roar subsided into the scraping of tiny claws. The pain had turned into a furry bright-eyed beast which was snuggling inside her, no bigger than a mouse. It nestled now in her armpits, now in her temples, now in her shoulder-blades. Then it started to crawl through her body like a swarm of scorpions. Then it fluttered over her head, separate from her body, like a bat. Then it flew into a tree and perched on a twig and watched her silently. She was free of the pain at last. It had left her for ever.

And now something that had always puzzled her seemed on the brink of elucidation. Just one more glimpse: one more hint: one more flickering of light in the leaves! And everything would be clear! Everything would be named and explained and identified! She would know whether her name after all was Elizabeth Nightingale, she would know who she was and why she was born and for what she was intended. With one part of her awareness, or what was left of her awareness, she knew that none of these questions really mattered in the eternal scheme of things. But with another part of her awareness she knew that they mattered tremendously and that the whole of the universe, the sun and the moon and the nameless stars, kept circling and glittering in the hope of an answer to these questions.

A purplish blur in the sky passed over the stars, like the wings of an eagle. She felt herself rising, sitting astride an enormous horse and the horse galloped skyward until it turned into a tower, from which a single white ray fingered its way across the sea. She heard music, like strings being plucked on a guitar, and then a voice: "Gently, now! Careful, darling! Careful, careful . . ."

"Yes!" she cried, "I'm coming back, just wait for me, wait for me, I'm coming!" The marvelous beauty of the music made up for all the rest of it, the confusion and the cold and the black everlastingness. And then the tower melted away into a huge foaming breaker, and the foam broke over her head and she sank into darkness.

VII

Daphne sat in the attic and looked at her face in the dusty mirror.

"You're homely," Barbara had told her. "You're the ugly one in the family."

She gazed at her freckled, rectangular face with a mournful curiosity. Her hair was tied into a bristling red braid around her head. Her mouth was sullen and reproachful, a little bit flabby. Her eyes had a foolish, hunted shimmer, like a rabbit's. She was ugly; it was obvious. She was the ugliest of all the sisters.

And as she stared into the mirror she realized that the ugliness lay deeper than the surface. She realized that she was bleak and charmless, without Augusta's strength or Barbara's beauty, without Consuelo's flair or Freya's gayety, without Grace's secret awareness. She felt drab and sluggish, without sparkle or delicacy, without even the vividness of slyness or malice. Gradually her features seemed to melt into the blistered oval mirror. They grew blurred and bulbous, as though her face had turned into a mask.

She turned away in a spasm of misery and ripped open a dusty drawer and started groping among the doilies and antimacassars and pincushions. She was desperately looking for something, looking for anything that was clear and definite. But the dirty lace and the pin-pricked satin had an evil, corrupted look to them: she hurled them across the floor and went racing down the stairway.

Out in the garden all was still. Most of the family was asleep. The sunlight floated over a cloud of blossoming honeysuckle.

She crossed the lawn and stepped out into the daisy-filled meadow. Then she stole through the cedars toward the rocks down by the inlet. Now and again she glanced back to make sure that nobody was following her. Finally she came to the Tree. She sat down in the shade and tenderly ran her fingers over the deep-rutted bark.

A frog sat beside her under a Jack-in-the-Pulpit. She reached out and cupped it deftly under her hand. She felt the membranous little body squirming and nuzzling against her palm. She picked it up by the waist and stared at it thoughtfully. Then, half gingerly and half caressing, she ran her fingers along its spine. "I'll call you Jimmy," she said. "We'll be friends, won't we, Jimmy?" Translucent lids folded sadly over the bulging golden eyes, the slimy little fingers groped imploringly at her thumb. She opened her hand and whispered, "There, you can go now, Jimmy." The frog took an enormous leap and she called out after him: "Goodbye, and don't forget that I let you go now, Jimmy!"

She rose, flicked the dust from her skirt and started to climb the Tree.

The part that was difficult was reaching the bottom branch. She carefully placed one foot on a knob in the trunk, gave a leap with the other and snatched at a twig halfway up; then she tucked her right foot into a hollow in the trunk, seized the neck of the bough and coiled herself around it. She bruised her knee against the bark and the blood came oozing but she hardly noticed it. Now she crouched on the bough and started to climb slowly higher.

Up in the crest of the Tree there was a delicate agitation. The twigs stirred lazily in the slow, brackish wind. A spiral of gnats went spinning past her in a parabola. A battalion of ants was marching along the bottom of the bough and a red-bellied spider scurried across his web toward a twitching mosquito. The Tree was a world in itself, busy and ravenous and bloodthirsty, and the world of men shone in the distance, limpid and comatose. White clouds trailed their shadows over the flesh-colored beach. Out in the bay a little sailboat passed slowly toward the isthmus.

A shadow was moving along the beach. It turned into a beetle and then a man. He crossed a dune, vanished from sight, and emerged two minutes later and sauntered up toward the grove of cedars. He glanced around furtively, then came and stood under the Tree. Daphne crouched motionless, peeping down through the latticework of leaves. He was a powerful, bull-like man with a mass of auburn curls. His skin was tawny with the sun; the hair on his arms sparkled like wires. He reached into the pocket of his corduroy pants and took out a pipe, patted the tobacco in the bowl, struck a match and held it cupped.

At that moment she caught sight of a woman crossing the meadow below the house. She was wearing a yellow dress and a crimson shawl over her shoulders. In one hand she was carrying a paint-box and in the other an aluminum easel. She came to the edge of the meadow, paused for a moment by the fence, then opened the wooden gate and followed the path toward the grove. She came to a halt when she saw the stranger. She placed her paint-box on the ground and carefully leaned the easel against a treetrunk. There was a tense, eerie moment when the woman and the stranger looked at each other, neither of them stirring, the woman with her hands raised casually to her throat, the man with the pipe held out in front of his chest: they looked spellbound, petrified in a strange, dark expectancy. Daphne felt obscurely frightened, she wanted to cry out to her mother, but then she saw her smile curiously and walk slowly toward the stranger, fold her arms around his neck and lay her head on his shoulder.

"You've been waiting?" she whispered.

"A while," said the stranger.

"You knew I'd be coming?"

"I hoped," said the stranger.

They sank gently to the ground and their voices grew mingled, as though they were gradually melting into each other. Daphne crouched on the bough and peered down at them, puzzled, appalled. A strange and sickening recognition seeped slowly through her brain, a sense not quite of viciousness but of a nightmare acrobatic, a kind of bestial, primeval grotesquerie.

She closed her eyes and clung blindly to the overhanging branch. "Oh God," she thought miserably: "let it be over, let it be over!" And then it finally was over, there was a whispering and a stirring and her mother leapt to her feet and flicked the dust from her elbows.

"Goodness, I'm late," she said softly. "Don't forget now. Next Thursday!"

"Same time. Same place," growled the stranger, buttoning his trousers.

VIII

She stood on the edge of the boulder and stared down at the water. Already the memory of what had happened was mysteriously eluding her. It spread out in little ripples that died in the sunlight. She had witnessed nothing and heard nothing, she had merely dreamed a horrible dream.

The water rustled among the reeds; it kept whispering through the stillness. And she knew it was speaking to her, it was sending a secret message to her. But what was the message? Something about time and repetition and loneliness; about the years still to come and the years already forgotten. But what was the meaning? Was there really a meaning? Was there always repetition? Were there always things happening in duplication of things that had already happened? Were things happening only a reflection of other things that had already happened and were lost in the dark echoing well of the past? And would there always be loneliness? Was there no way of getting closer to people? Of understanding other people and being understood by others? Of accepting the ugliness of others and of others accepting one's own ugliness?

When she came back to the house she saw Miss Malachi at the end of the garden. She was clipping the tea-roses with a pair of black shears. Daphne tip-toed around the porch and darted up the stairs. She paused for a moment at the landing and glanced through the stained glass window. The lawn below was a blazing yellow; Miss Malachi was lifting her basket. Daphne shifted her head a little. Now the scene was a deep sea-blue. Miss Malachi dropped her shears and was stooping down to pick them up again.

She moved noiselessly down the hallway and opened the door on the left. Grace was sitting on her bed, threading a chain of wax pearls.

"I've lost two of them, isn't it awful?" she said softly, gazing at her sister.

Daphne flung her arms around her and buried her face in Grace's neck.

"Goodbye, darling," she whispered, feeling her eyes fill up with tears.

Grace sat motionless, then drew away and stared at Daphne with her spaniel eyes. Her lips started to quiver; she lifted the pearls to her chin.

"I'm going away," said Daphne.

"Yes, I know," whispered Grace.

"Forever!" said Daphne.

"Oh, Daphne," murmured Grace.

"Nobody will care," said Daphne brokenly, "they all think I'm stupid and ugly. You're the only one that I'll miss. Don't forget me now, Grace!"

Grace looked at her solemnly, holding the chain of pearls in front of her.

"You're looking for something," she murmured. "Yes. I know. Looking for something . . ." Then she whispered: "Don't be long, dear. Come back. I'll be waiting."

Daphne closed the door softly and went back to her room. She turned the key in the lock and pulled down the blinds. Then she opened the drawer of the bird's eye maple dresser and took out a comb and her mother-of-pearl scissors. She leaned forward, squinting a little, and let down her braid. Then carefully, strand by strand, she clipped her hair with the scissors until it was almost as short as a boy's. It looked crude and stubbly but a look of triumph shone in her eyes as she gazed at the snub-nosed face in the mirror.

She picked up the coils of fox-like hair from the carpet, regarded them quizzically and dropped them into the basket.

Then hurriedly, almost frantically, she stripped off her clothes and tossed them over the rocking-chair that stood by the dresser. She flung open the closet door, ripped the jeans from their hook and pulled them over her legs with a blunt, coltish movement. She slipped on a T-shirt and on top of that a moss-green pullover. Now she glanced at the mirror again with a wide-eyed gravity.

She opened the leaf of the desk and took the earthenware pig, broke it open and scooped the quarters and dimes into a handkerchief. This she slipped into a trouser pocket along with the comb and a bar of chocolate. Finally she slid on her socks and her black Norway moccasins. Then she peeped through the blinds into the sunlit garden.

She turned the key in the lock and stealthily opened the door. The hall was empty. There was only the ticking of the grandfather clock. She crept to the edge of the landing, listened intently for a moment, then went rippling down the stairs like a trout down a waterfall.

IX

She kept walking toward the hill. The earth was dry and pebbly. The shrubs grew scrawny and after a while there was nothing but pines. On top of the hill there was still a halo of peach-colored light. It dissolved as she watched it. The comb of trees turned a mottled blue. Far below she saw a river winding through the valley, brown and scummy. A wooden bridge crossed the river and a road ran over the bridge, dipped sideways into the woods and reappeared in the distance, pale as gunpowder.

She started downhill toward the bridge and the river. The slope sharpened. Patches of gravel kept slithering under her feet. Once she slipped and fell headlong and the blood leaked from her palms. Then the earth grew mossy. The smell of swampland rose around her. It was dark all of a sudden and the stars began to shine. The moon peeped through the clouds and the fire-flies were sparkling.

A cliff rose in front of her. She groped her way along the edge of the river. Then her legs sank into a deep nest of slime up to her knees. She clutched at the twigs and scrambled up into the thicket.

She halted. Something was stirring very faintly among the leaves. She stood poised, ready to run. There was a sigh, low and husky, and then a plaintive whisper:

"Oh Lord. Lord A-mighty."

There was a dry little scratch. A flame shot from the match and by the dance of the flame she saw the face of a boy, both cheeks blotched with blood. She saw the collar of his uniform and the cap on the grass beside him, and the puff of cigarette smoke that rose in the air. And then all was dark again except for a tiny red glow.

A twig snapped. The glow darted. A timorous whisper: "Who are you?"

"Nobody special," stammered Daphne.

"What you looking for?" said the boy.

"What's wrong? Are you hurt?"

"Yep. Hurt."

"Bad?"

"I guess . . ."

She ducked through the shrubs and knelt on the ground beside the sailor. She could see his face staring up at her, just barely visible in the glow of the cigarette.

"Land sakes," she said. "Just look at you."

"Yep," said the sailor. "That's how it is."

"You've got to do something," said Daphne.

He closed his eyes and puffed at the cigarette.

She leaned closer. "What happened?"

"A fight," said the sailor, blinking.

"I'd better look for somebody . . ."

"No," whispered the sailor. "Don't. Don't please!"

"Lordy me," whispered Daphne, squatting on the leaves with a little moan. "I wish I knew what to do. You can't just stay here all night."

"I'm thirsty," muttered the boy. He tossed his cigarette into the darkness.

Daphne gazed at him thoughtfully. The moon rose over the trees and now it shone down in silvery patches through the leaves. His face was wet and distorted and his cheeks were clotted with blood, but she could see that he was a powerful, good-looking boy, with a dimple in his chin.

"There's some water down by the rocks," she said. "Just wait. I'll get some water for you . . ."

Down by the shore she found a gin bottle half buried in the sand, and she washed out the sand and filled it with the warm, milky river water.

"Here you are," she said, crouching over him. "It's clean and nice. Don't mind the taste of it."

He raised his head and tried to drink but suddenly his mouth squirmed sideways, he spewed out the water and sank back with a groan. She caught sight of the great black stain in the grass and was frightened.

"It hurts, doesn't it?" she whispered. "You poor little thing."

She spilled some water in the palm of her hand and stroked it gently over his forehead.

The boy gulped and panted. Then he opened his eyes and looked at her intently.

"Don't go away," he said pleadingly. "Just stay a while. Don't go away, honey."

"That's all right," murmured Daphne. "Don't you worry. I'll stay."

He smiled tenderly and said nothing and closed his eyes and lay motionless. She thought he had fallen asleep. But then he said with his eyes still closed:

"You're nice. You're real sweet."

"Just relax now," said Daphne.

"You're queer, ain't you?" said the sailor.

"Ssh. Relax," whispered Daphne.

"Put my head in your lap," mumured the boy in a far-off voice.

She lifted his head ever so gently and let it rest on her thigh. It felt heavy and damp; she ran her finger over his temples.

Now the moon shone straight down on them. A strange loneliness filled the night, so deep and uncanny that the world seemed utterly changed. The past fell echoing like a pebble dropped in a cistern, and all around her the shadows of an unfathomable future came welling closer. The moonlight turned the sailor's hair into tight little coils that shone like platinum.

The swaying leaves overhead stroked his face with their shadows.

He opened his eyes and stared at her with a childlike gravity.

"Guess I'm done for," he said.

"No," said Daphne, "don't say that!"

"I don't mind. I just want to lie here, that's all," said the boy.

"Hush," said Daphne. "Don't talk. Just try and sleep now."

"Kiss me, please," said the sailor hoarsely.

She leaned over and kissed him on the forehead.

"I ain't scared of it," said the sailor in a low, steady tone.

"No," said Daphne, full of terror. "No, no. I know you aren't."

"What do you think?" whispered the sailor.

"What about?" said Daphne pleadingly.

"When we're gone . . ."

"Yes?" said Daphne.

"I mean . . . is there anything left of us?"

"Yes!" said Daphne. "I'm sure!" Her voice deepened. "I'm positive!"

The boy turned his head and opened his mouth as though he were drinking.

Overhead a little bird was hopping delicately from bough to bough.

X

A sloping light hung over the hills, green, opaque, like the light in a fishbowl. Her clothes were soaked with the dew and matted with slime and torn by the underbrush. When she finally reached the road the light had deepened to an ugly purple. Far in the east, out over the bay, the waves of thunder were beginning to rumble.

The first drops were already falling when the green convertible came to a stop. The door swung open: "Get in, child," said a woman in sun-glasses. "There's a storm coming on. No use standing in the downpour."

Daphne got into the car and stared out through the swinging wipers.

"Mercy, child," said the woman, sharpening her gaze. "You're all scratched up."

Daphne nodded. She kept stroking her sweat-soaked bangs back from her forehead.

"You've been in a mess," said the woman, "haven't you?"

"I'm worn out, kind of," said Daphne.

"Come now, duckie," said the black-haired woman in a deep, ringing tone. "I could see it in a flash. You've had a crisis. Am I right?"

"Well, maybe," said Daphne. "Something awful just happened."

The woman nodded with competence, narrowed her brows and tightened her lips. Her face was broad and lined, a leathery brown, like a squaw's, and in her powerful mass of hair there were streaks of iron gray. She wore a green muslin dress, bulging slightly at the middle. On her chest there was a large golden starfish studded with corals.

"And he's still lying there, is he?" she said when Daphne had finished her story. "Well, there's nothing you could do. Better not get mixed up in it. It all sounds as though there were more than meets the eye in it, duckie . . ."

"He was so lonely," said Daphne softly.

"Well, things happen," said the woman.

"He was so frightened, so confused . . ."

"You can't keep them from happening."

"He never told me his name, even."

"Forget about it. Just forget about it. Things happen," said the woman stonily. "You can't stop them from happening."

The rain grew less for a while and then the thunder came

rolling again. There was a zig-zag of lightning over the plains to the east. And then a great violet cloud spread its wings and swept toward them. The smell of phosphorus seeped through the window; all the leaves started to flutter. There was panic in the air as a claw of fire shot over the road and then the storm was upon them in all its anarchy and clamor.

"My name's Mona," said the woman, staring intently through the downpour.

"Mine's . . . George," said Daphne thinly.

"Come now, child, stop pretending. You're not a boy, no more than I am. You can't fool Mona. You're going through a crisis. It's as clear as the palm of my hand. Don't you worry, I won't give you away. Just be frank with Mona, that's all she'll ever ask of you."

"Yes, you're right, I guess," said Daphne. "My name's Diana . . . Diana Jones."

"You're suffering from a shock," growled Mona, puffing vigorously at her cigarette. "Yes, I can see that you're baffled. I can see the panic in your eyes. Something else must have happened, even before you found that sailor-boy. Yes, I'm sure of it. There's been a crisis, a real, genuine crisis." She shot a fierce look at Daphne. "You're running away. Now it's a fact, isn't it?"

Daphne nodded. She leaned her head against the leather and closed her eyes.

"Yes, I know," said Mona relentlessly, "it's been a shock, whatever it's been, but you'll have to be brave, Diana, and not lose your perspective. Everything depends on perspective. Life is hell without perspective. If I lost my perspective, I'm telling you, Diana, I'd go mad. I'd go out of my mind."

The car went skidding across the asphalt. The storm roared and whistled. Great cascades were flooding the windshield and fists of rain battered the canvas.

"Fiendish, isn't it?" said Mona.

Daphne started to shiver.

"Yes, I know," said Mona placidly: "that awful loneliness.

That awful bewilderment. We all go through it. It's part of life. It's a part of America, isn't it? So wonderfully secure on the outside. So sickeningly insecure on the inside. So well-fed, so ill-loved. So steeped in sanity, so close to madness. Just contradictions, that's all, mysterious and endless contradictions . . ."

A gust of wind whisked the car to the opposite side of the highway. A big truck came hurtling through the downpour, headlights blazing: it missed them by a foot.

"This is ghastly," said Mona huskily. She steered the car back to the right side of the road, inched forward for another mile and turned into the driveway of a chromium-plated diner. They parked beside the entrance and went darting into the neon-lit heat.

Two beefy men in sweat-stained overalls were sitting at the counter, drinking coffee. A pouch-eyed waitress was flirting listlessly with a pimply boy in a cowboy hat. Flies hung seething over the pastries and were bouncing against the panes; coiling stalactites of flypaper were peppered with little corpses.

Mona ordered a glass of beer. Daphne ordered scrambled eggs. They sat down by the window and peered through the swarming dirty raindrops.

"People," said Mona, leaning back and folding her arms across her chest, "are very intricate, fantastically intricate, and nowadays they're more intricate than ever. We all reflect the dark and complicated things that are happening around us. We're all just echoes of the mysterious far-off things that are happening in the world. Some people say that we are what we are because of what we've inherited. Some say it's early childhood. Some say it's environment, or the tempo of life, or the triumph of machinery, or the lack of religion. Well, I say it all goes together, it's all a part of something bigger—something that nobody's found the answer to. Something much bigger than any of us realize!" She sipped at her beer and fixed Daphne with her formidable gaze. "You're looking for your soul, Diana. Am I right? Am I correct?"

Daphne stared at her feebly. "Yes," she whispered, "yes, Mona." She gazed dejectedly at the yellow paste which lay cooling on the plate in front of her.

"Poor child. You're all tired out. You're utterly exhausted," said Mona.

Daphne smiled, half shyly, half gratefully, then closed her eyes and leaned her head on Mona's shoulder. She felt nothing, nothing at all except two powerful arms gently enveloping her, sleek and irrestible as the tentacles of a sea-beast.

XI

Summer returned, and with it came the singing of insects out in the orchard. Six months had passed since Augusta's marriage and departure for Blue Hills and three since Elizabeth's death and two since Daphne vanished. It was Elizabeth's which was the saddest tragedy and Daphne's the most mysterious, but it was Augusta who left the house with the deepest sense of disorientation. Life had lost its cohesion and self-confidence in Bishop's Neck. A yellow haze crept over the fields and rolling pasturelands along the Chesapeake. A yellowish dust rose from the dessicated veins of the estuaries. The yellowed stubble was spotted with black, burnt-out patches; the bright plumes of goldenrod were scattering their yellow pollen.

The seventh of August was Mr. Nightingale's sixtieth birthday. Out came the old English silverware inherited from granduncle Horatio. The candelabras were washed and polished; the Italian napkins were laid on the table. Compotes were cooked, fondants were boiled, patties were baked and a turkey was roasted and over the house hung a tension, half festive, half melancholy. After luncheon Grace played the sonata *alla turca* in the drawing-room and Consuelo sat on the love-seat to comb the Persian cat. Barbara curled up on the couch with *The Mysteries of Udolpho* and Miss Malachi left a platter of fudge in the library. A faint breeze set the wicker chairs rocking on the veranda. The shadows of the pillars fell sloping across the ivy.

"For years," said Mr. Nightingale, with a curious look in his face, "I believed in improving the world. I believed in progress and equality. I wrote conscientious reports on the oppressions in Korea. I wrote earnest memoranda about the prevalence of syphilis in Macedonia. I pleaded for a better understanding of the Kurds and the Cypriots and the Fiji Islanders. Nobody listened. They called me a crackpot. They called me a crank and a communist . . ."

"And for years," said Mrs. Nightingale, "I've put up with mediocrity. I've tried in my own house to preserve a semblance of awareness. But what can one do? Look around! Nothing but cheapness! That's all I see, just the vulgar cheapness of second-rate thoughts and second-rate feelings. Millions of marvelous little capsules and fantastic little gadgets to prolong millions of meaningless, pointless lives *ad nauseam* . . ."

Freya beckoned to Peter and they sauntered down to the pier, where the row-boat lay anchored in a jungle of lily-pads.

The water changed color as they drifed from cove to cove. In the first of the coves it was a reed-tinted green and in the second little cove it was a dirty, slime-streaked coffee. Then the shore twisted suddenly and a row of willows leaned over the water, which had darkened into black, the color of the twisted, rotting willow-roots.

"Augusta's gone and deserted us," said Freya, staring at the water, "and Elizabeth is gone and Daphne's run away. Maybe Elizabeth is happy but I'm sure that Augusta isn't happy, and there's something about Daphne that will always keep her from being happy."

"Grace is happy," said Peter. "Even when Elizabeth died she wasn't sad, was she? Even when Daphne ran away she didn't seem to mind it especially."

"Grace," said Freya, "is a genius. Someday Grace will be famous. I feel it in my bones. Grace will be another Horowitz."

"It's Consuelo who'll be famous. Grace is much too retiring. Consuelo has the glitter. Consuelo will be another Pavlova."

"And Barbara?"

"Oh, Barbara." Peter glanced at the opposite shore where the sails of a yacht were floating slowly across the greenery. "Barbara's ambition is like a knife. She's not an artist like Consuelo, or a poet like Grace. But she'll be rich. She'll get what she wants. There's a glitter in Barbara's eyes."

"Isn't it sad," remarked Freya, "what keeps happening to people? Even if they're famous and successful, something ugly always happens to them. And if they're miserable and failures, there's another kind of ugliness. No matter what happens to people, it always ends by making them uglier."

"How do you know so much about people?"

"Intuition," said Freya, "I guess."

"And what is the answer, then?" said Peter.

"To live on an island," answered Freya. "Neither a failure nor a success. Away from the world. Free. Separate . . ."

The fireflies gathered. They rowed back and anchored the boat among the lily-pads. They strolled up through the orchard and there in the dusk, among the apple trees, Freya whispered, "Oh, Peter darling, life is so wonderful, I'm sure it's wonderful, we're so lucky to be born and it's so dreadful to think we'll die! Every morning when I look through the window, I feel lucky to be alive, and still, what is it, can you tell me, this funny darkness that lurks in everything?"

When they stepped into the garden and started across the lawn, Freya's hand tightened on Peter's and both of them knew that something had happened. The veranda door swung open and Miss Malachi rushed toward them, beating her arms in the air like some huge, black-hooded bird.

"Quick," she cried, "hurry, hurry! Oh, why did he do it? What made him do it?"

And they followed her up to the room where Mr. Nightingale was lying.

XII

Late that night, when the house was dark, Peter climbed the stairs silently and tiptoed into the guest-room where the corpse had been laid. A vaporous light shone through the window, filling the room with a fog-like atmosphere in which the light of the candles flickered dimly like beacons. A plaster bandage had been placed over the wound in the dead man's temple. He looked shattered but calm; there was a look of relief on his face. Peter leaned over the bed and kissed the corpse on both cheeks and then hurried from the room, which smelled of sea-weed and sea-urchins.

And later, when he looked again at Mr. Nightingale as he lay in the dining room, the shattered look had disappeared and the look of relief was also gone. He lay in a silver-mounted coffin which rested on a bier covered with wreaths of tuberoses. His sharp bony chin was resting on a white silken scarf and the hair was neatly divided and shiny with oil. There was an ambiguous aroma of perfume, chemicals, and molten wax. The eyes were closed tightly and the lids had a flat, immovable look to them and the kindly troubled face looked neither kindly nor troubled but merely alien and impersonal, transcendently strange.

On the following evening, which was a Thursday and the day after the funeral, Mrs. Nightingale called Peter into her half-darkened bedroom.

"Grace," she whispered, "has decided to stay and Miss Malachi is staying with her. The rest of us are leaving for Europe. Barbara and Freya and Consuelo and I."

Peter nodded politely and held his hands folded in front of him.

"You are a very good boy. We have grown to love you," said Mrs. Nightingale.

Peter stared at the floor. He was afraid to look at Mrs. Nightingale.

"We are leaving for Italy. You must come along," said Mrs. Nightingale.

Peter glanced at her silently.

"You'll come, of course?"

"Yes, Mrs. Nightingale."

"My darling," said Mrs. Nightingale, "all these years, these many years, and still you call me Mrs. Nightingale!"

Peter blushed. "I didn't know quite . . ."

"Come, kiss me," said Mrs. Nightingale. "We must struggle through this together."

Peter leaned over the chaise-longue and kissed her shyly on both cheeks.

Then he tip-toed down the stairs and wandered out into the garden. A ray of light from the library window gilded the roof of the little summer-house. But as he stood there alone, listening to the litany of the crickets, the light went out and the world was lost in the sudden immensity of the darkness. All that vastness! All that terror! All that black, impenetrable mystery! Was there any answer to the frightening loneliness of being a single human being? And as he stood there under the chestnut tree a strange thing seemed to happen. It was as though some alien pity or alien love had gently materialized, had slid out of the darkness and were nestling in his consciousness. It was as though, under the blaze of those hundred million stars, a new identity had suddenly sprung up in him and a new being had been created. The entire past floated away like the coils of mist by Cleghorn's Inlet and the breath of things to come welled out of the dark unmeasured wilderness.

Part Three

The Paganini was a prim little hotel on the Via Emilia, with a potted palm in the hallway and an agreeable view of the Pincian Gate. Here they lived for three months, visiting the churches in the morning, lunching at Mario's or Giovanni's, and taking their noonday nap like everyone else in the city. Consuelo was reading Dante, Freya was painting up at the Academy, and Barbara went strolling through the museums with Peter and her Baedeker. Mrs. Nightingale stayed in her room and read detective stories during the day and had coffee at Rosati's in the late afternoon.

In June Mrs. Nightingale detected a gathering strain on the family budget. Five hundred and fifty dollars a month was not enough for a hotel life. So she rented a four-room apartment on the Via Campagna, with a row of tall windows facing the bust of Belisarius. Here Freya and Consuelo shared a room overlooking the court and their mother shared a damask-lined bedroom with Barbara. Peter was put in the little narrow maid's room behind the kitchen. Every morning at eleven the cook arrived with her daughter Tina and for lunch they'd have *lasagne* or a *risotto con funghi* and for dinner a leg of lamb or a chicken with noodles. Seventy thousand lire a month for the apartment; twenty thousand for Assunta; one hundred thousand for the food and wine; ten thousand more for the gas and electric bills. That left enough for the opera at Caracalla once a week and an occasional excursion to Fregene or Nemi. But not enough for shopping sprees on the Via Condotti or the holiday in Venice which they all kept talking about.

"It is odious, being so poverty-stricken," said Barbara.

"And what exactly," said Mrs. Nightingale, "do you propose to do about it?"

Barbara stared at the umbrella pines. "I haven't quite decided."

"There is only one thing that you can do about it, my child," said Mrs. Nightingale, "and I am not in a position to make suggestions, as you will appreciate."

"Rome," said Barbara, with a shrug, "can be very depressing."

"You are feeling the Spectres," growled Mrs. Nightingale.

Barbara went wandering through the city with Peter every day. One whole day they spent on a visit to the Forum and the Palatine. Another they gave to the mosaics; a third to the catacombs. Once they wandered from fountain to fountain, ending up at Santa Maria in Trastevere. Occasionally they went for a prowl in one of the streets near the Pantheon or the tangle of alleys behind the Piazza Navona, poking their noses into the wine-shops, watching the cobblers hammering at their boots, peering into the puppet-maker's studio or the artisans' workshops. They watched the boys painting roses on porcelain door-knobs or folding sheets of gold-foil on the carved wooden candle-sticks. Once they spent the whole morning in the Protestant Cemetery and she sat in the shade while Peter read the *Ode to a Nightingale.*

In the late afternoon cascades of light poured over the hills. The walls of the Quirinale grew alive with a shower of copper. But the grandeur of Rome was not a grandeur that appealed to Barbara. There was a heaviness about it, a stagnation, even a certain vulgarity, and the ponderous façades had a curiously hollow look to them, as though the passions that lurked behind them had lost all their pungency. She loathed the desecration of the bill-boards; she hated the squalor of the neon-lights. She hated the leers on the Via Veneto and the scream of the Vespas along the Corso. She hated the pompous Victorian mustiness of the Via Nomentana and the cheap flabby modernism of the Via Parioli. But what she hated most of all was what the Romans called *la bella figura,* the perpetual strutting, the pseudo-elegance, the bravado, the vacuity, all that sour conglomeration of airs and poses that filtered through the streets like a mist from the marshes.

All the same, she vaguely sensed a certain undercurrent in the atmosphere. Something to do with the Roman people, with the Roman voices and the Roman bodies, with the way that the Romans looked at her and the way they moved in the crowded piazzas. Like animals; sly and graceful, over-civilized animals.

This flavor of animality seemed to filter even into the architecture. It hovered around the fountains, it clung to the pink façades. The naked river-gods in the Piazza Navona still shone with a lambent fleshiness. There was a leer of innuendo in the baroque cherubs. Even the ruins seemed infected with a furtive animality. A faint whiff of sex lurked in the caverns of the Coliseum.

"Don't you find them a little queer, all these Romans?" she said to Peter.

"Yes," said Peter. "They are very ambiguous. They pretend to be happy but they're full of sadness."

"They pretend to be passionate but they're full of boredom," said Barbara.

"And they pretend to be brave but they're full of terror," said Peter.

II

One Sunday in October they were asked to tea at Miss Polk's. Miss Polk was over eighty; some said that she was a hundred. She had been a friend of D'Annunzio and Eleonora Duse and Adelina Patti. She lived in an old palazzo on the Via Gregoriana over a courtyard populated with pregnant cats and glowering goddesses. A vast gray stairway wound up to the mouldy *piano nobile* where a liveried footman stood waiting in the velvet antechamber. Everything in the house was oversize. It seemed to have been built for a race of giants. Stupendous doors ten feet high, gilded thrones shaped for a Hercules, and the head of Polyphemus overlooking the towering drawing-room.

Miss Polk was sitting in a deep baroque couch in front of the fireplace, tremulously pouring the tea from a large silver samovar.

"Do you see that piano?" she said, placing her hand on Barbara's wrist. "It belonged to Busoni. Vladimir De Pachmann played on it once. Ravel played on it once and I have a violin that belonged to Joachim. I even have an old corset that belonged to Rossini!"

All around her stood the remnants of a decimated era. White-haired diplomats and courtiers, symbolist poets, crippled philosophers; a wizened ex-soprano who had been the mistress of Jean de Reszke; a monocled Grand Duke who had met Rasputin at the baths.

A tall man with a white goatee came and sat beside Barbara.

"You are a musician, I presume?"

"No," said Barbara, "not in the least."

"I beg your pardon. You have the brow of a very sensitive musician," said the gentleman. His hair floated like thistledown over his tapering head; his voice had a sombre, measured sonority. His eyes rested on Barbara with an ice-gray curiosity. "A pianist's brow, distinctly. But your ears. There's mischief in your ears."

"Are ears capable of mischief?"

"Ears, my child, are capable of anything. People talk about eyes," said the gentleman, "they talk about skulls and they talk about noses, but they fail to see the fateful significance of ears. The slope of an ear lobe tells me more than a volume of anecdotes. There's a definite wickedness in your ears, Miss Nightingale. Forgive me for having noticed it."

"It is odd," said Barbara, smiling, "for I never listen very carefully."

"Precisely," said the gentleman. "You ignore the words, for the words mean nothing. And you even ignore the thoughts, for the thoughts mean very little."

"And what is left? What else can one listen to?"

"The pulse," said the man, "of destiny! Some hear it, some don't. Some obey it, some rebel against it. If one is lucky enough to hear it, or unlucky enough, as the case may be, one can afford not to listen, one can afford not even to think."

"I have never been able to afford very much," hinted Barbara.

"Not, perhaps, in the usual way," said the gentleman, nodding.

Some days later she went for a stroll in the Villa Borghese. She had discovered a walled-in garden in the depths of the park, the Garden of the Lake it was called, transversed by alleys of ilex trees which hid the place in a musky stillness. Sparrows lit on the arms of a moss-tainted Niobe and the slime of dead water-lilies lapped at the Temple of Aesculapius.

Someone touched her on the elbow.

"I beg your pardon. I think you've lost something."

It was the white-goateed gentleman she had met at Miss Polk's.

"Thank you," said Barbara. She took the glove that he held between his fingers.

He walked slowly at her side. "Have you noticed their presence?"

"Whose?" said Barbara.

"The dryads! They still live in the Giardino. The castiron gates are locked at night so that the dryads can revel in peace and if you peep through the grating you can sometimes catch a glimpse of them. I've seen them only once. Long ago, when I was a baby. I still hear them now and then, singing away in their frog-like voices. If you happen to have an ear for subtleties, as I'm sure you have, my dear Miss Nightingale, you can hear what they say: prophecies of love and all the rest of it. I have an aunt who was warned by a dryad never to get married and she never did. One should do as the dryads say. They're always right. *Ils ont raison.*"

He glanced at her shrewdly. "I'm talking nonsense. Is that what you're thinking?"

"Not in the least," said Barbara solemnly. "I'd love to hear what the dryads say."

"Shall I speak more prosaically? May I mention the light, for example? There is a magic in this light. It is the light of lost illusions. I don't happen to care for Rome. I prefer Siena and even Florence, but this drowsy golden light, half sad and half happy—it is unique."

They circled the lake and turned back toward the Pincian Gate.

"You will think me unpardonably forward, but may I extend an invitation?" He stood stiffly by the gate, very gaunt, very gray-eyed. "I have a perspective by Borromini. I have some sketches by Raphael. I have a ceiling by Serenario and a small medallion by Giulio Romano. They're not quite of the first quality, not *chefs d' oeuvre,* you understand, but would you honor me by inspecting them? I live on the Via Giulia."

Barbara smiled. "You are very kind."

"You'll come alone?"

"If you'd rather."

"Thursday at five, then? I shall live in expectancy. My name is Prince Massimo, if you didn't happen to be listening . . ."

III

The Via Guilia was a long, dusky, haunted-looking street, tinged with the dampness of the Tiber and dappled with skeleton-like shadows. The silhouettes that lurked in the doorways or leaned lazily out of the windows had an ominous, lupine look: they seemed ready to pounce on her.

Halfway down the street, on the Tiber side, stood the Palazzo Massimo. It was a massive old building with an ill-paved court-yard. Small puddles of dirty rain-water still lingered in the corners. On the left was a disused stable; there was a faint musk of horses. Through the half-open door she caught a glimpse of dusty harnesses. The day was hot and dry but as she crossed the ill-lit corridor she felt the chill and the clamminess which clung to the walls.

The Prince was waiting in the library. He was wearing a velveteen jacket. He smiled and took her hand between his bony white fingers.

"I am delighted, Miss Nightingale. Please try to be indulgent. The house is badly neglected by American standards, I'm afraid. But it is massive. It is spacious. It is quiet. It is cool. And even the shabbiness has a certain solidity. There is nothing flimsy about it. Let me show you the rooms."

They passed through a number of adjoining salons, high-ceilinged and heavily-curtained, lit by a glimmer of little bulbs. At the end of the vista was the great "Napoleon" drawing-room with its three candelabras of twined Murano glass. She was surprised to see a fire burning in the big black fireplace. The dance of the flames shone on a row of armchairs shaped like seashells. Overhead was the "famous" fresco: the legend of Diana and Actaeon.

They sat down in front of a dolphin who was balancing a marble disc. The Prince tugged at a rope; the butler appeared with a tray.

"And a bit of lemon, please, Perugia. Americans take lemon in their tea," said the Prince.

Perugia looked like a character in an *opera buffa:* grotesquely thin, with martyred eyes and a nose like a tapir's. He wore a lavender frock-coat and faded nankeen breeches, green woollen stockings and an egg-shell colored cravat.

"I shan't bore you with any more chatter about Rome, Miss Nightingale. You can judge the city for yourself. It is gossipy and hypocritical. It is greedy and lascivious and lazy. And it is riddled with superstitions. I have my own private witch down in the basement, for example, a hairy old scrubwoman named Desideria. I doubt whether there exists in Rome anyone who is especially happy or kind or virtuous. Nevertheless it has its points. The light, for instance. Did I mention the light to you?"

"Yes, that light under the ilex-trees, I still remember it," said Barbara.

The Prince drew a flame-shaped gesture in the air. "I judge everything by light. I judge places by their light, I judge paintings by their light and I also judge people by their light. Paris has a blue-gray light that I respect but cannot love. Sicily has a lemon-colored light that I thoroughly detest. The light in the Alps is a glassy green; I abhor it. Venice has a peacock-colored light which I find a little gaudy. The light embodies the history, the philosophy, the very soul of a place."

"And people? Do you see a special kind of light in people too?"

"Oh, decidedly," said the Prince. "A coolish glow, or a mournful shimmer. Sometimes there's a vulgar glitter or a vague sickly gleam. And sometimes there is a horrifying deathly phosphorescence. I judge people by their ears, as I may already have mentioned, but I judge them even more by the light they exude!"

He passed her a plate of wafers, then put it back on the table again. "I am about to say something which may startle you, Miss Nightingale. I might mention that the occasion at Miss Polk's was by no means the first time that I happened to lay eyes on you. I saw you once at the Castello San Angelo. You were leafing through a guide-book. I saw you buying some violets one day on the Spanish steps. Once I saw you sitting by the Fountain of Trevi with a young American. I was troubled for just a moment; but then I realized that he wasn't dangerous. In short, I have arrived at my decision not abruptly or tempestuously, but by careful degrees and with cool circumspection!"

His elaborate way of speaking, courtly and mocking, a bit fantastic, and all of it conveyed in a coppery resonance: it was beginning to have a disturbing effect on Barbara. She felt shy and disconcerted, but also flattered, even a little bit titivated. And at the same time she felt unnerved, not only by a gathering embarrassment but also by an under-current of something like panic.

"You are beautiful, ridiculously beautiful, that is what struck me at first," said the Prince. He was watching her with a languid, ruminative smile. "But as I studied you I developed, shall we call it a subtler view? It was this view that led me to think that my suggestion might be acceptable to you." He leaned back, folded his hands and looked at the fire with sudden gravity. "I cannot offer you youthful passion, I'm afraid, Miss Nightingale. I cannot offer you physical pleasure, in the strictest sense of the word. I can only offer you the various things that you see around you—a shabby old palace filled with obsolete relics, a shrunken old man with a swarm of bees in his bonnet. I can offer you devotion, tolerance, patience, understanding—but those are things that you'd gladly toss into the waste-basket, and rightly so. I can offer you financial security, which you might do well to consider, and I can offer you a few old-fashioned decorations, such as a title for instance. After all, life is a series of compromises, don't you agree?" He rose from the chair and looked down at her with a mingling of affection and mournfulness. He bowed slightly.

"Thank you for coming, Miss Nightingale. And please forgive my outlandishness. I have phrased my offer very clumsily. I will comfort myself with the thought that an eligible young lady is rarely piqued at a proposal of marriage, even from a doddering old fool!"

IV

They lingered on in the Via Campagna for several weeks after Barbara's engagement. They lived in a state which Barbara habitually referred to as "penury," but the penury was made more palatable, even for others than Barbara, by the prospects of luxury descending on Barbara.

Peter still considered himself to be in love with Barbara and the thought of Barbara's marriage filled him with a kind of dutiful dejection. But the dejection was tinged with more than a hint of relief. It was as though, now that Barbara was safely beyond his reach, his love could afford to grow speculative, remote. He realized that in a way his love had always been remote: she had been a symbol and not a personality, she had been a vision and not a body, and there had always been something a bit uncanny in his feeling, as though it were not really

Barbara that he loved but a phantom that dwelled in Barbara, and his love were a ghostly revival of some deep ancestral memory.

Whenever they spoke of Bishop's Neck it was fleetingly and a bit disparagingly, and his memories of Bishop's Neck were already gathering a misty vagueness. Sometimes he wondered about Augusta and her black, brooding secrecy, and about Daphne's disappearance and Grace's pale phantoms. But the real world was Italy. He was discovering himself in Italy. Rome was turning him into a person, with personal opinions and personal attitudes. He was still very shy, rather passive and shadowy, but even these were qualities that gradually took on a personal, distinctive flavor.

And so his happiness remained untroubled. Just being in Rome made him happy. He found happiness in the Roman voices, he found joy in the Roman fountains, and he even found pleasure in the unpredictable Roman weather, which fluctuated between a drizzle and a harsh, brassy sunlight. He felt happy to be alive, he felt happy to be in Italy, he felt happy when the sky was blue and equally happy when the sky was gray. He felt delighted when he visited the churches on the Aventine or the caverns on the Palatine; he felt exultant when he watched the children playing in the Piazza Navona. He enjoyed sipping coffee in the arcades of the Galleria, watching the pimps and the gigolos, the wagging whores and the mincing pansies, who somehow were blended by the Roman light and the Roman tolerance into the omnivorous human climate which pervaded the city. He especially liked the Piazza della Minerva with its obelisk-bearing elephant and the little shops around it filled with ecclesiastical robes, cardinal's caps and black cassocks, episcopal headgear and ornamentation, things of intricate white lace and pink moiré embroidered with gold, all tinged with an indefinable clerical bleakness but at the same time giving a certain gayety and even giddiness to that bleakness.

Through the kindness of Prince Massimo he earned a few thousand lire giving English lessons to some ragamuffins who lived in the Palazzo Orsini, and through the kindness of Miss Polk he earned a few more lire reading aloud from Jane Austen to a blind old lady named Miss Fothergill. And now that Barbara had deserted him on his tours of the museums he took to wandering with Freya, usually with a paint-box and an easel. Freya had shifted from pastels and water-colors to oils. She was developing a "style": something halfway between pointillisme and a hazy, light-drenched cubism, and gradually this mixture of styles became another style which bordered on abstraction: there was still a suggestion of sun-drenched columns and rain-blurred porticos but more and more the shapes dissolved into a swarm of interwoven threads which made the columns look like ladders and the porticos like spiderwebs.

His own paintings on the other hand grew more and more "visual." He sensed that his talent was less confident and original than Freya's, but little by little he too developed a "style," neither dots nor cobwebs but a conglomeration of curves and angles, suggested by the warm, sensual curves of the Roman statues and the luminous angles of the Roman vistas. In Freya's paintings there was never anything that resembled a human figure. In his own there were always figures but they had the appearance of statues, or if not statues then an operatic look, like figures posturing against a baroque backdrop. Freya was a modern and he was a romantic; and yet in Freya's very modernism there was a probing romanticism and in his own mask-like romanticism there was a bleak, dehumanized modernism. But he knew that of the two it was Freya's paintings which were the more authentic, and with all her abstraction she came closer to human reality. He realized that in his own wistful nostalgia for the past, for the cherubs and cupolas and shadowy colonnades, there was less genuine passion than in Freya's fur-like patterns, which stirred and flickered with a zest all their own.

Furthermore, in spite of the mystical look in some of Freya's paintings and the highly formalized look in his own, it was really Freya who was concerned with form and he who was the mystic. And since form was attainable in painting and mysticism unattainable, there was an inadequacy in all his paintings which he couldn't quite identify, just as in Freya's there was something limited but perfect and self-sufficient.

"You keep painting an imaginary world," she said, "that pretends to be real. But it never was real. It only exists in your dreams!"

Whenever he was with Freya he felt peculiarly light-hearted, as though he were breathing the air on top of a mountain. Or the air on an island, maybe, since Freya was still obsessed with islands and kept speculating about Madeira and Cyprus and Sicily. The whole world seemed spacious and sunlit in Freya's presence, and he felt full of enthusiasm and gusto and enterprise. Which was odd, since it wasn't Freya but Barbara that he was infatuated with, and with Barbara he felt troubled, self-doubting, apprehensive.

"Yes," said Freya, "I know perfectly well that you're infatuated with Barbara, and I won't dispute that Barbara is beautiful to look at. But after all these years . . ."

"Yes?" said Peter, with a sidelong glance.

"You show remarkably poor insight, darling. You are enthralled by the surface. You see only the surface."

"Why do all of you hate Barbara? What has Barbara done to you?"

"Isn't it obvious?" said Freya, laughing. "We are jealous of Barbara! We are frantic with jealousy!"

"Even you?"

"Well," said Freya. "I'm beginning to get over it. I used to be jealous of Augusta but that also died away. I pity Barbara. Especially now. I see where all this is leading her. With all her cunning and all her ambition her life will be a failure."

Now and again he went with Mrs. Nightingale for tea at

Rosati's and she would pour out her heart with her usual candor and trenchancy. She was blending into the Roman climate with astonishing rapidity, not the climate of the ecclesiastics nor that of the piazzas, not the climate of the antiquarians and certainly not the climate of the cinema, but that musty Victorian flavor which still lingered in the background, with its residue of whalebone and antimacassars. She had abandoned her linen smocks and Mexican beads and Aztec bracelets; she wore lipstick and mascara and a rakish hat with a long black feather. When he was alone with Mrs. Nightingale Peter felt a mingling of embarrassment and gratitude, always tempered with awe as well as a certain native caution.

"I am deeply relieved," she confided, "about Barbara's engagement to Prince Massimo. It's one more worry out of the way. Or even two, if you count the money part. I don't suppose I'll have to be scraping and scrounging much longer. Prince Massimo is one of the wealthiest men in all of Italy." She squeezed her lemon into the tea, which was served in a glass in the Russian manner. "Augusta's been taken care of, not as romantically as one might wish perhaps, and Daphne's out of the way, bless her poor little soul, and Grace is best where she is, with all that music and Miss Malachi, and so it finally boils down to Consuelo and Freya. You have no conception, Peter darling, of what a strain it has been. Seven daughters, all included, and some of them well on the weird side, and the insufficiency of funds and that neurotic blood of the Nightingales." She leaned back on the banquette, placed a cigarette in a holder, and fixed her eyes on Peter with an osprey-like stare.

"I've been wondering," she said.

"Yes?" said Peter politely.

"Consuelo is leaving for Paris. She'll be studying ostensibly, but I know my Consuelo and her penchant for color and I see her very vividly in one of those Left Bank cafés. Consuelo is a romantic to the fibres of her being. Thank God, she's given

up the illusion of dancing and she's going in for poetry, which
is equally unreal but a bit less dangerous, and with all her
romanticism I have confidence in Consuelo. There is strength
in Consuelo. Consuelo will survive."

"And Freya?"

"Precisely. I suppose you realize that Freya is in love with
you?"

Peter blushed and stirred his tea. "Not really. Not seriously."

"Yes, it's difficult to imagine, you're sweet and gentle but
hardly a beauty, yet I've noticed the way she looks at you and
it's perfectly obvious. She adores you."

She stretched out her arm, with the long black cigarette-
holder at the end of it, and glared across the room with an
oracular expression.

"Life," she said, "is a rather queer sort of business, all in all.
The things I could tell you, Peter. The waste and the pangs and
the treacheries. I think of you as a son, my dear, and some day
I'll tell you the truth of it. But not now. You're too young. You
wouldn't understand it all, I'm afraid."

Three days before her wedding Peter went for a last little
stroll with Barbara. It was dusk; the streets were empty and
unnaturally silent. They crossed the Villa Borghese and followed the road into the Pincio, where the marble busts shone
through the leaves like a row of heads from the executioner's
block.

"You look puzzled," said Barbara.

"Yes," said Peter, "I feel puzzled."

"Don't you see?" said Barbara tensely. "Don't you understand? It's not just silliness! All my life has been tainted with
this horrible fear of failure. Father was a failure *au fond*.
Everything at home smelled of failure. Everything was dusty
and seedy and finally I grew terrified. I made a vow. To be
rich. To be calculating and ruthless. I couldn't bear the idea
of shriveling away in Bishop's Neck, of dwindling into mediocrity with nothing to show for it! Anything rather than that

drabness. Anything rather than another failure. You can think what you wish but I'm sick of drabness and provinciality!"

The sky darkened and the lights started to glitter in the Piazza del Popolo. Beyond loomed the light-dappled slopes of Monte Mario. And as they stood there, leaning silently over the balustrade, Peter felt something happening: he felt that they were shedding their personalities and were turning simultaneously into two completely different personalities. He felt himself mysteriously transformed, maybe by love or desperation, or maybe by some time-destroying chemical in the atmosphere, into someone with an alien virility and self-confidence. And for a fleeting little moment Barbara was also transformed, she became a creature of a spectral gentleness and pallor and submissiveness. He wanted to press her hand to his lips and wet it with his tears. A crazy hope surged up for a moment and he wanted to cry, "I love you, I love you!"

They stood motionless for several minutes, staring down into the Piazza. Night fell, the illusion melted, they were Barbara and Peter again and they walked through the park back to the Via Campagna.

v

A week after the wedding they abandoned the flat on the Via Campagna. Consuelo flew off to Paris. Freya rented a studio in the Via Margutta. Mrs. Nightingale moved into a green-curtained suite in the Grand Hotel and Peter took a room in a cheap little inn near the Pantheon. He still gave lessons in the Palazzo Orsini and read *Persuasion* to Miss Fothergill and he was able to pay his bills without borrowing from Mrs. Nightingale. One day the gipsy-like woman who ran the Obelisco galleries took three of his paintings and displayed them in her shop-window. He still painted in his ruin-haunted "romanesque" manner but something new was beginning to creep into the dim, nostalgic vistas. Gradually those tiny silhouettes which were dwarfed by the vast façades, like Piranesi's, grew larger and more vivid and the vistas kept growing smaller until they in turn were dwarfed by the bold human outlines. They receded into a delicate mosaic behind the tree-torsoed figures, who no longer were dressed in operatic crimsons and purples but in dirty brown rags, like the children in the slums of Trastevere. He developed a particular love of Caravaggio at this time and he used to visit the Galleria Borghese just to look at the Caravaggios. He loved the way the whole canvas was filled with his glowing bodies, which wore grapes or guitars or half-filled wine-glasses instead of clothes, or if they wore clothes they looked like an appendage to their flesh, which was so sexually alive that he could almost smell the secretions. And the same thing was true of the sculptures of Bernini, where the flesh took on an almost hallucinatory vividness. The river gods in the Piazza Navona looked so alive in their sun-licked laziness, it seemed as though their skin would give under the touch of his fingertips.

He kept prowling through Rome, no longer with a Baedeker and no longer in the Forum, but past dilapidated alleys and smoky warehouses and peeling tenements where the people were much more beautiful and alive than on the Via Veneto. He frequented certain ill-lit restaurants where he grew familiar with some of the celebrities, the painter de Paolis and the poet Gerbore, the actor Manfredo and the critic Rosenstock. And he gradually learned that behind the Roman hedonism there was a sickening misanthropy, behind the sexuality there was an emotional staleness, and behind that brimming cornucopia of art and tradition there was a vacuum of doubt and unease and disgust.

Just a week after the wedding a ball was given at the Palazzo

Grassi and Peter borrowed an ill-fitting dinner jacket from a sculptor friend of Freya's. It was nearly ten when they arrived in the enormous courtyard behind the Campo dei Fiori, which was filled with the gleam of torches on antiquated town-cars. Powdered footmen in satin stood on the mirrored oval stairway and the host and hostess stood by the door as the guests walked in. Old Miss Polk, looking like a mummy beneath her feathers and sapphires, took Freya by the hand as they strolled through the ball-room. "Look, child, that's the Countess Piaggio talking to Prince Pompini by the window. He's the richest man in Rome. His mother's a Bolivian. That's the Duchess of Capua, half Russian and a terrifying bluestocking, and that's old Lord Hennessy who has an estate down in Sicily."

Barbara stepped into the room just as the music began and Peter's heart tightened when he looked at her loveliness. She was wearing a long white gown of Chinese silk and in the middle of her throat there was a single large diamond. Her beauty was so great that she did not need to charm or smile; she was so beautiful that she instinctively tried to understate her beauty. She looked cool and distant and a little bit sullen. She was immediately surrounded by a group of handsome young Romans, and as she danced she tried gracefully to pass her partners on to Freya, who wore a dress of blue chiffon which used to belong to Barbara. Peter felt tense and rather miserable. He kept sipping champagne and stood in a corner with no one to talk to. Miss Polk came limping up and muttered hoarsely: "She's incredible, isn't she? Just look at her. They are terrified or her. She could be the leader of Roman society if she wanted, with that formidable poise!" Food appeared on the narrow tables that were scattered among the rooms. The candles shone on the naked demigods who surveyed the Ligurian lobsters, the bowls of caviar from the Caspian, the rosy fish varnished with aspic and the blood-red gelatines studded with scampi. The desserts were brought on by a column of butlers in perruques: rum cakes covered with almonds and crystallized cherries, ice-filled pineapples and blazing peaches and wreaths of pistachio floating over clouds of Chantilly. The Capodimonte plates had a border of gilded laurel leaves, with a sea-beast in the center surrounded by a ring of azure waves. A window was flung open and there was a whiff of far-off things—old hemp, salt and seaweed, decaying cargoes in a tropical harbor— but then it all dissolved in the stench of human corruption, the smell of dregs and sweat-soaked powder and old, sagging flesh. Rumpled napkins and greasy plates covered the wine-spotted tablecloths and a faint tinge of rot settled on the pastes and purees.

"Come," said Freya, "we'd better be going. We don't belong here any longer. I'm not sure where we do belong but certainly not here and certainly not now . . ."

They walked down the stairs and crossed the Campo dei Fiori, where the carts of fresh vegetables were already crawling through the half-light.

VI

The first of Freya's islands was a rocky island in the Tyrrhenian. As she stood on the crowded deck she watched it sharpening on the horizon, turning from a misty far-off lilac to an amber-streaked plum. The ship landed; little rowboats splashed about in the crystal water and the sun beat down on the wharf where the barefooted fishermen were selling their sea-urchins.

She took the squeaky little funicular up to the piazza. The bell was tolling. A column of choir-boys was solemnly crossing the square, threading its way through a tangle of sun-tanned vacationists. A baker's boy was balancing a tray of brioches on top of his head; a half-naked muleteer was leading his mule past the café tables. The exhilaration danced in the air like a swarm of sulphur butterflies. A smell of peppers and onions floated out from the pizzeria.

She left her bags at the Gatto Bianco, which was a white-washed inn in the adjoining alley, and wandered up the cobblestones past a row of tiny shops. Sandals, scarves, gaudy pullovers and flowered bathing trunks hung in the shop-windows. The road started climbing. The crowded shops gave way to villas. Flowering acacias cast their shadows on flesh-tinted walls. Finally the villas trailed off in a stretch of sun-baked vineyards and she reached the top of a hill where a ruined temple stood in an olive grove.

To the right lay the Sorrentine peninsula jutting gloomily into the sea, with the cliffs of Calabria faintly visible in the southern distance. To the left lay the Bay of Naples, all adazzle in the dying sunlight, and the blue of the sea was a preening, stultifying blue. She glanced across the cliffs, looking for an effect that might be paintable, but everything she saw was much too garish and conspicuous. The beaches grew shadowy and the slopes of Vesuvius turned to bronze. A goat-bell tinkled in the gully. She caught a whiff of the sun-soaked precipice. Dusk fell and the sea grew dark and Naples turned into a string of fireflies which flickered and danced on the cloudless horizon.

The exhilaration still was there and the laughter still was there, but under the laughter and gusto there was something faintly nauseating.

The following morning she took the long twisting mule-path down to the beach. It was a dry sparkling day, not a cloud was in the sky, and for breakfast there had been crescents and straw-berries under the convolvulus. The mule-path was hot with the smell of the pines. Small green lizards kept darting through the cracks in the garden walls. Finally she reached the rock-lined beach. A row of blue and white-striped cabins stood on a broad wooden terrace which overlooked the "Rocks of the Sirens."

For a while she lay basking in the heat of the rocks. Then she waved to the boat-boy and asked him to bring her a sandolino, which was a one-paddled skiff resembling a kayak.

She went floating lazily across the warm blue transparency, leaning over to stare into the depths of the glassy water, where forty feet below she could see the pebbles in all their exactitude, with rainbow-like shadows hovering nervously beside them. She paddled beyond the rocks which marked the end of the beach and here the cliffs rose wild and towering, with tufts of cactus nuzzling on the edges. Here the island was completely deserted, there was nothing but cliffs and water, and the vaguely cloying atmosphere of the island abruptly vanished. She felt the warmth of the chasms radiating from the cliffs, and the cliffs became a presence, hot and immanent, like a herd of animals. And the water was a second presence, not stiff and glowering like the cliffs but sly and casual, lapping away at the sandolino with its little tongues. And the third of the natural presences, the most insistent and insinuating, was the air, the sun-soaked air which weighed on the water like a golden blanket and enveloped her body in a heady exultancy. Her skin tingled in the lightly scurrying breeze as though it were wine. Clouds were gathering in the east and there was a flurry of sudden coolness, but then the wind died down again into a midsummer torpor. She followed the curve of the cliffs until she came to a rocky crevice. Here the shade of the abyss darkened the water to mahogany. She paddled closer and saw the grotto burrowing into the side of the cliff. The shadow of the cliff slid over her like a big umbrella. It grew suddenly chilly. A spray of gravel fell from the cliff and went splashing into the water close beside her.

She paddled up to the mouth of the grotto. Inside the grotto all was dark but as she peered into the darkness she could see a faint reflection of the sunlight which played on the hidden water and shed its glow on the dripping walls. She ducked her head under a tusk of stone and guided the skiff into the grotto and now the darkness in the grotto changed to a queer prismatic twilight. She could see the tunnel reaching deeper and deeper into the gloom. A faint, sucking echo traveled back from the heart of the grotto. She left the kayak rocking lazily against the wall of the cave and started to wade into the narrowing tunnel. A medley of burnished colors played on the finger-shaped stalactites, all kinds of red, an onyx red, a nasturtium red, a visceral red, and she felt as though she had been swallowed in the secret organs of the island and that the throb of the water were the pulsing blood of the island. She passed under an arch. Veins of white shone in the walls, which the blood-colored water transformed into a luminous rose. The air, cool at first, now grew clammy and stifling. The echo of the waves was dotted with the echo of falling drops. There was a magic in all this blood-hued vaginal seclusion but there was danger as well, something raw and rapacious. The water grew deeper, it was up to her waist now, and a feeling of panic began to creep over her. Deep in the core of the tunnel, amongst the lappings and gurglings, there was a deeper sort of noise, like the groan of a large animal. She turned back: the mouth of the grotto was only a tiny half-moon. She waded back cautiously, groping her way along the walls, and then she noticed the little moon growing rapidly fainter. There was a sound of rushing water as the waves slapped into the tunnel. She slipped on a slime-grazed rock and fell headlong into the water. She felt a tugging in the air, a powerful suction like that of a vacuum, and she started swimming frantically toward the mouth of the grotto. Waves came splashing over her head up to the roof of the cave. She hurled herself forward, diving down as she reached the opening, and found herself swimming along the edge of the cliff. The storm was hurling the waves against the stony ledges and the sandolino was bobbing to and fro below the cliff, with the paddle floating aimlessly some twenty feet beyond it. She swam up to the sandolino and tried to climb inside it but the weight of her body kept tipping it sideways and it was impossible to keep it balanced on the surface of the water. So

she swam out further and retrieved the white paddle and tossed
it into the kayak and started swimming back to the rocks again,
clumsily steering the kayak in front of her until she managed
to guide it into the inlet. She dragged it ashore and crouched
on the edge of a rock, feeling the rain drumming lightly on her
cold, quaking shoulders.

VII

"You're all right?" cried a voice.

She turned brusquely and looked at the cliff. A man was
squatting on a rock directly over her head. He was very blond,
extremely sun-tanned, too blond and sun-tanned to look quite
natural. He was wearing yellow shorts, more like a loin cloth
than swimming-trunks, and his body was dripping with the
pouring rain.

"Nasty, isn't it?"

She nodded gloomily.

"I was watching you with the boat. They're treacherous, those
little boats. But you were clever the way you handled it."

"Was I really?" she said cuttingly. She detested this cocky
stranger, with the round golden medal dangling from a chain
around his neck. "It didn't occur to you to come and help me
a little, did it?"

"Oh, you did it very competently. You didn't need help. You
were very efficient!" He looked down at her with a teasing,
conceited expression.

The sun shot through the clouds with a startling suddenness.
There was a rainbow for just an instant, a haze of colors bridg-
ing the chasm, and the rocks shone in the sunlight as though
they were freshly varnished.

"Queer, these storms," said the man. He spoke with a hint of a stammer. His accent was thick and broad, like that of a Dutchman or a Scandinavian. "They shoot up out of the blue and come rushing across the sea and five minutes later they're gone without a trace."

"You're German?"

"No," said the man. "I'm Swedish. From Uppsala."

"You've been here long?"

"Three months nearly."

"You like it?"

"Well, like isn't exactly the word for it. Either you love the place or you hate it. There's nothing halfway about this island."

"I see," said Freya contemptuously. "I wouldn't know. I've just arrived."

"You're staying a while?"

"Oh, a week."

"It isn't enough," said the man. "You won't get the feel of it till you've been here a month. After a month you begin to feel it. You feel the radiations."

"Radiations?"

"Oh yes, haven't you heard about the radiations? They ooze out of the cliffs and little by little they seep into you. They make you healthy and strong and full of carnal desires but after a while they make you feel a little bit crazy. They're famous, these radiations. People come to the island for the sexiness but after a while all they feel is this typical island craziness."

"Very interesting," said Freya.

"That's what happened to the Emperor Tiberius. He came for the baths and the sexiness, but he went crazy. It's the radiations . . ."

The rain had dried on the rocks and the air was bright with heat again. Freya climbed from her ledge and started to tug at her kayak.

"Wait!" said the man. "What's your hurry?"

Freya stepped into the kayak.

"Always hurrying!" cried the man. "Perpetually hurrying! You American women!"

She glanced back and saw him squatting on the edge of the rock, and his body as well as his eyes shone with a vain, grinning mockery.

Two hours later she was sitting in the piazza, sipping a sugary lemonade. Whistles were blowing; a radio blared; the bells started clanging. The carriages from the beach came to a halt at the edge of the piazza and the bathers, dazed with the sun, staggered forth with their beach-bags. The funicular arrived, disgorging a new batch of tourists. A chubby priest came waddling from the church, arms laden with silver candlesticks, and a hag raced through the archway with a coal-black rooster dangling from her wrist. The air smelled of sun-oil and coffee and oranges but still subtler and more insistent was another smell, a mineral smell, the smell of rocks saturated with sunlight and salt and the fishy sea, the smell of all those strength-bearing, lust-breeding "radiations."

"Do you mind?" said a familiar voice. The blond young Swede leaned over the table. Without waiting for an answer he drew up a chair and sat down. He was wearing a batik shirt and coral-colored trousers. His hair was combed neatly. There was a whiff of eau-de-cologne.

"I was rude, I suppose."

"Were you really? I didn't notice."

"One keeps forgetting on this island. One forgets one's manners," said the Swede.

Freya stared at the steeple and fondled the rim of her coffee-glass.

"I love this island," said the Swede, "because it's a world all to itself. One forgets the rest of the world. One forgets all those tensions. One stops worrying about Russia and China and Africa. One just sits in the sun drinking wine and munching almonds and all that matters is the things that are happening between human beings, trivial things like falling in love or a new pair of shoes or a bit of gossip . . ."

"The tensions exist," said Freya. "There's no point in trying to forget them."

"They exist where they exist. In the jungle of Africa. In the mountains of China. But here they are unreal. What is real is the wine and the sunlight and the people."

"Real!" said Freya. "What is real? Only the things you see around you? We're not savages. We are aware of the things in Africa. It can't be helped."

The Swede laughed. His beautiful eyes, blue as ice, glittered impudently. "We'd all," he said lazily, "be better off if we lived on islands. If we clung to the reality around us. If we forgot those far-off crises."

"Yes," said Freya, "I too love islands. I've always wanted to live on an island. The wine and the sunlight and the sea. Yes. They're charming. They're delightful. But what I'm looking for is freedom and there's no freedom in forgetting the world. And when an island becomes forgetting things it becomes an illusion. It becomes a prison."

"You are charming," said the Swede conceitedly, "and I love listening to you. Will you have a cocktail?"

"Thanks," said Freya. "I'll have to be going. It's nearly six. There's a chill in the air."

The Swede leaned over with a tense expression. "You hate me, don't you?"

"Why should I hate you?"

"I see it in your eyes."

"You are very clever!"

His ice-blue eyes grew pleading and soulful. "Tell me, please. Why do you hate me?"

"I hate vanity," said Freya.

"Am I vain?" said the Swede.

"Revoltingly," said Freya.

The Swede lowered his eyes. His voice grew wistful and delicate. "Very well. I shall try to change. I shall get rid of this horrible vanity."

"No," said Freya. "You will never get rid of it. You will always be vain. You will always be horrible."

"Come," said the Swede, "please be reasonable, you've jumped at conclusions because I laughed at you. I apologize. I was rude, I was stupid. Will you come and have dinner with me?"

Freya laughed. "Just as you wish. I can't abide you, I've already said so, but now that you've asked me I'll gladly have dinner with you."

They met in the piazza at half-past eight and strolled through the archway to a trattoria which looked over the harbor toward the lantern-fringed bay.

"My name," said the Swede, "is Erik."

"And what do you do for a living, Erik?"

"I do nothing. I used to be a tennis-player. I played in all the tournaments. I played in Cannes and St. Moritz and Viareggio and Baden-Baden and once I even got into the quarter-finals at Wimbledon. But then I decided there's more to life than hitting a ball over the net. I took up painting. I stopped being a tennis-player and I started being an artist."

"How very interesting," said Freya. "And are you happy, now that you are an artist?"

"Yes. I'm happy," said Erik.

"Tell me," said Freya. "Describe your happiness."

Erik looked at her and laughed. "How can one ever describe happiness? I can describe sadness or hate or jealously, but I can't think of the words to describe happiness properly. A feeling of peace. A sense of harmony. Nothing is ugly. Nothing is frightening. One hates nobody. One is envious of nobody. It all sounds meaningless. I haven't the words."

"Yes," said Freya, "there is something bland and insipid about mere happiness. Life is flabby if there isn't pain or distortion somewhere or other. Not too much, just enough to give depth, to give shadows. Without the depth and the shadows life is bovine and love is meaningless."

"Love," said Erik, suddenly alert. "Have you ever felt it? Seriously, I mean?"

"No," said Freya. "I've never felt it."

"Neither have I," said Erik mournfully.

They drank their coffee and Erik said: "I believe in telepathy, or whatever you call it. I keep on thinking that I've met you before. Years ago. In the middle of a forest. I saw you coming along a path all speckled with sunlight. You were wearing a pale blue dress and you were carrying a basket of strawberries."

"Go on, please," said Freya.

"It was long ago. Before we were born. We stood in the path. It started to rain. We hurried out of the rain into a deserted little summer-house and there we started to talk and all of a sudden I fell in love with you."

"Yes? And then?"

"That's all," said Erik. "Years passed. We were happy and suffered and finally we grew old and unhappy and died, and now we've been stranded back in the world again, looking around for what we lost before we were born."

"It's a dream, that's all," said Freya. "Half truth, half falsehood, like every dream."

"Dreams are a lunacy," said Erik. "Last night I dreamed that I was in Chile. There was a wall all around me and as I wandered along the wall I met a woman in a bright red overcoat, and the woman was carrying a bird and the bird cried out, in a piercing voice, 'Oh why did you kill me?' And a shudder went through my body, I was filled with desperation. What does it mean? Does it mean anything? Is it a prophecy? Is it a memory?"

"It's both," said Freya. "It's prophecy and it's memory and it's something else, I don't know what."

"Come," said Erik, rising from his chair. "Let me show you my horrible paintings."

He lived in a small pensione behind the Hotel Brittania, in a white-washed room overlooking a garden. His paintings were mostly landscapes and seascapes in a traditional manner: fishing-boats on the edge of a beach, fishing boys with their nets, peasant girls beside a fountain, rows of cypresses in the sunlight. They were exactly the sort of thing that Freya detested. Amiable and empty, picturesque, with a kind of corpse-like verisimilitude.

"You hate them," said Erik.

"I'm afraid so," said Freya.

Erik nodded. "I knew you would. You always hated whatever I did. You always despised me, even long after you fell in love with me . . ."

And later, as they lay together with their naked bodies interlaced, she once again felt that curious, trancelike disembodiment: that mirroring, echoing impression of timelessness. It might have been that in the rush of an orgasm human identity had shriveled; it might have been that somehow or other Erik was right after all, they had been lovers long ago, in another land and another century, and all the ritual and compulsion of that earlier love had come back again, as well as all the pangs, the reproaches, the hatred.

She slid out of his arms and silently slipped on her clothes and then she leaned over the bed where Erik was lying, his arms flung apart, smiling lazily in his sleep. His long girlish lashes were pressed to his cheeks. His lips were half-open; his chest rose and fell. She kissed his cheek lightly, feeling the warm sandy texture of it, and tiptoed out of the room and closed the door softly behind her.

She walked across the island, past the villas and vineyards, through the grove with its ruined temple and past the half-ruined chapel, where a small ray of light shone on the brightly painted crucifix. She walked past walls laden with asphodels and caught the aroma of prickly pears. The light leaked over the sea, all gray and leaden beyond Ischia, and as she walked back to the village she passed the muleteer with his mule. A girl was climbing the mule-path with a basket of blood-oranges. A sheep-dog came bounding and jumped up at the orange-girl. The basket fell from her head and the oranges went tumbling, dozens of bright yellow oranges which caught the sunrise in their pores, and they rolled and kept rolling down the path toward the sea.

When she reached the Gatto Bianco she crept quietly up to her room and started to toss her dresses into the cowhide valise.

VIII

Life in the palazzo on the Via Guilia was a little livelier than Barbara had expected. For a fortnight after the wedding the days were given to social activities—a ball at the Odeschalchi's, a fancy dinner at the Aldobrandini's, a round of canasta at Aunt Gina's and a visit to Monte Rotondo, where Aunt Susanna lived in a vine-covered romanesque convent. Orazio's manners were always of the greatest tact and delicacy; his caresses were covert and brief and apologetic. He redecorated her bedroom with a flood of pink damask and a row of marble obelisks was placed on the dresser. He bought her a Lancia as well as a Guardi and a Salvatore Rosa. And at night after he kissed her on the brow he said gently, "You are mellowing, my lovely. Soon you'll turn into a Roman!"

She spent her mornings in the library, which was lined with vellum-bound classics. She leafed through Petrarch and Boccaccio, Goldoni, Leopardi. Copies of the *Revue des Deux Mondes* and the London *Tatler* were scattered about. A "trophy room" adjoined the library. Here was the relics of Orazio's youth: equatorial birds of astonishing colors, snakes and lizards from Madagascar, a leather shield, a shrunken head, and on the mantle two Eritrean divinities, a little monster with a frog-shaped penis and a goddess with a moonstone set in her vagina.

Christmas came. She received a Fabergé egg from Aunt Gina and a mechanical nightingale from old Aunt Susanna. Orazio gave her a golden cigarette case from Bulgari's and some beautiful new dresses from the Florentine dressmakers. They drove to St. Moritz for a week in mid-January and visited Taormina for a fortnight in March. She found herself in the "Himalayas" of Roman society, as her mother put it; her mother being installed in a suite at the Grand. She made her entry into the ballrooms in a blaze of pearls and diamonds and the Duchess of San Pellegrino called her "the transatlantic Venus."

Mrs. Nightingale said to her once: "You should be sublimely happy, Barbara. You've got what you wanted. You're rich and you're a princess. There's nothing left, except, well—but you've never really cared for men, have you?"

"I am not a Lesbian," said Barbara drowsily.

"That is not what I meant, quite," said her mother. "What I meant is that you are frigid. You aren't bowled over by sex, like Consuelo. And I wouldn't dispute that you're right. Sex is good for the complexion but it's bad for the figure, and God knows that a little bit of it goes a very long way. Sex is an overrated commodity, I have finally decided."

It was true. She had all she could possibly have desired. A bouquet of red roses was sent to her room every morning. A Pekinese puppy, whom she called Otello, was waiting for her one day in the library. On her shopping trip to Paris she was given a suite in the Ritz and in April Count Gastoldi took her on his yacht to Sardinia. She developed an entirely new circle of friends. Consuelo had gone to Paris and Freya was in Naples and she rarely saw Peter, who was roaming about in the Apennines. More and more she was spending her time with the Romans, who kept flattering her idiomatic Italian, her taste in baroque, and her faun-like figure.

May arrived. The weather grew balmy, the balconies were

showered with wistaria and when she strolled along the Tiber she grew aware of an unusual brightness, as though the trees had been sprinkled with a coppery powder. A man was playing an accordion; a flower-girl tossed a rose at her; an old woman was combing her poodle and a little boy was doing cart-wheels. The most ordinary objects were encased in a shining vividness, so intense as to seem unreal, like a view seen through a stereoscope. Barbara felt herself moving in a new and heady atmosphere, breathing a sharper denser air, seeing the world from strange new angles. She felt the warmth of the crowds in the piazza as though it were the warmth of her own body. An ancient magnetism seemed to rise from the paving-stones, tugging away at her limbs, drawing her closer to the earth, instilling in her flesh a tingling lethargy. "Spring fever," she called it. She felt an expectancy in the air. She blushed without reason; she smiled at odd moments.

Aunt Gina said, "Barbara *carina,* I've never seen you looking so lovely," and Aunt Susanna said, "Believe me, you can be frank with me, *mon ange,* but don't tell me that it's actually going to happen so soon!" Princess Fabriziano said, "It's the Roman climate, it is capable of miracles," and the Duchess of San Pellegrino said, "She is developing a sense of fantasy."

One evening in early June Orazio's sister arrived from Mantua. She came with her son, Alessandro, and they were put in the "Borromini suite."

Vittoria Reali was a wolfish bony woman with a black moustache. She glanced at Barbara with a look that was both fierce and solicitous. Then she kissed her on the cheek and said in a hoarse, tender growl, "Your eyes are not American, your voice is not American, only your nose is American and, after all, what is a nose?"

Alessandro was a curly-haired boy with the neck of an ox. His head resembled the head of Antinous in the Vatican. His eyes, huge and brooding, were of a midnight blue. His lashes were like a woman's; his lips were thick and contemptuous. He stared at Barbara with a look of suspicion, almost of hatred at first, but then his face suddenly melted into a sweet, child-like smile.

That evening after dinner she strolled into the trophy-room with Sandro.

"The salamander is from Zanzibar; it has magical powers. And look at this viper, please. Orazio found it in Chile."

Sandro lingered close beside her, so close that he almost touched her. He kept casting sidelong little glances at her. She caught the smell of his ripe young flesh; like a plum left out in the sun.

"Here is a mask from the Madagascar. If you put it on you can fly like a bird."

"Yes, yes," he kept purring. "How very strange. How very interesting."

"You take pictures, I hear."

"Yes," said Sandro. "I am a photographer."

"What kind of pictures?"

"Beautiful doors. Beautiful stairways. Beautiful people."

"Nothing ugly?" said Barbara. "Ever?"

"Nothing is ugly," said Sandro, "if you look at it carefully."

"But some doors and some people are more beautiful than others, I take it?"

"Tell me, please," whispered Sandro. "Do you really love my uncle?"

"What a very odd question. Of course I love your uncle."

Sandro stared at her incredulously. "You're too young to love him. And too beautiful."

"Love," said Barbara, staring at the salamander, "has its spiritual side."

Sandro's eyes glittered impudently. "One can see that you're an American!"

As they walked back to the drawing-room she felt his breath on her shoulder; his hand grazed her fingers as she turned the bronze door-knob.

"You're not angry?" he whispered.

"Have I a reason to be angry?"

"No," said Sandro. "No reason!"

"All is well, then," said Barbara.

IX

The great heat fell on Rome. All the shutters were closed at day and the streets were deserted from two until four. A yellow vapor lay on the Tiber. Flies clung motionless to the fruit-carts. The roads to Ostia and Fregene were seething with traffic and a layer of oily bodies covered the pine-edged beaches. Only when the shadows grew longer and the breeze came down from the Pincio did the city itself gradually come back to life.

A moonlight picnic on the Via Appia was arranged for Sandro's birthday. Chinese lanterns were hung from the arches; a tigerish glow fell on the ruined sepulchres. Shriveling contessas and marchesas, dressed in tulle and black lace, drifted slowly among the tombs with their glasses in their hands. Two musicians in red velvet were strumming away at their guitars while the villagers lurked in the shadows and listened to the singing.

Freya had just come back from Capri; she took Barbara by the arm and the sisters sauntered into the meadow, where the evening fog was beginning to rise.

"Ghosts," said Freya. "That's all that they are. Beautiful sensual little ghosts. The dead have never been decently buried in Rome. Everywhere you see little bits of them—a head or an arm, a naked foot. Don't you feel them hovering about? With their meddlesomeness and malice? Even their lust, that famous lustfulness, there's something ghost-like about it!"

"And still," said Barbara, "they think they are realists. They keep their ears cocked to the ground."

"They cling to their so-called realism because their inner life has shriveled."

"They are capable," said Barbara, "of passion."

"Do you really call it passion?"

"And they are capable of wickedness," said Barbara.

"Not of a true spiritual wickedness!"

"They are beautiful, at any rate," said Barbara.

"Beautiful!" said Freya. "How you have changed, my dear. You are beginning to notice people. Yes, you even look different. Your eyes—do I see a strange little glint in them?"

"Have you heard," said Barbara, "from Augusta?"

"Not for weeks. Augusta is lazy."

"Bishop's Neck," whispered Barbara. "It seems so infinitely remote now, doesn't it? Sometimes I wonder if it ever really existed."

"Yes," said Freya, raising her glass so that the moon hung floating in the wine, "Bishop's Neck was only a sunlit fantasy, with a demon or two lurking in the background."

"And still," said Barbara, "it is strange, Bishop's Neck is like a dream, but the dream seems like the reality and it's Rome that seems like a fantasy. I feel I'm floating in mid-air, watching a witty little ballet being danced by a bevy of gesticulating phantoms."

"Yes, you've changed," said Freya mockingly. "You are turning into a poetess."

"In the old days," said Barbara, "I always used to envy Augusta." She turned her wine-glass upside down and watched the drops fall on the grass. "Augusta was shrewd and obstinate. She didn't go in for flights of fancy. But then one day I suddenly realized that Augusta was done for. Her life had turned sour. It had grown dismal and provincial. And I made up my mind not to fall into Augusta's trap. I was ambitious. I wanted grandeur. I wanted to be in the heart of things."

"You have succeeded," said Freya, "obviously."

"Do you think so?" said Barbara.

"You wanted power. I wanted freedom. Freedom was always the great intoxicant. I wanted to smell the seas and the mountains. I wanted to browse on sunny islands. Consuelo wanted freedom, but it was a different kind of freedom. You have the freedom of wealth and luxury. Consuelo has the freedom of her bohemianism. Daphne ran away, she wanted the freedom of isolation, and Grace, poor little Grace, she wanted a secret kind of freedom, she wanted to escape into music and dreams."

"And you? What kind of freedom," said Barbara, "are you looking for?"

"I don't know! And that's exactly what freedom means to me," said Freya. "Freedom of instinct. Freedom of impulse. Freedom to change at a moment's notice. Freedom to shed my entanglements, my loyalties, my principles, freedom to pack my things in a bag and head for another island."

Barbara balanced her wine-glass on the edge of a broken column. "You are glorifying your promiscuity with the airs of philosophy," she said. "Freedom! We talk about freedom. What we really want is security. There's no freedom in not knowing where we belong or what we believe. You are trying to escape from insecurity by plunging into insecurity."

"You are making a paradox of it. But it isn't a paradox," said Freya. "Yes, Augusta was caught in a trap. And there's a trap waiting for Consuelo. Poor Grace was trapped in her nightmares, and Daphne was trapped in rebelliousness, and even you are slipping into a trap. Look around. Don't you see it tightening? Don't you feel it beginning to strangle you?"

Barbara laughed. Her wine-glass fell to the ground and shattered. "Oh, Freya, my innocent Freya, you've always been an idealist. You are full of delightful theories but you're blind to the things in front of you. A trap? Oh yes, I agree, there's a trap here in Rome, there is something waiting to trap me if I'm silly enough and weak enough. I have my faults, I'm a vicious woman, much more vicious than you suspect, but I doubt whether I need to feel frightened of Rome."

"Who," said Freya, "is that beautiful young man who's been watching us?"

Barbara glanced around quickly. "I suppose you mean Sandro."

"He's in love with you, isn't he?"

"He is only a child," said Barbara carelessly.

Freya looked into Barbara's eyes. She started to say something. Then she turned and walked off into the misty darkness.

A silky hand fell on Barbara's shoulder.

"Did your sister say something wicked about me?"

"No," said Barbara. "Not in the least."

"But she said something, didn't she?"

"She said you were *molto bello*."

Sandro blushed; he caught his breath. His eyes shone like bloodstones.

"Please," he whispered, "will you give me a birthday present, *zia* Barbara?"

"I gave you that pretty little box of lapis lazuli."

"Something else," pleaded Sandro.

"Yes? What?" said Barbara playfully.

"Will you drive out to Ostia with me tomorrow?" said Sandro.

X

They turned left when they reached the sea and followed the road through the pine-woods. Through the screen of black trunks they could see the walls of the bath-houses. Finally they came to a deserted stretch of tea-colored dunes. Sandro parked his car in the shade and they took their beach-bags and towels and followed a path through the flowering underbrush.

The heat of the sand burned through her thin leather slippers. Bright green flies spun through the brambles; there was a sweet smell of sage. They crossed over a knoll and stood on the edge of the sea. The swarms of bathers in the distance danced like minnows in the waves of heat. Immediately behind them a wooden hut stood on top of a dune. To their left lay the long empty beach stretching toward Anzio. A shaggy fisherman gathered his tackle, waved to them briskly and vanished.

They folded their towels around their bodies and wriggled into their bathing suits. She wore a bikini patterned with heliotropes; he wore a tight azure triangle. They lay down on the pitted sand and stared up at the sky.

"Look," said Sandro. "What do you see in that cloud overhead?"

"I see the head of a woman. Her hair is streaming. She looks like an ogress."

"I see a helmet," said Sandro. "A silver helmet tufted with plumes."

"Look! She's turning into a dragon! She's breathing flames! Do you see her?"

"I see a piano with a lion crouching on top of it," said Sandro.

He spread his arms and closed his eyes. She glanced at him furtively: at the shadow of beard on his cloven chin and the little curls nuzzling in his armpit; the sheen of sweat on his belly and the indolent curve of his *cache-sexe*. Under the blaze of the summer sunlight human flesh lost its mystery. It looked clumsy and primitive, even a little bit repellent.

Sandro opened his eyes again. "What are you thinking, *zia* Barbara?"

"Nothing," said Barbara.

"Nothing at all?"

"I was watching the waves," said Barbara.

"How many sisters do you have?" said Sandro.

"Five," said Barbara, spreading her fingers.

"Are they beautiful? All five of them?"

"Did you think that Freya was beautiful?"

Sandro frowned. "Not beautiful, exactly."

"But you liked her? You liked her, didn't you?"

Sandro grinned. "Do you have any brothers?"

"No, no brothers. Only Peter."

"Who is Peter?"

"A friend of the family's, you might call him," said Barbara.

"I suppose you had an affair with him?"

Barbara laughed. "You Italians!"

"Is he handsome?"

"Neither handsome nor ugly," said Barbara.

"You love him. I can hear it in your voice," murmured Sandro.

She snatched at a handful of sand and let it drift through her fingers.

"A child, that's what you are," she said. "Just children, you're all of you children! Not the women, they're as clever as witches, but the men. They're nothing but children!" She stared angrily at Sandro. "It's a game, that's all it is for you! Just a silly, simpering game! Self-indulgence and vanity!"

"And Orazio?" said Sandro. "It isn't a game for Orazio, is it?"

"Orazio," said Barbara, glancing at the water, "is a philosopher."

Sandro laughed. "Come," he said, "it's too hot to be talking philosophy!" He scooped her up in his arms and carried her down to the sea.

The water was listless and tepid. It was like floating in a sea of feathers. She rolled around in the wavelets, beating at the foam with her toes. A surge of recklessness rose up in her, a dazzle of animal well-being. She shot out into the sea trailing the ripples behind her.

When they lay on the beach again she saw that the clouds had grown larger. Sandro was squatting at her side. Drops of the sea hung from his eye-lashes and rolled from his silky sun-tanned chest. A single drop as bright as a diamond was clinging to his nipple. He leaned over and ran his thick warm finger along her collar-bone.

"I had a dream last night," he said. "I was walking along the sea. It was dark. The moon was out. I heard a voice come out of the sea."

"A siren," said Barbara, "probably."

"No," said Sandro, "it wasn't a siren. The voice rose out of the water. It was a water-ghost calling."

"And what happened?"

"The waves parted and I saw a tunnel leading into the sea. I stepped into the tunnel. It was covered with marvelous jewels —sea-urchins and sea-anemones carved out of amethyst. The voice kept singing from the end of the tunnel. *"Aiuto!"* it sang. *"Aiuto!"* The jewels turned into sea-beasts, terrible medusas and octopuses, and the song kept growing shriller and shriller . . ."

"Yes? And then?"

"I woke up."

"And you never saw the weeping water-ghost?"

"She would have turned me into a fish if I'd seen her!" said Sandro, laughing.

The clouds were spreading, unfolding their plum-blue petals. There was a clap of thunder rippling away in the distance. A whirlpool of sand came dancing past them and then the rain shot over the dunes, tugging at the pines and flattening the thistles, digging craters in the peppery sand.

Sandro snatched at the clothes and started to lope toward the dunes. "Only a shower," he shouted. "Nothing serious! Only a sprinkle!" She followed him up the beach toward the little black hut. He tugged at the door; the rusty bolt sprang open.

A fisherman's net hung from a hook behind the door. An oval basket and a wooden bucket stood in the middle of the floor. In the corner lay a knife and an empty wine-bottle. The concentrated stench of the sea hung in the black hot stillness.

Sandro closed the door carefully and hung the clothes on the iron hook. The only light was a watery eye that peered through a little knothole. The rain let up for a moment. There was a tense, musty stillness. And then a second clap of thunder and the rain started to pour again, more powerfully than before, hammering away at the flat tin roof.

Part Four

There is an island off the coast of Florida, floating in the stillness of the Gulf, long and flat, shaped like a porpoise, stirred by dank and fishy breezes. The rippled sand, yellow as corn, slopes down toward an idle sea. The beach is fringed with a litter of shells, black, amber, puce, écru, from which rises like steam an iridescent blue light and a smell of old bones, sea-spiced and sea-battered.

The name of the island is Tortosa. At one end is an old plantation house, now shaggy with vines and misted with cobwebs. In the middle of the island lies a jungle where flowering bushes quiver with humming-birds. At the other end lie scattered the shacks of the fishermen and the bungalows of the spinsters. One of the bungalows facing the pier has a small

L-shaped annex and over the door of the annex is a pea-green sign: "Miriam's Place."

Here lived Mona and Miriam. Miriam was old and very tiny. She wore heavily-lensed glasses and rose-spattered dresses and her hair was tucked up into a thin white bun. She ran the café all by herself; Mona merely handled the money-part. She served coffee and hot-dogs and an occasional bit of pastry to lean, bitter ladies and sun-shriveled anglers.

When Daphne arrived she was given the bedroom behind the kitchen, with a row of little cactus pots lining the window-sill. She tied a polka-dotted apron over her faded blue jeans and served the guests in the afternoon. Not that there were very many of them, in fact on some days there weren't any at all. But occasionally toward dusk a couple of weather-beaten cronies dropped in, or maybe one of the girls who worked at the 'Tween Waters Inn.

It was all very casual, there was always coffee and Coca-Cola, on certain days there was pecan-pie and on others there was lemon meringue, and sometimes there was ice-cream and more often there wasn't. Sometimes Miriam sat on the veranda with her cards, playing patience, and sometimes Mona sat on the sofa with her green-backed thrillers, and under the casual monotony there was a strange bedazzled dreaminess, as though everything went on in a kind of sun-soaked delirium.

Months went by, nothing changed, and every morning after breakfast Mona and Daphne put on their sun-glasses and wandered along the beach. Sometimes a great new multitude of shells lay washed in by the tide and they'd kneel in the sunlight and grope for the beauties and rarities. Daphne learned to tell at a glance the single treasure among the thousands. There were the beautiful fan-shaped shells, some of them rounded and some flat, a marbled violet or a mottled crimson, a fleshy rose or a vaporous azure. There were the gnarled and varicose Lion's Paws, with their amber-hued knuckles, and above all there were the infrequent and exquisite Junonias, glossy scrolls white as ivory dotted with blood-red hieroglyphics.

"Shells," said Mona. "Aren't they marvelous? All washed clean by sea. Utterly clean. Pure. Lifeless. The mineral purged of the animal. Purged of everything corruptible, everything mortal scrubbed away. Only the pattern and the purity left, only the bone, the immortal element. I only wish, Diana, dear, that our own skeletons were the prettiest part of us! Well," she murmured, lowering her head as she knelt there, like a woman praying, "it may be that they are. Flesh, flesh, what's nice about flesh? Sometimes I wish that I were a skeleton, dancing along on the beach by moonlight . . ."

When they came back to the cottage Miriam put down her cards and peered at them.

"Did you find anything?" she whispered.

"Some nice little fans. Nothing special."

And they sat down to lunch in the trance-like stillness of noon.

"It's so quiet here, so still, nothing seems to be happening. It's deceptive," said Mona, her voice booming across the porch. "Things keep happening all the time, even when nothing seems to happen. In fact, it's then that the most important things of all are happening. In the stillness of the day the secret dramas unfold. Yes, the crucial things in life, the real dramas, the real turning points"—she raised her fork and fixed her black, brooding eyes on Daphne—"they happen when nobody is looking, in stillness and secrecy. The real crises come to a head when nothing at all seems to be happening, nothing that's visible to the naked eye. Such is life. God help us!"

After lunch Mona went back to her desk and picked up her pencil.

"What are you writing?" said Daphne cautiously.

"My thoughts," muttered Mona. "Every notion and every detail, every single thread of thought. That's the trouble with people. They only remember the big, plain thoughts. They forget all the millions of tiny quivering elusive thoughts. But the truth doesn't lie in the ordinary thoughts that you can talk about. It lies in those millions of squirming little thoughts that are like amoebas. Somewhere in that labyrinth of words I'll capture the truth, the real truth. I've filled fifteen volumes already. There'll be thirty before I die."

"It sounds fascinating," said Daphne.

"It is meaningful!" said Mona.

She bit her pencil and smiled at Daphne with her feverish, haunted smile.

II

There was stillness on the beach, not a breath, not a ripple, and all along the edge of the water lay the rainbow-colored shells. It was as though the whole island had been drained of actuality and lay rigid and hollow, reduced to a coiling stillness.

Way off, caught like an insect in the limbo of the Gulf, a lonely trawler lay poised on the dead horizon. A large bird hung in the sky overhead, pinned to space, absolutely motionless, and in the west a puff of cloud hung afloat over Florida.

She walked on. This was an unfamiliar part of the island. No cottages or shacks, not even a footprint in the sand. Yellow butterflies were waltzing over the sparse little bushes.

She sauntered slowly beside the water, stooping to pick up a shell occasionally or maybe a pock-marked chip of brownish glass. The beach curved. She stepped through the bushes and came to a halt. Directly in front of her, half-hidden by the shrubs, lay a naked body. It was a man, a young man burned as dark as an Indian. A yellow towel lay spread over his face. His chest kept rising and falling lazily.

She had never seen a naked man. She stood still, momentarily curious; then distressed and alienated, disgusted almost. It was a healthy young body but the maleness of it was too vivid. It was somehow bizarre, it was downright uncanny.

She turned away but at that moment the young sleeper turned over, rubbed his eyes, sat up, yawned, and tossed the towel across a bush. He glanced indifferently at the sea and then ran down to the water's edge and flung himself into the sun-glazed waters of the Gulf. He swam a few strokes, beating the lacquer into foam; he dipped and gamboled, kicked, dove, then swam lazily shoreward and climbed back on the beach, shaking the drops from his head.

He caught sight of Daphne. He grinned and shrugged his shoulders. Then he strutted across the sand and plucked the towel from the twig, tied it casually around his waist and strolled calmly toward Daphne.

"Looking for shells?"

Daphne nodded.

"Yes, they're beautiful," said the boy, "aren't they? I used to collect them myself but then one day I got disgusted with them. They're so empty, they're lovely and colorful but they're empty and dead. So I took the whole batch of them and threw them back in the water . . . You live in Tortosa?"

"Yes," said Daphne, "more or less, I suppose."

"I've got a hut back there in the bushes," said the boy, cocking his thumb. "I built it myself six months ago, all out of driftwood. I've been living alone there. It's queer, living alone like that, not talking to a solitary soul for days on end."

"Yes, it must be," said Daphne.

"I've been eating nothing but oranges. It's an experiment I'm trying. I'm fed up with civilization. Back to sunlight and water —that's the only salvation!"

He was a lean, light-haired fellow with a fanatical gleam in his eyes. When he looked at her it was with an impersonal and almost unseeing intensity, and his lips were frozen into a smile, half pained, half contemptuous.

He reminded her of the sailor whom she had found in the woods by the river. The same features, muscular and taut, and the same tawny curls, the same curious air of mingled expectancy and hopelessness. Only the sailor had been gentle and patient and yielding: this boy was rebellious and angular, there was a hint of frenzy in his eyes.

"Well," he said, glancing at the sea and running his palm across his nipples, "I hope you didn't mind seeing me sunbathing like that. You look sensible and broad-minded. People get used to it down here. What's the point of being here if you can't relax and be sensible?"

"None, I imagine," murmured Daphne.

"Come," said the boy, with a sudden smile. "Let's go and walk for a while." And they sauntered along the shore toward the sandy point which was called the Dolphin's Snout. There was a curious smell in the air, a mingling of hibiscus and rotting clams; a disconcerting bouquet, obscurely human, sweet, fetid.

"You just lie in the sun," said the boy, "and nothing else seems to matter. All your problems melt away. Your nerves get baked to a pulp. All you ever feel like doing is jump into the ocean. That wonderful cool green water. Sun and water. That's all I want."

"But you can't just live in Tortosa the rest of your life," said Daphne, "can you?"

"Maybe not," said the boy. "And that's the tragedy of it all. Sooner or later we get sucked back into civilization. We think we can escape and maybe for a while we do escape, but the awful thing is that the escape ends up by driving us crazy too, only it's a different kind of craziness from that terrible civilization."

Daphne nodded. "Maybe we're all just a little bit crazy."

"I don't mind," said the boy. "What's wrong with being crazy? With civilization the way it is maybe it's better to be crazy. My folks back in Brooklyn used to tell me I was crazy but I tell you right now, I'm a whole lot happier than I was in

Brooklyn!" He grinned at her mournfully. "Come. I'll show you my shack."

They followed a path through the undergrowth and entered a thicket. Here a makeshift little hut had been built out of driftwood. The roof was thatched with tufts of mossy shrubbery and sea-weed and there was no floor at all, only the cool yellow sand. There wasn't even a window, only the light that blazed through the doorway. An army cot stood in the corner, covered with a threadbare brown blanket. There was a stool, an easel and a table. On the table lay a pile of tools: knives, chisels and saws, tubes of glue and chipped kitchenware. There was a smell of wood and sawdust and a young man's odor, tart resinous.

"It's a bit of a mess," said the boy. "Well, who cares? My name's Pancho. I don't look like a Cuban but my dad came from Havana. He died two years ago. He was killed in a street-fight. That's why I ran away from Brooklyn and I've never been back to Brooklyn."

He watched her glancing around the room. He shrugged his shoulders and grinned. "Pretty primitive, I guess you'd call it. Look. See? That's what I'm working at."

He pointed to the wall which was facing the doorway. Here stood an array of sculptures, imaginary beasts and fanciful monsters, forms half-human and half-mythological, all made out of driftwood. Their heads were patterned with fish bones and pebbles and cork and their bodies were crusted with chips of broken glass and rusty fish-hooks.

"It's all what I've found on the beach. Nothing but what I found on the beach. See the colors? Everything blends. Everything's weathered and natural."

Daphne ran her fingers cautiously over the back of a sea-dragon.

"What," she said, "are you going to do with them?"

"God knows," said the boy. "I don't think of them as sculptures. I think of them as gods. Little water-gods and wind-gods, star-gods and moon-gods. They comfort me when I'm gloomy. They heal me when I'm sick. I'd hate to sell them but who knows, maybe some day I'll have to sell them . . ."

Daphne couldn't help glancing at his glimmering brown chest, where the water had dried in salty white veins.

"Don't you have any friends here?"

"No," said Pancho, scratching his armpit, "I keep to myself. I don't bother with people. What's the use of bothering with people?"

"I suppose," said Daphne gravely, "you're what's called a narcissus . . ."

"Well, maybe," said Pancho, frowning. "Maybe I'm really a narcissus, but I try to keep away from sex. Sex is ugly and it's dangerous . . ."

The sun was just setting when Daphne arrived at the bungalow.

"Lord," said Mona. "We've been worried. You've been gone three whole hours!"

She was sitting on the veranda in her poinsettia bath-robe, playing patience and blowing clouds of cigarette smoke through her nostrils. A glass of whisky stood beside her. Her head was lowered ominously. Patches of peeling red skin clung to her half-naked shoulders.

The radio was playing in the kitchen. Miriam was making *chili con carne* and the smell of beans and pepper hung in the dead evening air.

Miriam stepped out of the kitchen with a knife in her hands.

Mona glanced at her wildly. "What's wrong with me, Miriam? Do I look peculiar? I've been feeling very peculiar, I must say."

"You've been drinking," said Miriam.

"No," said Mona, "it isn't that. Two or three highballs don't faze me. It's much more insidious."

"Your nerves, dear," said Miriam.

"Yes, my nerves," whispered Mona.

"And the sun," said Miriam, owl-eyed.

"Yes, the sun, of course," said Mona.

She raised her head and stared at Daphne with something like terror. Then she lowered her head again and picked up a card with a trembling hand.

III

The days grew longer again. The sun grew warmer; the grass grew greener. The daffodils bloomed by the summer-house and the orchard began to blossom. Grace went limping each morning down the path to Frenchman's Creek, stooping to pick a wild strawberry or maybe a wild anemone.

She loved the forest. She loved the silence and the smell and the secrecy of it. Some of the trees had a friendly look, others were mournful and gnarled. Some looked giddy and disheveled and there were some that looked sinister. Some held out their arms in a welcoming way. Some stretched them skyward in hysterical gestures. The copper beeches wore capes that trailed behind them like a queen's. The birches wore veils over their naked white bodies.

Somewhere a mocking-bird was calling. But Miss Malachi had told her once: "A mocking bird, Grace, is never where you think he is." So she knew that the mocking-bird was not in the birches.

He called again. A mischievous note, with a tinge of desolation. This time it came from the junipers on the edge of the hill. So she knew that the bird was not in the junipers.

She kept thinking about the mocking-bird. She longed to be like the hidden mocking-bird. She yearned for its privacy and cleverness, to have a song but never to be seen, to have a voice that fooled everyone and did not give away her hiding-place.

Then she wondered what the mocking-bird was trying to say to her. Sometimes it seemed to be "Yes, dear," and sometimes it was "No, dear," and once or twice it seemed to be saying, "Come on, now, come on," but she knew that the mocking-bird was trying to say something quite different, something much more crafty and complicated and mysterious.

She kept limping through the forest toward the Eagle's Rock. And as she wandered she was continually waiting for something. Possibly a chipmunk or a quail, maybe only a swallowtail, maybe to hear once again what the mocking-bird was saying, but always there was this feeling of something about to happen. Something peeping through the leaves, someone creeping through the shadows.

The Eagle's Rock was a high gray barren sort of place. She took off her shoes and walked through the sun-flowers. Then she started to climb the rock. The chips of stone dug into her flesh but she didn't mind, she was used to it, she even enjoyed it. Drops of sweat blurred her eyes as she crawled over the boulders. Finally she reached the top of the Rock. Only the underbrush was growing here. There was the smell of fresh mint and of sun-baked granite.

No one else knew the Eagle's Rock. No one else ever went there. No one else was even aware that it was called the Eagle's Rock. Long ago they might have known about it, they almost certainly did know about it, but they were people who were dead now. The Mohawks, for instance.

No one alive knew about the Cave and probably even the Mohawks didn't know about the Cave. There was a heap of gray stones on top of the Eagle's Rock, and on top of these was a cluster of sumachs that danced in the breeze like a crown of feathers. Here, hidden by foliage, was the hole that led into the Cave.

She would squat in the Cave and spread out the pine-cones

she had gathered in the woods; or the pebbles, white as ivory, which she found in the brook. Then she'd lie in the darkness and start singing to herself. Now and then a Mourning-cloak came loping along or a Painted Lady. Once a snake slid past her and slithered away in the underbrush.

Only once had she crept into the depths of the Cave. It grew so dark she could hardly see; the air grew clammy, almost suffocating. The earth was treacherous with slime and a nauseating smell oozed from the crannies. She grew aware that there was a secret life going on in the Cave: subtle and intricate, soft as velvet, vicious as poison. She looked up and saw something that looked like an enormous black rose. It was a cluster of furry bodies clinging motionless to the ceiling. Or almost motionless. Here and there a wing unfolded and then contracted again; there was a momentary flicker, the glint of a tiny eye. The pest-like stink of the worm-infested corpses welled about her. She tiptoed back to the mouth of the cave. The air grew sweet and fresh again. The sunlight shone on the sprigs of mint and the brick-red sumach. But oddly enough, the stench of nightmare hadn't frightened her in the least, it had only deepened her awareness of things hidden and unfathomable.

IV

One day on her way from the Cave she slipped on the edge of a boulder. She lurched forward, snatched at a twig and went tumbling into the thicket. She sat dazed for several minutes. Flakes of light darted past. Everything in the forest around her looked suddenly wily, clandestine.

A piece of sky shaped like a scorpion shone through the foliage overhead. Next to that was another piece like a hand with six fingers.

"No harm done," she said softly. "Just a bruise. It's all gone now . . ."

At that moment she heard footsteps on the leaf-strewn path. She crouched in the bushes and held her breath. A Mohawk, maybe, or an Apache. A twig snapped: a towering young man in tattered overalls stood in front of her. Dusky curls covered his head and his face was thin and starved-looking, with velvety brown eyes that looked at her with a doe-like astonishment. At his side stood an Irish Setter with his tail cocked up curiously.

"Who are you?" said Grace.

"My name's Jasper," said the boy.

"Jasper," she said. "It sounds like a jewel."

"I'm from Chicatogue," said the boy.

"Sit down, Jasper. Lordy me. You're tuckered out," said Grace amiably.

Jasper knelt down beside her. "Look," he whispered, "your knee's bleeding."

"Nothing serious. Just a scratch. It's stopped hurting," said Grace.

"Somebody told me there's a treasure buried around here," said the boy.

"Yes. Goldpieces," said Grace.

"How do you know?" said Jasper eagerly.

"Mrs. Bontecue told me about it. So did Barbara. Everyone knows about it."

"But nobody's found it?"

"Not yet, they haven't."

"D'you know where it is?"

Grace smiled mysteriously.

"I'll bet you do!"

"No," said Grace.

"You don't want to tell me," said Jasper, bitterly.

"Well," said Grace with a stealthy expression, "maybe I'll tell you some day."

Jasper's head sank down mournfully. "I've been walking all day."

There was something rather odd about Jasper, she began to notice. His eyes shifted aimlessly. His jawbone twitched; his mouth squirmed. And in his voice there was a meandering, slightly feverish melodiousness. She felt a wave of elderly tenderness and a touch of pity as well, as though he were desperately ill or dying.

The Irish Setter kept nuzzling and cavorting around Grace. "Down, Pompey," the boy kept saying. But the dog wouldn't leave her.

She put her hand on Jasper's shoulder and rose to her feet with a little grimace.

"Does it hurt?" said Jasper, stuttering.

"No," said Grace. "Hardly at all."

"Wait, I'll carry you," said Jasper.

Grace looked at him intently.

"You're as light as a feather!" he cried as he picked her up in his arms.

"I'm small, you know," said Grace.

"You're as light as a doll," said Jasper.

She smelled his powerful young arms around her, like birch bark freshly peeled. Neither of them spoke as he carried her gently down the path toward the asphalt highway.

v

One April morning the entire bay of Tortosa was covered with fish. Dead fish and fish dying, millions of fish, white-bellied multitudes, so many fish that the Gulf of Mexico seemed to have turned to a seething mercury, deepening to a rippled gold at noon and to copper at dusk, and the ladies locked their windows trying to keep out the stench.

"An epidemic," said some of the people. Others said "A volcano." The local doctor said "Algae." Still others said "Fallout." But none of them knew what had actually caused the devastation and one old fisherman said that it was a deliberate mass suicide, there were too many fish in the Gulf, the lust for survival had perished.

For several days the beach was nauseating with the flood of rotting corpses. But finally the fish were carted away and the sea turned clear again and the mystery of the massacred fish was forgotten.

Daphne wandered along the shore toward Pancho's hut in the thicket. She had known him for over a month. She saw him every day. They used to lie on the sun-baked sand, Daphne toying with a Lion's Paw and Pancho with a piece of driftwood, and they talked about their lives, about Brooklyn and Bishop's Neck, about insanity and civilization, about dreams and hidden monsters.

"I couldn't stand the rest of the fellows on my street," confided Pancho. "There were the Buzzards and the Cannibals and I hated the sight of all of them. I hated the bragging and the filth. I hated the drinking and the dope. I hated the Rock 'n' Roll in the attic and the gang-bangs down in the cellar. I was afraid of the kitchen knives and I was afraid of the sexual diseases. I hated baseball and jazz. I had a record of the Pathétique. I read Van Gogh's letters and *The Brothers Karamazov*. I felt disgusted with everything and finally I decided to run away . . ."

"Yes," said Daphne, "I know how you felt. It was different at Bishop's Neck, I suppose, but in a way it was nearly the same. Seven sisters and I was the only one of the seven that felt alone. I was the only one in the house whom everyone pitied and despised. Even Grace, poor little Grace, we all secretly admired her. Barbara and Consuelo were beautiful, Freya had lots of charm and talent, Augusta was tall and athletic and Elizabeth was an angel. I was ugly and freckled. I was clumsy and terribly stupid. I could never get the gist of Miss Malachi's lessons in algebra. I roamed through the woods and climbed trees. I crouched by the streams, I crawled on the rocks. I never spoke to a single soul. I hated mother. I detested Barbara. I envied Consuelo, I was afraid of Augusta. The only one that I loved was poor little Grace . . ."

"Sometimes," said Pancho, "I have very complicated thoughts all of a sudden. Especially when I'm lying next to the sea and listening to the birds. It's a kind of divination, a kind of instinct, if you know what I mean, feeling things that I've never experienced, remembering way back into history, sensing what everything was like before Columbus arrived in America. Prehistory, that's what it is. I feel I'm part of prehistory. That's the reason I love the birds and that's the reason I hate the cities. Listening to the birds I sometimes feel I can hear the sounds of a million years ago . . ."

"Yes," said Daphne, "isn't it strange, I feel exactly the same as you. Except that sometimes, under it all, I feel a queer little panic. I love the sand and the water, I love listening to the wind and everything, but underneath there's something secret about it all that scares me. I feel I'm being bewitched. I feel I'm being trapped. There's all that space and sunlight and all this wonderful freedom but under it all, I don't know why, I feel I'm being hypnotized . . ."

She glanced at his body. They were both completely naked. After their first few days together they both lost their shyness, they stripped and lay in the sun in the secrecy of the thicket. There was celibacy between them; neither of them ever touched the other. There was no sense of guilt, there was nothing lascivious, and every so often they raced to the sea and slid through the coolness, dazed and exultant.

But today, as she looked at his body, she saw for the first time its beauty. His eyes were half-closed and his lips were all that was moving, his lips and the gentle heart-beat and the vein that throbbed in his neck. She looked at the sun-bleached hair on his chest and the flat, salt-ringed nipples and the faint golden haze that shone on his belly. She looked at him with a kind of tender and scrupulous curiosity, as though he were a Junonia or a very fine Lion's Paw.

He looked up and caught her gaze. He smiled lazily, ironically.

"We get along," he said, "don't we?"

"We feel natural, I guess," said Daphne.

"We think the same thoughts."

"We're both fugitives," said Daphne.

"You won't believe it," said Pancho rather tonelessly, "but I'm still a virgin."

Daphne stared across the sea. She lowered her eyes. "Yes. So am I."

"Queer, isn't it?" said Pancho.

"Yes, it's odd," whispered Daphne.

"Why are you trembling?" said Pancho.

"I don't know," said Daphne, frightened.

He flung his arms wide apart and whispered, "Come, let's see what it's like," and after a moment she sank gently across his sun-heated body.

When she sauntered back toward the bungalow she saw a small black shape in the distance, no bigger than a wasp, arms pressed to her side. When she came closer she saw the face gazing seaward intently and the look of desperation that was visible even behind the sun-glasses.

When she entered the cottage Mona was sitting on the couch with her highball glass. She was talking to Miriam, who was in the kitchen baking biscuits.

"The more I see of people," she shouted, not looking at Daphne, "the more I begin to grasp their miserable role in the universe. They're no better than the rats of Norway, they breed and keep breeding, all quite blindly and pointlessly, and then they race about in a frenzy and go plunging toward destruction. That's all, just proliferation and frenzy and self-destruction, and if you look at the sea and up at the stars the answer is perfectly obvious. They are beasts, nothing but beasts. They are doomed and their lives are meaningless."

She sipped at her glass, folded her arms and stared bleakly at Daphne.

"There's a funny look in your face, dear," she said, lowering her voice.

Daphne plucked at her shirt sleeve and stared through the window.

"Listen to me, Diana," said Mona quietly. "Tell me frankly. What do you see in him? He's a flibbertigibbet, he's a beachcomber, he's a peacock and that's all. Just a silly adolescent, if you want my opinion. All that arty pomposity and just a bunch of swollen muscles. There's nothing there, I'm telling you, Diana, there's nothing there at all. Behind those swollen muscles lies a sick female softness. I know the type, indeed I do. They're stupid but they're dangerous."

She shook her head, took off her sun-glasses and folded them thoughtfully.

"Don't delude yourself, child. Go and look at the mirror. No man will fall in love with that ugly little face of yours. I'm in love with it because it is strange and because it is poignant. But it's not a face that a normal man would want to kiss. I'm warning you, Diana. You are heading for a *désastre*."

She got up and strode slowly across the room and then back again. Her iron-gray head was thrust forward between her bull-like shoulders.

"Well," she said, coming to a halt in front of Daphne, "why don't you speak to me?" Her voice grew hoarse; she leaned closer; her eyes were burning. "Do you love the boy? I won't have it! Don't think that I haven't noticed it! I've been watching you day after day, I've been following you down the beach, and I tell you, I won't have it, I just won't have it!" Her voice rose to a shriek. Miriam stood in the kitchen doorway, peering wanly at them both through her thick-lensed glasses. "You belong to me, do you hear? Do you hear me, Diana? I won't have you go to ruin with that filthy little fiend! He'll bring you to destruction! I won't have it! I won't allow it!"

She turned and hurled herself on the couch and buried her head in her big brown arms. Her body kept shaking with the violence of her sobs.

VI

The apples rotted in the grass; coils of darkness dragged through the sky. The feeling of loneliness at Bishop's Neck grew deep and hollow, like the sound from a cistern.

Grace kept walking among the birches, hoping that Jasper would come back again. She stood by the bridge and called "Jasper!" But only the mocking-bird called back to her. And after a while she began to think that she had never met Jasper. She had made him up in a dream, with his tattered overalls and his tawny setter.

But all the same, she went on having her little chats with Jasper.

"Are you scared," she would say, "of spiders?"

"No," said Jasper, "I don't mind spiders."

Or she played him a minuet.

"It's lovely," he said, "like glasses tinkling!"

She played him Schumann's *Warum*.

"Yes," he said, "that's just what it's like! Something hidden around the corner, waiting and waiting, trying to say something . . ."

After her walks in the woods she sat by the piano in the drawing room. The house was utterly still; the haze of sunset seeped through the shutters. The dusty glass of the chandelier caught a dull reddish glow. On the card-table lay a pack of old-fashioned Swiss playing cards, marked with acorns and thistles, vine-leaves and shepherdesses. On the chessboard stood a set of Chinese warriors carved of ivory. By the window on a cast-iron stand stood a large white vase filled with peacock feathers.

There were times when she felt the music enfolding her like a vapor; the sound seeped into her blood and became the sound of her heart-beat. And the music was no longer a sound, it was an intuition which lurked in her body, a communion with the unspeakable, a distillation of silence. It was no longer merely Beethoven, it was an arrangement of inner stillness, it was the solitude and the search shaped into a pattern, made bearable.

Occasionally she noticed Miss Malachi sitting out on the veranda. Her head leaned toward the window as she listened to Grace playing. And after a while she dropped her knitting and came sneaking into the drawing-room. "Mercy, its time for dinner," she said. Or, "Look, dear. *Molto espressivo!*"

When the storms of winter arrived they would sit by the fire-place after dinner.

"Did you see him today?" said Miss Malachi.

"Who?" said Grace, with a furtive smile.

"That boy."

"Jasper, you mean? Yes, he was sitting by the bridge," said Grace.

"Did you speak to him?"

"I asked him about his family," said Grace.

"What did he say? Anything special?"

"He's all alone in the world, he says."

"Does he believe in God?" said Miss Malachi.

"Well, he does in a way," said Grace. "He's told me what he believes but I'm not quite sure that I understand it. He believes in a kind of Providence that hangs in the air, like smoke from a fire."

"He sounds puerile," said Miss Malachi.

"He is a poet," murmured Grace.

"Has he ever tried to kiss you?"

"Lordy no!" said Grace, agitated.

Miss Malachi opened the drawer of the walnut chest and took out a brush. "There, sit down in front of the mirror, Grace. I'm going to brush your hair." And as they sat in front of the mirror she felt a glow of pride, almost of vanity. The silky waterfall of hair fell rippling down over her shoulders and the dwarf-like face peered back at her knowingly. "You've got marvelous hair," said Miss Malachi. "Much too much but quite marvelous. I don't know how that little head of yours can carry all that hair!"

And after a while Miss Malachi murmured: "You need love. That's what you need."

"I have love," said Grace, motionless.

"No, that's not what I mean," said Miss Malachi. "A man, that's what I mean. The way you did the Appassionata, for instance. The Brahms and the Schumann, yes. The Fauré, yes. But the Beethoven, no!"

Grace kept sitting beside the fire long after Miss Malachi had gone to bed. She watched the flames licking at the logs and then the logs gradually crumbling into flakes of reddish gold that slowly faded and died. Her shadow stirred nervously on the wall behind her. She kept staring at the fire until the dance of the flames grew into an elaborate melody, dimming and brightening like the pulse of her blood.

And gradually the rhythm of the fire melted into the rhythm of water. She felt herself floating among the coves, *en bâteau*. But then the grip of the whirlpool seized her; she went circling faster and faster. Only the most desperate control would keep the boat from tipping over and spilling her into the blackness. And yet she was secretly yearning for the boat to tip over, the continual spinning made her dizzy and the strain of the effort was so agonizing. There was something restful, even alluring in the thought of sinking into the whirlpool.

She closed her eyes. She started to doze. But a crackling ember woke her up again. She felt a spear of cold air, as though a window had been flung open. The room had darkened. Only a flicker still clung to the logs. The écru curtains stirred uneasily beside the window. Her hands tightened on the arms of the chair. Somewhere in the room something was moving. She turned quickly. There! What was it? Something had darted behind the table. She could have sworn that an ivory pawn had moved on the chessboard.

She heard a rippling little noise, like the patter of feet on the veranda: and then a claw-like scratching at the pane, followed by a plaintive little whimper. One of the curtains was lifted slowly, as though drawn by a hand. A head peered through the pane: the head of a dog: an Irish Setter.

She sat without stirring. The curtain fell back again. The whimpering died away in the depth of the night. The fire darkened as she watched it and a feeling of guilt rose slowly up in her, as though she had committed some indefinable but unpardonable act of betrayal.

VII

Sometimes Miss Malachi would say, "It's a miracle, an absolute miracle. Play that passage again, child. You have touched the heart of the music . . ."

And Grace herself was aware that a mysterious gift had suddenly flowered in her. Her fingers had developed a steely strength as well as a supple caressiveness, and she knew by some unfaltering instinct how to dive deep into the music. Her fragile fingers accompanied this instinct with an eerie agility, and it was as though there were three separate impulses at work instead of one: her fingers rippling over the keyboard and the attendant spectre of the composer and an occult third presence, some latent grandeur in her sensibilities. She moved effortlessly from a Chopin ballade to a Brahms intermezzo, from a bagatelle by Beethoven to a *moment musical* by Schubert. But she was always at her best with Schumann and Debussy, and her favourite pieces were the *Kinderskenen* and the first book of *Préludes*.

Now and again she would go and have tea in Miss Malachi's room. Miss Malachi had studied with Mademoiselle Boulanger in Fontainebleau, and she still had some souvenirs of those days scattered about—an autographed album of *Les Indes Galantes,* some frayed little snapshots of picnics in Barbizon. On her shelves slender volumes by Colette and Claudel were tucked amid sets of Daudet and de Maupassant.

"Dust, dust!" cried Miss Malachi. "Everything turns into dust!" She ran a piece of felt over her bust of Couperin. "Except," she murmured in her hoarse low voice, "my beautiful floating darlings." And she turned to drop a wafer into the octagonal fish-bowl.

Grace knelt on the rug in front of the bowl. Tiny grottos and arching bridges rose in the murky green water through which the Japanese fan-tails moved with a swirl of golden draperies, faintly lit by the oblong bulb which was hidden behind the bowl.

She had never cared for these luminous water-monsters, in spite of their wraith-like beauty and fragility. She detected an ugly glint in the eyes of the goldfish, a suggestion of savagery, an almost murderous greed. But whether this depravity was a part of living in an illuminated bowl or simply a part of being a beast from the seas, that was something she was never sure of: but she feared and hated Miss Malachi's goldfish.

One gray morning Miss Malachi said: "I have arranged a

recital in Belleville. The Ladies' Horticultural Society is renting the Beasley Auditorium. I have spoken to Mrs. O'Malley. They are dying to hear you. It will be a memorable occasion for both of us, my puss . . ."

Grace smiled and nodded vaguely. She didn't seem to be listening.

Three weeks later Mrs. O'Malley came and fetched them in her Oldsmobile. It was pouring. Far-off thunder came from the hills by Frenchman's Creek. When they arrived at the auditorium Mrs. O'Malley led her to the Green Room and said: "Don't be nervous, you'll be magnificent, I'm perfectly sure of it." Mr. Byrne, who taught at the High School, slid his head through the door and whispered: "I can't wait for the suite, my dear! The *Passepied* will be the pinnacle . . ."

And Miss Gooch, a thin white woman dressed in an Indian sari, said softly: "We've been hearing rumours of a Revelation!"

As she limped on to the stage she heard the clapping of brittle hands. Miss Malachi sat beside her and opened the album. "Just ignore them," she whispered. "They're all imbeciles, they won't know the difference."

The rain slashed at the windows; there was a smell of wet rubber. The lights grew soft. Grace gazed at the murmuring cavern below her. It suggested to her fancy the gaping jaws of a sea-monster, studded with tiers of disintegrating, weed-entangled teeth. She smiled blandly and nodded. She felt calm, almost casual. Miss Malachi flattened the page. She embarked on the *Passacaglia*.

She closed her eyes as she played. She felt serenely, triumphantly alone: infinitely removed from Mrs. O'Malley and Mr. Byrne, even Miss Malachi. She felt herself floating in a smoke-like spiral toward the candelabras, and when she opened her eyes the audience, which was feverishly applauding, was lost in a torrent of sea-green shadows.

After the Bach came the *Variations in f* by Hadyn, and these were followed by the Waldstein Sonata. It was in the opening

movement of the sonata that she began to feel the Presence. It
was not yet distinct, it was merely an impersonal magnetism
which was deftly but powerfully drawing her attention toward
a certain spot in the auditorium. It was in the second movement, the adagio, that the Presence grew unmistakable. In the
very front aisle, slightly to the left of the centre, she caught sight
with the corner of her eye of something luminous, like a burning candle. She fixed her gaze on the keyboard; she felt Miss
Malachi's protective nearness. A hand rose tactfully beside her,
turned the page and retreated again. But the shadow of that
hand, encased in violet wrinkles, kept hovering at her side as
though it were warding off some dark antagonist.

She began the third movement, the rondo. Suddenly the keyboard crumbled in front of her. The rectangular flakes of ivory
broke into small fiery fragments. Someone spoke, someone was
saying something. She turned her head in a spasm of terror.
Directly below her shone a face, intensely familiar yet horribly
strange, haggard, dilapidated, with smouldering eyes looking
balefully up at her. "Have you forgotten me?" he whispered;
she could hear his voice through the fading music. She jumped
up from the stool and ran crying from the stage.

The rain had stopped when they entered the narrow road to
Bishop's Neck. The sun was setting. The rain-soaked reeds were
tipped with orange, like burning knives, and then a cloud covered the sun and everything was gray, calm, familiar again.

"No wonder," said Miss Malachi, tightening her grip on
Grace's fingers. "All that tension, all those strangers, and then
that dazzle of the variations! It was much too much to expect.
Forgive me, Grace. It was vanity, vanity . . ."

VIII

A dawn-smelling mist hung over the moss-colored water. Daphne hurried along the board-walk without looking back. She passed MacNamara's Market and the 'Tween Waters Inn and took the short-cut through the cat-tails down to the pier at the edge of the cove. Nothing stirred, not even an insect. A breathless stillness covered the island. It looked desolate in the morning greyness: bleak and littered, depopulated.

"There you are," muttered Pancho, looming up through the mist. "Everything's ready. Watch your step. We'll head straight for Ophira."

The row-boat went gliding through the reeds into the sea. In the distance the mainland hung afloat like a mirage. A lazy brightness spread through the air and the spice of dawn had a wonderful pungency. The water was sleek as a seal, swaying in the slow greenish swell. The only sounds were the swish of the oars and the squeak of the oarlocks. They turned the point. The Dolphin's Snout shone like a red-hot needle as a geyser of sunlight gushed out of Florida.

She looked back. The scattered bungalows caught the blaze in their windowpanes. She caught sight of Miriam's cottage, half hidden by hibiscus, and then to her horror she saw a figure step through the door and stand motionless on the steps, stiff and faceless, like a blackened matchstick.

"Look," said Daphne. "There she is. She's capable of murder, I shouldn't wonder."

A fish jumped out of the water. Suddenly the whole sea was ablaze as the full flood of sunlight poured over the shoreline. The air grew hot instantly. The delicate misty smell gave way to the flat hot breath from the Gulf.

A wail came echoing across the bay: "Di-ana! Di-ana!" She hardly recognised the voice, it was so disfigured by grief and ferocity.

Her fear was tinged for a moment with a pang of longing for Mona; for Mona's deep-ringing philosophy, her speckled flesh, her passion, her misery. But then a ripple of wind sprinkled the sea with gold-pieces and remorse gave way to a rush of joy and expectancy.

Pancho was wearing his khaki pants and T-shirt and sneakers. A canvas bag lay tucked in the prow, beside a heap of driftwood monsters.

Pancho smiled at her cunningly.

"She'll be lonely without you, won't she?"

"She's always been lonely. She's used to her loneliness."

"She's got Miriam anyway, hasn't she?"

"Miriam's a spectre," said Daphne.

"It's terrible to be so bitter, isn't it? I mean Mona's kind of bitterness."

"Oh, she's proud of her bitterness. She worships her bitterness. It's her religion."

It was nearly seven when they landed at the pier in Ophira. Pancho fastened the stolen row-boat to one of the stakes and they strolled down the asphalt to the end of the street where a row of rusty cars stood parked in the shade of the palm trees. He tossed his bag in the back of a derelict little Studebaker. Then he hopped into the front, turned the ignition key and stepped on the starter. There was a squeak, a grunt and a rattle: finally the motor began to splutter and the car went lurching down to the pier where they picked up the sculptures and tucked them in the car under a piece of burlap. Then they drove through Ophira toward the cement highway to Belshazzar's Beach.

"We'll head north," said Pancho, "and we'll keep on going as long as we can. I know a fellow in Maine who's got a house on the edge of the ocean. I'm sick of the Gulf. All that heat and stillness. We'll head for the north, all windy and cool . . ."

They drove on through sizzling marshes, droning orchards, steaming villages. They had coffee and cornbread in a town called Frog Harbor. Toward noon they crossed into Georgia, two hours later they reached the Atlantic. They had started with thirty dollars and they still had twenty-seven.

"Five bucks a day. That's all we can spend. We've got to be careful," said Pancho.

They drove through Georgia and toward dusk they rolled into the meadows of South Carolina. They had hamburgers and sarsaparilla in a village called Beatitude.

They had twenty-four dollars left. "We're spending too much," said Pancho. "We'll eat nothing but apples and plums for a couple of days."

When darkness was falling they followed a side road into the hills. They crossed into a valley where all was still, not a light was burning. A beast darted across the headlights and vanished in the underbrush. A freight-train wailed in the distance. It was like the whine of a pterodactyl. After a while they started climbing again until they came to the edge of a stream. Behind the trees they heard the gurgling of a small mountain waterfall and when they looked they saw the starlight glide like a snake through the braided water. They took Pancho's blanket and spread it out on the grass. The breath of the dampish woods came welling through the tree-trunks.

They lay silent for a while. Then Pancho whispered: "Listen. Do you hear something?"

"Just the wind in the leaves, that's all," murmured Daphne.

And a little later Pancho said: "Do you think you'll sleep all right?"

"Yes," said Daphne, snuggling close to him. "All that peacefulness and stillness."

And a little later Pancho said: "Don't you hear it? Down in the bushes?"

"It's only a possum. Or maybe a weasel," said Daphne.

And later still: "It's not like the sea, is it? All those creeping things in the bushes."

"They won't hurt you," said Daphne. "They're just moving around in the darkness."

The crickets were squealing. A bull-frog started to bellow. She folded her arms around him and pressed her lips to his cheek.

IX

On and on, continually northward. They drove up through North Carolina and near a town called Cook's Corner they stole some peaches from a fruit stand. They crossed into Virginia in the bronze of the afternoon and had frankfurters and beer in a little hamlet called Peppertown. The air grew gradually cooler, plumes of cloud filled the sky and when they came to the Chesapeake they had nineteen dollars left.

And as they drove she thought of her sisters, for the first time in weeks. She thought of Augusta and her arrows. She thought of Barbara and Consuelo. She thought of Elizabeth and her serpents and of Freya with her birds and of poor little Grace with her luminous bat-eyes. She thought of the house with its crackling columns and dirty rugs and faded curtains and it all seemed like a dream from some earlier incarnation. She felt nothing at all when she thought of it, nothing at all or almost nothing, only a twinge of pain so quick that it was gone in a second.

"Isn't it queer," she said in the dusk-light, "how things move away from us? Everything keeps moving away from us, people and places, even ourselves. I remember the way I used to be, all angry and vengeful, but somehow I know that it isn't me any longer. Odd, isn't it? And there's something else. Did I ever tell you? I'm really a twin. It was me and Dorothea but Dorothea died in her cradle and I've felt ever since that I'm only half a person. I keep looking for the other half, I keep looking for Dorothea and sometimes when I'm dreaming I think that I've suddenly found her. But then I wake up, I know it's a dream and I feel like crying. And sometimes it's queer but I almost feel that I'm Dorothea. After all, twins are special, they're really the same individual and there's nothing so strange about me turning into Dorothea, is there? Sometimes I think of Dorothea and the way she would have been, gay and graceful and delicate, just the opposite of myself, and I feel sort of comforted because one half of me at least was beautiful. But then, like everything else, I know it's only an illusion. Dorothea is dead and gone and there's no point in looking for her. But even then, when I think of Dorothea dead and gone forever, I feel a kind of serenity, I feel that death isn't so horrible. Dorothea went through it somehow and there's still the sun and the starlight, the hills are the same as ever, nothing changes, the trees keep growing, and if only one could manage to stop thinking about oneself then death wouldn't matter, it would stop being so horrible . . ."

The light faded away from the tufted blue promontories and as the highway turned east she said:

"Pancho, will you do me a favor?"

"Yes? What?"

"Turn right, please. Down by the gas station."

He turned right and ten minutes later they were on the road to Bishop's Neck.

"I just want to make sure that it really exists," said Daphne.

He parked the car on the edge of the road, where the sycamore was struck by lightening, just beyond where the path turned off to Frenchman's Creek.

"Just wait for me," said Daphne.

"Don't be long now!" said Pancho.

She crept along the hedge until she came to the kitchen driveway and now it was nearly dark, there wasn't a soul to be seen. She walked softly into the orchard past the bed of asparagus. The grass was high and wild; the apples crackled under her feet. Then she tiptoed into the garden and sneaked past the rose-bushes, keeping close to the shadows, her arms raised in front of her. The smell of the dead chrysanthemums seeped through the stillness. "Lord," she whispered. A furry shape scampered past, grazing her ankle. It was only a cat, a little white one spotted with black.

She walked on through the tattered weeds and came to a halt under the chestnut tree. The swing was still hanging there; she caught the smell of the weathered rope. In the house a single light was shining in the library window. She sat down in the swing, which sagged gently under her weight. She heard the creak of the rope and the squeak of the bending bough. Under her feet she felt the familiar dusty unevenness of the ground. She swung back and forth and as she sat there swinging the darkness seemed to melt and her eyes grew blinded with tears. A shadow crossed slowly in front of the library window. She kept swinging and thought, "Queer, queer, but that's how it is. Everything happens by accident, one meets people by accident, one goes to places by accident, one is happy or unhappy by accident, one falls in love by accident and I suppose one dies by accident. And still, under it all, what is it, why is it, I had to be here on this particular night of all nights, I had to come and sit in the swing here, feeling queer and listening to the katydids . . ."

She crossed the lawn and peered through the library window. The room was empty. The beaded lamp dropped a circle of light on the table and in the glow shone an empty glass, an open book, a dusty Buddha. Beyond the brightness rose the shelves, shadowy tiers of dusty books, and on the wall over the fireplace hung the painting of Notre Dame, faintly visible in the gloom, like two great thumbs thrust out of the wall.

"Was anyone there?" said Pancho when she stepped back in the car.

"Not a soul . . . Well, yes, I suppose there must have been somebody."

"One of your sisters," said Pancho.

"Yes. I guess so," said Daphne.

"Funny," said Pancho, "going back like that."

"Yes," said Daphne, "and no one knowing."

They drove slowly under the trees. A twig snapped under a tire. The smell of the cedars flickered past them: then it was lost in the smell of the marshes.

x

There were moments when it occurred to Grace that she might have died already, that what seemed like existence was merely a fitful illusion; that a woman named Grace might already have passed away and that this sequence of divinations was simply the texture of immortality.

But then something or other reminded her that she was living after all. A cup of coffee spilled on the rug; an aching tooth; a fly on her nose. And a ripple of panic shot through her: still alive! And life so short! *Hurry, hurry,* someone was whispering. *It's growing late! No time to be wasted!*

And she jumped from the love-seat and ran to the window. But all she saw in the garden was the wind stirring in the chestnut tree, or a sparrow sitting on the edge of the sun-dial.

She had abandoned the piano. The memories of Belleville were still painful to her. They had left a dark stigma on the shining splendors of Beethoven. And there was something else too. More and more she found that music, no matter how subtle or insinuating, seemed to draw her into regions no longer her own, no longer safe. She took up drawing. Here the kingdom was entirely her own. She used pencils and colored inks and sometimes bits of crayon. Everything she did was in lines: nothing was solid, nothing was painted. She drew people with enormous head-dresses, fern-like plumes and palm-shaped tiaras, towering combs shaped like flamingoes or wigs that billowed like smoke, and the faces were drawn in geometrical patterns, with jet-black eyes that looked like arrow-heads. Some of these creatures bore a resemblance to those tattooed savages in the *Trip to the Fijis,* but they also, with their tubular torsos, might have come from the *Journey to Saturn.*

Miss Malachi would tip-toe into the library and stand behind her chair.

"Look, you forgot to put fingers on that hand, didn't you, dear?" Or: "What's that thing on the lady's back? It looks like a centipede, almost."

One day she said: "Lordy, Grace, you're as thin as a praying mantis! All your clothes are just dangling on you. Look—there's a hole in the bottom of your shoe. What will I do with you, tell me! Eating nothing but bits of cornbread . . ."

"Listen!" said Grace, turning to the window. "Did you hear someone calling?"

"It was only the wind in the trees, I shouldn't wonder," said Miss Malachi.

And a moment later: "There! Again! Don't you hear it?" said Grace.

"Hush, child. It's only the kitchen door squeaking," said Miss Malachi.

But her illusions kept growing continually more alive to her, gathering precision and expressiveness until they were just as real as Miss Malachi's goldfish.

Three things she was used to seeing. The first was an object beside the bed. When she awoke in the middle of the night she saw it lying in front of the night-table, a furry sort of thing, maybe a mastiff or a gorilla, with enormous red eyes that burned in the darkness. The second was a creature she glimpsed in the orchard, usually at nightfall: a pale hopping thing, like a kind of giant toad, with a growth on its head that resembled a lady's bonnet. The third was the Bearded Man. He would stand at the head of the stairs or poke his head through the library window, or steathily open the door of her bedroom: usually just as she was getting ready to go to bed, and as often as not while the clock was striking. But the terror that had accompanied each of these visitors on their first appearance began to dwindle as they grew familiar, and after a while she lost her fear of them entirely. Indeed, she began to look forward to their periodic calls on her, which carried with them an aura of lost, beseeching intimacy.

One windy day she climbed to the cave on top of the Eagle's Rock. The air was brisk; autumn was full; the sumachs were bright as the wings of a Cardinal. As she sat near the mouth of the cave, singing Schubert's *Der Lindenbaum*, she caught sight of a thin white object in one of the recesses. She crept deeper, ducking her head to avoid the loping bats, and made her way into the stench-ridden alcove.

She knelt down and said tenderly: "Pompey. Poor little Pompey." She fondled the crumbling skeleton and muttered, "Yes. It was all my fault . . ." She grasped the fact that the wandering dog, like his master before him, had died of grief: the grief not only of loneliness but also of spiritual deprivation, the grief of never finding his role, his private harmony in existence. She took off her alpaca jacket and carefully wrapped up the bones in it and carried them down to the shady grove by Frenchman's Creek.

XI

The two women were sitting on the veranda, drinking their noonday coffee. "Tell me, Grace," said Miss Malachi. "Would you mind answering me a question?"

Grace put down her cup. "What is the question, Miss Malachi?"

"Are you subject, my child, to the usual appetites?"

Grace stared at a caterpillar which was crawling across the coffee pot.

"I am not," said Miss Malachi, "in the habit of prying, as you know. But I can't help detecting a certain restlessness in you."

Grace blushed; she fondled her coral necklace furtively.

Miss Malachi was wearing an embroidered dress with a black lace collar. She sat rigid, hands folded, with a treacherous gleam under her bushy eyebrows. There was something about her of an animated mosaic. Stiff, beaded, symmetrical, she looked like some dark Byzantine virgin.

"Did you ever, for example," she said, "feel attracted to our dear Peter?"

"Honestly, Miss Malachi," said Grace, glassy-eyed, "I don't know what you're talking about!"

"I used to think," intoned Miss Malachi, "that you were intended by the Lord for celibacy. At least I hoped that you were. Life would have been so much easier. But I've noticed these last few weeks a certain feverishness about you. I am not a prude. I know the symptoms. I know these simperings and fidgetings." She looked grimly across the lawn. Then she bared her teeth slightly. "There is a demon lurking in all of us and there's no point pretending. Life is dark and it's transitory. We are what we are. Forgive my frankness. May I suggest that you have an affair, *ma petite?*"

"An affair?"

"It would be for the best," said Miss Malachi hoarsely.

"You mean," said Grace, stuttering.

"I do indeed," said Miss Malachi. She narrowed her eyes, which were glittering with an almost frenzied intensity. "Sexual intercourse, or call it copulation if you wish, is not, as I try to visualize it, an especially dignified performance. But whatever we may think of it, it is an exceedingly common one. Flesh is flesh, blood is blood, we're mortal beings one and all of us. Would you like," she said in a whisper, leaning forward on the sofa, "for me to make some discreet little arrangement for you?"

Grace's face was twisted with horror. "Lordy no, please, Miss Malachi!"

"Oh, don't bother to protest, Grace. *Qui s'excuse, s'accuse,* you know."

"It isn't that," stammered Grace, "it's just that I'm so . . . unattractive-looking!"

Miss Malachi leaned back again, shrugging her shoulders.

"Just as you say. I was merely making a therapeutical suggestion."

She swirled her spoon around in the cup and swatted a fly that lit on her bosom.

"When I try to look ahead," she said, "and see what is coming to us, I see clouds of fiery blackness, yes, it's all quite unmistakable, I see those very scenes which the mediaeval artists put on their canvases, strips of skin peeling from corpses, testicles aflame and eyeballs dangling, only the whole thing transpiring in the world of the living instead of the dead! But what I see beyond it all, when a flash of lucidity comes over me, is something quite amazing, a metaphysical oneness that falls over the race, a permeating harmony of soul not like anything we have hitherto visualized, something stranger and deeper, yes, I think you're beginning to grasp it, the time will come when we'll be revealed as something other than beasts. And I see us all struggling, maybe blindly and a bit hysterically, but constantly struggling toward that oneness, the thing that will bind us all together, and we'll finally stop suffering the pangs of our separateness. We'll blend together in a single consciousness, if you can imagine such a thing. We'll end by thinking identical thoughts and by feeling identical feelings, and the fate of the one will be inseparable from the fate of the many, and there no longer will be some who are lucky and others who are unlucky. Yes, I often suspect that it's beginning to happen already, and after all there's nothing bizarre about it, if you've ever studied the bees, or even the flocks of birds which come swirling around in the evening . . ."

That night as she lay in bed, Grace experienced another Vision.

The breeze flowed in through the window and the curtains stirred lazily, in a way that reminded her of Miss Malachi's fan-tails.

She lay motionless. She grew aware of a slightly rancid, oppressive warmth. Then she noticed a furry mass blocking the center of the window. Something black and immense was thrusting its head through the chiffon curtains. A filmy brightness shone from the moon: two giant horns caught the light on their tips. They reminded her of the ivory scimitars that hung in the library. A tangle of mud-caked hair burst from the base of each horn and under the horns two bloodshot eyes were fixing their gaze on the core of her body.

She shrieked: "Jasper! Help me!"

The Vision started to melt. The eyes grew dim; the head receded. The curtains fell into place again and only the aroma lingered on, the stench of some sickening phallic ordure.

Part Five

I

On the western slopes of the Apennines there is a town called Brancaccio and here Peter decided to settle and work on his paintings. A road wound up a hill from the dusty brown countryside. The leaves of the trees shone like flames in the web of sunlight. At the gateway into the town there was a pitted yellow arch surmounted by a sad, corroded lion and a limp old dragon clutching at a shield. Goats with bloated black udders grazed on the rocks below the walls and the donkeys stood in the sun with their vast pudenda dangling like blood-sausages.

His room in the inn had a single bulb hanging from the ceiling, which shed its barren light on a stained engraving of Saint Veronica. He slept in a narrow bed beside a wall which rustled with rats. He drank the wine of the mountains and ate the dark dry bread of the peasants and every morning he walked in the hills, occasionally taking along his paints but more often only his sketching-pad and a volume of Vasari which he read in the shade.

It was a relief to be in Brancaccio. There was a dryness in the air. There was nothing of the Roman laxity, of the Roman strutting and self-indulgence. The people in Brancaccio were hard and plain and bony. He felt happy just to sit in the piazza and watch them go by. He grew familiar with the faces of the local tradesmen and dignitaries—Signor Corradi, the spectacled mayor, and the red-cheeked arch-priest Monsignor Spada, and Signor Pucci, the little doctor, and old Battista the cross-eyed notary. There was Vincenzo, the village idiot, and old Marcella, the village witch, and Carlotta, the village slut who stood chuckling beside the fountain.

Peter was happy but behind the happiness there was an occasional stab of loneliness, and the loneliness made the happiness seem all the purer and more authentic. Sometimes he wondered about the future. He wondered what would eventually happen to him, and he couldn't quite visualise just where he fitted into the scheme of things. He had always felt as though he were dangling. He had never gotten a foothold. He had dangled when he lived with his grandmother and he had dangled in the asylum, he had dangled among the Nightingales and he was dangling away from the Nightingales. He had dangled in Maryland and he dangled in Rome. He felt nowhere that he was a part of things; he felt nowhere that he belonged. He kept worrying about money and about earning a living but he worried even more about where he belonged. For some ill-defined reason he had never felt like a part of America, and for perfectly obvious reasons he had never felt like a part of the Nightingales. He had never felt like a part of Rome, of the Roman artists or the Roman expatriates, and he wondered whether he could ever be a part of any place, since he had no visible roots and belonged to no visible background and even his thoughts seemed to hang in mid-air, rootless, haphazard. And the only answer he could imagine to all this dangling and rootlessness was to become a member of the entire world, the human world that had no boundaries, the world of humanity regardless of place or of background. But just how to achieve this membership was difficult to imagine, and the only way seemed to be by attaining a kind of inner purity, by painting without prejudices and thinking without prejudices and by loving everything equally, irrespective of place or background. This was the answer that he visualized but it was a vague and elusive answer, and it seemed impossible to achieve without endangering its very essence, namely to feel and create with utter freshness and spontaneity, without *arrière-pensée,* without dogma or doctrine.

The wind blew eddies of dust along the narrow winding road and the cypresses looked as though they had been sprinkled with cinnamon. The air was smoky and mountainous. The hawks had fled from the sky, which looked hollow and drained, like a bowl turned upside down. The woman Carlotta came shuffling down the road and she stopped beside Peter and stared at the canvas.

"What's that you're doing?"

"Painting," said Peter.

"Why?" she chuckled. "What's the point of it?"

"I like it," said Peter.

"Oh you like it!" she said mockingly. "You like it! *Bravissimo!* But what's the use of it, will you tell me?"

She was filthy and foul-smelling but in her way she still was beautiful, with those adder-like eyes and that blood-red mouth that looked ready to bite him. She was rotting with syphilis but the beauty was still there, a dark tremorous beauty that bordered on lunacy. There was even a certain savage innocence about her, made all the more poignant by the foulness in her body.

"Let me tell you something," she said, squatting down under the ilex. "When the soldiers came through the village—it was years ago, I was only a child—they dragged me into a barn with my sister Anna. Men are beasts! Just listen to what I'm telling you. Anna was whimpering and holding her baby but they snatched away the baby and smashed its head against the wall. Then they threw us into the hay, first me and then Anna, and the baby lay on the floor with its brains splashed over the wall. Men are monsters! Can you believe it? Just rotten devils, that's all they are! And when they were gone Anna took the fish-knife and ran it through her belly and I ran down the road and cried all night under the olive trees.

"And after that do you know what happened? We were poor, as poor as grasshoppers. A sick old mother and a drunk old father and four brothers and myself, and a bowl of minestrone for all of us and never enough of it. So they brought home their friends to make love to me in the evening. Can you believe it? Men are devils, nothing but devils! Damn their souls!"

She scratched her thighs and said grimly, "Sometimes they tell me how they pity me. But what is pity? What good is pity? It doesn't cost them a penny to pity me! I'm growing old, I'm nearly thirty, my breasts are shriveling like a hag's! They can keep their stinking pity! God's curse on their souls!"

She looked up with a crafty glitter and said, "Come on, what are you frightened of? You're a sweet little man, I won't hurt you, I'll make you happy!"

She cocked her thumb toward a gooseberry bush and whispered, "There! Lie down in the shade, why don't you?"

But Peter blushed and stammered, "Maybe another time, Carlotta."

She bared her fang-like teeth and her belly shook with laughter. Then she lay down in the grass and a moment later she was fast asleep.

The vines grew ripe and heavy and the carts came creaking from the vineyards, filled with grapes which dropped in the dust and were crushed by the cart-wheels. The smell of crushed grapeskins filled the village every evening. Girls came walking along the path with juice-stained baskets on their shoulders.

Down in the valley the women were treading the grapes as they sang and their legs were purple as ink with the grape-juice. The whole village was laughing, drunk with the smell of the grapes. Everything was stained with their juice, everything smelled of broken grapes. Everywhere there was laughing and singing and even the long-horned bullocks were splashed with the juice as they climbed up the slope.

It was dusk when Peter wandered past the vineyards back to the village. The lights were beginning to gleam in the little piazza. He paused by the edge of the road and listened to the singing down in the valley and he noticed Carlotta fast asleep under a bush.

He stepped closer and said, "Carlotta! Wake up! It's nearly night!"

He saw the ants crawl over her face; her mouth was stiff and gaping; a tiny green fly was settling on one of her nostrils. He picked up her withered hand but the life had gone out of it. He held it a moment and let it fall into the dust again.

As he walked through the gate he heard the boys teasing the watchman.

"Been catching any thieves, Bastiano?"

"Mind your business," said the watchman.

"Been catching any fleas, old fellow?"

"Go to the devil," growled the watchman.

The boys started laughing and darted around the corner and down below waves of mist were rising up from the shrunken river-bed. There was an empty black tower on the opposite shore of the river and it looked as though it were floating on top of the mist.

II

The wind grew sharp in the Apennines. The village looked bleak and empty, and one gray morning Peter packed his bag and got on the midday bus to Rome. But Rome was bleak and windy too and the piazzas were half-deserted and the shores along the Tiber were almost as dismal as the Apennines. Freya had gone to Amalfi and Barbara had gone to St. Moritz and Mrs. Nightingale was taking the waters in Montecatini. So he cashed the little check which his paintings had brought from the Obelisco and packed his bag again and took the third class to Paris.

And Paris was also bleak, caught in the grip of an icy winter, but the bleakness was more interesting and alive than the Roman bleakness. The trees were squeaking and shuddering on the quays like old hags and lumps of brownish ice drifted miserably down the river. But all the same there was a magic about that wintry desolation. There was a depth and suggestiveness in the lilac-colored gloom.

He usually spent the morning in his dingy room in the Rue du Bac, but when the oven went out, which usually happened at noon, he used to go to the Louvre and sit on a bench of dirty velvet and dangle his feet over the hot-air register. And when he finally felt warm again he started to wander along the galleries, trying to detect something new in that battalion of masterpieces. He spent hours in front of the Titians and Tintorettos and Raphaels, trying to reach into the subtleties of line and color and facial expression, trying to see how the lines and the colors were interwoven with the attitudes and how the attitudes expressed themselves in the lines and the colors. The most subtle of all these paintings was Giorgione's *Concert Champêtre;* the naked girl with the flute and the naked girl with the water-pitcher, and between them the two youths gazing intently at one another, all blended into a dream-like vision of lust and happiness, the happiness poised over the darkness like the pitcher over the well, and the lust lurking in an ambiguity of gestures and glances, so that the happiness as well as the lust were suspended in an atmosphere of terror, all the darker because of the trance-like tranquillity of the scene. And similarly the Veroneses, though much less subtle than the Giorgione, in their very lavishness and splendor created a mood of desolation. In *The Wedding of Cana,* for instance, with its bevy of grayhounds and blackamoors and its whole steaming cataract of silks and brocades, the figures looked peculiarly stiff and expressionless, as though a glacier had engulfed them in the midst of their festivities. And the same sense of nightmare infected Uccello's big battle scene, in which the pattern of yellow spears and black hooves and mask-like helmets built up into a climate of murderous phantasmagoria. And the most despairing of all was the Saint Sebastian of Mantegna, in which the body was sheathed in a marble-like grayness and the blood that flowed from his wounds looked like leeches clinging to the marble: everything was stiff and frozen and even the faces were frozen with pain and the clouds in the distance looked like ice-floes in the Arctic. It was as though in their obsession with human beauty and human flesh the Italian painters had grown obsessed with the suffering and decay that awaited the flesh, and even in the ripeness of the Titians and the elegance of the Bronzinos there was the same pervading sadness, the sense of corruption behind the loveliness.

After the Italians he turned with a certain relief to the Frenchmen, where the very realism of the paintings made the suffering seem more tolerable. There was a cynicism behind the flattery of Nattier and Largilliere and decay was implicit in the powdered flesh of Fragonard, and even in Ingres there was an acid pessimism behind the cold, sharp perfectionism. But the pessimism was that of reason rather than of dreams and desires, and the French acidity was much less saddening than the Italian sensuality. There was a celebration of human death in the spectacular *Raft of the Medusa,* where the bodies were washed in a sulphurous gray light, and the marvelous *Burial at Ornans* was also a rhapsody on death, with its black and white pattern of weeping women and haggard pall-bearers, but in both there was an austereness and a lucidity behind the spectacle which made death seem like a part of the pattern rather than a terror behind the pattern. He was especially fond of Poussin's painting of *Orpheus and Eurydice,* in which an apprehensive Eurydice was following a leering Orpheus out of hell into an Arcadia filled with lyre-playing shepherds and naked bathers. He also loved Claude Lorrain's *Le Débarquement de Cléopâtre à Tarse,* with its enchanted evening light shining on a galleon-haunted harbor. But the fantasy of these painters was very different from the Italian fantasy; it was a dance of the intellect rather than a delirium of the senses.

Every time that he went to the Louvre he discovered something new, whether it was the humble geometry of a loaf of bread in Chardin or the grand mosaic of Thermopylae in David, or maybe the shadow-streaked cunning in the peasants of Le Nain. And each time it was the same exhilaration that came over him, since the sense of suffering in the greatest art was always strengthened by a sense of nobility, so that the suffering never had the effect of defeat or degradation but on the contrary, it made life seem all the more precious and all the more venerable. Even in a trivial little still-life like Bauguin's *Le Dessert de Gauffrettes* the tapering glass and the lilac cloth and the plate of curly wafers were painted with such enthusiasm, such a delight in their mere existence, that it became a song of praise to human habits and human artifice.

There were three paintings in the Louvre that he came to love more than the others, and whenever he stood in front of them he felt a joy which was hard to define, not merely joy in technical miracles but the warmer and more mysterious joy of being drawn into the heart of existence, which before he had felt only with Rembrandt and Goya and Michelangelo. *The Coronation of the Virgin* of Fra Angelico was like a rush of morning sunlight next to the thunder and savagery of Giotto's vision of Saint Francis. The arch-like hierarchy of halos, each encasing an angelic head which nestled in the gold like a jewel in a casket, rose into a sky so blue and so intensely innocent in its blueness that a final victory over evil seemed very nearly plausible. But when he walked a few steps further and looked at the Condottiere of Antonello da Messina, a humdrum thing compared to the blue and gold sublimity of Fra Angelico, the vision of heaven dissolved in the passionate vitality of its human features, the jutting chin and ruthless mouth and aggressive, glittering eyes, which concentrated in a few square inches such a virile intensity that the people strolling through the gallery looked like a crowd of somnambulists.

But the most moving and magical of all the paintings in the Louvre was the painting by de la Tour called *Saint Joseph Charpentier,* in which a deep tragic grandeur glowed through the tenderness and humility. He felt a chill run down his spine whenever he looked at this masterpiece. The light of the candle shone through the hand of the watching child, transforming the upheld fingers into a luminous rosy parchment, and it fell on the wrinkled brow of the sad old carpenter, which said all worth saying about goodness and endurance. It was a scene of a barren and somber simplicity but it burst into flame from the sense of wonder that hung over it, so that the flame of the candle looked like a soaring exclamation point shining on the whole impenetrable mystery of human existence.

III

He kept looking for Consuelo but Consuelo had vanished. Neither the concierge nor the consulate nor the university could
give him her address. So he spent his time alone. He was used to
being alone, and when he went out for dinner he took along a
book or a newspaper. He had learned that there was a difference
between loneliness and solitude: he had felt lonely and miserable in Chicapasco but never solitary, and in Bishop's Neck he
had felt neither lonely nor solitary but strangely isolated. In
Brancaccio he had felt isolated as well as lonely and solitary,
and in Paris he felt solitary and occasionally lonely but never
isolated, since the very intelligence of the city provided a kind
of companionship.

One morning in the Louvre a young man with a black mus-
tache was standing in front of the Virgin of Baldovinetti, which
Peter especially liked because of the Virgin's resemblance to
Barbara.

"Hideous, isn't it?" said the man.

Peter looked at him curiously.

"Oh, yes, you think I'm just saying it to shock you," said the
man defiantly. "But I mean it. It's vapid. It's shallow and artificial."

Peter looked at the Virgin with a thoughtful expression.

"The purpose of art," said the stranger, "isn't to comfort or
reassure us. It isn't to strengthen our prejudices. It isn't to tell
us what we know already."

"Yes? What is it?"

"It's to liberate us! To destroy all the claptrap! To deepen
our sense of the dark and the chaotic!"

He was a shifty-looking man in a dirty red pullover with a black silk scarf carelessly tucked under the collar. His skin had an oily Levantine sheen to it and his eyes were tense and clever and penetrating. His name was Quilico and after their meeting in the Louvre he and Peter used to stroll along the boulevards together.

"That's the thing with modern artists. Maybe they're frauds, many of them," said Quilico, "but at least they're hacking away at our prejudices. They're doing away with all this claptrap about goodness and beauty."

"But don't you think . . ."

"Christ," said Quilico, "just look around. What do you see? Do you see any traces of the good or the beautiful?"

"Yes," said Peter, "I keep seeing it in people's longing for the good and the beautiful."

"You're quibbling," said Quilico. "People aren't longing for goodness and beauty. Goodness and beauty have grown meaningless in this preposterous new world of ours. What they want is narcotics and drugs and rituals, anything to give them a foothold in the torrent that swirls around them."

Peter suspected that Quilico's theories were based not so much on a search for truth as on his venom against society, and his hatred of "prejudice" was really a passionate prejudice of his own against any kind of established authority. By "prejudice" he meant faith and tradition and order and his whole desire was for anarchy and absurdity and negation. And when he argued with Peter his desire wasn't for truth but simply to prove his own astuteness and superiority. He was obsessed with the spirit of contradiction and whatever Peter said Quilico found grounds for refuting it.

And yet Peter detected in Quilico a furtive yearning for approval, and even for luxury and popular acclaim, in fact for the very things which he so viciously condemned in others, provided they worked to his own personal benefit. In short, there was a streak of hypocrisy in Quilico, but there was also something pathetic and lovable about the fellow, with his high piping voice and desperate, foxy eyes.

"And don't you think," said Peter, "that goodness or beauty can give a meaning? Or happiness? Or even love? Can't these things give a meaning?"

"Love!" snarled Quilico. "People chatter about the opium of the people but the biggest opium of all is what people call love. Love is an illusion, that's all. There's lust, there's jealousy, there's rage and hatred, but love is merely an illusion that's waiting to be shattered. When people say they're in love they're just waiting to wreak their vengeance and rip the thing that they love into pieces!"

"I wonder," said Peter.

"That's what's wrong with you," said Quilico. "You keep wondering and speculating but you never take a position. The artist nowadays must take a position. He must be involved. He must take sides. He must be a destroyer. You're merely an amateur. There's no passion in your paintings, only a kind of childish romanticism, and you'll never be an artist until you forget this so-called beauty and step outside of yourself into the chaos around you!"

Peter knew that there was a certain truth in Quilico's criticisms, in spite of their venom and exaggeration. There was something lacking in his character. He was too easily impressed, too easily influenced. He sometimes wondered whether he had the stubbornness and crudity that were necessary to an artist. He had abandoned the baroque vistas of his Roman paintings and he had abandoned the rock-strewn landscapes of the Apennines. But when he tried to discover a new manner and a new material he found himself slipping into derivations and mannerisms. Neither the grandeur of Rome nor the grimness of Brancaccio had matured him sufficiently and he sensed that something violent was necessary to turn him into an artist.

Once he said, "You don't believe in a God, do you, Quilico?"

Quilico laughed. "Poor little Peter! You keep longing for reassurance! You keep hoping that peace and happiness really exist in this world!"

"But isn't it you," said Peter sadly, "who are running from reality? Isn't it you who refuse to look at people the way they are? Wherever I look I see happiness and hope in people's faces and not the misery and despair that you always keep talking about. Oh yes, the misery exists and the despair undoubtedly exists, but men keep looking for something else which is more natural and human."

"Yes?" said Quilico, with a look of sarcasm. "And what do they keep looking for?"

"For an answer," said Peter. "There's no answer in hate and chaos. If God exists, and only God can ever be sure that He does exist, then God must be the only possible answer to death and chaos. If God exists then He must delight in the existence of other things than Himself. And that's the point of being alive, isn't it? To delight in other things than oneself?"

Quilico laughed and shrugged his shoulders. "You're a child, just a child. You're clinging to phantoms. You recoil from the torrent of reality!"

IV

Peter was walking along the Rue de Rennes one sunny morning when he saw a youngish woman stepping out of a bakery shop. She was wearing black slacks and a green-plaid jacket and she was carrying a long loaf of bread under her arm.

"Consuelo!" he cried.

She wheeled around with a look of panic. Then her face suddenly melted and she ran toward Peter and kissed him affectionately.

"Darling," she whispered. "How long have you been here?"

"Over a month now," said Peter. "I've been looking all over the place for you. What happened? Whom are you hiding from?"

"Yes," she said, "it's perfectly true. I've been hiding from everybody. Nobody knows where I'm living. You mustn't tell them you've seen me!"

"I won't," said Peter obediently. "But why in the world . . ."

"Come," said Consuelo, taking his arm, "we'll have a chat over a cup of coffee and then you'll forget that you ever saw me."

They stepped into the red-tiled brasserie around the corner and sat down on a bench and ordered a *filtre*.

"Tell me," she said, "how is mother?"

"She's doing splendidly, except for her liver."

"And Barbara?"

"She's doing brilliantly."

"Happy?"

"Obviously."

"Poor Barbara!"

"Freya's somewhere near Naples."

"Happy?"

"Of course. She'll always be happy."

"Any news from Bishop's Neck?"

"A card from Miss Malachi. Everything as usual."

"And Augusta?"

"Also a card. She won a prize at the Baltimore dog show."

"That leaves Daphne," said Consuelo. "I wonder what happened to poor old Daphne."

"Maybe Daphne is happier than anybody."

"Isn't it marvelous?" said Consuelo. "Everybody happy, in spite of everything! All those problems among the Nightingales and all of them working out so beautifully!"

She looked teasingly at Peter and said: "And you? What about you?"

"Oh, I'm happy," said Peter. "In my queer little way."

"It *is* queer, a bit," said Consuelo, cocking her head. "You were always a part of other people, watching other people and admiring other people, and I never was sure what was really at the bottom of you."

"Neither was I," said Peter sadly.

"You were like a dragon-fly," said Consuelo. "Hovering in space, with nowhere to settle. Long and thin and translucent, with thousands of tiny eyes peering down at the rest of us."

"And never quite understanding any of you," said Peter.

"But always watching," said Consuelo. "Always wondering. Always wandering."

She had changed but it was difficult to tell just what had changed in her. She looked thinner and older and her skin had a different texture. Her eyes glittered nervously under the dark languid eyelids and her mouth had a rich, vaguely voluptuous look to it. Her cheeks narrowed down to a pointed, capricious chin with a mole on the end of it, like a small blue beetle.

"Well," she said, "I've behaved abominably. I'm worse than Daphne, running away like this, but life is short and I'm not going to ruin it like Augusta or Barbara. I was always the vagabond in the family. The slut, the trollope, the good-for-nothing. But I have my own morality and in my way I'm a terrible puritan and I deeply disapprove of the wickedness of Augusta and Barbara."

"Are they wicked?" said Peter.

"All of the Nightingales had a streak of wickedness. But at the same time there is also a marvelous innocence in all the Nightingales. Even Barbara is profoundly innocent. Even Augusta has a kind of innocence. But it's terribly easy for someone innocent to slip into wickedness."

Peter could see something secret lurking in Consuelo's eyes and he knew that what she was saying was about herself and her new secret.

"Are you studying?" said Peter thoughtfully.

"Oh, certainly," said Consuelo. "I'm reading Schopenhauer

and Hegel, not to mention Heidegger and Kierkegaard. As soon as I grasped the fact that I'd never be a dancer I hurled myself into philosophy and I've decided to be a philosopher."

"Very admirable," said Peter, nodding.

"They need a philosopher among the Nightingales. Father had a certain philosophy and Mother has her own philosophy, but having a philosophy is one thing and living by it is another, and I've decided I'm going to try and build my life on a philosophy."

"Very wise," murmured Peter.

"Well, we'll see," said Consuelo. "Maybe the philosophy will work and maybe it will crumble into pieces. But at least I'm going to try. Life is short and I'm going to try."

She got up from the bench and kissed Peter on the forehead, and then she took the loaf of bread and tucked it under her arm.

"Nothing," she said, "is especially easy for me and it's never easy to say goodbye, but since I've turned into a philosopher I've learned to say goodbye!"

She smiled and waved her hand and hurried out into the street again, and that was the last that he ever saw of Consuelo.

v

One night Consuelo was sitting in a tavern near the Panthéon, listening to a beautiful young Negress singing to the music of a mandolin. Snow was falling and the light from the window shone on the slowly falling flakes. Now and then a jet of air slid through a crack in the pane and the flame of the candle shot fiercely into the air.

She was sitting beside a broad-cheeked ashen-haired girl who was staring at the ceiling with a rapt expression. Now and then she looked at Consuelo with a smile and nodded. Once or twice she glanced at her wristwatch and shrugged her shoulders.

Consuelo had been living in the Rue Verneuil for several months. She went to the lectures at the Sorbonne in the morning, lunched on coffee and a brioche, sat in the reading-room in the afternoon, then met Tania in one of the nearby cafés and had dinner in some bistro on the Rue Jacob or the Rue du Dragon. She read her Plato and Aristotle, her Pascal and Montesquieu, she read her Valéry and Gide, she read her Sartre and Camus. She read the white-backed periodicals that were for sale in the Left Bank kiosks and after dinner she sat with Tania and talked about Webern or Giacometti. She wore dark woollen dresses and black cotton stockings and her hair hung in velvety strands over her shoulders. She felt neither happy nor sad, neither excited nor bored, neither liberated nor imprisoned, neither baffled nor illuminated. She felt all of these things momentarily but none of them for long, and while she felt that she was reaching toward some role in existence, toward some recognition and purpose and even a kind of fulfillment, she also felt that some indefinable barrier was preventing her from achieving it: a barrier that loomed sometimes as dark as a fog in midwinter, sometimes as tall as a street at midnight, and sometimes as imperceptible as a thread of steel.

The door opened. A gust of ice-cold air swept into the room. Two men strode up to Tania's table, shaking the snowflakes from their overcoats. They greeted Tania in Russian and flung their coats over a chair and sat down next to Tania with a casual glance at Consuelo.

"This is Dimitri. My friend Consuelo. And this is Giorgiu. My friend Consuelo."

They shook hands, Dimitri vehemently and Giorgiu very gently. Their hands were as cold as ice. Their cheeks were flushed with the icy wind.

"Well," said Tania, "what's been happening?"

"Nothing much," said Dimitri. He muttered something in

Russian and then, with a glance at Consuelo, slipped into French again.

"You've heard from Boris?"

"Not a word," said Tania.

"Or Jaroslav?"

"Not yet."

"It's getting late. There's not much time left."

"Don't be nervous. You'll be hearing from them."

"Horrible weather," put in Giorgiu in his mild, caressing voice. The waiter came up to the table. They both ordered a cognac. Dimitri turned in his chair and stared tently at Consuelo while Giorgiu scratched his head and listened to the monotonous plaintive music.

Giorgiu was a man in his middle forties. He had a good-natured face with smiling wrinkles around his mouth and large brown eyes that were vague and dreamy but also, at intervals, sly and observant. A Chinese-looking beard hung from his bald, egg-shaped head. He had large hairless hands with thick white fingers and dirty fingernails.

Dimitri was in his thirties; he created an impression of strain and violence. His face looked split in two. The upper half, with its Tartar-like eyes, looked cool and ascetic as a hermit's. But the lower half looked almost brutal with its thick wild lips and jutting chin. He wasn't handsome but there was a passionate vitality in his face, a blending of blind aggressiveness and slave-like vulnerability. His hair was ruddy and coarse. His fingers kept drumming at the table. He wore a turtle-neck sweater and a golden bracelet around his wrist.

"Who are you?" he said softly, leaning over toward Consuelo.

"I am nobody," said Consuelo, smiling.

"You don't exist? Is that what you mean?"

"Very nearly," said Consuelo.

"Come," said Dimitri, baring his teeth a little, "let's stop chatting in enigmas. What do you do? Where do you live? Do you have a lover? Do you have a sense of the Infinite?"

A secret warmth was beginning to glide through Consuelo, half pleasant and half disturbing. She glanced furtively at Dimitri. There was in his blunt, half-savage face something that mysteriously delighted her. And at the same time she felt alienated, repelled, a bit alarmed.

"You're quite right," she said mildly, "there's no point in enigmas. I do nothing, to be quite frank about it. I have no home. I don't have a lover."

"No home," said Dimitri mournfully, "yes, that I can understand. No lover—it's odd but even that I can understand. But doing nothing—that is terrible. That is criminal, I tell you! Doing nothing means feeling nothing, believing nothing, hoping for nothing!"

Consuelo nodded wistfully. "Yes, yes, you are perfectly right. It is wicked. I agree. I believe in nothing, I feel nothing. But hope—that's a different matter! I keep on hoping!"

Dimitri looked away with an irritable air. But a little later, as they rose to leave, his deepset eyes wandered back again. They rested on Consuelo with a muted, inquiring look. Slowly his hand moved over the table and covered her own very gently. He looked tensely into her eyes. His lips melted into a smile—a sweet, childlike smile that was also feral and ruthless.

As they stepped through the snow Dimitri turned and whispered to her:

"Please, please, may I come home with you? Or will you come home with me? Which is it?"

VI

Dimitri's flat on the Rue Saint-Dominique was shabby but bizarre. It belonged to an Egyptian lady who was staying in Mallorca and had rented it to Dimitri for a negligible sum, along with the Maltese cat and the canaries. There was only one big room. Turkish draperies hung from the walls and there was a furtive but persistent odor of stale lingerie and sandalwood. The curtains were frayed along the edges and faded to a streaky, suspicious violet. The rug was spotted with stains and the upholstery was in shreds. The gilt had chipped from the snakes' heads on the arms of the chairs. The ceiling sagged and a dying palm stood in the jardinière in the corner. A small gray bathroom which also served as a kitchen branched off to the left of the corridor.

Just one week after she had met Dimitri Consuelo moved into his flat. She hung her dresses in the closet and scattered her books across the table. She still took the Métro to the university every morning but no longer went to the Flore with Tania, no longer dined in the Rue Jacob, no longer lunched on a brioche, no longer talked about Giacometti. Instead she went with Dimitri for a glass of vermouth to a nearby bar, then came home with him and cooked a bowl of risotto or a dish of noodles. And she spent the rest of the evening listening to Dimitri and his friends talk about Glinka and Moussorgsky, or about Gogol and Gorki.

She detected, after a week or two, something queer in the atmosphere, but Tania said: "Don't be upset, don't pay too much attention to Dimitri's oddities. He is lovable, he is naïve, he is soulful, but he is crazy. Don't try to understand him. His character is as slippery as a drop of mercury . . ."

So life went on in the Rue Saint-Dominique with an air of outward domesticity. Once a month she went to the bank to pick up her allowance, which wasn't much but enough to indulge occasionally in something special—a lunch out in Bougival or a bottle of champagne. She used to prowl through the little market-place behind the Rue Amélie and peer at the piles of pink and white fennel, the dusty artichokes, the clusters of dates and the wizened peppers, the pumpkins and cauliflowers and the blood-oranges from Sicily; and in the nearby "Comestibles" there were fine red lobsters, chickens in aspic, rosy hams and vol-au-vents, great membra of bologna or mortadella dangling above a shelf of cheeses crusted with grape-seeds or sheathed in wax.

Sometimes Dimitri disappeared for several hours in the middle of the day. Occasionally there were phone calls while he was gone and a strange, choked voice spoke to her in an unintelligible language. Sometimes parcels would be delivered by a mousy little man—shabby manila envelopes or bundles of pinkish-gray paper. Sometimes a woman in the building opposite leaned over and peered across her flower-pots. Sometimes a gentleman in a long brown overcoat hobbled by with a cane, nodding his head. And after a while Consuelo couldn't help suspecting a hidden significance in the malacca cane or the pots of begonia, but Tania said: "Don't fret about Dimitri. He is crazy, he gets obsessed with things. He gets involved with all sorts of people but he lands on his feet. He's like a cat . . ."

One evening in the middle of March she was sitting with Dimitri and Giorgiu, drinking coffee on the quay directly opposite the Louvre.

"My moral feelings are one thing," Dimitri was saying, "my political feelings are another and my feeling of fate, or history, or inevitability if you prefer, is still another. Which am I to trust?"

"Trust none of them," said Giorgiu, gently stroking his beard. "Just trust your natural spontaneous feelings. The throb of your blood. Your human impulses."

"Human impulses! Good God," said Dimitri excitedly, "what are they?"

"Your heart," said Giorgiu, with a sigh. "Your love of life. Your love of people."

"A heart is a vague sort of organ," said Dimitri. "Especially when it comes to making decisions."

Giorgiu sipped at his coffee silently. He turned to Consuelo and looked at her probingly.

"Listen," he said. "I'll tell you what happened down in Bucharest, my friend. Right after the war, in 1945, we were all very tired, my friends and I. We were poor, our clothes were in rags, the food in Bucharest was deplorable but still we were cheerful, we felt hope, almost enthusiasm. We felt that a fresh new life was beginning, not particularly easy in many ways, even a bit disturbing here and there, but still it was a beginning. It was a clean fresh start for us. There was hope in the air.

"The new men came into power. New laws were passed, new regulations. Old things were prohibited. It didn't all seem quite necessary but still we were hopeful. We accepted it. We nodded our heads and smiled. One fine morning we suddenly realized that we were no longer free. The men from the East had seized the libraries, the bookshops, the printing works. They screamed orders at us all—at Petru, at me, at poor little Dinu. They told us, rather gruffly, that we must educate the people. We must tell them that the prisons are empty and that everything is beautiful and right in the best of worlds. But we looked around and knew that absolutely none of this was true, the opposite in fact was true, the prisons were full and our hearts were empty and the air around us was swarming with lies. It didn't seem quite right to us but still we didn't give up hope. 'Patience,' we said. 'Give them time. After all, it's only a beginning.'

"Years passed. Now and then it seemed that things were getting better. But then after a while they always got worse again, much harder and dirtier and uglier. Poor Dinu was told that he mustn't write love poetry any more. Petru was told that his stories must speak only of the golden dawn and the happy factory workers. More years went by. We did our best, just keeping quiet, keeping our thoughts to ourselves, still hoping that things would sooner or later loosen up a bit. Well, two years ago it finally came to a head. There was a new wave of terror. God knows why. It just happened. The air was so thick with lies that it stank like a corpse. Petru was killed one fine morning as he stepped out of an elevator. Old Panaït was thrown into a prison somewhere in Cluj. Poor Dinu committed suicide in the hills of Moldavia. And why? Because we knew. We finally understood. We at last grasped the fact that there was no hope of things improving. It was simply a part of the system that there must always be lies, there must always be hatred and a fear of men who love truth, there must always be treachery, there must always be oppression. We almost forgot what it was like to live without fear but the fear was still ugly, it still hurt us, it still offended us. We almost forgot what the truth really looked like but all those lies made us long for it all the more desperately. Life went on, oh, yes, it went on all right, we ate our bread and drank our beer but we did it under the shadow of silent despair.

"One day I went out to buy a head of cabbage for dinner and when I came home the house was empty. My sister Clara was gone. Her husband Constantin was gone. I looked around. I asked the neighbors. None of them knew. Nobody knew anything. And then I noticed that when they spoke to me there was a funny look in their eyes. That night I scraped together the rest of my money and took the bus to the edge of the town. I walked a few miles till I came to a little fishing village. I bribed an old fisherman—it wasn't much but it was enough. Two nights later I landed in a rocky bay on the coast of Turkey, just a stone's throw south of the Bulgarian border. I won't bore you with all the rest of it but, frankly, do you blame me for being a little sceptical about that beautiful golden dawn? . . ."

VII

The second of Freya's islands was much larger than the first, too large to be really an island; it was more like a separate kingdom.

First of all there was the steamer. It was a dismal gray day. The seagulls whirled and the horn kept hooting, the ship rose and fell, and a dull Victorian glow shone on the varnished maple doors. Stewards and waiters in dirty uniforms rushed by in the second-class dining room, serving cold ravioli and oily little veal chops. She wandered dismally along the deck, smelling the smoke that shot from the funnel and the stale black grease that oozed from the machinery.

After the steamer came the train. In the third-class compartments there were soldiers and peasants with their sausages and wine-bottles. A child started to bawl. Another child started to vomit. There was a stench of dirty boots, of vomited milk, of baby urine. The track wound over the hills and a clammy drizzle filled the air. The lemon groves were filled with lemons and the olive groves with olives but there was a look of destitution and sterility in the faces. The donkeys wore scarlet plumes as they drew their painted carts but the faces looked crushed and sad, hard as stones, wrinkled as medlars.

Finally they reached the volcano. It rose like a ghost out of the sea, with a cloud pinned on top of it, like a plume on top of a donkey. Even in the volcano there was something sad. It looked eerie and brooding. On the lower slopes there were farm-houses and scrawny little orchards, and below the orchards rose the cliffs and below the cliffs shone the sea, so blue, so desperately blue that it seemed to conspire with the white volcano to create an illusion of hope over that miserable stony earth.

She found a room in a small pensione for three hundred lire a day. There was an earthenware wash-bowl, a cracked oval mirror, a splintered wicker chair and a creaky bed with a straw mattress. Every morning she carried her easel down the path beyond the town, looking for something suggestive and hidden in the landscape. Above the town rose a monastery, a rambling mass of ochreous stucco, and beyond lay some columns among the straggling mulberry trees. The sea was not paintable and the volcano was certainly not paintable, even the drab squatting houses and the broken columns were not quite paintable. She was developing a new manner, patterns of long spidery threads weaving delicately across a background of white and black pebbles. And so she painted the barren land, a land of stones and dead stubble, and the olive trees were stylized into a pattern of writhing threads which floated over a labyrinth of speckly gray gravel. The effect was abstract but something of the bleakness was reflected, the threads of mystery and unearthliness playing over the dryness and poverty.

After the drizzle of the first three days there was nothing but sunlight. White dust rose like steam from the rolling cartwheels. The whiteness covered everything; it was almost like frost. The trees were coated with fine white powder and the goats looked as though they had been dipped in flour. The slopes of the volcano seemed to throb in the heat-waves and the bells in the monastery sounded like an echo of the heat.

And after a while it seemed pointless to keep on painting the stony land. She stopped looking at the land and started to notice the stony people, who before had seemed like shadows moving through the misery of the landscape. She noticed the dirt and the poverty, which was more than the poverty of the landscape. The latrines were nothing but holes dug in the slope behind the shrubbery. Heaps of garbage lay in the heat, seething with little green worms. The feeble-minded children wore bandages on their hands to keep them from chewing at them, and the women past forty had turned into witches: worn and scrawny and vindictive, with wisps of hair curling like wires and feral eyes peering into the unknowable.

One day there was a procession through the medieval alleys. Files of peasants went straggling and stalking through the heat, carrying a great wooden cross and a masked Christ in chains. The women wore hoods and the boys held flickering candles and the white-robed attendants wore masks over their faces. She detected something pagan and prehistoric in this ceremony, as though the people were mourning for some long-lost divinity.

Once a haggard old woman ran up to her on the mountain.

"What do you want here?" she cried.

"Peace," said Freya. "And solitude."

"Oh, you'll find it!" shouted the woman, shaking her fist in the air. "The peace of a tomb! The loneliness of a sepulchre! Don't worry! You'll find it!"

VIII

The moment one leaves the highways one steps into the past: into the Middle Ages or into antiquity or even the times before antiquity. Tiny cart-roads branch from the highways and narrow mule-paths branch from the cart-roads, and the mule-paths end up in one of those rocky little villages that sit perched like a buzzard on the crest of a hill, with a tumble-down castle rising up in the middle of it. Pigs nuzzle in the gutters and naked babies play in the dirt and unfortunately even the architecture is nothing illustrious—no baroque or romanesque, nothing Greek or Byzantine, just the residue of the past without a name and without a history.

Such a village was San Stefano, about an hour's walk from the coast. One day Freya climbed up to San Stefano and set her easel on the edge of the hill. She started to paint in her usual way—a maze of gravel covering the canvas and multi-colored cobwebs weaving at random across the gravel. There was nothing in the painting that resembled the landscape except for the interplay of colors and something bony about the atmosphere.

She saw a man come down the path and pause beside her in the shade. He wore a striped worsted suit and a tiny hat of greenish velvet. He was a cripple, a hunchback; his face was heavily wrinkled and his eyes shown with a twisted look that was like a reflection of his twisted body.

"Yes," he said, "that's what it's like if you look under the surface. Just chaos. Just a jumble. That's what it's like on Saturn or Jupiter."

Freya smiled at him and suddenly there was a sweetness in the cripple's face. The parched, self-pitying face grew tender and imploring.

"Well," he said, "it's a perfectly sensible way of painting, I'll admit. People won't be existing in the world for very much longer and you might as well paint as though the people had stopped existing. That's the way that things look through the eyes of a lizard, I suppose. Just a crazy wild jumble that only a lizard can interpret."

"Well, I wonder," said Freya.

The hunchback laughed. "You're right in wondering. The lizard wouldn't see the point of bothering to put it on canvas. Still, colors have a huge advantage over words, when you come right down to it. With words you're stuck for good with the human ways of thinking. Maybe the paintings will still be alive when the holocaust is over but the poems will mean nothing, they'll just be scrawls on a piece of paper."

"Do things need an audience to be beautiful or meaningful?"

"What did Sophocles say? One has to wait until the evening before one finally realizes how beautiful the day was. One has to wait for a man to die before one really can judge him. And human history looks like a tangle of bloodshed and tyranny but who knows, when it's over maybe it will suddenly take on a pattern. Nobody will be left to appreciate the pattern but the pattern will be there, all beautiful and vivid, like a marvelous epitaph."

"You write poems, did you say?" said Freya.

"Did I? I've forgotten. Maybe I did. Yes, I'm a poet I suppose but unfortunately not a very good one. I write poems about things like the snow on Mount Aetna, but there's nothing left to say about the snow on Mount Aetna and my poems are just echoes, just sad little echoes . . ."

After this Freya returned from time to time to San Stefano and sat in the piazza and drank wine with the hunchback Virgilio. Whenever she sat with Virgilio she saw new meanings in the things around her, not so much because of Virgilio's words, which were sometimes a bit occult, but because there was something about him made things seem more intense to her.

"I still keep trying to have visions," said Virgilio, staring into the distance, "but I'm tired and the visions no longer seem to materialize. I used to have marvelous visions, glittering steppes and cataracts and glaciers, but now all I see is a lump of bread and a dirty bottle. I can't seem to transform the drabness of the world any longer. The words are stale, the music is dead, and even Dante is growing meaningless."

"But life still has a meaning, I can see it in your eyes," said Freya gently. "Maybe the poems have lost their meaning but being alive still has a meaning, even if the meaning has grown just a little bit sinister."

"It still has meaning," nodded Virgilio, "but I have to lie to myself about it. I have to lie to find brightness or comfort in that meaning. I say to myself, the stars are beautiful, the sea is glorious, the lion is noble, but I know they're all lies, the stars aren't beautiful and the sea's not glorious and even the poor old lion isn't exactly noble. It's all just sentimentality, it's all just human artifice and the only thing that's left is the horrible reality of dying."

"Well," said Freya, "if death has a meaning, then living also must have a meaning."

"If only," said Virgilio, "one could say, this is life, this is the way things happen and things will even out in the end and what is lovely eventually withers and what is terrible grows less terrible, and the beautiful pay for their beauty and the ugly are blessed for their ugliness—oh yes, if one could say this and really believe it, then one could probably cultivate a very charming philosophy."

"Why do you keep brooding about beauty and ugliness? There are plenty of other things than beauty or ugliness."

Virgilio leaned closer and looked tensely into Freya's eyes. His bony hands were shaking nervously on the edge of the café table.

"I repel you," he whispered, "don't I?"

"Why do you say so?" said Freya.

"It's obvious. I'm hideous. I'm a monster!"

Freya looked away and said nothing.

"Do you deny it?" screamed Virgilio. "You'd shudder if I touched you! Isn't it true?"

Freya looked at him sadly. "You ought to know better. Being a poet."

"Poetry! Poetry! Who cares about poetry? You can throw your Dante into the sewer! Poems exist because people try to run away from their ugliness but what they want isn't grandeur, it's love. Ridiculous, isn't it?"

Late one night Freya was sitting in the loggia of the Pensione, playing chess with a young Austrian who was writing a book on Taormina.

A woman's voice called, "Signorina!"

Freya looked into the garden. A girl in a checkered dress came running up the stairway.

"Signorina! Please hurry! He's been asking for you! He keeps on asking for you!"

A tumble-down taxi drove them to the edge of San Stefano and they climbed up the path that led to the walls of the town. She followed the girl up the slope and finally they came to a tiny house that clung like a barnacle to the walls of the castle. An oil-lamp was burning and a gray-haired woman stood in the doorway. Tears shone on her cheeks. She took Freya by the hand.

"Forgive me, signorina. He kept calling. Please forgive me."

Virgilio was lying on a rumpled wooden bed beside a window. He turned his head as she entered but he didn't seem to see her. His face was mottled with fever and his body lay curled under the sheet like an animal's.

"Virgilio," she said.

But he didn't seem to recognize her. She sat down by the bed and folded her hands and waited in silence.

Down in the valley a lamb was beginning to bleat. The smell of the Sicilian night flowed in through the window—a smell of lemon trees and rocks, of burning oil and human refuse. Nothing stirred and as she stared at Virgilio's face it seemed already to be turning into a broken fragment of antiquity.

The gray-haired woman and the girl kept muttering away under their breath, and after a while the door opened and an elderly priest entered the room. Freya stayed by the bed and kept looking at the dying poet, hoping somehow that just by looking at him she could comfort him a little. But he obviously didn't recognize her and the women kept on praying and finally she said "Good night" and walked back through the darkness.

IX

March came to an end. The cuckoos sang in the woods and in the crannies, like leftover snow, the wild narcissus were blossoming.

From time to time Dimitri suddenly had to go somewhere in the country, and now that he was beginning to trust Consuelo he took her along. They drove out in his old Citroën to a villa in the suburbs or some inn on the banks of the Seine or maybe an empty mill in the middle of a forest. There he would leave her for a while and go and do what he had to do, and she would saunter through the trees or over a crumbling stone bridge, waiting for him to drive up again and fling open the door.

Once he left her in a little gray town not far from Chartres. She strolled under the plane-trees through the arcaded square and watched the farm-women laying out their vegetables in the stalls. He came back an hour later. As she jumped into the car he muttered:

"Did anyone see you?"

"Oh, I suppose so."

"I mean, did anyone watch you?"

"I doubt it," she said.

"Nobody at all?"

She shrugged her shoulders. "An old fisherman walked by with a basket."

"Did he say anything?"

"Well," she murmured, "he might have said good morning."

"And did you answer?"

"I nodded."

"But you didn't say anything?"

"No, nothing."

That evening she went with Dimitri and his friend Ivan and a man named Krauss to a cheap little bistro on the Rue du Bac called Le Tigre. They drank wine and ate mussels; heaps of black, oily shells lay shimmering in the dirty bowl in the middle of the table. Ivan wiped the edge of the bowl with a crust of gray bread and Krauss kept sucking at his brick-red mustache. It all looked rather mournful and strangely pointless—the gaping black shells and the scattered gray crumbs and the white wisp of garlic clinging to Ivan's cloven chin.

"What disgusts me," said Ivan, "is the terrible theoretical-mindedness. Even the very word abstract—it's just a cackle, all dry and shriveled. What in the world is abstract, will you tell me? What in the jungle is abstract? What in the ocean is abstract? What in our hearts is abstract? *Mamma mia,* how I long for a world where things are just to be touched and tasted! A world without dogmas, without doctrines, without theories!"

"There is no such world any more," said Krauss. "Even the Hottentots have doctrines."

"Maybe they always did," said Dimitri.

"It's the Curse of Man," said Krauss.

They rose from the table. Krauss looked wanly at Dimitri.

"It's all set, then?" he said.

"Three o'clock sharp," said Dimitri.

"And you've got the name? You're positive?"

"Yes. The Mogador," said Dimitri.

X

The following day was a Tuesday. The sky was a melancholy gray and shortly after noon a cool, thin drizzle started to fall —or rather, not quite fall, it was so misty and weightless that it seemed to hang in mid-air, clinging to the cheeks like a veil.

"Well," said Dimitri, glancing at his watch, "I think we'll pick up Professor Borisov."

"Who is Professor Borisov?"

"A scoundrel," said Dimitri, looking at his fingernails.

So they got into the car and drove slowly down the Boulevard. Presently they entered the long dingy vista of the Rue du Cherche-Midi. Now and then a few drops went spraying across the windshield and then suddenly the clouds parted and the sun fell shining on the mottled pavement. And then it vanished just as suddenly and the thin gray drizzle started all over again. They stopped in front of a shop where a sign said: "Martin. Pharmacie." Dimitri got out. He glanced around and crossed the street. Then he beckoned to Consuelo. She walked over and joined him.

"There," said Dimitri, turning his head to the left imperceptibly. "D'you see that sign? The Mogador? You'll be so good as to enter the café. You will see an elderly gentleman sitting on the banquette next to the bar. Thickish face, clean-shaven, dark blue suit, azure tie. You will recognize him by a very slight scar over the eyebrow. You will say to him, in English, mind you, 'I beg your pardon, did you find an umbrella?' and he will answer, if I'm not mistaken, 'Are you a member of the Astronomical Society?' That is all. You will nod politely and he will follow you to the car."

Consuelo said: "I see. That scoundrel, Professor Borisov?"

"Never mind," said Dimitri. "Please do as I've told you."

Consuelo turned the corner and entered the Mogador. A dull gray light filled the place. For a moment it looked empty. Then a waiter popped out through an oval-glassed door and simultaneously she saw, like a shape emerging through the fog, a dark little figure sitting in a corner left of the bar. She walked up to him casually. He was not quite what she had expected. His suit was dark blue and his tie was a sultry lavender but his face was singularly colorless, broad and flat and finely wrinkled, with nothing to distinguish it but a certain indefinable brutishness and at the same time a rather seedy, downtrodden expression.

She walked up to him, leaned forward, and said in a liquid tone: "Pardon me, sir. Did you find an umbrella?"

The man blinked, cleared his throat, and in an Oxford accent murmured: "Ah, I gather that you are a member of the Royal Astronomical Society?"

Consuelo smiled coyly. Professor Borisov rose from the table. He picked his raincoat from a hook and followed her out into the street.

They drove slowly through the drizzle in the direction of the quay. Professor Borisov sat in the front of the car next to Dimitri. Neither of them spoke to the other but now and then the Professor turned his head and said to Consuelo: "Beastly day!" or "Have you been to the Louvre lately?"

They followed the quay all the way to the Place des Invalides. Then they turned left. A narrow street branched off to the right behind the Invalides. It was beginning to rain harder now. The light had a dismal oyster tinge.

"Spring," said Professor Borisov, "is a detestable season, don't you agree?"

A little later as they waited at a corner for the lights to change, Borisov murmured to Dimitri:

"You know Pamfilovitch, I suppose?"

Dimitri nodded. "I had an unusually nasty cup of tea with Pamfilovitch three days ago."

They drove on. Something seemed to have gone wrong with the motor. The car lurched and stammered. A croaking noise came out of the engine.

The street was deserted. On the left stood a kind of warehouse, a long faceless building of yellowish stucco. On the right rose an aisle of humdrum bourgeois houses built of dirty gray brick, with peeling shutters covering the windows.

Professor Borisov kept glancing to the left and the right. Consuelo detected a gathering nervousness in the back of his head. Once he turned around sharply and caught her eye, rather pleadingly. She smiled blandly and said:

"Are we running out of gas, I wonder?"

The Professor looked startled. He looked tensely at Dimitri.

"Well, I think . . ." he began.

But at that moment Dimitri stepped on the brakes and drew up in front of a narrow door. He nodded his head and said quietly: "There. Number Forty-two. That's right, isn't it?"

A peculiar agitation had seized Professor Borisov. He shook his head quickly. His thin blue lips were beginning to tremble.

"I wonder, would you excuse me, I just want to make sure that . . ."

But before he could finish his sentence the door of 42 swung open. Two men in black raincoats stepped out and strode toward the car. With great rapidity and at the same time an air of casual authority they opened the door of the car, took the Professor by both arms and half led and half carried him across the sidewalk and up the steps. A tiny cry, half-strangulated, seemed to escape from Professor Borisov. The door closed behind him and he vanished from sight.

Dimitri released the brakes and drove quickly down the street. Just as he turned around the corner a dark-faced woman in a knitted shawl came running out of a shop and waved both her arms at them. But Dimitri drove on. When they entered the quay the sun peeped through the clouds and the budding trees started to glisten.

XI

That same evening, as they sipped their coffee, the telephone rang. A woman's voice spoke to Dimitri in rapid, agitated tones. Dimitri listened and nodded, said a word or two in Russian, then put back the receiver and turned quietly toward Consuelo.

"You'll have to pack rather quickly, I'm afraid. We'll be leaving in ten minutes."

"Oh? Where?"

"I don't know."

"We'll be back soon?"

"Who knows?"

She folded her dresses into the suitcase, tossed her Baudelaire on top of them, hurriedly wrapped up her toilet articles and tucked in a box of almond wafers. She snapped the lock.

The two canaries were asleep in their cage but the cat, Cléopâtre, was watching her impenetrably.

She slipped her passport into her coat. Dimitri turned out the lights.

"Ready?" he said.

She smiled and nodded. He turned brusquely, put down the bags, tightened his arms around her waist and kissed her on the mouth.

They drove through the evening haze toward the Porte d'Italie and entered the straggling deteriorating outskirts. People were milling about in the dusk. A man with a monkey was playing a hand-organ. A little boy with a balloon crossed the road directly in front of them. The brakes squealed, the car veered, Dimitri missed him by an inch. They passed the squalor and melancholia of drab cafés and neon-lit gas-pumps and then the road suddenly narrowed and became quite empty. They followed the weather-beaten wall of an old country cemetery. Through the gate they caught glimpses of castiron crosses and marble angels. Night gathered. They entered the forest of Fontainebleau. A powdery blue fell over the trees. There was very little traffic. Great trucks came thundering occasionally with their headlights blazing but in Sens, at a curve in the highway not far from the cathedral, Dimitri turned left abruptly, flicked off the headlights and came to a halt.

He waited for several minutes. Then he turned on the headlights again and followed a side street toward a pebbly country road.

There was no traffic at all here. They went winding through the meadows. In the distance, like a firefly, the window of a farm-house twinkled faintly. A lonely sheep, lost from its flock, wandered slowly through the mist. A sudden chill swept through the air. Fog was gathering all around them.

"Do you think he was following us?"

Dimitri shrugged his shoulders.

"It's sad, isn't it?" she said.

"What is sad?" said Dimitri.

"Living like this. Doing things that one doesn't want to do, just out of hatred."

"It isn't hatred," said Dimitri.

"What is it?"

"Faith," said Dimitri.

The road dipped into a valley and now the fog grew so dense that almost nothing could be seen. They were crawling through a thick white nothingness. The glow from the headlights was diffused in an opaque jelly. Here and there the trunk of a tree loomed for a moment and was gone again. A train whistled behind them, they could hear the growl of the engine, and then, like two little pearls, two headlights moved toward them. A car passed them slowly, a rattling old station-wagon, and then it vanished and Dimitri suddenly jammed on the brakes: they had stumbled off the road and were stuck in a ditch.

"It's hopeless," he said.

"Let's wait," said Consuelo.

So he shut off the motor and they sat in the car and waited. All they heard was the bellowing of a cow in the distance. Once she thought she heard footsteps and the snapping of a twig but that too was like an illusion, nothing was real anymore. The world had collapsed into a death-like vapor.

"Tell me," she said, "what is the world going to be like a hundred years from now?"

"There will be stillness, that's all I know. Just a great mass of stillness."

"No people?"

"Oh," said Dimitri, "there will be people. If you'd call them people."

"Barbarians?" said Consuelo.

"Monstrosities, more likely. Clutching and driveling little beasts with three legs and half of an eye."

He reached under the seat and took out a bottle of wine. He pulled out the cork and passed the bottle to Consuelo. The wine flowed down her throat, cool yet warming, reassuring. She closed her eyes and leaned her head against Dimitri's shoulder and felt his hands move slowly under her dress.

"Tell me, Dimitri, it's a silly question, I know. But tell me . . ."

"Yes?"

"Do you believe in a God?"

"Be more explicit, please," said Dimitri.

"I mean, do you believe in something wiser and better than all of us? Than our laws and desires? Do you, frankly, Dimitri?"

"I don't know," said Dimitri. He sucked at the neck of the wine bottle; she could feel the throbbing of the wine as it flowed down his gullet. "I only know that we ought to be happier and nobler than we are, but whether this will be our own doing or the doing of a sort of God, well, I really don't know. I've often wondered. I just don't know."

"Then you keep on hoping?"

"I don't think. I don't hope. I only know that I've got to keep fighting in my miserable crazy way against what is ugly and false and cruel."

"Look," said Consuelo, "the fog's lifting!" And sure enough, all around them with an uncanny swiftness the haze was beginning to dissipate. It flowed southward across the field like a ghostly cascade. A balmy wind came out of the north, the smell of the earth grew fresh and tangy; a moment later the stars were aglitter in the widening blackness.

Part Six

I

Ripples pass over the bay but they pass in an aimless silence.
The streams keep flowing on but they flow along in secrecy.
The mosquitos swarm in the reeds and the hornets buzz in the
orchard, but over it all hangs this silence and under it all lurks
this secrecy. Other states have a natural stillness, the woods of
Maine, the sands of Florida. But Maryland has an unnatural
stillness which is like the stillness of a dream. There are echoes
of things still faintly remembered from another continent, and
there are echoes of things when the land was still virginal. Beads
of resin like topaz ooze from the wrinkled black trunks. The
rocks along the shore are streaked with onyx and mercury. It is
almost as though the whole landscape were hypnotized, waiting
for the moment to come back when the realities of the world are
once more visible.

Time passed, but the passage of time left this hovering still-ness unchanged, and even the changing of the seasons left the landscape unaltered. It merely seemed, under the passing fluc-tuations of light and color, to intensify the deep, desolate same-ness at the heart of things. And yet, under this very monotony there lurked a slumbering uneasiness whose hidden churnings were like lava bubbling away in a crater.

Augusta spent most of the summer playing tennis down at the country club. She played in the tournament in Richmond and was runner-up in the lady's singles, and the audience applauded her spearing drives and subtle volleys. And then she played in the tournament in Baltimore and again she lost in the finals, but they applauded her stylish backhand and powerful smashes. By the end of each tournament she was dizzy with nervousness and when they asked her to play in Wilmington she was stricken with panic. And after that she began to lose her ambition in tennis and spent most of her time down in the kennels with the dogs or else taking walks with her favorite bitch, whose name was Bessie. When Bessie was in labor, which happened in Au-gust, she sat all night long helping her through the convulsions of child-birth. She often loitered in the stables with the cows and the mares. She loved the smell of animal bodies, she loved the glow of their gentle eyes. She loved the musk of their breath and the tender feel of their fur, she loved their warmth and their silence and their ruddy, submissive gentleness. She even enjoyed the stink of dung and the acrid smell of cow-piss, it all seemed clean and healthy compared to the stench of humanity.

And as for Cyrus, an icy aloofness had risen up between them. They no longer spoke at the breakfast table and after a month of this tension she decided to have her coffee sent to her bed-room. They didn't speak at the luncheon table and they hardly spoke at the dinner table and after a while she took to drinking White Ladies before dinner. A cocktail or two took the edge off her vengefulness and a third made the boredom in the house seem almost tolerable, and a nightcap after dinner made the ways of the world seem less sinister. It was only when she was back in her room after midnight that a spasm of fear shot through her and she threw herself on the bed. "Oh God," she thought, "anything! Anything at all, I don't care what! Just not this horrible nothingness that's lurking around the corner!" It was a terror that seized her more and more frequently of late, a terror of the void, a *horror vacui,* as though she were standing on the edge of a precipice and her grip on the world were crumbling.

One day she went walking along the creek with one of her bloodhounds. It was a clear August day, the fields were brilliant with goldenrod. Down by the waterfall two boys were diving into the pool. She caught a glimpse of their sun-tanned bodies through the web of trailing ivy.

Finally she came to the hunting-shack. The wooden door was ajar, someone had ripped off the lock, and she stepped into the darkness. The place was beginning to rot. Cobwebs hung from the ceiling. It was obviously being used as a place for surreptitious pleasure, and the detritus of past amours lay scattered across the floor—an empty beer bottle, a hair-pin, a rubber disc, a shriveled handkerchief. There was a peculiar salty odor, a faint smell of shellfish. The dusty window-sill was littered with the stiffened bodies of daddy-long-legs. She caught sight of a small tin whistle lying by the door. She picked it up and blew it: a raucous squeal, like a sea-gull's.

She sat down on the creaking steps, as she had done long ago. She picked up a twig and drew a pattern in the earth—a bulging heart with a long sharp arrow piercing the center of it. She laughed aloud. "A bleeding heart. Sick with desire. That's what I am!" She dug her heel in the ground; the heart went up in a puff of dust.

A strange sensation came over her: a feeling of mysterious duplication, an awareness of a hidden counterpart to everything she was doing. She felt a shadowy *doppelgänger* hovering close beside her, both eerily present and disturbingly absent. And this pendant, this *doppelgänger,* was both herself and not herself, it was a reflection of what she was, bored and lonely and purpose-less, and also a reflection of someone else who was buried inside her. The air was like a mirror, it reflected the scene just as it was, with only the faintest variation in time and décor. But this subtle variation was crucial and overwhelming: it seemed to embody the very essence, the very meaning of existence. This impression grew so vivid that she felt herself being severed, be-ing split into two halves, half shadow and half substance: half of herself sitting on the steps, watching a spider dangling from the windowsill, and the other half still sitting there and still watching the spider, but infinitely removed in time and space; blissful, transfigured.

A rusty pen-knife was lying on the ground in front of her. She picked it up and prodded open the blade with a stick. It was bubbled and black, as though it were matted with blood. She drew the edge of the blade along her arm absent-mindedly.

A twig snapped. She looked up. At first she saw no one. Then she noticed a man standing motionless under the trees. He was a heavy-set man with thick reddish curls. He was wearing a lum-berjack shirt and heavily stained corduroy trousers.

He smiled and strolled casually across the clearing.

"Better be careful," he said.

"What about?" said Augusta tensely.

"That little knife. It's pretty rusty. It wouldn't be nice if you went and cut yourself."

"I just found it," said Augusta sullenly.

"Yes, I know, you just found it. I been watching you through the trees and I seen you pick it up."

"Is it yours?"

"No," said the man. "It ain't mine. It wouldn't be mine."

"Who are you?" said Augusta.

"Nobody special," said he, grinning.

"I said: Who are you?" said Augusta furiously.

"I just told you," he answered gently. "I'm nobody in particular, ma'am. I'm nobody you'd notice. My name's Cleophas, in case it'd interest you. I live down the road a way. I've seen you plenty of times but I guess you never noticed me."

"I've never seen you before," said Augusta.

"Maybe not so as you noticed me. But you seen me from a distance without aiming to notice me."

"What are you doing here?" said Augusta.

"I heard you blowing that little whistle. I thought somebody might be calling and that's why I came."

"No," said Augusta. "That's not what I meant. What do you do? What's your job here?"

"Nothing much," said Cleophas casually. "I keep bees down the road and I sell my honey up in Euphoria. It's a peaceful kind of life here. I can't argue that I'm specially busy."

Augusta watched him intently. There was something familiar about his face. His furry voice sounded familiar but she couldn't quite place it. She grew uneasy. She was irrationally afraid of the stranger and yet she felt a furtive pleasure in hearing his voice and feeling him close to her.

She got up. "Well, I'd better be going, I guess."

"Don't go," said Cleophas tenderly. "I watched you sitting there, so quiet, I almost thought you was asleep. You needn't go. I won't be troubling you."

"Do you come here often?" said Augusta, looking intently at the man.

"Not so often," said Cleophas. "Now and then. As the spirit moves me."

She picked up her cane and whistled softly for the bloodhound.

"I'll be seeing you," said Cleophas, smiling lazily as she crossed the clearing.

II

When she arrived back at the house again the sun was just setting. The drawing-room was aflame with a last blaze of light. Through the curtains she could see the obelisks of privet. On the lawn lay the bitch with her nuzzling puppies, fast asleep.

The light began to fade in the room as she stood there. It ebbed across the table where Meissen figurines were standing. There was Europe, a queen-like woman in a flowing blue cape with a dove on her outstretched fingers and a crown on her head. There was Africa, a beautiful Negress with a headdress of plumes, with a lion dozing peacefully at her feet. There was Asia, a sloe-eyed warrior in a scarlet turban, with a tiger at his side and a scimitar in his belt. And there was America, a red-skinned Indian in a robe of gaudy feathers, carrying a bow under his arm and a giant hawk on his shoulder.

She caught sight of Mr. Aspinwall sitting on the couch by the fireplace. He put down his book and looked at her quizzically.

"The more I read," he said softly, "the more puzzled I become. This business of love. It's very mysterious. What has happened to it? Does it still exist? I keep hearing about love, I keep reading about it in novels, people sing about it in operas and poets write about it in their poems. But where is it? Will you tell me? Has it shrunk into boredom? Has it withered from over-exposure? Has it vanished from the face of the earth?"

"It still exists," said Augusta. "I don't know where but it still exists."

"In the jungles, maybe," said Mr. Aspinwall.

"All around us," said Augusta.

As she climbed up the stairs she met her husband on the landing.

"I have something to say to you, Cyrus."

"Yes?" said Cyrus, recoiling a little.

"Have you ever thought of taking a trip, dear?"

Cyrus looked startled. "Where, for instance?"

"Oh, anywhere. Guatemala. Haiti. Bermuda. Just the two of us."

"I don't get the point, I'm afraid," said Cyrus carefully.

"We need a change," said Augusta. "Both of us."

"You're bored, are you?" said Cyrus.

"Not bored," said Augusta. "Worried."

"Going on a trip won't help," said Cyrus. "Things are what they are. It can't be helped."

"How do you know?" said Augusta tensely.

"Why fool ourselves? You've never loved me. You'll never love me. There it is. It's all over. It can't be helped."

"And what do you suggest?"

"Nothing," said Cyrus. "Just being polite. Just being mannerly."

"It's all my fault," said Augusta. "I made a blunder. A ridiculous blunder."

Cyrus's voice shook a little. "Would you like a divorce, Augusta?"

"There's no point," said Augusta, "in being hysterical, is there?"

"Very well then," said Cyrus. "Let's just try to be mannerly."

"Life is short," whispered Augusta.

"Thank the Lord," muttered Cyrus.

Up in her room she flung off her clothes and turned on the bath water. After her bath she sat down in front of her dressing table. She took longer than usual with her lipstick and eyebrow pencil. There was something very odd about her face, she suddenly noticed. The peach-colored lamps gave her flesh a feverish tint. There was a brightness in her eyes, a Turkish-looking glitter. And the lips looked swollen and bruised, as though someone had bitten them. She looked down at her massive breasts and down at the creases in her belly. She was growing fat. There was no mistaking it. There were bubbles of fat above her hips and her thighs were taking on a limp, puckered texture.

"Flesh, flesh," she muttered. "Nothing but flesh. Putrid flesh."

The light that fell on the table seemed to sharpen a little, as though the electric current had grown more powerful. The porcelain bowl and the scent-bottles, the combs, the scissors, the files and tweezers: they lay scattered across the glass like hieroglyphics. They were trying to convey some deep and urgent message to her; but the lettering was too abstruse; the message was illegible.

She put on a dress of red silk which she had never worn before, as well as the ruby ear-rings which Cyrus had given her for her birthday.

"Goodness me," said Miss Aspinwall when she entered the drawing-room. "You look like an Assyrian princess, positively."

"What would you like?" said Cyrus thinly. "A White Lady, as usual?"

"No," said Augusta, "something new, I think. How about a Daiquiri?"

III

Three days later she walked back into the woods behind the inlet. She followed the path along the creek, just the same as before. When she came to the waterfall she paused for a while. The spray from the torrent floated above the mossy rocks. It was shot with prisms of sunlight; a rainbow hung over the pool. The hissing and crackling of the water sounded like human voices—little whispers and moans, sudden gasps of excitement.

Two boys were sitting on a rock by the bridge with their fishing poles. They were stripped to the waist; their faded levis were splashed with water. A shaggy dog sat beside them. He jumped up and barked furiously. Then he wagged his yellow tail, whimpered softly and sat down again. The boys started to whisper; they peeped at her furtively. One of them reached into his pocket and took out a pack of cigarettes. He struck a match, cupped his hand, and tossed the match into the stream.

The path climbed a slope. Five minutes later she came to the clearing. She paused for a moment in the shade; then she stepped into the sunlight.

"Fine day, isn't it?" said Cleophas.

"Yes, it is," said Augusta.

"You can smell the maples," said Cleophas.

Augusta nodded sullenly.

"I knew you'd come," said Cleophas, smiling.

Augusta said nothing. She walked across the clearing and sat down on the steps beside Cleophas.

"Yes," said Cleophas, "I was sure of it. I felt it in the air. I said to myself 'Today she's coming,' and sure enough, here you are."

"Autumn," said Augusta. "One more month and the leaves will all be gone. I hate Autumn. I've always hated the rain and the chilliness."

"I don't mind it," said Cleophas. "I don't mind anything especially. That's your trouble. You're too sensitive. You keep minding the way things are."

"Because they're ugly and sad, very often," said Augusta.

"It's only the way you take things. Nothing is ugly if you just accept things . . ."

She felt the tension in the air but it wasn't the tension of pain or oppression; it was expectancy, it was alertness, it was almost exultation. She glanced covertly at Cleophas. He was staring into the trees. She noticed the leathery texture of his sun-darkened face, with its broad, bristling cheeks and delicate ear-lobes. She noticed the fleshy lips and the finely curved chin. She noticed the hair on his forearms, shining in the sun like copper wires. She caught the smell of his body, intimate, sap-like. And sitting so close beside him, feeling his warmth and solidity, all the tension and agitation in her melted away.

"You can look at things gloomily and you can look at them cheerfuly, it don't change them, you just got to sit back and accept them."

"Do you accept them?" said Augusta.

"There's no way but to accept them. You can't keep on fighting against the things that's only natural. What's the use of being born if you're going to fight against what's natural? There's only one good reason for living and that's the joy of being alive, and if you're fighting against what's natural you might as well be dead."

"But sometimes," said Augusta, "there is something horrible in what is natural."

"No," said Cleophas, "it's never horrible, it just looks horrible because you're scared of it. If you get to accept what's natural nothing looks horrible any more. Even pain and sickness and death stop looking horrible. Even a corpse rotting in the sunlight isn't horrible any more. What's the point of being alive if we keep worrying about what's horrible?"

Augusta rose. "Come," she said. "Let me see where you're living."

They walked silently down the path until they reached the road to Euphoria. A narrow drive led up a slope to a wooden shack half-hidden by shrubbery. Behind the shack, surrounded by berry-bushes, stood a row of six bee-hives. "There's a lot you can learn here," muttered Cleophas, "about what's natural."

He struck at one of the hives with his powerful brown fist. And instantly thousands of bees started to buzz around him fiercely, whirring and sizzling around his head in a menacing manner. There was a spicy smell of honey that rose from the alighting board. She felt the aura of heat that was shed by the buzzing of the bees.

Cleophas opened the partition of one of the hives and she peered into the bottom of it. Clusters of sleek quivering bees were scrambling about on top of another, working with a kind of bubbling intensity, building at the combs and storing the honey. Then Cleophas showed her the middle partition, which was the nursery of the bees. Here there were thousands of insects sitting motionless, as in a temple, mutely witnessing the creation of life, the rituals of generation. Then he showed her the top of the hive, and there were rows and rows of bees, tireless, scrupulous, intent, perfecting and sealing the waxy edifice.

"Here," said Cleophas. "Look at this one. The queen is dead. The hive is dying."

Augusta looked into the dying hive. Here too the bees were buzzing about but the buzzing was aimless and scattered and desultory. There was a fragrance of honey but it was a stale, withered fragrance. Cleophas struck at the hive but there was only a listless circling of the miserable bees. Everything was broken and dirty and disorderly in the dying hive. The bodies of the degenerate bees lay scattered on the floor, and there were hornets and wasps and even bumble bees prowling amongst them, stealing the left-over honey which the bees no longer fought to defend. Some sickly-looking bees still flew about languidly, corrupt and demoralized, knowing that the hive was disintegrating.

"And all," said Augusta, "because their queen is gone? Is that the reason?"

"That's the reason," nodded Cleophas. "When the queen is gone there's no point any more. There's no hope. There's no orderliness. There's nothing to work for and nothing to fight for. There's no purpose in anything. They grow sick and lazy and cowardly . . ."

She followed him to the shack and he opened the door for

her. She was startled by the cleanliness and tidiness of the place. The dishes and glasses were neatly stacked on the shelves. The bed was freshly made and the flowered curtains looked freshly laundered. There was a row of books on the table. She glanced at the titles. They were mostly books about bee-keeping, some nature guides and seed-catalogues.

"There ain't much to drink here," said Cleophas apologetically. "Just some cider and some port. Let me give you a glass of port. It ain't nothing special but maybe it'll cheer you up a little."

He sat down close beside her and flung his arm over the back of her chair.

"Many a time," he said softly, "I been watching you from a distance. You never noticed me, did you? I always kept to the shadowy places. I watched you riding through the woods even before you got married. Maybe there's some that wouldn't think you were specially beautiful, but to me you looked beautiful, so big and mournful and sort of lonesome. I often used to wonder why you were so queer and lonesome. You looked sulky and proud but there was always this lonesomeness."

Augusta looked at the ceiling and said quietly, "I know. Everyone thinks that I'm proud. Everyone thinks that I'm bitter. And it's true. I hate people because I'm frightened of people."

"And what is it," said Cleophas, "that scares you about people?"

Augusta hesitated. Then she said: "Superstition, I guess you'd call it. Something to do with bad luck. From the time I was a child I had an obsession about bad luck. Something or other made me think that I always brought bad luck. If I planted a plant it was sure to die. If I played a game I was sure to lose. If I tried to help somebody, like Daphne, it was sure to end in a calamity."

"You were scared of yourself," said Cleophas half-teasing, "it sounds like."

Augusta nodded. "Yes. I was. I always felt I was doomed. I tried to shrug off the feeling and that's the reason I married Cyrus, but the feeling lingered on and I couldn't get rid of it. I felt something hideous would happen if I fell in love with somebody, and so I tried not to love people, I tried to hate them and despise them. And hating and despising people also brought misery, but it was a sluggish, monotonous misery, not a wild and bloody misery. That's why I kept to myself. I kept to the woods and the animals. I tried to ward off the impending calamity."

"Don't worry," said Cleophas. "There's no calamity if you fall in love with somebody."

Augusta stared at her hands. "Love," she said. "It's an easy word. There are different kinds of love, just like different kinds of weather. It can be sunny and smiling, it can be cloudy and depressing, it can be drizzly and misty, there can be thunder and lightning. It can be cold to make you shiver and hot to make you sweat. It can be anything and everything and there's no way to define it."

"You say you never been in love. But you seem to know a lot about it."

"Everybody knows about love. Even if they've never felt it," said Augusta.

She closed her eyes. She already knew exactly how it would happen. She felt his hand on the back of her neck, warm and heavy, like the paw of an animal, and then the gentle insinuation of his hand between her breasts, and then the feel of his thick firm lips on her throat and the melting power of his arms as they enveloped her. It was exactly as she had always known it would happen, but all the same, what really happened was like nothing that she had ever imagined. She had anticipated it all, she had visualized it all, but the pang, the thrust, the ugliness, the sudden delicacy, the lingering sadness—these things she had never imagined but when they happened she mysteriously recognized them.

IV

The stillness of Maine was a crisp salty stillness, very different from the dazed, tropical stillness of Tortosa. When Daphne stood on the shore and smelled the foam that splashed on the rocks she felt a rush of wild, birdlike energy surge through her; and when the wind came suddenly whirling, kissing her cheeks with flakes of spume, she flung out her arms like a bird spreading its wings.

They found a small log-cabin on the edge of a cliff, just across the oval bay from where Jason had his tower. Below them the Atlantic kept crashing against the rocks; behind them rose the evergreens, all stiff and black on the narrow hillside, and down to the left lay the scythe of sand which circled the bay toward Jason's tower.

The cabin had two rooms. One was the kitchen, which they called the "den," with red cretonne curtains and a stove in the corner. The other was the bedroom, which they called the "studio," with corduroy draperies and a large brick fireplace. Summer guests who rented the cabin paid sixty dollars a month for it but Mr. Purvis, who owned the cabin and lived in Mackerel Point, let them have it for thirty a month if they took it the whole year round.

And so Jason, who was rich, lent a hundred dollars to Pancho and arranged for Pancho to leave his sculptures down in Ogunquit in a gallery that belonged to a certain Miss McDiarmid. There were plenty of people in the neighbourhood who were interested in art, said Miss McDiarmid, especially in things like involuntary actions and dream-assemblies.

The driftwood centaur, she said, might bring a hundred

dollars. The scylla was labeled fifty and the pegasus seventy-five. The swan and the cerberus were priced at forty dollars and the two little porcupines at thirty a piece. The polyphemus, she hinted in her cool gray way, was a bit too vivid. Next summer there might be a client for it, Mr. Baines or Mr. Casella.

So they settled in the cabin and Pancho worked on his sculptures while she curled up on the couch and read *The Possessed*. For lunch she made sandwiches, salami or tuna-fish, and for dinner they usually wandered along the beach to Jason's tower, where there were powerful martinis and charcoal-grilled steaks and occasionally lobsters and one of Sado's weird little puddings. Jason was working on an ambitious long poem called *Aquarius* and after dinner they all squatted in front of the fire, sipping highballs. They would listen to opera records, *Elektra* or maybe *Orfeo*, and after a while Jason would read them a page from his poem.

The weather turned cooler, the last leaves were falling and the smell of woodsmoke and clams filled the air. The waves beat more powerfully against the barnacled boulders, spraying the cabin with tufts of yellowish foam and salty mist.

And when they came back from Jason's, sometimes long after midnight, the sea rolled into the bay with its white-maned breakers, which shivered like phantoms when the sky was clouded and blazed into silver when the moon came out.

"Oh, it's lovely," said Daphne, "but so weird and ominous! One of these nights there'll be a storm ripping the house into pieces!"

When they lay in bed together and the lights were out Pancho whispered:

"Your body never relaxes. It's all twitchy and frightened."

"It's chilly," said said, "a little."

"Are you scared of something?"

"Yes."

"What?" said Pancho.

"I don't know."

"A man? Or a woman?"

"I don't know."

"Maybe yourself," muttered Pancho. "Something in yourself begins to scare you."

"Maybe," she said. "I don't know. Maybe the winter coming on. Maybe the cold and the dark. And that tower, that funny tower . . ."

She took long walks in the mornings so that Pancho could work in peace. She walked inland toward the hills or down the road toward Mackerel Point or over the sand-strewn rocks, continually watching the water.

More and more she came to be fascinated by rhythms, by patterns. She began to see patterns in almost everything around her and little by little she saw patterns even in things like twigs or boulders. She picked up a feather and parted its delicate fern-like ribs; or she picked up a tiny skeleton, and there was a strange resemblance between the feather and the skeleton. There were shells, very different from the beautiful shells in Tortosa, black shells, ugly shells, shells with the stormy north engraved on them, and she threw them away because their pattern was crude and desolate and there were times when she longed for the daze and stillness of Tortosa. She would pick up a leaf and scrutinize the pattern, the narrow veins spreading out from the dark central artery, and the leaf then resembled both the feather and the skeleton. Even the clouds had a pattern, sometimes difficult to detect, but a flock of little clouds had a casual but unmistakable rhythm and even a big single cloud, continually shifting and dissolving, had a mysterious and beautiful rhythm in its dissolution, like music. And even the waves, as she watched them gushing among the rocks, had a pattern embossed on them, part foam and part water, with salty veins arrowing out from a bubbling artery. And the more she studied these patterns the more she saw their similarity, and even the imprints on the sand had a pattern that blended with the rest of them, a rhythm, a coherence, a branching of veins from a central artery.

But what she finally began to see in all these patterns was something else—not coherence or continuity but change, perpetual change, not the sprouting and spreading of life but death, decay, decomposition, until in the end it almost seemed that death and decay were a part of the pattern and just as beautiful, just as symmetrical, just as significant and vital as the patterns of living things, such as the fish and the sea-gulls.

But then she realized a moment later that there was something false in this analogy, there was something wrong and even dangerous in visualizing beauty in decay, there was a sinister fallacy in detecting a rhythm in corruption, since the only rhythm in corruption was the anguish of things perishing. And death in fact was the very epitome of the destruction of patterns, the real enemy of patterns and the ultimate destroyer of all patterns: and patterns and rhythms, however rigid or monotonous, were the pulse of life, the persistence of life, and even in death the echoes of life.

v

One morning when she awoke the whole coast was covered with snow; the rocks and the trees and the sickle of sand were all covered with snow. The only thing that wasn't white, except for the sun-swept Atlantic, was Jason's tower out on the point, black, erect, like a hooded witness.

After breakfast she went out for a walk in the foamy snow. The sky was stupendously blue and the sea blazed with sunlight and the snow was so blinding that for a while she could hardly see. The rocks had been changed into diamond-bright clouds, soft and rounded and so light-looking that they seemed to float in the air.

She had forgotten Tortosa and she no longer longed for the palm trees, she had let her hair grow long again and wore dresses instead of jeans. She was vaguely aware of some mysterious change inside her body. And she had finally come to love all this bleakness and austerity. What was beautiful in this landscape was the asperity, the inhumanity. Air, clean air without thoughts, wintry hills without memories, trees towering and unpruned, stones gray and untrodden, everything casual and clear and inhuman as spring-water.

That evening at dusk they waded through the snow to Jason's tower. A fire was blazing in the fireplace, sprinkling highlights over the cocktail glasses. Jason was sitting at the piano in his Chinese kimono and Sado sat on the floor in his sweaty jerkins, shelling walnuts. Jason was tall and very lean, with a dark Etruscan head, a tiny brown beard and a nose like a hermit's. Sado was squat and fleshy and Mongolian. He was naked down to the waist and his pubis bulged in the tight blue denim. He had eyes like a child's or an animal's, black and clear, both stealthy and innocent. He finished shelling his nuts and while Jason played a toccata he started to do his exercises in front of the fire. He did twenty-five push-ups and then he did the crab; he twisted his legs around his neck and then he stood on his head and glared at the flames.

Pancho watched him with a deep brooding look in his eyes.

"Why do you do these things, Sado?"

"To be strong," said Sado, tittering.

"You're strong enough, aren't you?"

"No," said Sado in his sing-song voice. He glanced tensely at Daphne and ran his palm over his chest. "I'm weak. I have to be stronger. I'm afraid of the demons!"

After dinner they listened for a while to *Ariadne auf Naxos* and then Jason took out his manuscript and read from his poem.

After a while Daphne said:

"I don't understand it, Jason. Are you purposely obscure? Or is your meaning so terribly complicated?"

"Poems," said Jason, frowning a little, "aren't meant to be understood. They aren't meant to have meanings. They are meant to be listened to. Does a Chinese vase have to be understood? Does a fugue by Bach have a meaning?"

"But poems are words," said Daphne, kneeling by the fire, "and words are meant to have meanings, aren't they?"

"The Chinese vase had a purpose too, it was meant for flowers," said Jason slowly, "and Bach's fugues had a purpose also, they were meant for clavier practice, but when something becomes art the usual purpose no longer matters and when a poem becomes art the words stop having the usual meanings."

"But still," said Daphne, spreading her hands, "don't poems have a purpose, like a vase?"

"A hidden purpose, maybe," said Jason, "but soon the poet forgets the purpose."

"But don't you want some kind of audience?" said Daphne, peering at Sado.

"No," said Jason. "I don't want an audience in the world I see around me."

"But then," said Daphne, lowering her head, "you're willing to live and die unknown?"

"I despise the world around me. I don't care what it thinks of me."

When they finally came back to the cabin Pancho muttered: "Look, you're quivering."

"I'm cold," said Daphne, "I guess."

"You're scared, aren't you?" said Pancho.

"Oh, yes, you're right," cried Daphne, throwing her coat across the couch. "I'm scared! I'm scared of rats and I'm scared of tarantulas! I'm scared of toads, I'm scared of lightning and

I'm scared of men with beards! Do you know what I'm really scared of? I'm scared of being nothing! Just a lump of flesh hanging around whom nobody loves and nobody needs!"

"You're weak," said Pancho coldly. "You have no will-power, that's the trouble. You're just like Jason's poem, you have no purpose, you just exist."

"Oh, God," said Daphne softly, "you're right, you're right, I'm dangling in nothingness! And I'm scared, yes, I'm scared that you're drifting away from me, darling . . ."

The following morning the sky was dark when she looked out of the window. She went into the kitchen and lit the flame under the coffee pot. She broke two eggs in the frying pan and put the marmalade on a tray and then she lit the gas oven to heat up the biscuits. Then she sat down by the window and stared over the sea. The smell of coffee and of burning butter seeped through the deep wintry grayness.

When Pancho entered the room in his pyjamas she said softly:

"Listen, Pancho. Have you ever thought of getting married one of these days?"

Pancho looked at her emptily. "How funny to hear you say that."

"What is funny?"

"You. Married."

Her mouth began to quiver. "You're stupid, Pancho. You're stupid and childish! You have all these theories about art and philosophy but you notice nothing about people! Absolutely nothing at all! You make your crazy statues and you live with your childish fantasies and you notice nothing of the depravity around you!"

His mouth sagged; he looked puzzled; there was a look in his eyes that frightened her. The sea growled in the rocks and the flame danced feebly under the frying pan.

Her voice grew tender and pleading. "Listen, Pancho, listen to me, please. I love you, believe me, I love you. I want you to have friends and to be happy but there is something evil, there

is something downright sinister in the atmosphere around here.
I want to find a way we can keep on living together and the
only way is to be sensible and try to keep away from all
this . . ."

"What are you driving at?" said Pancho in a dull heavy voice.

"We must stop seeing Jason and Sado," said Daphne.

Pancho was staring at her with a cool, far-off look in his
eyes. His lips tightened strangely and he rose from the table,
walked slowly into the bedroom and shut the door quietly.

VI

The wintry cold continued and the snow grew deeper and
deeper. There were days when everything was gray, the sky
looked like a prison and the ocean spread out into a great heaving gloom. And there were days when the sky was cloudless,
the whole Atlantic was a blaze of light and the hills were white
and cloudy, like a world freshly created.

One evening Pancho put on his machinaw and wrapped his
head in a muffler.

"Where are you going?" said Daphne.

"Out for a walk," muttered Pancho.

"Over to Jason's?"

"Jason's gone down to Boston," said Pancho.

And he stepped into the dusk, which was full of white whirl-
winds.

She still loved Pancho, she was sure of her love, but it was
a torn and ambiguous love. It was a love tinged with suspicion
and self-torment and anarchy. She felt exiled, excluded, mysti-
fied; and since love feeds on mystery her love grew still sharper
and still more chaotic. And since love blurs one's vision her

notions of Pancho grew still more torturous and there were times when she felt that she didn't understand him at all. In a way she loved his body, it was crisp and clean and lovable, but in another way she resented it, she felt an envy and exasperation toward it, not only when he was lying listless and sleepy beside her, but even when he made love to her, which now was only occasionally, and she detected in his lust something alien and scornful.

On this particular evening she felt more than usually restless. She leafed lazily through a record catalogue and then she opened a can of peaches. Then she turned to the window and stared out over the bay.

Finally she put on her coat and galoshes and stepped out of doors.

There was always a shaggy splendor about the coast in the winter, there was something grand and unlimited about the quality of the light. The trees rose out of the snow with a grim and stubborn blackness and in the evening, now for instance, the shore was bathed in a blue transparency that didn't come from the sky but seemed to rise from the depth of the sea; and the clouds gradually dissolved as the threat of the night wandered closer, they sank down into the horizon like wisps of pink smoke, and the evening stars flickered, very sharp and very separate, and the vastness grew intimate and piercing like a lamentation, and the bleakness of the stones took on a poignance, even a hint of tenderness.

As she walked she caught sight of a shadow in the distance, a curious black shadow that was crawling over the hill. Her mouth started to twitch. "Am I mad?" she wondered. "Am I feverish?" The shadow drew closer, faint as a comma at first and then curved like a question-mark, and suddenly vivid and abrupt, like an exclamation point.

Her heart pounded wildly. The light died on the water. For a moment she thought of running, her panic was so violent. Then she turned and walked quietly back to the cabin, entered the kitchen and turned on the light and dropped the latch on the door.

She sat down in the rocking chair by the stove and waited.

Five minutes later, maybe ten, there was a knock on the door. She didn't move. She sat in the rocking-chair with her hands gripped together.

There was another knock; then silence; then a rap on the windowpane. She glanced at the window and there was the broad dark face with its glittering eyes, frighteningly familiar and at the same time strangely altered, almost unrecognizable.

She went to the door and lifted the latch. An icy gust swept into the room. Mona stood in the doorway, dappled with snowflakes. Her face was red with the cold; rheumy tears rolled down her cheeks.

"God, what weather," she growled, striding up to the stove. "How people can stand it I refuse to imagine."

Daphne stared at her motionlessly. "Why did you come here, Mona?"

"Goodness, child, don't ask questions. Hurry, get me a drink." She flung her coat on the couch and took off her astrakhan cap and started rubbing her freckled hands over the stove.

Daphne took out the ice and mixed her a bourbon highball while Mona kept puffing cigarette smoke through her nostrils.

"What a time I've had! Lord!" she said in her low, ringing voice. "No taxis at the station, not a soul but that idiot ticketman, he'd never heard of Diana Jones or even of Mr. Lopez. It took me over an hour and a half to get here. I had to ask at the Copper Kettle. What a horrible woman runs that place!"

Daphne kept staring at her with a hypnotized expression.

"How did you find out where I was?"

"Never mind," said Mona grimly. "You can find out almost anything if you just keep on trying."

She turned and lifted her glass and gazed thoughtfully at Daphne, tilting her head to one side, as though looking at an abstract painting.

"Do you realize," she murmured, "what you did to me, Diana?"

"You had no right to come here," said Daphne, very slowly.

"No right! Good God, no right! Do you call it no right when I've given my whole life to you, when I've made you the center of everything, when all my thoughts and all my plans circulated around nothing but you—you call that no right? You've gone straight out of your mind!"

She looked broader than usual, her iron-gray hair had turned paler, there were signs of fatigue in that leathery face, dark as a Seminole's. She clutched the glass to her bosom and dropped the ash from her cigarette.

"Diana, allow me to tell you something. You're a coward pure and simple. I know what lies beneath your behavior. Cowardice sheer and unmitigated. You're afraid of your own impulses. You're trying to hide from your own nature. But you're doomed to defeat, I tell you. This is only an interlude, this Pancho thing, it's only a hiatus. And you know it deep in your heart. You know it perfectly well. You don't really feel attracted to that ridiculous little ephebe. Of course you don't. You're just pretending. You're bored to distraction. I can see it in your eyes. This snow and ice! Why, it's worse than Alaska! Come back to Florida, Diana. You're not meant for this horrible climate."

Daphne lowered her eyes and rested her hand on the kitchen table. She could feel Mona's strength encircling her, those formidable blood-warm coils.

She reached out laboriously, as though groping through a gelatine, and picked up the big kitchen knife from the table.

"Mona, you've finished your highball and you've warmed up enough now. It's late and Pancho's coming. You'd better get going."

Mona's lips started puckering. "Come," she whispered. "Come back to me!"

Daphne lifted the knife and held it pointed in front of her.

"Please put on your coat now, Mona. If you don't get out I'm going to kill you."

Mona took a deep breath. She blinked her eyes and raised her head a little and stared at a spot six inches to the left of Daphne's shoulders. Her face was drained of expression, she looked suddenly very old, she had the majesty and pallor of a very old woman.

She put the glass back on the cabinet, bent down and picked up her coat, put her cap on her head and moved slowly toward the door. She glanced down at her feet for a moment as though she were studying the linoleum. Then she nodded her head abruptly, as though in sudden recollection.

Then she opened the door and stepped out into the night.

VII

The snow melted. March came, and with March came the storms of the equinox.

It was a heavy, uneasy night, the sky was overcast with clouds, purplish clouds which kept coiling and uncoiling over the sea. But the rain didn't fall though the smell of thunder filled the air. The pines groaned and whistled in the sharp jets of wind. And then finally there was a sound of far-off galloping over the sea, a mighty gust pierced the atmosphere and lightning broke on the horizon and the full force of the storm fell crashing over the coast.

Daphne closed the shutters tight when she felt the house beginning to tremble. Suddenly the lights all went out and there was a muffled roar, like a dynamite explosion.

She lit the kerosene lamp and sat down to gather her thoughts. Then she set the table for supper and lit the oven to put in the apple pie. She poured the dill pickles into a little glass bowl and then sat down by the stove and started to leaf through *Anna Karenina.*

The rain kept on pounding. An hour went by, then another. She closed the book and stared at the stove. "He's over at Jason's, I guess," she thought.

It was ten; then eleven. Finally the clock struck midnight. The wind was as wild as ever but the rain started to lessen. She opened the door and peered out into the night. But the gale ripped through the kitchen and blew out the lamp, so she quickly closed the door and lit the lamp again with trembling fingers.

She waited the whole night long. She'd fall asleep for little spells but then she'd suddenly wake up again and listen to the roar of the ocean. The wind tore through the pines, the panes squeaked and rattled and through it all she could hear the clattering and booming of the surf.

She woke up the next morning all alone in the bed. All was still, the wind had died, there was a clamminess in the air. Through the storm-streaked panes the world looked utterly limp, all flattened and battered, bathed in a streamy half-light.

A little later the sun came out and the clouds drifted away. The mud and detritus lay shimmering in a cool gray radiance.

When she stepped out of doors it was startlingly warm. The smell of the earth seeped through the aftermath of the tempest.

As she climbed down the rocks she felt a strange exultation. "It's all right, the storm's over, he's waiting at Jason's," she thought; and then, "Well, either at Jason's or up in town somewhere, probably." She felt the gayety of relief, the noise and the nightmare were over and the air was full of smells, unidentifiable little smells, as though the storm had dug into the ocean-bed and released its hidden secrets.

A man on a spotted horse was riding along in the distance. For a moment it looked like Pancho but then she knew it couldn't be Pancho. The man rode over the dunes and then slowly up the slope and then he disappeared behind the bulge of the hillock.

She climbed over the rocks and wandered down to the edge of the water. There was a circle of stones here, a rocky pool ringed with barnacles. Usually it was stagnant and half-empty but now it was filled with yellowish water and the heave of the sea kept spilling into the pool.

And something about this pool suggested the blindness of existence; the opaqueness and misunderstanding, the imprisonment, the savagery. It seemed that everything in life had been twisted and obscured, that people were strangely helpless in struggling against the obscurity, that words were helpless and energy was helpless, love was helpless, art was helpless, and the answer to it all lay somewhere far in the future, when the storm would be over and human life would have to start all over again.

Directly in front of her stood another rock, shaped like a fist. Little flecks of dirty foam were still clinging to the top of it. She circled around the rock and as she happened to glance behind her she caught sight of Pancho's body in the shade of the rock. One arm was flung sideward and the other clutched at his chest; his swollen blue face was half-covered with seaweed.

She stood still, startled by something like the howl of a dog. Then she realized that the howl was the sound of her own voice. She sank down on the sand, not daring to touch the body, not daring even to look at it, not daring to do anything. She pressed her hands to her cheeks and stared out at the heaving ocean, feeling the sun on her back and hearing the stuttering of the water.

VIII

"Tell me, Miss Malachi," said Grace one evening. "Did you ever have a sweetheart?"

Miss Malachi tightened her lips; her coal-black eyes grew gently luminous.

"Why not? Certainly I did."

"What did he look like?"

"Pale. Tubercular."

"What was his name?"

Miss Malachi paused. She fingered an album and said craftily: "Alastair."

"What did he do?"

"He played the harp."

"And he loved you?"

"He adored me."

She laid her embroidery on the wicker table and decorously folded her fingers.

"Why didn't you marry him?" said Grace.

"He died," said Miss Malachi, "on a trip to Corsica."

She sat in her cinnamon-colored robe, looking unusually gaunt and narrow. Her eyes had a dangerous glitter; her nose was as sharp as a tomahawk.

"Grace, my child. There are certain women who were never intended to be loved by men. I am one of them, judging from the evidence, and quite conceivably you are another, and though to most of the hoi-polloi it may seem like a terrible deprivation I can assure you that it has its own inestimable advantages. You'll be spared some terrible ravages. You'll be spared the pangs of childbirth. You'll be spared the humiliation of seeing a man lose his love for you. And in the end you'll discover some unexpected sources of joy and fortitude!"

It was one of Miss Malachi's philosophical days, apparently. She rose and stared thoughtfully into the bowl of goldfish.

"There's a spirit in this house, how shall I put it, not of tragedy exactly, but of inexplicably and incorrigibly bad luck. Bad luck that borders on self-destruction. I've noticed it repeatedly. Take Augusta for instance. Augusta is grim and bitter, she has ruined her life and she knows it. Consuelo is given to spasms of suicidal melancolia. Barbara is selfish and greedy: she will suffer for it eventually. Freya is resilient and gay but, oh, that childish romanticism! Daphne I will not enlarge upon but I'm sure she's headed for trouble. Elizabeth was the exception that proved the rule, alas, poor darling."

"And what about me?" said Grace.

Miss Malachi ignored her question. "A family," she declared, "can be a strange and sinister affair. Especially a family of women. You are all alike and all unlike. You all feel threatened. You all feel isolated. You are all of you looking for love. And yet you're frightened of love, though for a variety of reasons. You are waiting for a revelation of truth and yet you're frightened of the truth, for a variety of reasons. Only Elizabeth was strong and pure and at peace with the world and she died young. The rest of you are perpetually looking. With all the betrayals. The hallucinations."

"I don't think that I know what you mean, quite, Miss Malachi," said Grace.

"I'm not sure that I do myself. I feel like an oracle, sometimes," said Miss Malachi.

She tossed a log on the fire, then reached down behind the bookcase and brought out the Ouija board and laid it on the table. The two women sat down at the table, hushed and grave and expectant, with their fingers poised on the counter as though on a dying chord of music.

Ten minutes went by. The embers burst in the fireplace. Miss

Malachi's head started to nod; she suddenly jerked it up again. Grace lifted her eyes and glanced toward the window. There was a flash in the octagonal bowl: a darting fish caught the leap of the flames.

"Is Someone present?" said Miss Malachi.

The counter stirred, then came to a halt again.

Miss Malachi repeated rather hoarsely: "Is Someone here? Is an Intelligence present?"

The counter zigzagged under their hands and spelled out hesitantly: Y-E-S.

Miss Malachi nodded rapidly. "Good," she said in a clear, cool tone. She paused a moment. Then she said distinctly: "Please tell us your name."

The heart-shaped counter trembled a little, then gathered energy and shot toward J. It returned to the centre, moved to A, then back to the centre, then toward S. It wavered briefly, not quite sure of itself. Then it crept to P and on to R, this time without bothering to return to the centre.

Grace whispered, "Is it you, Jasper?"

The counter spelled Y-E-S.

"Are you happy where you are, still?"

The counter replied: I A-M W-A-I-T-I-N-G.

"Waiting for what?" urged Miss Malachi.

The counter paused awkwardly. It crawled slowly toward R and then back again to E.

"Re-something," murmured Grace. "Return? Reply? Resuscitation?"

The counter moved falteringly toward I and then to N. It moved half-heartedly back to C. Then it came to a halt, exhausted.

Miss Malachi was frowning. Her wrinkled lips moved to and fro. Then she muttered: "Reincarnation, could it be, do you suppose?"

The counter jumped gratefully, then shot swiftly toward Y-E-S.

Grace said gently: "What will you be when you're back with us, Jasper?"

The counter shook with excitement and spelled out vigorously: B-I-R-D.

Grace nodded. "I thought so." She lowered her head toward the board. "Jasper, tell me. Do you have any news of Daphne?"

For two or three minutes the counter refused to stir. The two women sat motionless, their heads bent over the board. And once again, as though some electrical force had been generated under the table, some palpitation from the uncharted realms of the Beyond, the counter started to quiver, then shot into motion. It spelled out its message in a quick sharp zigzag: P-A-N-C-H-O D-E-A-D. And it added rapidly: K-I-L-L-E-D I-N A H-U-R-Y-C-A-N-E.

Miss Malachi stared at Grace. "Who is Pancho, I wonder?"

Grace leaned back and closed her eyes. She listened to the embers crackling in the fireplace. Even the fire was trying to say something, cabling its messages across the room.

And as she sat there, listening to the embers, she felt the breath of a second Presence. Nothing with a name, nothing describable, nothing from the world of "human" phantoms, but something that was like an aura from her own crippled body. It was something that was halfway between an enormous bleeding emptiness and a tiny, twitching insistency, no bigger than a mushroom. She sat motionless; the thing crept closer; it hovered over her; she felt the heat of it. The blood rushed into her temples. Sweat poured down her cheeks.

Finally she cried: "Help me, Jasper! I'm all mixed up! What shall I do?"

The counter started to move again in fitful parabolas. It spelled out: T-W-O T-W-E-N-T-Y S-E-V-E-N M-E-L-P-O-M-E-N-E S-T-R-E-E-T.

"*Très bizarre,*" said Miss Malachi. She looked probingly at Grace. "What does he mean? Melpomene Street. I've never heard of it I'm sure."

A misty smile was slowly creeping across Grace's face. "Thank you, Jasper. Melpomene Street. Two twenty seven. I'll try to remember."

IX

Things were falling into disruption. Mrs. Bontecue came only on Thursdays and in the kitchen the dishes and bottles kept piling up. Hordes of cockroaches went scampering across the sink. Once Grace saw a large purple rat lurking under the icebox.

Miss Malachi lamented: "I can't imagine what he was thinking of! A hundred dollars a month, even with the mortgages paid off . . ."

They couldn't afford to have new panes put into the attic windows and the rain kept slashing in, seeping down into her bedroom. Flakes of plaster kept sprinkling from the drawing-room ceiling. The dangling crystals of the candelabra were foggy with spiderwebs.

One evening as she crossed the lawn with her croquet mallet under her arm, Miss Malachi said: "It's odd, but I've been feeling a wee bit shivery."

Grace said, "You do look frail, just a little, Miss Malachi."

"Nothing seems to agree with me," said Miss Malachi bitterly.

"Could it be," said Grace tactfully, "the pineapple tid-bits?"

"My pleasures are few," snapped Miss Malachi, "and innocuous." She crouched forward, cocked her eye and hit the ball through the wicket.

"It lies deeper," she said.

"Too many thoughts," suggested Grace.

"More than likely," said Miss Malachi.

"One oughtn't to think," ventured Grace.

"There are things," said Miss Malachi, stooping to pick up her ball, "that need thinking about, unfortunately. Come, child. The dew is settling."

They sat down on the veranda and watched the half-moon creep through the mist.

"Sometimes, you know, Miss Malachi," said Grace, rocking thoughtfully to and fro, "I can't help thinking that we're all of us just a single girl really. Some of us are different from others, Barbara for instance, Barbara is beautiful,—but even Barbara is really me. And even Augusta is really me."

"There was always," mused Miss Malachi, "something calamitous about Augusta."

"She hasn't phoned us for weeks."

"She has her quandaries," said Miss Malachi.

"Consuelo," said Grace, "had an eye for the exotic, didn't she?"

Miss Malachi nodded regretfully. "Consuelo," she said, "was a voluptuary."

"Even Daphne," insisted Grace, "was really me, when I think of it."

"Such a tragedy," moaned Miss Malachi. "That Spanish boy killed by a tornado."

"And poor Elizabeth," said Grace.

"We all," said Miss Malachi, "shared little Elizabeth."

"Only Freya," said Grace, "was a mystery. So terribly queer, with all that happiness . . ."

"Things happen," announced Miss Malachi, and her head sank over her breast. "Things happen the way they happen because they were always meant to happen. Nothing can keep them from happening; somehow or other they're bound to happen. Sometimes at night I hear a throbbing sound, like the earth spinning around or maybe it's only the house falling to bits, as I've long suspected . . ."

"Or footsteps," said Grace. "It might be footsteps climbing the stairs."

"Or a volcano," hinted Miss Malachi. "Something bursting in Mexico."

They tucked their mallets into the box and Grace went for a stroll down to the inlet. She knelt on the pier and stared down at the murky water. It was only the water, she realized, that could tell her what she looked like. Her bedroom mirror merely reflected a wizened gnome-face, with streaks of brownish hair dangling over a fevered-looking forehead. But in the water she saw a countenance, not bright and clear but sombre and mythical, a goat-like silhouette against a sky of dark mercury which seemed to recede into unearthly distances: so that her face was no longer her own but that of some brutish, wild divinity.

She grew obsessed with the idea that she had ceased being Grace, and that the assumption of being Grace was only a ritualistic stratagem; that she had long ago abandoned the whole pretence of being Grace and had turned into something fluid, primeval, impersonal: an element, as it were: a part of the intangible universe.

Two small episodes occurred in the summer, neither of them intrinsically alarming, but both of a nature calculated to deepen her convictions.

The first was in June. It was dusk; the light was fading. She was crossing the small wooden bridge by Frenchman's Creek. Under her arm she was carrying a basket of wild raspberries, those rosy, aromatic ones which grew on the knoll by McCaffery's Pond.

A twig snapped. She looked behind her. A young man stepped through the foliage and came to a halt at the edge of the creek. For just a moment she thought it was Jasper. But then she knew that it wasn't Jasper. Jasper was dark and very tall. This boy was stocky and red-headed. He was dressed in a deteriorated powder-blue flannel, something resembling a uniform, with thick brass buttons down the front. His boots were crusted with mud, his breeches were torn and muddy. His finely cut jaws were tufted with wisps of golden beard. He looked tensely at Grace and pointed to a spot beneath his feet. He nodded; he seemed to say something; but what he said, if he really said something, was no louder than the rippling of the creek over the pebbles. And then gradually, as she watched, the powder-blue turned to green, the flannel turned into leaves and the face into mist.

She crossed the bridge and walked cautiously to the place where he'd been standing. There were no footprints in the mud, not even a broken blade of grass. But she noticed behind a stone the solitary imprint of a boot, with the gash of the heel dug deep in the clay.

"Yes," she thought. "That's what it is . . . But I wonder why he suddenly . . ."

She crouched by the stone and started digging with a piece of rock. With the very first thrust she struck at something metallic. She scooped off the soil, blood-red handful by handful, and tugged at the edge of the rust-splintered box. The lid sprang open, effortlessly almost: and under the lacquer of slime she caught the lustre of innumerable golden scales.

"Yes," she whispered. "I knew it. But I can't help wondering why he suddenly . . ."

She closed the lid scrupulously, put the box back in its cavity, sleeked it over with clay and washed her hands in the warm bright water.

Then she picked up her basket and walked thoughtfully over the bridge again.

The second event was the following.

One morning, it was late in August, she climbed out of bed a little earlier than usual. There was a restlessness in the air, the dew was sparkling on the goldenrods. She strolled past the petunia beds, which were all in weeds, like the rest of the garden.

She passed the derelict greenhouse and the shattered summer pavilion. Then she climbed over the fence that shielded the orchard from the woods.

She was standing beside the fence to pull a splinter out of her thumb when she saw her sister Elizabeth standing under a tree, ten yards away. She waved her hand casually. It seemed quite natural, completely plausible. Then she remembered, as a kind of after-thought, that it was years since she'd seen Elizabeth.

She cried softly: "Elizabeth!"

Elizabeth smiled and lifted her arm. The upper part of her body was clear and distinct. She was wearing a pink lace dress with a golden locket hanging from a chain. Below the waist her body trailed off in a greenish transparency, as though she were floating in a kind of woodland vapor.

Grace stood motionless for a minute or two. Then she moved toward Elizabeth. But Elizabeth shook her head and raised her finger to her lips. In her eyes there was a bewildered expression, half reproach and half apology. Then she turned around slowly and vanished among the tree trunks.

x

Three days later Miss Malachi took to her bed. Dr. Scarborough drove out from Belleville, glanced at her tongue and applied the stethoscope. His heavily lensed glasses gave his eyes a troll-like expression. He prescribed a diet of semolina and soft-boiled eggs and then drove off again.

But Miss Malachi kept growing thinner. Her face resembled a skull. Her insomnia reached a point where she could hardly sleep at all, even in the daytime, what with the rhythmical thrusts of pain and her desperate bird-like nervousness. She kept asking for her bed to be shifted from room to room and Mrs. Bontecue, who was coming daily again, would drag the blankets up to the guest-room and then down to the library, then back into Freya's bedroom or Consuelo's or even Daphne's, and finally even into the pantry or the dusty old dining room. It seemed that Miss Malachi wanted to escape from the thoughts that came over her, all the thoughts about death coming and the various things she had done wrong in life, and each of the rooms where she lay and kept thinking these gloomy thoughts grew finally intolerable: and she insisted on moving into another.

And in the meanwhile Grace's strolls in the afternoon grew longer and longer. She limped barefoot along the shore, feeling the mud ooze through her toes, watching the dragonflies flying in tandem or the grasshoppers squatting in couples, listening to the innuendoes of the quail or the firm staccato of the woodpecker, watching the ripples perpetually rearranging their serried patterns in Cleghorn's Inlet. She finally realized, with a triumphant certainty, that not only the battalions of the dead but even the whole ascending hierarchies of nature itself were struggling to commune with her and that each insect and bird and even each little ripple were involved in a grandiose process which was trying to express its intentions to her.

One night, after kissing Miss Malachi good-night in the drawing-room, where her bed had been placed directly behind the grand piano, she started up the stairs. She came to a halt on the landing. There was a slithering, scraping sound on the second-floor corridor. Only the tulip-shaped bulb on top of the Mercury was burning. A streaky mauve light played on the lily-patterned wallpaper. Something long, dark and sinuous was moving along the wall; not crawling precisely, it was more of an undulation, like the movement of water spreading in the wake of a boat. She pressed close against the bannister. A flat, gleaming head, poised several inches above the floor, peered carefully around the corner. It blinked its eyes in the dusty light.

Then it continued on its way: an abnormally large snake, almost as thick as her thigh, with a pattern of hexagons engraved on its back. It paused again at the head of the stairs, flicked its long black tongue appraisingly, then started down the stairs in a marvelously graceful and coordinated motion, its head still raised slightly, its eyes fixed in space, each ripple of its body maintaining a suave and casual discipline. It passed Grace without seeming to notice her, without a flicker in its ruby gaze. Then it was lost in the shadows of the downstairs hallway.

She felt no fear, strangely enough, not even a twinge of uneasiness; only a tremor of delight at the serpent's majesty and decorum. She wondered vaguely: was it heading for the drawing-room? But then she realized, by the keen and relentless look in its eyes, that it would go where it wished to go, there was nothing that could stop it. And she sensed that there was nothing dangerous or malignant in the snake, it was a beast like any other, a creature embodying a natural force, perhaps more powerfully than most, maybe more ruthlessly and harmoniously, but neither sinister nor vicious but imperially splendid.

XI

The following morning, on her way to breakfast, she heard a low, half-strangled voice calling her name. She hurried into the drawing-room and saw Miss Malachi lying on the sofa, propped up on a heap of pillows, with her eyes fixed straight in front of her. The bed by the piano lay disheveled and empty. The curtains were drawn over the three French windows.

Grace limped slowly toward the sofa and knelt silently on

the floor. Miss Malachi looked weirdly diminished under the wrinkled gray sheet. Her bony hands lay folded on her chest: they were knotted with thick black veins. She turned her head slightly and clutched at Grace's hand. Her lips started to move. She was trying to say something. Grace noticed that one of her eyes had lost all expression but the other had a pleading, almost agonized look in it.

Grace leaned closer and tried to hear what Miss Malachi was saying. "Forget it all, forget it," she kept muttering, or something of the sort, and then another word, half audible but repeated several times: it sounded like "love." She twisted her body to the left and made an effort to sit up but then she slumped back again with her arms flung out sideways. Grace moved back but Miss Malachi kept staring at the spot where Grace's head had been, and then she whispered something that sounded like "Open the windows!" Then she started to gasp, there was a throbbing in her throat and her great inky eyes seemed to drop into their sockets.

Grace stepped out on the terrace and crept down to the bottom of the garden. There was a nook, half hidden by forsythias, from which she could see the opposite shore, with the smoke rising in the distance from a passing freight train. Here she sat for a very long time, feeling the sun slowly rising and the heat gradually spreading from the windless orchard.

Someone was crying, "Miss Grace! Oh Lordy! Miss Grace!" Mrs. Bontecue came running across the lawn with her apron fluttering. "Quick! Miss Grace! Hurry up!" Grace got up and walked back to the house. Miss Malachi was lying on the sofa, looking unusually calm and stern. Grace bent down and kissed her gently on her dark, wrinkled forehead. She glanced guiltily at Mrs. Bontecue, whose cheeks were streaming with tears: but she herself felt no grief, the only feeling that welled up in her was neither love nor compassion but a pang of distaste toward this alien body, which no longer was Miss Malachi and no longer had anything to do with Miss Malachi, which no longer suggested or even symbolized Miss Malachi. She whispered something to Mrs. Bontecue, she wasn't sure what it was, and then she opened the door and walked out into the garden again.

That night she came back to say good-bye to the corpse. Not that this visit had any meaning, since the corpse was no longer Miss Malachi, it was no longer even associated in her mind with Miss Malachi. But she felt that something or other, she wasn't sure what, still had to be done. A candle was burning on each side of the sofa and a black lace shawl had been draped over the body. Mrs. Bontecue had washed and perfumed the dead woman's face and had placed a rhinestone-studded comb in her hair.

Grace sat in the arm-chair, listening to the crickets in the garden. She wasn't thinking of Miss Malachi: she had already forgotten Miss Malachi. She was thinking of some little errand still unperformed that lurked in her mind.

The flames writhed uneasily in a sudden jet of wind. A purring noise crept out of the dark, like the rumbling of far-off breakers. Grace leaned forward, tightening her grip on the arms of the chair: she recognized that uncanny heightening of the atmosphere. She found herself gasping. The air in the room grew almost suffocating. The shadows rippled across the walls, higher and higher, like a gathering flood.

There was the sound of measured footsteps. Grace turned her head slowly. The flames flattened in the draught as the door swung open. A dark-haired woman stood in the doorway. She was totally naked; her hair hung to her hips in a tangled torrent. Her cheeks were abnormally flushed. There was a glitter in her eyes.

"Who are you?" said Grace.

"You know who I am," said the woman wearily.

Grace leaned forward. "So soon, then?"

The woman smiled; then she nodded.

Grace whispered: "Was it worth it?"

The woman lifted her head a little. Her eyes gleamed triumphantly. "It took time," she said gently. "But yes, it was worth it. It was enough. In spite of everything . . ."

She closed the door carefully and the flames shot back toward the ceiling.

Part Seven

The Camargue is a lonely and desolate sort of land. It is a land of shining marshes and flat bubbling lakes, long-necked birds, coal-black bulls, crouching bushes, heathery breezes. It is a land of flamingoes and gipsies; of scorpions and wild horses. The earth is smooth, swelling occasionally into a dismal gray hillock. White clouds float from the delta and dissolve over the swamps. The tang of the sea spreads inland, salty, dank, flickering with mist. It clings to the brushwood, it drips from the rushes. Toward sunset the wind sometimes sounds very strange; it gallops and neighs; it chirrups; it sobs. Gusts of fog come loping over the plains like great wild ostriches. There is a moaning of giant owls and out of the west when the sun is setting marvelous mirages rise from the earth, great cathedrals, herds of elephants, or just a corpse swaying limply from the branch of a tree.

Dimitri rented a house in the lonely wastes beyond Arles. It was a *mas,* a rustic cottage of ruddy stone thatched with straw. There was a tapering white fireplace under an arching ceiling; burlap curtains, black chests, bulging chairs, vats of ivy. An elderly woman named Sephine came bicycling down the road every morning with a basket of vegetables and maybe a fish or a chicken. She wore a dirty lace cap and a golden cross over her bosom. She had a face like a transvestite's, beaked and hirsute, netted with veins, with an ogling and slightly contemptuous gleam in her eyes.

"It's funny that you should come here," she grunted. "D'you really like it?"

"Well, there's something," said Consuelo, "the tang of the wind, the wild horses . . ."

"It's the birth-place of the world," said the peasant woman. "Here's where the whole thing started. Just the wind and the swamp and those little white worms. And then the bugs and the wasps and after a while the fish and the birds, and not long after the horses and then finally one day the gipsies. That's what my father used to say, it all started in the Camargue, all the nastiness and the dirt, all the cheating and fornication. They invented it all down here and to be frank, it's odd you should come here. How on earth can any one want to come to the Camargue?"

They spent their mornings playing dominoes out under the plane tree and in the afternoons they walked over the flat gray spread of marshes. In the evening, after Consuelo had set the coffee in front of the hearth, Dimitri opened a book and started reading aloud. He read the poems of Pushkin or maybe a story by Turgeniev. Consuelo would sit listening on a cushion by the fire-place. He read in Russian and strangely enough, even though she'd never studied Russian, she began little by little to understand the words: maybe it was because Dimitri's voice was

so musical and suggestive, or maybe the strength and the passion he found in the words seeped across to her. At any rate,
the poems and stories grew strangely alive to her, she didn't
grasp the details but she caught the swing, the pulse, the flavor.

Summer came. June passed without a single drop of rain.
Stringy clouds would go drifting over the sky every morning,
and sometimes it seemed that the rain was about to fall. But it
didn't fall. The clouds vanished, a great heat clutched the
prairie and a circle of orange mist clung to the edge of the sun.
The stubbly plains were yellow and brittle. The ponds were
brown and parched. Dust rose in lazy puffs when the horses
raced by. Even at night there was no coolness. The bulls lowed in
the marshes and there was nothing left to graze on in that
stifling gray dust, which stung at the eyeballs and seeped into
the lungs. The cowboys rode past with handkerchiefs tied over
their noses.

Old Mathieu, their only neighbor, dropped in occasionally
with his shaggy dog.

"Life is short," he said gloomily. "Soon it's over. We all die.
I keep saying to my children, why be wicked or sinful? Once I
was wicked and sinful myself but now I'm old, I know better.
There's no point in being sinful, none at all, none whatever. It
just makes you miserable in the end, it's just a blind alley . . ."

"We all die," said Consuelo, nodding. She gazed across the
room. She caught sight of her reflection in the mirror which
hung on the wall over the table. She was startled: she looked
so old, all dry and bony, like a peasant woman.

She suddenly felt dejected. She turned to Mathieu. "Tell me,
Mathieu. Do we die forever?"

Mathieu twirled his mustaches and cleared his powerful
wrinkled throat. There was a twinkle of gayety in his old,
mournful eyes. "Of course it's not forever, no, of course not, my
dear little lady, but who is there amongst us to lay down the law
about it? Maybe we'll be just blades of grass growing from the
soil in God's sunlight, maybe we'll be grains of sand shining on

one of His stars, maybe we'll be just a wave moving across God's ocean, or maybe we'll be just a passing little thought in somebody's mind. Yes, who knows, but one thing's certain. It's not forever and that's the fact of it!"

After Mathieu had gone home Dimitri sat with his pipe in his mouth. He picked up his pencil and started to scribble away at his "memoirs" while Consuelo sat with some canvas embroidery in her hands.

"What are we having for dinner tonight?"

"A chicken," said Consuelo.

"We're running low," muttered Dimitri.

"Yes, I know," said Consuelo.

"I'll write to Krauss. It's a trifle risky but there's nothing else to do."

"I'll write to Barbara," said Consuelo. "Barbara is rich. She can afford it."

She went into the kitchen and lit the stove. Then she washed the lettuce and started to mix the dressing. Through the window she could see the darkness beginning to loom and a great cloud of birds crossing the plain, like the shade of a hurricane.

She came back into the living room and started to set the table.

"Those birds," she said softly. "Millions of birds. Where do they come from?"

Then she turned to Dimitri and cried: "Oh, Dimitri, we can't go on like this, just waiting for something to happen! Just waiting to be discovered! Just waiting to be trapped!"

"Waiting is better than some other things I can think of," said Dimitri.

She flung out her arms. "Why can't we just go and . . ."

"Yes? Go and do what?" Dimitri's voice started shaking. His eyes glittered dangerously. "You're free to go! Why don't you go? You're free to leave me whenever you want!" He got up from his chair, strode to the door and flung it open. "Yes, go! I don't need you! I didn't ask you to share your life with me! Go, why don't you? You might as well! You'll be happier back in Paris!"

Consuelo walked toward the table and set the glasses beside the plates. She said softly, "I'll never leave you. Not as long as you'll let me stay with you."

Dimitri walked slowly across the room and stood by the fireplace. He picked up a twig from the floor and started to twist it in his fingers. Drops of sweat were shining on his forehead. The veins in his temples were throbbing visibly.

"Women," he muttered, "they're all idiots! They've brought me trouble, nothing but trouble. You mean well but you're stupid. You meddle in things you don't understand." His voice sank into a kind of melancholy sing-song; he kept on stroking his Adam's apple. "You want love without pain. You want security without meaning. You want all the airs of humanitarianism without any of the dirt, the sweat, the sacrifice! Oh, yes, you read your Dante, you think your fine lofty thoughts but at heart you're just another petulant, pampered American!"

His voice softened, it grew calm and reasonable all of a sudden. He folded his arms and watched Consuelo as she laid out the napkins.

"I tell you, you live in a dream! That's all it is, just a dream. Your world is disintegrating but still you cling to your naïve faith in happiness." His voice started rising again. "Don't you understand? Don't you see? A new horror has entered the world! Or maybe it isn't really new, maybe it was there all the time, just lurking in the shadows, waiting for things to ripen a bit. I'll keep fighting, I tell you! I won't give up! I'll keep on fighting! What's left to being alive if one doesn't keep on fighting? Even when it looks completely hopeless I'll still keep on fighting. And if I ever stop fighting, well, then you'll know that my soul had died."

II

No rain fell, not a drop, the whole delta was suffocating. Little clouds of yellow-jackets went bobbing over the river-bed. The flamingoes scrawled their hieratic patterns on a cavernous sky, the heat of the sun swayed in the sheen of the salt-deposits.

August came. There was still no message from Krauss or Ivan. A week went by and another. No word from Barbara; no word from Augusta. They seemed to be the last survivors in an echoless world. Nothing reached them from outside, not even a ripple of anxiety.

There were moments, in the grayness and flatness of this dismal landscape, when it seemed that Dimitri was right, a whole world was disintegrating and all the things she had valued—all the poetry and the aspiration—were no more real than the grape-colored mirages on the horizon. The ornamentations of the western world, the poignant sonnets and soaring symphonies, had no more permanence than the wavering calligraphy of the birds. Yes, even the whole moral fabric of her attitudes, the lingering notions of "progress" and "tolerance," the sanctity of "art," the glory of "thought," the whole assumption that human life was created for "fulfillment"—all these notions seemed strangely irrelevant in the wide gray stillness of the Camargue, where a fly settling on an apple had a sharper aura of reality than the eloquence of the *Purgatorio* or the pangs of the *Pensées*. There were moments when she thought that maybe Dimitri was right after all, that at the core of existence there was something blind and obsessed, that what mattered in the end was struggle, just a blind hot struggle, what won out in the end was passion regardless of truth; and the symphonies and the sonnets, far from deepening a sense of illumination, merely disfigured it and trivialized it by detracting from the very thing they were meant to exalt—the whole immediacy of living, the always raw and sometimes savage sensation of being alive; the screaming of the birds, the smell of sweat, the glare of the salt-deposits.

Late one night, just as she was putting away the dishes on the shelves, there was a knock on the kitchen door. Dimitri peeped through the curtain. Then he pulled up the castiron latch on the door.

It was Mathieu. He leaned forward and closed the door behind him scrupulously. Then he blinked his eyes and murmured, somewhat hoarsely:

"There's a message."

"Oh? From whom?"

"No idea. Just a message," said Mathieu. "Jeanne got it this evening over the telephone from Arles. Tell the man with the American girl-friend that his Aunt Mathilde is dying. That's all. That's the message. Your Aunt Mathilde is dying . . ."

He stroked the ears of his dog and kept peering at Dimitri, as though curious to see the effect of his announcement. Dimitri turned pale and took his pipe out of his mouth.

"A pity," he said carefully. "She's a splendid woman, my Aunt Mathilde."

"It's quite clear then?" said Mathieu. He seemed to be chuckling to himself. He ran his black forefinger along the bottom of his nose.

"Oh, quite clear," said Dimitri briskly. "Perfectly clear. Thank you kindly. Good night. My regards to Jeanne! There, watch your step, Mathieu . . ."

He waited for a moment after the door had closed again. Then he said somewhat dreamily: "Well, I hope we've got enough petrol."

Consuelo nodded and put down the tray. "I'll start packing. Anything special?"

"That bottle of Calvados," said Dimitri.

"Yes. The Calvados," she said.

"And the dominoes," said Dimitri.

"Yes," she said. "Of course. The dominoes."

She felt a surge of exhilaration. It was like a wave of cool air, so sudden, so unexpected that it made her slightly dizzy. She skipped into the bedroom and pulled the bags from under the bed. She started humming to herself as she packed the skirts and the underclothes. Then she hurried into the kitchen and took out the bottle of Calvados. Dimitri was already beginning to turn out the lights.

"Leave the kitchen light burning," he said. "It won't do any harm." He too looked elated, there was a purr of relief in his stealthy voice. "There, the blanket. We might need it. I'll go and start the car. Yes, and the map. Where's that map? And don't forget the sun-glasses . . ."

III

Not far from the Palazzo Massimo, just beyond the Campo dei Fiori, there was a small triangular piazza with a fountain in the middle of it. Behind the fountain during the day a row of stalls was set up: silver candlesticks and pots, copper cake-moulds, and warming pans, old engravings of Burmese monkeys or Polynesian savages. Every morning Barbara used to wander across the little square, buying a cameo or maybe an ikon, which back in the palazzo would promptly be buried in a drawer. Once or twice she saw an old woman lowering her mail-box from a window or a woolly black dog hurrying home with a basket of onions. A yellow cat with swollen teats dragged her body across the pavements; or a wounded rat lay on a doorstep, all covered with flies.

But these scattered hints of darkness left her only with a fleeting impression of some dusky little brushstroke on a sunlit landscape. The darkness she sensed in Rome was not the darkness of suffering or poverty, it was the gloom of moral hollowness, of spiritual exhaustion. Once she saw her face reflected in a baroque mirror on one of the stalls and was horrified to see that it was her own face she was looking at. The lines of lust, scorn, cynicism—there they were, unmistakable. She was perfectly aware of it: she had changed incredibly, shedding exactly those qualities—ambition, aloofness, calculation—which a year ago had been uppermost. The Roman climate seemed to operate like a photographer's chemical, brightening the weaknesses, darkening the virtues, transforming the soul into its very opposite.

The summer deepened. The whole city began to look uncanny. The Tiber was bathed in a reddish glow. The columns floated like clouds. Voices penetrated the air like the sound of bells under water. Wherever she was—down in the Corso or up on the Pincio—she grew aware of a shudder of unease among the shadows; a silhouette in a cellar window, a stealthy rustling among the ivies which rippled away like waves from a gong.

Every night, long after Orazio had kissed her on the cheeks, she turned on the light again, flung a robe over her shoulders, glanced at the mirror, raised her brows and ran a comb through her hair. Then she opened the door and tiptoed quickly down the corridor. She crossed the empty gallery and the moonlit loggia, paused for a moment at the door of the library, and climbed the circular stairway. A tiny shape loped past her: one of the Siamese cats. She passed the "tropical conservatory" and the "room of the puppets," stopped at the door of Sandro's bedroom and softly turned the knob.

The room had been transformed into a kind of photographer's studio. Ribbons of film were dangling from a string across the window. The only light was the dirty haze seeping up from the courtyard. She closed the door, turned the key and walked slowly toward the bed where he was lying, dark as a savage, with only his teeth shining white in the gloom.

Once she whispered, as they lay with their naked bodies intertwined: "Do you know what I think? Someone is watching me. Someone is spying on me. Who is it? One of the servants? Simonetta, do you suppose?"

"It's your fancy," said Sandro.

"Or my conscience," said Barbara.

"Or one of those dusty old ghosts that are lurking in the palazzo."

"Yes, Orazio told me the story. Two centuries ago, or was it three, a little girl named Teresina . . ."

"Teodora," corrected Sandro. He leaned over her in the darkness. "Tell me, what does he think of it?"

She kissed his palm. "Nothing, probably."

"He knows, I'm sure of it," said Sandro.

"Does it matter," said Barbara, "especially?"

One day Orazio was sitting in the library, drinking his coffee. The morning light fell on the tapestry which hung over the couch—the Judgment of Paris, with armored cupids floating above an ivied temple.

He looked up when she entered the room. "You're looking unusually beautiful, my dear. What has happened? Has one of those Goddesses climbed down and kissed your cheek?" He smiled teasingly. "You're blushing. Was it Minerva, the Goddess of Wisdom? . . . Come, sit down. Have some coffee." He tightened his robe around his shoulders. The sunlight fell on his face, accentuating the weariness and the wrinkles. He looked unusually old; worn and sickly and melancholy. The parrot was perched on his shoulder. He spread his emerald wings, glared balefully at Barbara and folded them again.

"My dear child, yes, forgive me if I think of you as a child, you are a woman and a very beautiful one but I think of you as a child. I've been feeling a bit unwell. I'm old and that's a part of it. I'm old, I've had my pleasures, more than an ordinary share of them, and I have no wish to deprive you of yours. There is a question in my mind which it is difficult for me to phrase properly. It has nothing to do with gossip, with discretion, with respectability. I have no interest in anything other than to spare you suffering. I'm not blind. I've noticed the way you've been looking at Sandro. Sandro has been here for two months now. A little longer than was expected. I'm not sure that he takes his photography very seriously. If I felt there might be happiness in it I'd say to both of you, do as you wish. Happiness, mind you. There is always a price to be paid for mere pleasure. You have a right to your share of it, I've said so already. I don't begrudge it. I give you my blessing. You are welcome to his caresses. It is only when I detect those sinister little omens . . ."

Barbara gazed at him quietly. She brushed a gnat from her sleeve.

"Do I make my point?" said the Prince. "I know Sandro. I know his impulses. I know exactly how he felt and how he feels and how he's going to feel. He is not in love with you, I assure you. He may think he is but please remember, he's from Mantua and he's young and he's vain and stupid. He will never be in love with you. I don't say this to reproach you, Barbara; I merely say it to warn you. Don't be startled, my child, if suddenly one morning . . ."

Barbara took Orazio's hand: it was limp and weightless, like an empty glove. "I'm not worried about anything that Sandro may do to us," she said.

She got up, kissed him on the temple and stepped into the loggia.

IV

September came. Nuts fell from the dusty trees in the Villa Borghese. Sandro said to her one evening: "You are growing tired of me. I can feel it."

Barbara laughed and kissed his earlobe. "Nonsense, child. I'll never grow tired of you."

"You are growing bored," insisted Sandro. "You think I'm a stupid little animal."

"You're not a bore, dear. Nor an animal. But there are moments when you're blind, a little."

"With Orazio you talk about Proust. With me you chatter about Magnani."

"I feel happy, utterly happy," whispered Barbara, "whenever I look at you."

Toward the end of the month there was a series of thunderstorms. The Tiber was littered with leaves; the chrysanthemums lay crushed in the garden. One night they listened to the rain dripping from the eaves and Sandro murmured:

"If Orazio were to die . . . Forgive me for saying it! I shouldn't have said it."

"Go on. What were you thinking?"

"What would happen if Orazio died?"

Barbara looked at him silently.

"Would you sail with me to Tahiti?"

"Are you tired of Rome?" said Barbara.

"I am tired," said Sandro, "of all this hypocrisy!"

Two nights later Sandro said: "I've had a letter from Mantua."

"Yes?"

"My mother."

"What does she say?"

"It's time to be leaving, she says."

"I see."

"She misses me. My father misses me. My sister Giulietta misses me."

"You have a very affectionate family, apparently."

"Don't tease me, please, Barbara. My mother is right. I cannot live on the Via Giulia for the rest of my life."

"Kiss me, darling," said Barbara.

Sandro pressed his lips to her belly. Then he crouched close beside her and stared through the darkness.

"There! You see! I'm not a character. I'm not even a human being to you. I'm only a phallus, a great hungry phallus!"

And finally one night in the middle of October Sandro said: "They've been gossiping."

"Who?" said Barbara.

"Oh, they've guessed it! They're vicious, these Romans. I can see it in the way they look at me. I can see them waiting for the catastrophe."

"There will not," said Barbara tensely, "be a catastrophe."

"I've decided to take a studio in Frascati," said Sandro.

"Are you frightened of gossip?" said Barbara.

"I am a realist," said Sandro.

"Very well. Do as you wish." She turned her head on the pillow.

The south wind was blowing through the half-open window. But instead of bringing freshness it brought tension and oppression. She heard the whine of the traffic along the Lungotevere and the tittering of the servant-girls down in the courtyard.

"You're annoyed!"

"Of course I'm annoyed."

"I'll come and meet you whenever you wish."

"Whenever I wish! How very obliging of you."

"I've been in the Palazzo three months. Do you think they're

all idiots? Do you think they haven't noticed? You're fooling
nobody but yourself, my kitten."

"What in the world does it matter? Orazio accepted it long
ago. And as for the rest, you said it yourself. They're all vicious.
Who cares what they say?"

Sandro knelt in the bed beside her. His voice shook with fury.

"You're selfish! You're disgustingly selfish! You say you love
me but I know that love of yours. Luxury! Power! That's all
you're after! You want to turn me into a lap-dog, something you
can cuddle and kiss and throw away when you're tired of it. I
refuse! Do you hear me? I'm not a gigolo! I have my pride!"

"I see," said Barbara quietly.

"You despise me," said Sandro, "don't you?"

"I am in love with you," said Barbara.

"I don't believe you," said Sandro.

"Very well then," said Barbara. "Do exactly as you wish.
Keep your pride. Take your nasty little studio in Frascati."

V

The third of Freya's islands wasn't really an island but it had
the remoteness and the blue, windy separateness that belong to
islands. Instead of water all around it there were snow-filled
ravines, and instead of a steamer to get there she took a small
cabled railway. The village was tucked on the slope of a mountain, floating high over the furrowed expanse of snowy valleys,
which turned in the evenings into a deep, translucent violet that
spread like a sea toward the faraway peaks, mighty cones that
still burned with a fiery brightness after the rest of the land
was lost in shadows.

She lived in a cheap little inn called the Pension Alpina and her window looked down over a snow-covered forest. At first she sat by the window and painted in her usual manner; she painted a criss-cross of needles sprinkled with rosy-white flakes. But after a while these tree-like patterns no longer seemed interesting and she started to draw crystals like the frost on the window-pane—exquisite crystals shaped like fans or ferns or sea-anemones. But then the crystals grew monotonous and she painted a series of animals, delicately etched creatures of a scaly blue or a feathery yellow that floated in a net of ripples or a cage of red branches. Neither the fish nor the birds looked like real fish or birds; they were spun out of ice or woven out of crystals, but even so they created an effect of brightly colored beasts trapped in the chill and rigidity of the Alpine winter.

She painted until eleven and then she climbed up the slope and put on her skis and went skiing for a couple of hours. There was a restaurant on top of the hill where the sportsmen gathered for lunch. Deck-chairs were spread in the sun, which was as warm as the sun in summertime, and young people in scarlet ski-sweaters drank beer and munched sausages, and there was laughter and coquetry and a snipping of cameras.

After lunch she went skiing for another couple of hours and after that she went down to the village for a cup of coffee and some pastries, which were especially delicious at a place called Hutzelmeyer's, marvelous almond cakes and plum cakes and poppy-seed strudels. After that she went back and worked for a while on one of her canvases, or else she lay on her bed and read *The Conquest of Mexico*. At seven she took her bath and then she walked to the Goldener Hirsch, where she usually dined with two Bavarian girls, Irmgard and Ingeborg.

In the corner stood an oven made of shiny green tiles. On the dark wooden shelves stood rows of plates painted with roosters. Red cushions lay on the benches and checkered tablecloths on the tables. A cat with a litter of kittens lay in a basket by the oven. There was dumpling soup to start with, or an eel soaked in capers, and then a goulash or a goose, and rolled-up pancakes for dessert. A man with a yellowish beard sat by the door playing the accordion, and after a while one of the boys in a flame-colored pullover came up to the table and bowed politely and asked her to dance with him.

She kept smiling as she danced; nothing here seemed to matter; neither the man with the accordion nor the boy in the pullover; neither Irmgard nor Ingeborg nor the kittens in the basket. Everything around her had a flavor of meticulous coziness. There was nothing that hinted at thought or intensity. So that in the end the very coziness somehow created an atmosphere of a childish and slightly grotesque unreality.

She went back to the table and sat down with her friends. At that moment the door swung open and a gust of snow swept into the room. A tall man in a fur-lined overcoat stepped into the tavern, shook the flakes from his sleeves and hung his coat on the coat-rack. He glanced casually across the room, where the tables were already crowded, and strolled up to Freya's table and nodded curtly.

"May I sit down?"

VI

"Certainly," said Freya. "If you wish."

"Thank you kindly," said the stranger. He was a man in his middle forties, slightly gray at the temples, with a cleft in his chin and a scar across his cheek.

He looked at Freya and said: "You're American?"

"Yes," said Freya. "I'm American."

"I thought so," said the stranger. "You have that look of utter indifference. Only American women have that look in their eyes of absolute indifference."

"You're Austrian, I suppose?"

"I'm from Heidelberg," said the stranger. "I was born down in Dresden and we had a castle in the woods of Saxony. But now Dresden is done for and Saxony is done for and these last seven years I've been living in Heidelberg."

"Are you happy in Heidelberg?"

"Happy?" said the stranger. "I don't think about happiness. I ignore this whole ridiculous notion of happiness."

"I see," said Freya, rather mockingly. "Then you've never been happy?"

The man shrugged his shoulders. "God knows. I can hardly remember. Long ago as a child there were things that made me happy. But happiness is distinctly démodé, I'm afraid. Being happy has no relevance to the world we see around us."

Freya laughed. She found it impossible to take things seriously up here in the mountains. Everything seemed a little absurd and bizarre up in the Alps, with all their air of dangerous majesty and their meticulous humdrum coziness.

"Well," said Freya, "I'm perfectly happy, or I believe I'm perfectly happy, and if one believes in one's happiness then it must be real, don't you think?"

"There is an illusion of happiness," said the man, "when one lives in a torpor. But it isn't happiness. It is only a temporary absence of pain."

"Do I live in a torpor?"

"We all live in a torpor."

"Torpor," said Freya. "What is torpor? Religion is a torpor. Art is a torpor. Eating is a torpor and drinking is a torpor and sex is an utter torpor. Anything that takes us away from the horror of things is a torpor."

"Words, words," said the stranger.

"Yes, just words," agreed Freya.

"Anarchy, wilderness, chaos! That's what's waiting for the world!" The stranger's eyes glittered, his voice grew impassioned. "It's quite obvious. All the symptoms are plain to the eyes, unmistakable. The storm's drawing closer. There's sulphur in the air and we feel a thrill of horror but we're secretly longing for it. All this drawn-out tension is becoming too much for us. Our nerves are growing frazzled. We know it's going to come and we're appalled but we secretly long for it. And why not? It will be a blessing in disguise, that's my opinion. It will be the end of a rotten and suicidal civilisation. It will be the end of all this substitute for life we've concocted, it will be the end to the staleness and verbiage and disgust. The only hope for humanity is to destroy the whole concoction and go back to the sea and the earth like savages. Destroy the television, destroy the pain capsules, purge away all the stink of refrigeration and anaesthetics and bring back the good old stink of sweat and excrement, and then maybe there'll be a meaning to happiness again. So you see," said the stranger, "I'm not a pessimist, I'm really an optimist! I see hope! I see salvation! I see joy after the purgatory!"

Three days later Freya went skating with the tall gray stranger, whose name was Ottokar. They climbed down the path from the grand hotel which stood by the lake and put on their skates in the skating pavilion. The stars were beginning to shine sharp and cold, like sparks from an anvil. The boys in their astrakhan caps went swirling about on the ice, leaving scars that shone under the floodlights like streaks of platinum. She skated arm in arm across the lake with Ottokar, and then the radio in the pavilion started to play *The Blue Danube* and they waltzed with their scarves fluttering gayly behind them. Finally they sat in the pavilion and drank punch by the candlelight and Ottokar muttered:

"It's the horrible cold that turns it into pleasure!"

"You and your pain," said Freya, laughing. "You see nothing but pain around you. You revel in pain. You glorify pain."

"Oh, you people across the ocean," said Ottokar with vehemence. "You think that pain can be eliminated. But pain can't be eliminated. Pain is pure and it's real, it's all that is left that still is real. The human spirit feeds on suffering and without suffering we'd be beasts. We'd be jellyfish floating in a great sea of boredom."

"You're perverse, that's the trouble. You make a mysticism out of pain. You raise suffering into a religion instead of building a religion out of suffering."

"Words, words," muttered Ottokar.

"Yes," said Freya. "Nothing but words."

She looked at Ottokar. There was a strange, helpless, struggling look in him, as though he were bleeding. What she disliked about him was his mouth, which was both sneering and obsequious, and his eyes, which were ruthless and at the same time intensely vulnerable. And this mingling of the contemptuous with the pleading, of cruelty with vulnerability, made him alien and unpleasant but at the same time somehow pitiful.

On New Year's Eve they hired a sleigh and went riding in the woods. A row of torches lined the road that led down from the market place and the torchlight flickered on the heaps of snow and blazed in the icicles that hung from the eaves. It was fearfully cold. The ice crackled under the runners. There was a spine-chilling creak in the snowy ruts as they entered the forest. Even the fur that was flung on their laps grew stiff and spiny, like a porcupine. The sleighbells kept tinkling with a thin icy sound and the hooves of the horses crunched rhythmically in the snow. Shafts of moonlight threw their shadows across the snow-covered knolls, even the sleighbells cast a nervous little shadow as they passed. Here and there in the snow there was a sprinkling of deer tracks or a pit of orange urine or a black ball of horse-dung.

They came to the top of the hill and far below they could see the lights of the hotel reflected in the icy lake. A cloud covered the moon, there was a rush of cold wind and small bluish flakes started to fall through the air. The lights in the village grew hazy and mottled. A layer of whiteness covered the balls of horse-dung. Soon the flakes drew a veil over the entire forest and the runners stopped squeaking and the hooves grew muffled. Everything was hushed except for the glass-like tinkling of the bells. The head-lamps on the sleigh shone on the slow-falling flakes, obscuring the woods beyond, hiding everything except the snowflakes. Then the flakes stopped falling and the woods grew visible again: mighty firs drooping with snow, shining in the lamplight like frozen geysers. The wind kept tugging at the manes of the horses and their tails were crusted with flakes of ice.

Ottokar looked at her intently. "How much longer will you be staying here?"

"Oh, a week maybe," said Freya.

"And then?"

"I'll be going to Munich."

She saw his breath streaming through the air like a gust of cigarette smoke. His cheeks were flushed red and his eyes were watering a little. The hair on the horses' coats was curly with sweat and along their flanks it was covered with hoar-frost. She could smell the steam that rose from their bellies. They were both panting heavily under the snow-spotted shaft-bow and the driver sat motionless, crouching forward like a sphinx.

The road climbed a little and the trees grew fewer. They came to a wall and in the middle of the wall there was a gate. A snowdrift had blown over the road just by the gate and the cold on the hilltop grew suddenly intense. The driver turned around and Ottokar nodded. The sleigh slowed down and turned right through the open gate. Some clothes hung frozen from a laundry line in the courtyard, flapping stiffly in the wind, as though they were carved out of wood—a red woollen petticoat and a pair of grey underpants.

They stepped from the sleigh and entered the tavern while the driver backed the sleigh under a roof and tied up the horses. It was hot inside the tavern with a dense, unnatural heat. A mastiff growled as they walked into the bar-room. They sat down at a slate-topped table and ordered some coffee and a woman with a goiter set a tray of pastries in front of them.

They sat quietly for a while. The snow melted from their boots and gradually the heat in the room drove the cold from their bodies.

Ottokar leaned over the table and said softly: "You are very beautiful."

Freya glanced at the floor. "It's not true," she muttered. "I am perfectly ordinary."

"What is wrong?" said Ottokar tensely. "Why do you insist on being aloof?"

"Am I aloof?" said Freya, smiling. "I have no wish to be aloof. All I wish is to be left alone. To be separate and independent."

"Yes, but why?" insisted Ottokar. "Why alone? Why always alone? I've never known a woman who kept wanting to be alone."

"All my life," said Freya slowly, "I've been living with sisters. I've been chained to my sisters. I've been suffocated with sisters. Wherever I looked I saw sisters, hundreds of sisters, nothing but sisters. I felt myself turning into a replica of my sisters. Now I want to become separate. Somebody with opinions. Somebody with attitudes."

"Opinions! Attitudes!" Ottokar laughed. "That's the trouble with your paintings. Charming colors, charming lines, quaint little whimsies and conceits. Oh yes, you have plenty of opinions, you have charming little attitudes, but they're like the birds in one of your paintings, they flutter around behind a cage. And do you want to know why? I'll tell you why. You refuse to yield. All this struggling for separateness is draining the warmth from your blood and it's draining the vitality out of your paintings!"

"Yes," said Freya, "there's a price to be paid for being separate."

"And you still insist on being separate?"

Freya smiled. "Yes, I do."

Ottokar's pupils grew pointed; his lips began to tremble. His face grew frozen in a struggle between misery and exasperation. He picked up his cup and held it balanced on the palm of his hand and stared into the empty, frost-streaked blackness beyond the window.

VII

The sparrows started to twitter in the almond grove, and when Consuelo looked through the window, she saw the leaves beginning to gleam, the drops still clinging to the grapes and the wasps buzzing lazily.

It was much like their life in the Camargue, all in all—the sunlight, the waiting, the scraping and scrounging, the white-eyed dominoes and the chicken with rice. Only the sky was an iris blue instead of a cloud-streaked azure, there were cliffs and yellowish chasms instead of the flat gray marshes. No wild horses went galloping past in plumes of dust, there were only the burros climbing the path with their bundles of faggots, and at dusk as they sipped their sherry they could hear a voice welling up from the bodega, that weird flute-like voice blending with the throb of the guitar.

They walked down the black, crumbling steps to the market-place where a couple of glowering peasant-women still squatted with their baskets. They passed the alms-house with its row of lime trees and then Pepe's café, where the click of the billiard balls punctuated the drone of the radio. Finally they came to the wine-shop and sat down under the dangling light-bulb and listened to Pedro plucking away at his guitar.

There was nothing in the bodega but three huge wine-kegs, some hemp-seated stools and a black wooden table. On the wall hung a photograph of a smiling young cavalry officer, now brownish with age and speckled with fly spots. Pedro grinned as they entered. He was a fine-looking fellow, still dark-haired and elastic, with a toreador's buttocks. One of his eyes had faded to a blind blurry opal. He wore dirty linen slacks and a clinging gray jersey through which one could see his black, bulging nipples.

"I hear the world's in an ugly way," he said, scratching his Adam's apple. His voice was as tender and as high as a eunuch's. "It's one big volcano. They're all waiting for it to explode. Cordoba, Seville, Valdepeñas—they'll be nothing but rubble."

"They'll spare Valdepeñas," said Pia, plucking at her beard. She was a soot-faced old woman who sat in the corner behind the wine-kegs. "There's a mosque in Cordoba and a palace in Seville but there's nothing but mischief in Valdepeñas.

"Well," said Pedro, "I'm not worried. I know a place up in the Pyrenees, a tiny village, miles from nowhere, nothing but caves in the side of a mountain."

"I have a nephew out in the Canaries," said Pia bleakly. "A fruit-merchant."

"And there's Chile," said Pedro. "We can all go to Chile."

"They have earthquakes in Chile, hordes of snakes crawl out of the marshes . . ."

"Or Haiti," said Pedro.

"They have vampires in Haiti!"

"Never mind," chanted Pedro. "There'll still be people, even after the explosion, there'll be plenty of singing and dancing and the other thing, you know what I mean, and if there's fewer of us left to do it all the better. Why shed tears if some stinking old cathedrals go up in flames?"

"I'm the old one, I've suffered the losses, I'm the mournful one," said Pia plaintively, "but you're the cynic. You've always been lucky and still you're cynical. You have no reverence."

"Oh," said Pedro, "I'm not cynical. Don't call me cynical, Pia, I beg you. Do you know what I saw last night? I was crossing the lower bridge. Way down in the bushes the cicados were squealing and do you know what I saw? A nun came riding by; she was riding a donkey, not a sliver of flesh was left on the beast, not even a hank of hair, he was just a green skeleton, and in her arms she was carrying a newborn baby with a head like a werewolf's."

"Terrible things," grunted Pia.

"I have reverence!" moaned Pedro.

He stepped out of doors and stood on the edge of the cliff. They could hear him making water into the hissing nettles.

When they came back to the house Dimitri dipped his head in the basin. Then he slipped off his clothes and stood naked in the doorway. Way below, on the edge of the abyss, twinkled the lights of the village. The clock down in the plaza started to chime.

"Twelve o'clock," said Dimitri. "Do you want to know what I feel like doing? I'd like to take a sledge hammer and break it all to pieces, this whole miserable madhouse that men have built for themselves! Sooner or later it will crumble anyway, that much is certain, and the sooner the better, while there's still some spark of dignity left to us!"

A big moth with wings like a mask came swimming through the darkness. It settled on his shoulder for a moment, then floated away again.

He turned around and stared at Consuelo. His eyes were bloodshot; his jaw was shaking.

"Do you think I didn't notice it? Those sneaking looks that he gave you? And you grinning back at him, ogling and squirming like a bitch in heat! And it's not the first time either! That one-eyed braggart with a woman's voice! Well, go with him, why don't you? Go on, I'm not keeping you! You're dying to find out what he's like, you're aching to taste another man, aren't you? Oh, those soulful eyes of yours when you're listening to Pushkin, those eyes throbbing with insight when you don't understand a word of it! Go on. Try him out. He's down in the bushes waiting for you. But don't come whimpering back to me when you've found out the truth about him. That's all I ask. You're free to go, just go and follow that crazy itch of yours, but leave me alone afterwards, don't pretend that you're still in love with me! I know better, I see through you, you rotten little harlot!"

She was sitting on the steps just below the terrace. All around hung the brightness of the Andalusian stars, that dry close-up glitter that was like sparks rising from a bonfire, little sparks that kept fading and brightening back to life again, and all around floated the sickly sour sweat of the ripening limes.

She got up and walked toward Dimitri. His thickset body was silhouetted in the doorway. Behind him the kerosene lamp shone on the empty bottle and crusts of bread. She came closer. She caught the smell of his feverish wet flesh—a peculiarly slavic odor, it seemed, with a hint of wild goats' milk. He spread his arms with a kind of half-stifled groan and folded her close and covered her shoulders with kisses.

VIII

The almonds fell, the limes ripened. The tang of the harvest was in the air.

"There'll be a letter any day now," Dimitri kept saying. "Those idiots. They're badly organized, that's the trouble. I wrote Krauss again last week. It's two months that I haven't heard from him . . ."

When they strolled down to the village they could hear the bells echoing in the gully—great whirlpools of sound circling deeper and deeper. The hides lay spread out on the sunlit terraces of the tanners. Under the bridge the old women were beating away at their laundry. From the slaughterhouse came the baby-like squeal of stuck pigs and the shouts of the boys as they ran to the trough to wash the blood from their arms.

She had never seen such a blue as the blue of Andalusia—it reverberated like the sound of those death-like churchbells. Sometimes it looked to her like the iris of some calm, stupendous eye, fixing its gaze on the haggard cliffs, on all the wickedness and the praying. The autumn air rustled in the leaves like a giant sigh, but whether of joy or of misery it was difficult to say. It was hard to be sure of anything in this Saracenic landscape. She was no longer sure of Dimitri. She was no longer sure of herself. Dimitri was going through some subtle but sinister metamorphosis. Some secret corrosion was at work in his character, and sometimes his face grew twisted with pain, like that of a man struck with cancer. And she herself was changing too. Dark nervous lines appeared on her face and her mouth had a puckered, snout-like look to it. One day, as she glanced into the mirror, she gave a quick gasp of horror. Her eyes, glittering and sunken, looked exactly like Pepita's, the disheveled little whore who used to hang around the bodega. She grew aware of an inner violence that was spreading through her tissues, leaving its blight on the twitching eyelids, the greedy lips, the frozen chin. It wasn't merely that she was terrified for Dimitri's existence. It was rather that these terrors, once palpable and plausible, had grown into a climate, a whole way of life. The flavor of fear was tightening its grip on both of their characters, heightening the tension and sapping their strength, sharpening their passion but also poisoning it, distorting everything around them so that she began to doubt Dimitri's sanity, and there were moments when she herself seemed to be hovering on the brink of madness.

Once she sat on the terrace stirring her cup of coffee and a wasp fell out of the sky and landed in the cup. And as it lay

there, wriggling viciously, it looked like some desperate signal
of warning. A thread of smoke from the tavern scrawled a
shadow across the stucco and it looked like some cryptic mina-
tory message. She felt treachery in the stink of the slaughterhouse, she saw treachery in the flight of a crow, she heard
treachery in the dry, thin rustle of a grasshopper.

But her love for Dimitri kept growing all the stronger, tinged
as it was with a deepening pity as well as a mounting anxiety.
His eyes when he looked at her didn't seem to see her at all,
they were staring at some spectre, some suspicion or apprehension, a glimpse of something that might have happened or was
about to happen.

Once they stood on the bridge on their way back from Pia's.
Way below them the chasm yawned into blackness and she felt
that she was looking into an abysm of time as well as space,
where gorilla-faced men were still snoring in their caves. And
a second later it seemed that the chasm had shot into the future,
that billions of termites were squirming in the gloom and the
Time of Man was gone and forgotten.

"Tell me, please, Dimitri," she said.

Dimitri blinked, as though suddenly awakened.

"What exactly do they want to do to you?"

"Do to me?" He laughed. "Why, kill me, of course."

Her voice grew listless. "Oh God, Dimitri, what good would
that do them? What earthly good does any of this do, this
stupid vengefulness, this killing? What possible good did it do
to kill that poor old Professor?"

"Not only," said Dimitri, sharpening his voice a little, "was
Borisov a monster. You would vomit if I told you some of the
things that he's done. But he was also extremely dangerous.
He was a threat to all of our lives. If that snub-nosed little
Professor had had his way poor old Ivan would be rotting away
in the Seine. But more important, though I don't imagine that
you'll grasp my point, with your limited intelligence, is the
fact that he was a symbol, he was a clear and tangible symbol,

and killing that monster gave us pride, it gave us hope, it gave us dignity."

"How very curiously you sometimes use your words, Dimitri, darling. Dignity! Pride! So you feel that they were suddenly restored to you? Just by killing that little wretch you became a man again, did you? And what about this?" She flung her arms out over the chasm. It was one of those moments when she sensed him growing frail and vulnerable, and a mysterious surge of strength rising up in herself; as though, as sometimes happens in passionate relationships, they had suddenly exchanged roles and she was the aggressor and he the victim. "Living here in the middle of nowhere, clutching at our pesetas, waiting for ambiguous messages! Hanging around that dreary bodega and wondering what's going to happen to us! Is there pride in this? Is there dignity? What have you achieved? Will you tell me?"

He said nothing. He turned around and looked at her tensely. It was the first time in weeks that he really seemed to be looking at her. He took her hand in his own and they walked through the plaza.

As they passed the café his grip tightened suddenly. The radio was playing a tango; she heard the click of the billiard balls. A group of men was sitting at one of the tables, slapping the cards on the marble, and at another sat Pepita, eating a strawberry ice. At the third sat a lean little man in a pince-nez. He was studiously reading a newspaper with his thumb on the edge of the sherry glass. A mangy old sheep-dog came wandering along the gutter, sniffed mournfully at a little puddle and went lumbering around the corner.

"Come," said Dimitri very quietly, and they started up the stairway.

IX

The road went winding through a desolate plateau with a few little lime groves scattered in the distance. Here and there a couple of goats stood on the edge of a cliff. And then the land grew still emptier and bleaker than before. The slopes were littered with chips of flint and the trees were torn like the trees on a battlefield. The road dipped into a prairie of oyster-blue clay and then ran toward the horizon, where the sun was floating like a great balloon. They drove straight into the blaze. On the edge of the plain shone the roofs of a town. The houses against the sunset looked black and grim as abandoned ware-houses.

They entered the town. This was the border of Andalusia. Directly below them shone the ripples of the Guadiana and on the other side of the river lay the pastures of Portugal. It was dusk when they boarded the ferry, which was merely a raft run by a pulley and stained with dried up patches of cow-dung and horse-urine. The other passengers were a purple-nosed man with a pair of mares and a grim-eyed little woman with a child and a rooster. The ferry started to crawl over the biscuit-brown water.

"It never changes, it's always the same," muttered the ferry-man, nodding to Dimitri. He was a hyena-faced fellow in a striped woollen cap. "East to west, west to east, day after day, it never changes." His face was covered with sores and part of his nose was torn away. "People coming and going, week after week, year after year. What a life! What's the point of it? Spain's as miserable as Portugal and Portugal's no better than Spain, I can promise you, and still they keep on coming and going, day after day, as though there were some point to it . . .' "

The dying light combed the water with threads of a dirty brass. Over in Portugal a pair of oxen was trailing through the haze and in Spain a bare-legged boy was walking with his scythe on the fiery banks.

The boat shook a little, then it came to a grinding halt. It turned around slowly, and started to drift in the muddy current. The cable squeaked uneasily around the wheel of the pulley. "It's the rope," moaned the ferryman. "It's broken again, so God help us!" He crouched over the pulley and started to tug at the severed rope. The ferry kept shuddering in the grip of the current. He grunted and belched as he fingered the strands and started to weave the hemp together again.

One by one the little farm lights started to glimmer in the distance. Night fell. The oily water grew black and sultry. The mares kept pawing nervously at the splintering deck and the fiery-feathered rooster tucked his head under his wing. The woman sat huddled on a bundle of rags. She was picking the lice from the baby's hair.

"I'll tell you what," said the ferryman, turning his pock-marked face toward Dimitri. "If there's a war there's a war. It's not politics or guns that will do it, it's not problems or conflicts, it's not ideals, it's none of those things. Do you want to know what it is? It's the fate of man, that's what it is. Ten years ago I crossed the river once a day and it was enough. Three years ago it was three times daily and now it's five and it isn't enough. They keep on coming and going the whole day long. And why? I'll tell you. Too many people all over the place. Too many people wanting to see if life looks better elsewhere. Too many people being conceived and being dropped out of the womb, being healed and pampered and saved from death and living too long. Wherever you look, too many people. Is it useful, señor? Is it agreeable? I leave the answer to your own sagacity." He gave a yank to the mended rope and started to draw it over the pulley. "If there's a war it's just plain fate. The reason's clear to both eyes. Too many people. There's no way but to go ahead and slaughter them. And then when they've all been slaughtered we can breathe fresh clean air again and learn to be alone with our souls . . ."

The man with the two black mares spat contemptuously into the river.

"Souls! Souls! They're elegant words, Carlos, but you're a fine one to talk about souls. No one believes a word you say. Nonsense, that's all you ever talk. As though we could stop the poor little bastards from being born!"

"The truth is dark," growled the ferryman, "and people just don't like to hear it. They have their pieties. They have their prejudices. When they hear the truth they look away."

The light of the lantern fell on the river which churned past them, tense and noiseless. The hook-nosed man stood on the prow, picking away at his teeth and patting one of his mares on the rump occasionally. The woman had fallen asleep; her head nodded rhythmically. The ferryman's face beside the lantern looked like the face of a corpse, with its gaping nostrils and the flesh all in tatters.

Slowly they drifted toward Portugal. The dew shone on the pulley. The sweet smell of evergreen started to sift through the smell of cow-dung and tar.

The stars were on fire when they finally headed through the woods of Agarve. Now and then the walls of a stable shot up in front of the headlights, and then the woods rose up again, and after the woods a range of hills. It was uncanny. The whole atmosphere around them had utterly changed. It was as though the river were flowing between limbo and purgatory. There was a pine-scented stillness, an air of seclusions, of abandonment. The squat little shepherds along the road looked like sleepwalkers.

Dimitri hadn't said a word since he called good-night to the drunken customs-officer. Finally he said: "There's nowhere to stop. We'd best keep on driving." He reached into her lap, picked up her hand and kissed it gently.

"You're tired?" he said.

"Not yet . . ."

"Go to sleep," said Dimitri softly.

Now and then through the dark she heard the sound of a sheep-bell. Once she thought that she heard the rippling voice of a nightingale. "So far to go," she kept thinking, half-asleep beside Dimitri. Her head swayed uneasily against his shoulder. "So far to go, so much to do. So much to learn and the troubles waiting . . ." But then she opened her eyes for a moment and stared out into the night and she realized that what she felt was merely nostalgia, merely the worries of self-pity and not the bright clean pang of insight. She was dimly aware that something menacing still lay ahead of them and that she somehow had to learn, in loving Dimitri and forgiving him, to forget herself utterly and to crush her self-pity and to reach toward a compassion that was deeper than mere forgiveness or mere tenacity.

When she woke up again a pinkish mist hung in the air. The road twisted sharply. They were entering a valley. A tiny village with a wall around it lay tucked in the curve of a narrow river. When she turned she saw the sun peeping over a wooded hill-top. There was a clear, tinted delicacy in this early morning sunlight, as though it were exploring one frail tint after another, like fingers plucking at the strings of a guitar. But the mist floated away, the colors blazed, the shadows sharpened, and the heat of the autumn spread out over the valley.

X

More and more the Roman air was producing a hallucinatory affect on Barbara. The whole city was beginning to strike her as an elaborate design in *trompe l'oeil:* a series of sun-lit vistas hiding the rot underneath. The big blue domes and colonnades, the splashing fountains, the preening water-gods, everything was drenched in a slightly pock-marked sensuality. It wasn't a breathing sensuality, it was only a marble camou-flage, as though the splendor of façade were the only thing that was tolerable to the Romans, the only thing that could hide the horrors of death and decay. And her own passion likewise, after its phase of self-discovery, gradually turned into a series of pantomimes and strategems. The sensual zest began to lessen, the exploration lost its pungency. Only the core of suspense kept growing sharper and deeper. Whatever she did, glancing through a window, lowering a curtain, smoothing a pillow, it was linked with his presence or absence, it shivered with hope, it burned with terror. Everything else shrank away into staleness and pointlessness. The presence of other creatures grew more and more distasteful. She hated Perugia's simpering ways and Simonetta's nervous giggles; she was bored with her dog Otello; she hated the parrot Sinibaldo. And even Orazio himself was beginning to depress her a little, with his long ivory hands and his vaporous serenity. He was wilting away in front of her, his face was like a skele-ton's: it was as though, in an inverse ratio to her own growing hunger, he were losing all desire and were drifting away into limbo.

One windy evening in November she called up Sandro in Frascati.

"Sandro? It's you? . . . This is Barbara . . . You didn't? Really? I've been smoking too much, I suppose. . . . No, nothing's been happening. I'm rather worried about Orazio. The doctor says it's anemia but I'm sure it's more than anemia . . . Well, let's hope so. . . . Yes. Definitely . . . By the way, what are you doing tonight? . . . You are? . . . Oh . . . I'm sorry . . . You've been taking aspirin, I hope? It's the weather. Very treacherous . . . Yes, darling. I understand perfectly . . . No. Of course not . . . Absolutely . . . Do call me tomorrow . . ."

She hung up the receiver, walked listlessly across the room, struck a match, lit a cigarette and sat down at the writing table.

After a moment she picked up the pen, dipped it in the well and started writing.

"Sandro. I can't go on like this. No, I am not being hysterical. Maybe it's Rome. I've had too much of it. The place is beginning to frighten me. I can't bear being with Orazio—he is like a spectre, he's rotting away. The whole city looks tainted. Nothing seems real any longer. Even you. Do you really exist? Do you really love me? Did you ever love me? Or is it all just a mirage, like everything else in the city? I must see you. Can you meet me at the Rivoli on Friday at five?"

She put down the pen and glanced at the mirror. She sat tensely, without moving. "Good God," she said softly. Something fearful was happening. She was growing ugly: it was obvious. There was a sickly tinge in her cheeks. Her brow was hacked with delicate creases. Her mouth was twisted and bitter and her eyes stared back at her with a bleak intensity.

"Love," she muttered. "Is this what it's like? Is this what it does to one?"

She kept staring into the mirror. The room behind her melted away. The chairs, the curtains, the bowl of roses, everything swayed, simmered, fluctuated. At that moment she grew aware of a delicate stirring in the corridor; a hurried tapping, like raindrops or the padding of tiny feet.

The mirror shook imperceptibly, as though a draught had passed through the room. Something suddenly caught her eye, slightly to the left of her shoulder. It was the porpoise-shaped doorknob, which was turning very slowly. The door opened slightly. A darkish object slid through the crevice. It was only a glimpse, only an impression. It might have been the fluttering of a hand or the intrusion of a head, but of a fabric as misty as the stirring of a cobweb.

She turned sharply. The door was closed. She pressed her hand to her cheek, then crossed the room and opened the door. The corridor was empty; there was nothing at all.

For several minutes she stood in front of the window and stared into the garden. The leafless vines were black and glossy. A spiritless rain had started to fall. There was a hissing of tires on the cobbled pavement of the Lungotevere. The lights of the opposite shore were dancing restlessly in the water.

She walked back to the writing table, took her letter to Sandro and tore it carefully into little pieces. Then she picked up a ring of keys from the dresser, glanced about, and stepped into the corridor.

Somewhere a window was open. There was a sharp, clammy draught. A door slammed. A voice screamed: *"Attenzione! Mamma mia!"*

She caught her breath. It was only the parrot, Sinibaldo. She crossed the dark hall and knocked softly at Orazio's door.

A brittle voice said: "Who is it?"

"It's Barbara," she said.

A tiny pause. A rustling noise, then a click of something falling. And then Orazio's voice again, unusually frail: "Come in, my dear."

He was lying in bed, propped up on satin cushions, surrounded by a litter of books and periodicals. He was suffering from insomnia; he spent most of his night in reading, waiting for the monotony of words to lure him to sleep again. In the corner behind the bed stood a statue of Pan; on the red damask wall hung a painting of Saint Sebastian. There was a faint smell of camphor tinged with a whiff of human secretions.

"Are you feeling better?"

He didn't answer. His eyes moved slowly in their sockets. They were filled with a listless mournfulness: it might have been reproach, it might have been indifference.

"You've taken your powders?"

"How stupid. I'd quite forgotten."

"Where are they?"

"In the mirror cabinet. Top shelf. Way to the left."

She stepped into the bathroom, filled a tumbler with luke-warm water, took a spoon and a bottle from the cabinet, then stepped back into the bedroom.

"How much, dear?"

"Just a spoonful," said the Prince. "Slightly heaped."

The powder fizzed as it fell in the water; there was a thick greenish foam. Orazio winced as he drained the glass, then leaned back on the cushions.

"It's partly the weather, I'm sure," said Barbara.

"The sirocco," said the Prince.

"Doctor Bronchi will be coming tomorrow."

"Is he? I forgot. There's not much point in it."

She leaned over and kissed him on the cheek. It felt dank, curiously unpleasant. He was sweating heavily, she noticed; she caught the mushroom-like scent of it.

"Good night, darling."

"Good night."

She paused at the door.

"By the way . . ."

"Yes?"

"Were you asleep when I knocked on the door?"

"Was I? Yes, I suppose I was."

"I'm sorry. It was thoughtless of me."

"No matter, my child. No matter."

"Good night, then," said Barbara.

"Good night," said the Prince.

XI

She buttoned her coat, pulled on her gloves and stepped into the car. The rain had dwindled into a misty drizzle. The lamplight shone on the stone Apollo. Tears dripped from his chin, a mossy mask covered his cheeks.

She glanced at her watch. Ten forty. She leaned forward and pressed the starter. She drove cautiously through the narrow archway; there was only a foot to spare on either side. Then she followed the Via Guilia toward the Corso Vittorio.

On a curve near the Quirinale the car suddenly skidded: there was a shrieking of brakes; she nearly hit a Lambretta. She drew up beside the curbing, turned off the motor and lit a cigarette. "*Attenzione,*" she said, aloud. Her whole body was shaking. She closed her eyes for a minute. "Better be careful," she whispered.

She crushed the cigarette and glanced around listlessly. The car was standing in front of a pharmacist's shop. Through the rain-streaked windows she saw a bald little man in a white jacket. He was carefully arranging a row of bottles on a shelf.

She got out and entered the shop. The little man nodded wispily.

"Yes. Exactly. For the sirocco especially. It's stronger than aspirin, of course, but harmless . . ."

"And something else," said Barbara vaguely. "Something for rats. We're troubled with rats."

The pharmacist looked at her with a tearful expression. "Rat poison? I see. Exactly."

He took a round yellow box from a shelf and peered at it scrupulously.

"Anything else?"

Barbara hesitated. "Yes. A package of throat lozenges."

The pharmacist nodded; he jotted some figures on an azure pad.

"Twelve hundred and twenty, signora. Exactly. Thank you. Good night."

She began to feel better when she entered the open country. The sickening tension had left the air. There was a scent of rain-soaked hay. The road wound casually through a grassy stretch of pastureland, then started to climb into the vine-studded foot-hills. The lights grew sparse. The little farm-houses were al-ready dark. Frascati itself was shining on the edge of the hill in front of her, a scattering of lights shaped like a cornucopia. The road was a familiar one; she had traveled it before. But to-night there was something strange in the undulating landscape. It looked wild, oceanic. A chilly wind flowed in from the sea.

The road climbed sharply past a monastery and skirted an alley of cypresses. Then it swung abruptly into the middle of the town. An arc-light dangled over the puddle-flecked piazza, shedding its cold dreary light into the deserted café windows. Two young priests hurried past as she turned into the Via Gari-baldi. She turned left, parked the car, switched off the lights and crossed the pavement.

It was a nineteenth century palazzo which had been con-verted into "studios": gray and massive and graceless, with heavy grills on the ground-floor windows. She looked up at the pair of windows over the central balcony. They were dark. The whole building looked deserted except for a milky gleam be-side the entrance. She glanced at her watch. Nearly midnight. She paused at the door, tucked her gloves in her pocket, and pressed the small ivory button marked "Portiere."

The sound of the doorbell echoed dismally inside the build-ing. A dog barked. A shutter creaked as it swung on its hinge.

She caught the smell of old wine-kegs seeping out of the darkness. She looked up. The clouds were breaking, stars were shining through the shaggy crevices.

She tried the doorknob. It clicked; the door opened silently. She stepped cautiously into the hallway, which was dark except for a hazy rectangle which fell through a half-open door on the left.

She called softly: "Is any one here?" No one answered; nothing stirred. As her eyes grew used to the darkness she recognized the ponderous furniture—a large chest on the left with a leopard's skin flung on top of it, and on the right a huge mirror in which she saw herself reflected—a faceless silhouette, half menacing and half pathetic. She tightened the collar of her coat and started to climb the huge stairway.

She moved lightly, almost soundlessly, but the stillness was so intense that the click of her heels echoed like hammer-blows on the marble. The whole house seemed to be listening, to be watching and waiting. But for what? For some statelier, more momentous arrival, surely. But as she climbed through the darkness she felt the intimacy in the air, the curiously personal expectancy, the eerie tautness of recognition which emanated from the pillars and candelabras. She paused again on the landing and glanced down into the entrance hall, where the rectangle of light in the corner had suddenly widened. The shadow of a torso emerged in the lime-green brightness, stood motionless, arm raised, then slowly drew back again. There was the click of a door. Then absolute darkness.

She kept climbing. "Too late," she said to herself, half aloud, without knowing in the least what she meant when she said it. "Too late," she repeated and a wave of terror swept over her, so dense and so potent that she clung to the balustrade to keep from falling.

She opened her bag and groped for her cigarette case. It wasn't there. Had she left it in the car? Obviously she had. Never mind. She walked crisply toward the end of the corridor, where Pallas Athena caught the haze of the night through an oval window. She came to a halt at Sandro's door and bent instinctively in front of the keyhole. It was dark; there was nothing at all; he must be out; or asleep.

She fondled the knob. And once again the door swung open without effort. The living room lay to the left of a hexagonal foyer. She caught the smell of photographer's chemicals and sulphur-tinged celluloid. The dull sheen of the half-moon seeped into the room through the balcony window.

She saw a camel's hair coat tossed over an arm-chair, limp as a corpse. She reached down, took the sleeve and pressed it gently against her cheek. It was soft as a kiss. And a stab of longing shot through her, more piercing, more sickening than she had ever known it.

"*Attenzione*," she said softly; still not knowing what she meant by it.

At that moment she noticed a thin thread of light under the bedroom door.

"Yes. Of course," she said, nodding. She crept soundlessly across the living room, pressed her hand to the wall to steady herself, and opened the door.

The light in the room was so bright that for a moment she was blinded. She caught her breath, stifled the cry in her throat, then closed the door again.

XII

The road dipped sharply into a steep wooded valley. The steely rope of a waterfall sparkled suddenly in the headlights and the fresh chilly smell of the mountain laurel welled about her. She turned left. The road narrowed. An iron crucifix loomed in front of her. She slowed down and turned left again; the pebbles crackled under the tires.

Now she knew she was lost. The road grew soggy and deeply rutted. All around rose the thicket. Not a light was to be seen. She slowed down, looking for a widening of the road to turn around in. The growl of a mountain torrent rose from the darkness.

At that moment the motor died. The car scraped to a halt. She pressed on the starter; no use; the motor refused to start again. "Out of gas," she thought listlessly. She leaned back in the leather seat and ran her hand over her forehead. It was dripping with sweat. The feeling of vertigo grew sharper.

She reached into her bag, then remembered the missing cigarette case. She flicked at the light in the dashboard and looked around anxiously. A wave of panic surged up in her; her hands fluttered hysterically. "I've lost it," she moaned. "Oh God, I've lost it, I've lost it . . ."

The delicate spiral of nausea slid up toward her gullet. She flung open the door and staggered across the road. She knelt on the moss, clutching miserably at a sprig of laurel. Her head dangled limply; tears trickled across her cheeks.

She got up and walked dizzily over a small wooden bridge. A gust of cold air shot up from the torrent. The pebbles were slippery with dew and the grasses were soaked with dew. The road twisted down through a copse of scrawny aspens and then opened unexpectedly into a long narrow valley. A small building, a ruined barn perhaps, stood in the middle of a stony pasture. A group of figures sat crouched by an open fire behind the building.

She groped her way through the brambles and walked up toward the fire. The circle of faces turned slowly; the firelit eyes gazed wonderingly up at her. They looked like waifs. They might have been shepherds or maybe ploughboys. They were dressed in gray tunics or threadbare brown overcoats, two or three of them with woollen caps and tattered shawls flung over their shoulders. One of the group was a little older than the others; a bearded, powerful fellow in a thick blue pullover. The rest were boys in their teens and one of them was only a child; he lay on a blanket and was leaning his head on a large black spaniel. A pock-marked boy was stirring away at an earthenware pot.

The man in the pullover jumped to his feet. He scratched his cheek and looked at her thoughtfully.

"Good evening, signora! You look troubled!"

"Good evening," said Barbara wanly.

"Is there anything wrong, signora?"

"Yes," said Barbara, nodding wretchedly.

"You've lost your way?"

"Yes," said Barbara. "My car broke down on the hill."

The stranger's face grew wrinkled with sympathy. "It's a pity, signora, a burning pity! Here in the darkness and the cold. And all alone. Where's the car?"

"It's up on the road, just after the bridge."

"The bridge? It's up by the bridge, is it?" His eyes glittered craftily. Then he whispered: "It broke down, did it? Yes, there's wickedness in those woods. Last year it was Benedetto who had a knife stuck in his belly and now it's something new, it's a lady's car that's broken down!"

He stared at the sky and shook his head. Then he looked at Barbara with an ox-like gentleness.

"There," he said, "just sit down and wait with the boys here, signora. Those woods are no place for young ladies to go roaming in . . . Come, move over, Arcangelo. Let the lady sit down with you!"

The child crept over a little and put his arms around the spaniel's neck. He peered shyly at Barbara as she sat down beside him. The rest of the boys kept staring at her with an awestruck solemnity. The man in the pullover said, "There, don't worry, I'll be back." He tightened his belt and went trotting off in the darkness.

One of the boys, dressed like a scarecrow in a torn army over-coat, got up and threw a handful of twigs on the fire. The scent of pine-smoke mingled with the honey-like smell of the pasture-land and the warm fleshy smell that hovered around the shep-herd boys.

After a while another of the boys, a dark fellow with a face like a gipsy's, turned to the boy in the army overcoat. "Go on, Tullio. What happened?" The boy in the coat glanced around, hastily crossed himself and muttered: "I didn't move. I sat on the rock and said my prayers while she stood and leered at me. She had claws like a rooster's. Her cheeks were like a pumpkin. She said 'Ooo-oo' and made a snatch at me and then she squealed like a pig and tucked up her skirts and went flying over the tree-tops . . ."

"I have an aunt down in Procida. She turned into a bird one day," said Tullio.

"We lived in Matera before my mother died," said the boy with the gipsy face.

"My own mother was very wise. She could see into the future," said Arcangelo softly.

"Mine died in a fire. She was crushed by a bomb," said a boy with a harelip.

"Matera!" said the boy with the gipsy face. "You won't be-lieve it if I tell you. It's got palaces bigger than Rome. With doors that are shaped like elephants! My father was a copper-smith down in Matera."

"In Procida," said Tullio, "they had cakes shaped like drag-ons."

"Is there any more bread left?" said another boy, peering at the soup-pot.

"Here," said Tullio, reaching into his pocket. "There's a piece of *provolone*."

"Look!" cried the child, clutching at his dog. "There's a star falling down on us!"

"Somebody dying," whispered Tullio. He looked tensely at

the boy with the harelip. "Make a wish, quick, Pierino. Some-body's dying! Make a wish!"

All of the boys raised their faces as they made their wishes: childish faces, sly little faces, ugly as trolls or beautiful as an-gels, but all of them touched with the stains of an early cynicism which was suddenly transformed by the magic of hope.

The pock-marked boy lifted his spoon and said in a husky voice: "More wood, Pierino, quick. The fire's already dying." He dipped his spoon again and looked shamefacedly at Bar-bara. "Are you hungry, signora?"

"That kind of soup isn't for ladies," said Tullio with dignity. "There's no meat in it. It's only radishes and onions," he said apologetically.

"Listen!" said the child, raising his forefinger. "Did you hear something wailing?"

"Sounds like an owl, maybe," said Tullio, who was steaming the lice from the seams of his coat.

"Have you ever seen a wolf?" said the child Arcangelo, with a look of terror.

"Once in the wintertime," said Tullio. "He was crouching under a bridge. He was as big as Peppone's bull. His teeth shone like knives . . ." There were footsteps in the grasses. "Look, here's Franco again!"

The bearded fellow in the pullover stepped from the darkness. "Go," he said, turning to Tullio, "you've got a strong pair of legs on you, run down to the village and tell Maurizio there's some work for him." He smiled briskly at Barbara. "Maurizio's a genius. Everything he touches springs to life again. He'll take a look at that little car of yours, he'll know what's wrong with it right away, he'll just pat it on the rump and off you'll go as though nothing had happened!" He peered cautiously at Bar-bara. "You're shivering with the cold, my poor lady. Come on home. I'll give you some wine. You need some wine to warm you up again . . ."

XIII

They crossed the field and followed a thin stony path through an olive grove. At the edge of the grove rose a wall and behind the wall stood a long low building. It was something between a farm-house and a tumble-down manor-house, built of yellowish brick, with a castiron gate leading into a courtyard. Franco paused in front of the door and pointed to the sky.

"Look," he said, "how it's brightened. Do you smell the wet rosemary? The wind's shifted to the north. Good weather coming, up in the Abruzzi anyway." He took out a key. His voice grew warm and confiding. "Do you know the people in the Abruzzi? They're the only real Italians. They were here long before the Romans and the Neapolitans and the rest of them. They've got love in their souls, they'll spill their blood for a friend but they'll slit your throat if you ever betray them!"

He lit an oil-lamp in the kitchen, which was obviously the room where he lived. A fire was burning in a large cylindrical stove in the corner and beside it stood a narrow rumpled bed with an oaken bedstead. There was a smell of smoked ham, of crumbling mortar, of masculine occupancy. The kitchen table in the center of the room was covered with a dark green oil-cloth. Three hemp-seated chairs stood facing the table, which was littered with dirty glasses, old newspapers and playing-cards. A large black cat was dozing on a shelf; a pot of basil stood on the windowsill.

"You live alone here?" said Barbara.

"Oh, there's plenty of room," said Franco. "It's big enough for a regiment but it's dark and it's gloomy. It's lonely up in the hills nowadays. Once this house was full of life and I still remember when I was a child here, all the feasts and celebrations when the family gathered at Christmas time. But they're dead, the house is empty, nobody bothers to come back again. And why should anyone come back? With all the emptiness and the dreariness?" He opened the door of the stove and poked briskly at the fire. Then he took a bottle of wine from the shelf and set it on the table. "When I was a boy I groomed the horses and after that I tended the vineyards but when the Baron died ten years ago the family moved to Naples. And now there's nobody left, the place is crumbling and what can one do for it? Here, signora, I'll fill a glass for you. You'd better drink or you'll catch a fever." He sat down at the table opposite her; he laid his thick dark hands on the oil-cloth. She noticed the knotted blue veins below his knuckles.

The cat sprang up in his lap. He kept stroking it lazily, still smiling with his eyes fixed intently on Barbara. But as the wine warmed her body she grew less and less sure whether it was a smile of delicate protectiveness or of casual animality or even perhaps of a cold feral cunning.

"You speak like a Roman," he said. He filled her glass again. "But you're not a Roman. You could be from Milano but your eyes aren't Milanese. You could be from Bologna but the Bolognese women are full of laughter. There's gold in your hair, it could be the hair of a Venetian. You're sad, that's what puzzles me, you're almost sad enough to be a Sicilian!"

An uncontrollable, half-crazy recklessness was rising up in her, a warm resilience that swept away the misery and the nausea. "I'm sure that you know what I am. You knew it instantly. I could see it in your eyes. I'm too spoiled to be English and too stupid to be French. I'm too pale to be Spanish and much too nervous to be Scandinavian."

"Yes, I know," said Franco, nodding. "Our young Umberto married an American woman. That was just before the war and they went to Egypt for their honeymoon. The old Baron shook his head and said that nothing but grief would come of it but he couldn't stop Umberto and they flew off to Cairo."

"And what happened?"

"Who knows? One day they went on a picnic to the pyramids. Maybe they quarreled. Maybe there was a crisis. Maybe it was only an accident. Or maybe it was something deeper, something no one will ever know about. He was found in his bed that night with a bullet between his eyeballs. The Baron was perfectly right, of course, a horrible grief did come of it, but nobody knows what happened and the bride sailed back to America."

"A terrible story," said Barbara.

"So it is," nodded Franco.

"Might it," said Barbara, "have been suicide?"

"It might, of course," said Franco.

He leaned forward and poured the ruby-dark wine into her glass. Then he leaned back in his chair again and looked at her quietly, without speaking.

A powerful drowsiness swept over her. The glasses swayed on the moss-green oil-cloth. A rosy-cheeked knave leered up from a thumb-worn card. Her eyes closed; her head nodded and all she remembered was the wine-smelling arms that carried her gently across the room.

XIV

She opened the door. All was still; everything was exactly as usual except for the long black overcoat flung over the chest in the hallway. The bowl of roses in front of the mirror was beginning to wilt, she noticed. The Siamese cat lay curled in the chair; it blinked at her drowsily. She crossed the hall and glanced casually at the morning mail on the console table.

A fly was crawling slowly across a long manila envelope. Something stirred in the back of her brain; a tiny enigma was struggling to be solved. She watched the fly cross the *demi-lune,* pause at the edge, then dart into space. At that point she grew aware of a leaden heaviness in the atmosphere: as though a flood had been accumulating in the upper stories of the house, waiting to burst through the ceilings and come gushing down the walls.

"Principessa!" It was Perugia racing headlong down the stairway, wringing his hands and rolling his eyes, his lavender coattails fluttering behind him. "Where have you been? Quick, quick! Principessa! We've all been looking for you!"

She threw her coat in his arms and hurried up to Orazio's room. He was lying with his hands crossed over the yellow coverlet, symmetrical, motionless. The priest was standing in the corner, muttering obsequiously to Doctor Bronchi. Beside the bed sat Aunt Gina, who shot an electric look at her as she entered. A sickening smell filled the room: a mixture of rot and disinfectant. A flake of sunlight fell on the little painting of Saint Sebastian but the curtains had been drawn and most of the room was in darkness.

Her first impression was one of an elaborate hostile conspiracy. The scene had been staged; they had all been waiting; they were all of them watching her. Even Orazio, lying so still there —he was waiting and watching, on the lookout for some microscopical sign of self-betrayal. She suddenly realized with sickening vividness exactly what had happened. Doctor Bronchi turned and faced her. He was about to say something but then he glanced at Aunt Gina and lowered his eyes discreetly.

She stood by the bed and stared down at the corpse. The sleeping face looked calm and waxy, suffused with a faint tinge of mustard. The lips were slightly parted; it might have been a smile or a sneer. Her jaws started to tremble. It wasn't sorrow she felt or love, it was more like some piercing and scarifying recognition, a feeling of kinship too fearful to be identified.

She leaned down and kissed his brow. And at that moment she felt his being, his soul, his character, his essence, or whatever it was, abruptly receding with lighting-like speed. It had merely been waiting for this tiny contact before finally vanishing. And she felt that he had always been, as he was now, an absolute stranger, she had never known him at all, the feeling of closeness was illusory and her whole relationship with him was nothing but a mirage. Father Fabbri and Doctor Bronchi and Aunt Gina were only illusions and she was standing all alone in a dark, empty room.

Part Eight

I

Life changed very little at Bishop's Neck after Miss Malachi's funeral. The house seemed stiller than usual; the rooms looked smaller and darker. And for two or three days a vague aroma lingered in the hall, a smell of something musty down in the cellar, like decaying apples. But Mrs. Bontecue spent the weekend and aired the place thoroughly, she washed the sheets and the pillow-cases and sprinkled lavender in the drawing-room.

And oddly enough, an air of security, of almost the commonplace, came back to the house. Old Jim Beasley drove over from Pendleton's to mow the lawn and weed the flower-beds and a man came from Euphoria to repair the broken windowpanes. The goldfish were given to Daisy O'Haggerty, who ran the grocery store. Grace phoned for the piano-tuner to come out from Belleville, and every night after dinner she sat down with her Scarlatti, whom she now preferred to Schumann and even Debussy: she liked the antiquated precision, the twirling delicacy of his patterns.

When the clock struck ten o'clock she folded the album and closed the lid. It was then that she opened the doors to her pale-bodied visitors. The smell of the brackish water drifted in through the windows, the moths came fluttering through the lamp-light, the crickets started to chirp. She laid out the cards for a game of patience and after a while she heard those shy, leaf-like rustlings on the veranda. With one part of her mind she knew that her visitors were only phantoms. She knew it in a sidelong, almost incidental way. But she ignored this little knowledge, which seemed to her irrelevant. She ignored it because the beauty and the power of her phantoms was so great to her. They had a reality of their own which was clear and exact as quicksilver. And that other reality, in which they were exposed as merely phantoms, was a lesser and a limited reality, a squalid reality, a chaotic reality.

She knew of course that the world outside would think of her visions as a form of lunacy. There had been a time not long ago when the thought of madness desperately frightened her. But it frightened her no longer. She was in control of her "awareness." She knew quite placidly, almost gayly, that the world she had entered was a world of phantoms. But this didn't lessen its brightness or persuasion, its miraculous power to console. As she sat under the chestnut-tree in the hazy September twilight, swinging lazily to and fro, digging her heels in the yellowish dust, or at those times in the dusky drawing-room when the queen of spades slid from her fingertips, she felt something that was close to a pantheistic blissfulness. And the only thing that still troubled her in these cool autumn days was a lingering thought in the back of her mind: of something to be done still, somehow or other.

One night she put on her hat and took the bus down to Belle-

ville. She walked past the gas-works until she came to Melpomene Street. She studied the numbers on the doorways: Two-
ten, two-twelve, two-twenty. She crossed the street and stood
facing a narrow four-story building, a dingy house of nasturtium
brick with thick lace curtains over the windows.

"Yes," she thought. "That must be it . . ." She walked up
the white steps, straightened her hat and patted her skirt a
little, then pushed the brass door-bell.

One of the curtains stirred slightly, footsteps crackled on the
linoleum. The door opened and a corroded, mannish woman
stood in front of her. She looked Grace up and down and fondled her necklace suspiciously.

"Well," she said in a gravelly tone, "just whom might you be
looking for?"

"You're Mrs. Bull?" murmured Grace, snatching at the name
almost at random.

"Yes," said the woman. "I'm Mrs. Bull. And who sent you,
may I ask?"

"Mrs. Mulholland," said Grace with gravity.

"Oh," said the woman. She relaxed a little.

"It's a special situation," said Grace.

"So I take it," slurred Mrs. Bull.

Grace blushed. "I'd be happy to pay, of course."

Mrs. Bull lifted her head. "We don't run that kind of establishment, Ma'am. As it happens."

"Oh," said Grace, with an anguished look, speaking softly
and very rapidly, "don't misunderstand, please, Mrs. Bull, it
isn't that, it isn't just lechery, it's only this once and I'll never do
it again. Just this once, a nice clean boy who'll be a father to
my child, and I'll never see him again and I wouldn't dream of
making trouble for him. It's only just this once, I promise you,
and it's not just voluptuousness, and maybe the sum of twenty
dollars would be acceptable, Mrs. Bull?"

"I see," said Mrs. Bull, picking at her teeth. "A special situation."

"I took the bus all the way down to Belleville," pleaded Grace.

"You're definitely not," said Mrs. Bull, somewhat insultingly, "the usual dish."

"Yes," said Grace, lowering her eyes. "Augusta called me the elfin type."

"It's not the type so much as the attitude," said Mrs. Bull, relenting a little.

"Lordy me," cried Grace despairingly, "I'll do my best, Mrs. Bull! I'll do whatever you tell me, just give me a pointer or two! I'm scared, I'm just plain scared but I'll do like you say and would twenty-five dollars be an adequate compensation, Mrs. Bull?"

Mrs. Bull scratched her armpit and reflected a little. "I could let you have the rose room. We'll give it a try. It's Friday night, there's usually someone who ain't too particular."

"Someone young, please?" said Grace. "Or else I'd be terrified!"

"Come, I'll take you up to the rose room," said Mrs. Bull, smiling maternally, "I'll fix it all cozy-like, nobody drunk or nasty-minded. One of those boys from Camp Lawler, so just relax and act natural. The payment will be in advance, please, I like things to be reliable, and you'll wait in the rose room till I bring up the gentleman . . ."

II

It was a narrow little room, papered with a latticework of petunias. A taffeta-shaded lamp stood on the chipped walnut dresser. Over the bed hung an oleograph: "The Wreck of the Hesperus." A hovering suggestion of sandalwood was mixed with the odor of disinfectant.

Grace glanced at the mirror. "Land," she murmured, "I plum forgot." She put her bag on the dresser and snapped open her vanity-case. She pursed her mouth and carefully smeared her lips with a blood-red lipstick. Then she daubed her cheeks with a heavy layer of *Bon Soir* face-powder.

She sat down on the bed and looked at her face from a distance. It looked like a mask: Japanese, enigmatical. Her eyes were peering back at her with a mischievous expectancy.

She got up, turned out the light and sat down on the edge of the windowsill. The lazy night air ruffled the sleeves of her fuchsia dress. It was a dress she had inherited from Freya, with white embroidery down the middle and a velvet ribbon on each of the shoulders. The smell of coal-gas and tar rose from the dimly lit street. Across the way a sign kept blinking, O'DOO-LEY'S CAFE, and the blue of the neon-light throbbed faintly among the petunias. Over the buildings in the distance hung a dirty red haze. From somewhere behind her came the growl of a freight-train.

There was a knock on the door.

"Who is it?" said Grace.

The door opened. A young soldier stood in the doorway, blinking his eyes. He was thin and intensely nervous; he wore a crew-cut and glasses. His face looked stealthy and worried, evasive.

"Just sit down," said Grace festively, "and make yourself at home, dear!"

"Thanks," said the soldier, smiling a twisted little smile.

"What's your name?"

"Melville," said the soldier.

"What a beautiful name," purred Grace. "Melville. Why, it rhymes with Belleville! How very appropriate. It's almost destiny that you came to Belleville, isn't it, Melville?"

"Well," said Melville, turning his cap in his hands, "if that's how you look at it."

"Yes, it is!" said Grace excitedly. "I look at everything with a feeling of destiny. Maybe I got it from Miss Malachi. Things happen the way they happen because they're bound to happen, she used to say. There's no way around it. It can't be helped, said Miss Malachi."

The soldier smiled shyly and laid his cap on the dresser.

"Well, I guess I never thought about it but maybe you're right," he said dreamily.

"My name is Anastasia," said Grace, lifting her chin a little.

"It's an unusual kind of name," ventured the soldier, "for a girl like you, isn't it?"

"For a harlot? Is that what you mean?" said Grace, gleaming brilliantly.

"Oh, I didn't exactly mean that you . . ."

"Why, bless you, you can say what you mean, Melville. You won't hurt my feelings. It's an age-old profession, they even practiced it among the Babylonians. I read it in a book that belonged to Miss Malachi. There's no reason to be ashamed of it. They were called hetairas in ancient Greece. Sometimes they were ladies of considerable culture. Lordy, Melville, there's no point in being puritanical!"

"I'm not," said Melville, flushing a little, "a puritanical person, really."

"No, honey, I know you're not," said Grace, with a soothing look. "Flesh is flesh, blood is blood, we're mortal beings every one of us. Were you born in Virginia, Melville?"

"Massachusetts," said Melville.

"Oh," said Grace with delight, "I've always wondered about Massachusetts."

"Fall River," said Melville.

"Come, sit down," said Grace hospitably.

She smoothed out a place at the bottom of the bed for Melville to sit on: then she leapt on the pillow, curled up her legs and leaned on the bedstead. She fixed her luminous eyes intently on Melville.

"Are you lonely?" she asked mysteriously.

Melville glared at the carpet.

"You're Jewish, Melville, aren't you?"

Melville took off his glasses. He folded them silently and tucked them into his pocket.

"I thought so," said Grace. "You look wounded. Like a deer. And at the same time intellectual, sort of. You read a lot, don't you?"

Melville wrapped his bony arm over the base of the bedstead.

"Well," said Grace, widening her eyes, "there's one thing that's important. Not to feel sorry for oneself. That's the thing that's important. Goodness me, if I ever started to feel sorry for myself, honestly, Melville, I don't know where I'd stop. I'd probably go and commit suicide. Once I even considered suicide, there was a bottle of iodine in the bathroom. But when you really stop to think about it, what's to be gained by committing suicide? It's silly to give up, isn't it, just because we're not beautiful?"

"Not beautiful?" said Melville, startled. "Why, you're beautiful, Anastasia!"

Grace lowered her eyes quickly. Her mouth started to tremble.

"Not only beautiful," cried Melville adoringly, "you're so marvelously understanding! What you said about the iodine, well, I've felt exactly the same, only I never had the thoughts and the understanding like you did. Honestly," he said, lowering his voice to a note of apology, "I never dreamed that I'd meet a whore with a soul, right here in Belleville."

"*Tout comprendre,*" said Grace delicately, "*c'est tout pardonner.*"

"What's that?" said the soldier nervously.

"Oh, just something of Miss Malachi's. Miss Malachi had a philosophy. It was cynical, maybe, but it was a philosophy."

"A philosophy," said Melville tensely. "Maybe that's what we need."

"Come, darling, lay your head in my lap," whispered Grace.

III

The leaves fell. October came with its salty gusts and billowing rains. Clouds of blackbirds went screaming over the field by Cleghorn's Inlet and the copper beech behind the summer house looked black and hairy, like a great tarantula.

Grace's life was taking on a new detachment, a new tranquillity. She had finally learned, almost by accident, to detect the loneliness in other people, and to see it as something that was incurable and everlasting. Her heart no longer responded to other people in terms of longing or bewilderment, or even in terms of delight or speculation; but with compassion and acceptance, with recognition and impersonal love. She saw the pangs of personal love reflected in the people all around her, in their eyes and their voices, even their gestures and footsteps. But the questions "Why is it?" and "What will come of it?" no longer disturbed her.

Every day she carried a basket to the row of shacks behind O'Haggerty's grocery store, things like vegetables and eggs, and occasionally flowers and medicines, and now and then some biscuits or a Lady Baltimore cake. She left the basket with Miss Salina or else Mrs. Boone, and they'd give what they didn't need to old Jim Potts or the crazy Prentices. Sometimes she couldn't help noticing that they threw away the bottles of aspirin, and that the spinach and chrysanthemums shriveled away on their windowsills, and when she gave them a dollar it usually went for beer and popcorn, and she'd say, "Honestly, Salina, if you had any sense you'd be eating healthy things like celery and asparagus," but Miss Salina sat by the radio and drank beer and ate potato chips, and she explained: "I'm too old to be changing my habits, Miss Grace!"

One evening, it was early December, she was sitting by the upstairs window. All the leaves had fallen from the trees; the woods looked naked and melancholy. One of those wet-smelling days, it was, when the light had a threatening gold to it. The leaves in the orchard lay in soggy black layers and the clouds over the Chesapeake were fringed with pink edges.

Far away, on the lonely pathway from Pendleton's Landing, she saw an old woman crossing the hill. She was limping along rhythmically, rather nimbly for a very old woman but with her left foot trailing slightly, like a wounded animal's. As she gradually came closer Grace could see that she was wearing a frayed black overcoat and a man's fedora hat, very old and very shabby. She crept up the driveway and came limping across the lawn. Then she halted below the porch and stared up at Grace's window.

"Come on down and open the door for me, Miss Grace, why don't you, honey?"

Grace called, "Just a minute!" and hurried down to open the door.

The old Negress was so decrepit that there was no expression left in her face: just yellowed eyeballs with purple veins stuck in a mask of hungry wrinkles. Her hair clung to her scalp like a dirty white wig.

She wiped her nose on her sleeve and sat down on the veranda steps. "Sit down here, Miss Grace. I just wanted to come and look at you."

Grace sat on the steps beside her and said softly: "Who are you?"

"I ain't nobody, Miss Grace. I'm just coming to pay a call on you!"

She took off her hat and laid it neatly on top of a flower-pot. Then she whispered: "I'm Mrs. Pope. That's my name. Hattie

Pope." She leaned forward till her face almost touched Grace's own; her shrunken old fingers trembled lightly on Grace's cheek. Then she drew back again with a tender, cadaverous smile.

"There now. I went and done it. I just wanted to come and look at you. I'm so old, you oughtn't to mind if I come and just look at you. There's things that I know, Miss Grace. I sit in my rocker the whole night long, just sitting and knowing the things that I can't help knowing. There's plenty of other things too but those are the things I don't worry about. It's only a scattering of things I remember but I remember them proper!" She sloped her head with a gleam of pride. "How old do you think I am, now?"

"Well," said Grace, "just on a guess I'd as like as not say eighty."

"That ain't so far wrong, it's pretty near," said the Negress. "Nobody knows how old I am but on a guess it might be eighty. It might be ninety or even a hundred and that's a plain fact. When the years go so slow one can't help losing count of 'em. One year's as slow as another and they're as like as peas in a pod. Yes, Miss Grace, my liver's fine and my kidneys don't betray me—what's a woman like me to go and do with herself? One gets up in the early morning and fetches a pail of water, one tidies the room a little and sits down in the rocker. And then? It's all that thinking, that's the trouble with growing old!"

"Yes," said Grace, "too many thoughts, that's what I said to Miss Malachi."

"I ain't never been in jail, not even once," declared the old woman. "I never killed nothing except hornets and little bugs. I never scared nobody and the only one I slapped was Justus. That's the day he came home after he stole those two chickens. Don't I have a right to feel peaceful? At my age you ought to feel peaceful. If you don't feel peaceful at eighty there's no point in even trying . . ."

Her eyes darted about in a sudden panic. "It's cold here," she said. "Gettin' cold, don't you think? I need some shoes, but what use is a pair of brand new shoes to walk in? I'm not long for this world, Miss Grace. I won't be seeing the house where I was born again. See how thin I've suddenly got? Anyone knows when they're going to die soon. And who's goin' to come to my grave and weep on the gravestone, will you tell me? It's a fact, a sad fact. There's nobody left to come and weep for me, only you, poor Miss Grace, will you come to my grave and weep for me?"

Grace nodded. "I'll come and I'll weep for you, don't worry, Mrs. Pope."

"Goodness me," said Mrs. Pope. "Listen to that whippoorwill calling. It's time I got going and it's late, dear Miss Grace. How can we know about people till it's over and they're dead? How can we tell about a man if he's good or wicked till he's dead? There's so much that can happen in those last few minutes! It's the things in those last few minutes that decides it, Miss Grace."

She picked up her hat and placed it scrupulously on her head. She bent over, gripped at the steps and rose slowly to her feet.

"There, that's done it. Shoes, shoes. Who cares about shoes? Just come, that's all I ask, and weep a while for your poor old granny!"

Grace rose and leaned forward and folded her arms around the old woman. She kissed her on the cheek and murmured, "It was a lovely visit, wasn't it?"

Mrs. Pope tightened the threadbare coat around her body. "Getting cold," she grunted, "ain't it? Colder and colder every year." She limped over the lawn and then slowly down the driveway. Finally she vanished along the pathway to Pendleton's Landing.

Grace walked into the kitchen where Mrs. Bontecue was baking a pie. The evening light fell through the blinds on Mrs. Bontecue's face. She was a handsome woman still but bony and barren, antagonistic. There was something almost vengeful in her eyes as she looked at Grace.

"There's a chill in the house," said Grace.

"Yes, there is," said Mrs. Bontecue. She looked meaningly at Grace. "You ought to be careful now, Miss Grace!"

"Do you have a family, Mrs. Bontecue?"

"Oh, I do indeed, Miss Grace. My husband's gone away but I have a family, yes indeedy. Two boys off in the Navy and a little girl down in Roanoke."

"Where did he go?"

"Who?"

"Your husband. Didn't you say he's gone away?"

"He just went," growled Mrs. Bontecue.

"And he never came back?"

"He came back," said Mrs. Bontecue, "only once, just to look at me. I could see it in his eyes. He just wanted to make sure. He wanted to make positive that he didn't want me any more. He stayed for one night. I was proud, that was the trouble. And he left at the crack of dawn. I just laid there and watched him going. He slipped a ten dollar bill under the sugar-bowl and that was the worst of it. He never came back. Pride's my weakness, it always was."

She leaned over and peered into the oven and brushed a wisp of hair from her forehead.

"Who's that woman I seen you sitting out on the steps with, Miss Grace?"

Grace shook her head craftily. "I oughtn't to tell you. It's a secret."

"I seen her before," said the woman suspiciously. "Down by the creek."

"She's old," said Grace lovingly.

"Crazy and old," said Mrs. Bontecue.

"She's a relative of mine," said Grace.

Mrs. Bontecue glared at her. "One shouldn't go talking about it, Miss Grace, right in the open like that!" She dropped the frying pan in the sink and turned on the water. "All those things long ago, one shouldn't drag them out in the open!"

Grace looked at her gravely. "It's nearly done, isn't it, Mrs. Bontecue?"

"Five more minutes," said Mrs. Bontecue.

"Smells like pumpkin," said Grace thoughtfully.

IV

Time passed, time kept passing, and though nothing seemed to be changing it was obvious that some deep and invisible upheaval was occurring. The leaves were dying; the grass was withered; the pathway cracked under her feet. The creek shot over the waterfall but the ferns by the fall were black and shriveled. Nothing changed at Blue Hills but there was something in the sheen of things that suggested a gathering tension, like that of a far-off hurricane. Outside the window of Augusta's bedroom the autumn light grew heavy and deep. The shadows spread from the trees until they joined a larger shadow, which was the darkness of invisible distances, the brooding depth of the horizon.

She turned on the peach-colored lamps that flanked the mirror. Her face, tinged with the brightness, looked thin, bold and sinewy. She kept staring at the reflection, trying to detect what looked so odd in her. And as she stared she saw the dark glittering eyes fall back into their sockets, the skin grew dry as parchment, a sickening sneer distorted her lips. And she knew that time was passing, time was murderously passing, and what she was looking at in the mirror was the nightmare of time passing.

After this she developed an obsession against mirrors. One by one she removed the mirrors all over the house and stored them in the attic and down in the cellar. Neither Cyrus nor Mr. Aspinwall seemed to notice this especially but Miss Aspinwall kept saying, "What's been happening to the mirrors? I miss those mirrors!"

The Chippendale mirror in the drawing-room, the walnut mirror in the hallway, the Venetian mirror in the powder-room, the Queen Anne mirror in the card-room, one by one she took them down and had them lugged into the attic. Even the mirror on her dressing-table she covered with an embroidered shawl and the only mirror that was left was the cabinet mirror in her bathroom.

And after the mirrors all were gone she developed an obsession about clocks. She couldn't bear to look at the clocks, those chilly reminders of things vanishing. She couldn't bear to hear their ticking, which sounded like treacherous little footsteps; she couldn't bear to see those round, gnome-like faces leering back at her.

So she took away the clocks all over the house one by one. And neither Cyrus nor Mr. Aspinwall seemed to mind it particularly but Miss Aspinwall murmured plaintively, "How will we know when it's time for cocktails, dear?" The Empire clock in the library, the Baroque clock at the head of the stairs, the Regency clock in the drawing-room and even the grandfather clock in the hallway, all were quietly removed and stored in various closets, and the only clock that was left was the cuckoo clock in the kitchen, which nobody seemed to notice and which had stopped running anyhow.

With the deepening of fall the woods grew muddy and dark and when she went for a walk she wore her coat and galoshes. She usually walked alone now, she preferred to leave the dogs at home, and she usually took a roundabout way that circled the inlet. She had a feeling that now with the trees all naked and leafless people could watch her from a distance and follow her movements.

And these obsessions with clocks and mirrors and clandestine witnesses were associated in her mind with something else, not shame exactly, not guilt exactly, but a feeling of something bestial which was linked with her passion for Cleophas. It was passion, not love. It was closer to hatred than to love. She hated him for his power over her, his power to humiliate and degrade her, not only with the actual gymnastics of sexual intercourse but even more with the images he instilled in her brain, those shaggy and bestial images which both fascinated and revolted her. She grew obsessed in particular with the image of the phallus, which gripped her imagination with a spectacular vividness. That perfectly ordinary and utilitarian bit of flesh began to swell in her mind into a legendary enormity. It crouched on the horizon like a mosque; it shot skyward like a minaret; it soared with the darkly veined intricacy of a cathedral. "Good God," she thought, "am I really as vile as all this? Do other women suffer from these visions? Or am I alone in it? Am I disintegrating?"

One day in late October she took the path toward the hunting-shack. Violet clouds hung over the bay, crows were fluttering across the meadows and the tang of wet cedars welled up from the copses. A chilly breeze was blowing in from the marshes of the Chesapeake and the scarecrow in the rye-field was fluttering his arms. It was nearly five o'clock when she arrived at Cleophas's house. A fire was burning in the fire-place and the room was unusually warm. Cleophas, stripped to the waist, was sitting on the bed playing the banjo. Sweat was trickling down his neck, in which an artery was throbbing. She could smell the powerful musk from his shaggy dark skin.

"You look mischievous when you play," she said.

"I'm feeling mischievous," said Cleophas.

"You're never mischievous," said Augusta. "You're gentle and calm and thoroughly sensible. And still, seeing you sitting there, there's something mischievous in your face. Have you ever," she said softly, "done anything wicked?"

"Being wicked," said Cleophas, "is just a way of being sad.

I'm never sad, don't ask me why. I done plenty of hard, mean things in my life but I never felt wicked. To be wicked you got to brood about it. Whatever I done, I never brooded about it."

He took hold of her arm and drew her down on the bed beside him. She felt the slow, sly, delicate insinuation of his hand and the warm, stealthy prowling of his fingers across her body. She felt the thrust and the urgency, she felt the pang and the twist of the orgasm, and as always there was the desolation and the self-disgust afterwards.

"Odd, isn't it?" she said, breaking the silence of their listlessness. "It's so clumsy and ridiculous, all this business of copulation. It's an absurdity of nature that something so ugly should be so important, isn't it, and that life should originate in something so dirty and degrading, and that love should find its joy in the ugliest parts of the body."

"Are they the ugliest? You're sure?" said Cleophas, grinning.

"What looks beautiful," said Augusta, "is often just a part of something ugly."

"No," said Cleophas. "What looks ugly is just a part of something beautiful."

"Very well, then," said Augusta. "They're both the same. The ugly and the beautiful."

V

"And what's bad," said Cleophas, "is often a part of something good. Something terrible happens, or what looks like it was terrible, and then we see that something good finally came of it. And often what looks like something good turns out to be vicious in the end. The viciousness brings suffering and the suffering brings gentleness, and the goodness brings blindness and the blindness brings cruelty."

"But you can't deny," said Augusta angrily, "that there's wickedness and goodness. Some things are wicked and some are good and there's no use denying it!"

"Do you think what we done here between us is wicked?"

"I'm not sure," said Augusta. "Maybe it's good and maybe it's wicked. It's natural, that is obvious, but I don't quite share your conviction that everything that is natural is inevitably for the best. Is envy natural? Is hatred natural? Is wanting to hurt people natural? I'm afraid they are. But they aren't for the best, they are foul and disgusting."

They were lying on the bed with the firelight shining on their bodies. Through the window she could see the trees gleaming in the sunset. The logs crackled lazily and the flames danced uneasily; she could see the leap of the flames reflected in Cleophas's eyes.

"Life," said Cleophas, "ain't just a neat little split into good and evil. The very people that are the best often cause the biggest misery, and the ones that are the worst sometimes cause something good to happen. It's as though what is good is merely another part of evil. They're like Siamese twins. The one grows out of the other. And that's the way that nature seems to have wanted it, somehow."

"Tell me," said Augusta, pressing her hands into a tapering pyramid. "I have a very strange feeling. There's something you haven't told me."

"There's something in everybody," said Cleophas placidly, "that they never talk about."

"Something special," said Augusta. "I sense it in the way you're looking at me."

Cleophas lifted his head and peered down at her lazily.

"I killed a man. Is that what you sensed?"

"Yes," said Augusta. "That's what I thought it was."

"It all happened in a kind of dream," said Cleophas, looking through the window. "Sometimes I think it never happened and it was all my imagining, but then I know that it really happened and it was just like anything else. Just an accident or an incident, like swatting a fly or killing a turtle. Just something casual and commonplace and I try not to brood about it."

"Who was it?" said Augusta.

"A sailor," said Cleophas.

"Why did you kill him?" said Augusta.

"It just happened," said Cleophas, shrugging. "He came wandering into the house late one evening, kind of drunk. He was lost, he was looking for something, and there was something he tried to steal from me. And so I hit him over the head and he staggered into the woods again."

"And what happened after that?"

"Nothing much. Nothing I'd know about. I didn't know that I'd killed him but they found him three days later. He was lying all bloody down in the woods by the creek."

"And that's the end of it?" said Augusta.

"That's the end, I guess you'd call it. They never learned what really happened and when they asked me I couldn't help them. I'm a quiet sort of man, I got quiet regular habits. And I took the broken bottle and I buried it in the woods."

"I see," said Augusta softly. "And don't you think it was something evil?"

"It was just an accident," grunted Cleophas. "Not good and not evil. It just happened. Maybe it was sad in bringing an end to somebody's life, but who knows, maybe in the end something good finally came of it."

"Very well, then," said Augusta. "We just do whatever we do. What happens just happens. There's no point in struggling. There's no use in trying to be wiser or nobler than beasts. Is that what you think? We're just beasts? Just a part of nature?"

"Yes," said Cleophas, "that's all we are. Just a part of a huge, black nature. Everything we do, fighting in the darkness, fighting to break away from nature, it's all just a part of the great black design. We're too small and short-lived ever to see the design, and besides, it's a design that wasn't meant just for people. People are only a tiny part of it, like the grains of dust in a desert. The design behind it all is much too big for people to grasp it."

"Fatalism," said Augusta. "Fatalism. Just surrendering to the way things happen. Maybe to you it comes naturally but to me it seems terrifying."

"There's something else," said Cleophas softly. His narrowed eyes were watching her tensely. "There's something else you ought to know. It wouldn't be right if I didn't tell you."

Augusta raised herself on her elbows and looked at him fixedly. She had never understood Cleophas. There was always something that eluded her. In his very strength and serenity there was something dusky and elusive. He was staring at her calmly with his powerful deep-set eyes and she realized that she was afraid of him, she had always been profoundly afraid of him, and this deep, festering fear was at the core of her infatuation.

"Well," said Augusta, "what is it? What do you feel you've got to tell me?"

"Listen carefully now," said Cleophas. His voice began to tremble. "It was all long ago. It began at the very beginning. I was a part of you all and still I wasn't really a part of you. I belonged to the family and still I wasn't allowed to belong to it. I was the son of your father but I wasn't allowed to share in it. It was only by luck that I finally found out about it but I knew it all along, I sensed it, I suspected it, and from the beginning I had this funny longing, I wanted desperately to be a part of you and to be accepted in the heart of the family. I used to hide in the bushes and watch you playing on the lawn. I used to follow you down the path and see you wading in the creek. Not only you but all the rest of you, Consuelo and Barbara and Daphne. I watched you all, I was just your age, maybe a year or two older, and all seven of you looked beautiful and clean and kind of magical, and I knew that I was a part of you but I wasn't allowed to share in it. I felt ugly and dirty and low-down and scoffed at. There were times when I used to sit in the dark and cry about

it. After all, I was nothing but a poor little bastard. But gradually I grew older and finally I got used to it. But I still felt this
hunger, this crazy curiosity, and I still kept wanting to be a part
of you. I felt hypnotized, almost. I used to follow you secretly
when you went out riding. I peeked through the trees while you
played on the tennis court. And finally I decided there was only
one way I'd ever be a part of you, and I thought about it and
brooded about it, and the craving grew stronger and stronger.
And that's how it happened, yes, I finally was a part of you, and
the craving I felt for you wasn't a craving for your body, it was a
craving to share in what secretly belonged to me . . ."

VI

When she arrived at the house the lights were already lit. The
light from the library windows fell sloping across the lawn, and
far beyond, over the inlet, there was a zigzag of lightning. She
could see Miss Aspinwall's silhouette against the curtains of an
upstairs window. Down in the kitchen she could see Josepha sitting motionless in front of the television.

She crossed the hall and peeped into the dining-room. It was
empty and dark. She walked quickly to the sideboard where the
decanters stood in a row, and poured herself a glass of something or other at random. She held up the glass against the window and sniffed it. Rye, apparently. She drained the glass in a
single gulp.

Then she tiptoed up the stairs and locked the door of her
bedroom and turned on the lights and started packing her bag.
When she stepped into the bathroom she happened to glance
into the mirror. She was appalled by what she saw—she looked
like a woman confronting a murderer, hair streaming, jaw sagging, eyes jutting and bloodshot.

She rushed back into the bedroom and flung her toilet things into the bag, hurled her dressing-gown on top of them and snapped down the lock. Then she picked up a pencil and scrawled hurriedly on the lavender note-paper:

"Cyrus. Forgive me, I've been horrible but there's nothing we can do about it. I'm leaving Blue Hills and I'll never be back. Have my things sent over to Bishop's Neck as soon as it's convenient. Give my love to your father and Aunt Carrie. Augusta."

VII

The first drops of rain started to fall as she entered the highway. Two minutes later the storm came galloping from the Chesapeake. All she could see in the glow of the headlights was thousands of flame-white arrows. The rush was so powerful that even the windshield-wiper was useless, swinging pointlessly to and fro through the pounding cascade. The tires kept skidding uneasily on the flooded pavement.

She drove very slowly. Finally she came to a halt. She flicked on the radio but there was only the blare of static. She lit a cigarette and leaned back in the seat and listened to the growling and bellowing of the thunder.

Sitting in the storm-enveloped car, encased in all that rush and clamor, she felt eerily at peace, impregnable, inaccessible. It was like sitting in a hut on top of a snow-swept mountain. The rest of the world dwindled away; human chaos dwindled away.

And suddenly, as she sat there, something very strange happened. She crushed her cigarette and closed her eyes for a moment. And at that moment, for a fragment of time electrically brief yet weirdly spacious, she experienced a kind of dazed transmigration, as though an alien awareness had seized her body and her own awareness had entered another body. She felt it with a vividness that was absolutely exact, absolutely convincing, but so shocking to her metabolism that it was like an onrush of delirium. She felt that someone was sitting beside her, a squaw-like woman in a dark green dress, and this woman was quietly talking to her in a low guttural voice. She was saying something about a "crisis." She kept repeating the word "crisis," and then the illusion dissolved and Augusta opened her eyes again.

The rain had lessened. She released the brakes and started to drive cautiously. A sheet of mud covered the road and the wheels kept slithering and skidding. She crossed a long cement bridge and headed for Pendleton's Landing. At the cross-road to Euphoria she caught sight of the gas-station. It was gleaming mistily through the racing downpour.

She tried to recapture the fleeting presence of the woman in green. She somehow sensed that it carried some special prophetic significance for her. But even as she tried to pin it down, to recall the details of the vision, it slid away, it dissolved into smoke; nothing was left of it, not a trace.

She stepped on the brakes. The road in front of her was blocked by a fallen tree. She started to back up the car and turn around in the opposite direction. At that moment the rain stopped falling and the landscape grew clear again, abnormally radiant in the glow of the headlamps. The trees were lacquered with an ice-white luster; the dripping boughs were like molten silver.

She noticed the lights of a diner down the road a little distance. She turned off the motor and opened the door and stepped into the darkness. The only people in the diner were a Chinese-looking waitress and an elderly couple who were sitting in a booth.

"It's awfully expensive down there, isn't it?" said the waitress, glancing at Augusta.

"Oh, there's plenty of nice reasonable places," said the husband.

"I've always thought of Miami as terribly expensive," said the waitress.

"Not if you know where to stay. There's lovely places," said the wife.

She was a gaunt, hawk-nosed woman with azalea-colored hair. She wore anchor-shaped ear-rings and a sea-blue dress patterned with convolvulus. Her husband was a famished little man with horn-rimmed glasses; he wore a mustard-colored sport-shirt and a green tweed jacket.

"What'll you have, ma'am?" said the waitress, looming drowsily over Augusta.

"A cup of coffee, please," said Augusta.

"Black or white?"

"I beg your pardon?"

"Cream in your coffee?"

"Black," said Augusta.

"Nasty storm," said the man.

"Equinoxious," said the woman knowingly.

"That's the reason we're heading for Florida. Life's too short to be suffering from the weather. I get aches when there's a storm. I'm growing old, Lola keeps telling me. Yep," said the man, removing his spectacles and wiping them carefully, "I'm going to stop all this worrying about money. I'm going to stop this worrying about the kids. I'm going to sit in the sun with Lola and enjoy what time there's left for us."

"Very sensible," said the waitress pleasantly.

"Yes, isn't it?" said the woman.

"Life's too short," repeated her husband.

"One ought to relax, don't you think?" said the woman.

Augusta rose, paid for coffee and stepped into the night again. The stars were already out, a fragrant briskness filled the atmosphere. She got into the car and started the motor and drove back to the gas-station, where a narrow dirt road branched off in a short-cut to Frenchman's Creek. There was a boy in the gas-station, sitting at a table and reading a newspaper. The rhythm of a Malagueña came rippling over the radio. She thought of stopping for gas but then she glanced at her watch and turned into the dark woody road to Frenchman's Creek.

"Two more miles," she thought vaguely. "Ten more minutes. Or maybe less." The tires gurgled gently as they passed through a puddle. There was a clattering of planks as she crossed the wooden bridge and then she shifted into second and started uphill.

Halfway up the car skidded and squirmed clumsily across the road. She stepped on the brakes. The car sank and slipped backwards a little. She shifted into low and stepped cautiously on the accelerator. There was a sizzle of spinning wheels and a rattling of mud-soaked gravel. She threw the gears into reverse and tried to back on to the road again. The car refused to budge. It was trapped in a bowl of mud.

She got out, locked the doors and started climbing through the woodlands. The road was a quagmire: the mud rose over her ankles. Once she slipped and fell on to her knees and her hands dug into the slime. But she hardly even noticed it and rose to her feet mechanically and went plodding along until she reached the top of the hill.

Immediately below her, on the left, lay the rambling pattern of Bishop's Neck. A single small light was shining in one of the windows. The wet transparency of the atmosphere made it look very close. Way beyond, on the edge of the bay, the lights of Euphoria were sparkling. She started downhill. The trees rose all around her, hiding the view of Bishop's Neck and blotting the lights of Euphoria. The wood was full of noises, tiny rustlings and drippings. Broken twigs and dislodged pebbles lay scattered across the road. And over it all hung this aura of delicate peace after upheaval, of old things dismembered and new things waiting to rise again.

Her shoes were heavy with mud; she kept slipping and stumbling. She walked down the hill with the dazed obliviousness of a sleep-walker. The road dipped into a hollow and twisted through a copse. Suddenly she found herself standing at the white-washed gateway.

Here also the storm had created a shimmering, disheveled novelty. The flower-beds were a chaos of clay and torn-up roots. A broken bough was dangling from the side of one of the chestnut trees and over the lawn hung a luminous aromatic sweetness, as though the stars were only a reflection of the dappled glitter that covered the earth.

She crossed the veranda and looked in through the library window, which was the only window in the house that was lit. At first she saw no one. The room was deserted. Then she noticed something lying on the floor in front of the fireplace. It looked like a bundle of clothes, all rumpled and shapeless. Then she realized that it was a body; the body of a woman. She rapped sharply against the pane. But the body didn't stir. She screamed: "Grace! Gracie darling!" But still it didn't stir. She lunged violently against the window and dug her elbow through the pane. There was a crackle of broken glass; the warmth of the room swept through the window.

Grace rose from the floor and looked around in a daze. Then she walked toward the window and peered out at Augusta. Her face grew bright with joy. She smiled lovingly and knowingly.

"Yes, it's you, that's who I thought it was," she murmured, blinking her eyes a little. "Oh, I knew you'd be coming, I was positive you'd be coming, but I didn't know you'd be coming quite so soon, Augusta darling . . ."

VIII

It was a brisk cloudy evening, a few last leaves still hung from the trees and a powerful spice filled the air, a whiff of maple and laurel. The road to Pendleton's Landing was covered with rain-soaked leaves. Through the coal-black lace of the branches the evening sun shone like a forest fire.

Daphne put down her suitcase and paused in front of the Bachelor's Button, which was a gray wooden structure at the end of the highway. Her face was tired and sunken. Her cheeks shone with sweat. She opened her handbag and took out a handkerchief, paused and glanced into the bar, then slipped the handkerchief back in the handbag. Then she picked up her suitcase and stepped into the bar.

The room was empty except for a baldish little man behind the bar who kept reading his newspaper without looking up. A jungle-like wail poured out of the juke-box. There was a smell of stale-beer tinged with the whiff of cigar-smoke.

She left her suitcase by the door and walked up to the bar. The man peered over his glasses. He was a man in his fifties, ashen-faced, German looking, with an unhealthy flush in his eyeballs.

"Evening ma'am."

"I'd like a beer, please."

The man reached under the bar and opened the ice-box and took out a bottle.

"Beautiful weather. Indian Summer."

"Yes, it's warm for October, isn't it?"

"Travelling, ma'am?"

"I'm down from Washington. Yes, travelling, I guess you'd call it."

The barman planted his elbow on the streaky mahogany. He puffed at his cigar, flicked a fly from his hairy wrist, then looked at Daphne with a veiled suspicion mildly mingled with melancholy.

"It's kind of late for Pendleton's Landing. Most of the folks have gone home. A couple of cottages still occupied. It's been a lousy season." He lowered his voice. "Rain, rain. And now it's fine and the place is empty." He belched, pursed his lips and thoughtfully lit her cigarette for her. "Well anyway, everything's changed. There's a new kind of people. A Japanese man and his wife down at the end of Royce's Road and a couple of artists took the McIlhenny cottage. It's been quiet, not much doing, not much money floating around, queers mostly from Baltimore, you wouldn't think they'd see much point here, and then rain, all that rain, a bit of rain brings people in but not that lousy perpetual drizzle, day after day of it, like down in the Solomons."

"You've been in the Solomons, Mr. Schultz?"

"Yes, in the war, Guadalcanal, ma'am. That's down in the Solomons. Seems pretty long ago now." He stared at her face with sudden interest. "How did you know I'm Mr. Schultz?"

"It just happened to come back to me," said Daphne with a far-off look. She pushed two coins across the bar and picked up her suitcase.

The road went twisting along the bay for a quarter of a mile. At that point, near an empty barn, a small dirt road turned off to the left and curved through the woods toward Frenchman's Creek. A stealthy whispering filled the woods, the leaves kept rustling under her feet. The road dipped over a stream and then gradually climbed up again and there was something haunted and half-recognized in the atmosphere, not so much in the look of the place but in the smell of it, the sound of it, the cracklings in the stillness and the hint of things in the shadows.

At one place in the woods the road passed through a kind of tunnel, where the rhododendron was so thick that the sky was completely hidden. The ruts of the road were all furry with grass and her feet kept sinking into the oozy black earth.

She came to the gateway at last. Vines had climbed over the broken sycamore. The hedge along the driveway was shaggy and unkempt. The paths were thick with weeds, the panes of the greenhouse were broken and the plants inside were all ragged and scrawny. A broken bough hung trailing from the side of the chestnut tree. Down by the shore at the end of the lawn the wooden pier was floating sideways, half under water and covered with slime.

She climbed the steps and crossed the porch. The shutters of the drawing room were locked but as she reached to ring the bell a light went on in the library window. She put down her suitcase. A throttling feeling rose in her throat, a rush of guilt and alarm but at the same time a pang of joy so violent that she leaned against the wall and covered her eyes.

When she looked up again she saw that the door had opened. A tall dark woman was standing in the doorway. Her face was hidden in the gloom but her eyes pierced the shadows. She stared at Daphne without moving and finally she whispered: "There. At last . . ."

IX

"You look exhausted," said Augusta. "Give me your hat. You'd like a drink, I guess?"

Daphne shook her head vaguely. "Just let me sit for a while, that's all."

Augusta sat down opposite her in the big red chair with the sphinx's claws. She was wearing a woollen dress, very plain and dark green, and a broad black belt with a silver buckle around the waist. She wore her hair drawn back tightly from her looming white face and bound in a great swirling knot on top of her head.

"What made you finally come back?"

"Loneliness," said Daphne, blinking her eyes.

"Funny reason," said Augusta bitterly. "There's plenty of loneliness right here. If it's loneliness you're trying to get away from you shouldn't have come to Bishop's Neck."

"I just had to," said Daphne. She lowered her head and stared at the pillow, where a feather was peeping through one of the seams. "One gets frightened of cities. There's a nasty smell in all those cities."

"Which cities?"

"Oh, Cleveland," said Daphne rapidly, "and Boston and Baltimore. I tried them all. I was a waitress in Cleveland, I sold gloves in Baltimore and records in Boston."

"Sounds grim," said Augusta.

"It's so ugly, being poor," said Daphne. She raised her head with an earnest look. "I ate in the cafeterias and the automats. I was terribly poor. I really was."

Augusta got up and walked slowly across the room. Her outstretched hand came to rest on the little bronze Buddha.

"What made you run away, Daphne?"

"Oh, Lord, I can hardly remember. I was miserable," said Daphne. "But it's all so long ago, I can hardly remember. I thought that nobody loved me. You got married, Augusta, and you were the one that I needed, it's a fact and you know it. And then Elizabeth suddenly dying and Barbara being so mean to me, and then on top of it all . . ."

"Yes?" said Augusta, standing motionless.

"Well, anyway," said Daphne, "it all sounds childish I suppose but I had to go and find myself, to burst out of my shell . . ."

"And did you?" said Augusta, glowering.

"Oh, I did all right," said Daphne. "I lived in Florida on a strange little island and then way up in Maine, not far from Ogunquit . . ."

"You got around," said Augusta tensely.

"Yes," said Daphne, "I really did."

She looked up at Augusta. Some of the fear still was in her but when she saw Augusta's face she was filled with a wave of pity, a pity that was discreet and yet at the same time warm and penetrating. A great change had come over Augusta. The glow from the lamp shone on her face, brightening her neck and her cheekbones, hiding the look in her eyes. There were bags under her eyes and cracks in her cheeks. The hair on her temples was turning gray. But even so, even in the darkness that shrouded her eyes Daphne could see the delicate alertness, the reaching out in Augusta's eyes, the look of things explored and of things painfully abandoned.

"I suppose you realize," said Augusta, "what a terrible thing you did?"

"Was it terrible?" said Daphne pleadingly. "Tell me the truth. Did any of you miss me?"

"That isn't the point," said Augusta. "Maybe we did and maybe we didn't, but that isn't the point. You violated a pact."

"A pact? Was there a pact?"

"There was," said Augusta quietly. She walked back from the table and stood motionless in front of Daphne. "Whatever the reasons or the justifications, and don't think that I'm not aware of them, the fact remains that you deserted us. We treated you badly but, still, you deserted us."

"Out of misery," said Daphne.

"Out of weakness," said Augusta.

"You're wrong, you're wrong," cried Daphne, grasping the arms of her chair. "You're the only one that could help me, you're the one that I needed, you knew it, Augusta, and still you went and got married!"

"I never deserted you," said Augusta softly, placing a finger on her chin. "Maybe you thought so, you were always so panicky. But it wasn't so."

The light shone on the faded red damask on the walls, but it was a deteriorated light, nothing emerged very clearly. Even the fluted bronze inkwell and the star-shaped paperweight looked faded, as though the passage of time had involved a loss of distinctness, and even in Augusta there was something blurred, as though the intensity had drifted inward so that only a gleam of it was left, like the reflection in a well.

"And now?" said Augusta.

"May I stay a while?" said Daphne.

"All those years," moaned Augusta. "All those years, those wasted years!"

And suddenly she started to cry, great hot tears flowed down her cheeks, her head fell over her breast and her body kept shaking. She looked old and very worn. Her powerful body looked soft and sagging.

Daphne sat with folded hands. Then she rose to her feet and put her arms around Augusta and kissed her on the neck.

"There," she said. "I know, darling. I know. Don't think that I don't."

The two women stood silently, clutching each other in their arms. Finally Augusta said hoarsely: "Time, Daphne. Time and patience."

x

At that moment she heard the delicate rippling of the piano in the drawing-room. Augusta took her face between her hands and stared at her with a piercing scrutiny. Then she drew away brusquely, strode to the sideboard and poured a glass of sherry.

She handed the glass to Daphne. "Go," she whispered, "go and talk to her."

Daphne stepped across the hall and opened the door to the drawing-room. The dusty light from the chandelier fell over the big rose-patterned carpet. Shadows danced on the walls as the pendants swayed in the draught. Grace was sitting at the piano, dressed in a pale blue smock. She was playing a barcarolle. She glanced casually at Daphne and smilingly turned the page of the album.

Daphne stood by the door while Grace kept on playing. A

speckled haze seeped through the mass of honeysuckle that covered the two windows. The great room, except for Grace's presence, looked as though it hadn't been touched for months. A layer of dust covered the marble table-top and the two Chinese vases.

Grace finished her piece, clapped the album shut and whirled around on the stool.

"It's getting cool, isn't it?" she cried in a wispy voice. "Winter's coming!"

"That was lovely," said Daphne. "Go on, darling. Keep playing."

"My," said Grace, suddenly grave. "Let's take a look at you. You've grown!"

She got up from the stool and skipped sideways toward Daphne, placed her hands on her shoulders and stared up at her questioningly.

She looked smaller than ever, like a midget almost, with her large brooding head with its enormous brown eyes set on a shrunken little neck, like a flower too heavy for its stem. Her twitching body swayed uneasily, he hands fluttered quaintly and her glossy hair, cut in bangs, danced up and down like a rooster's feathers.

"Oh, it's nice that you're back!" She squeezed her hands together. "Just yesterday I was thinking to myself, Daphne's coming, and sure enough!"

"Honestly, Grace, you play beautifully, I'm amazed," said Daphne.

"I can't get over it, you've grown so, you're a whole head taller than I!"

Daphne glanced around the room. "Is everything all right? How's Miss Malachi?"

Grace smiled rather furtively. "She's wandered away. Into Glory . . ."

"Oh," said Daphne, nodding rapidly. "Yes. I see. How terribly sad."

"It wasn't sad," said Grace, startled. Her eyes shone. "Tell me, Daphne."

"Yes?"

"Did you find what you were looking for?"

Daphne ran her hand over the coal-black head very gently, then sank to her knees and folded her arms around Grace. "Grace, child, I'm so happy. Just to see you again, that's all." She looked up and said softly, "What's your secret, Grace, honey?"

"I don't have a secret," said Grace touchily.

"You look so peaceful, so terribly calm."

"I've stopped worrying, that's all," said Grace. She dropped to the floor beside Daphne and leaned her head against her shoulder. "Do you remember how we used to sit like this out in the yard and watch the grasshoppers?"

"Yes," said Daphne.

"Lord," said Grace, "I used to be scared of the dark, do you remember?"

"Yes, I do."

"And those nightmares!"

"Yes," said Daphne, "I remember."

"I'm not scared of the dark or of dreams any more," said Grace. "There's nothing scary about the truth, and the dark and the dreams are a part of the truth."

Daphne stroked Grace's shiny black head and said nothing.

A gust of wind shot through the door. The crystal pendants started to tinkle and Grace laid her head in Daphne's lap with a happy smile.

XI

Things were different in Bishop's Neck with Augusta and Daphne home again. Breakfast came at regular hours, there were muffins for lunch, the cobwebs were whisked away and the *Ladies' Home Journal* came to the house. Augusta drove up to Belleville for a bridge game every Thursday and Daphne brought home a baby spaniel from Euphoria.

Occasionally Mrs. Bontecue said to Grace: "You look pale, child, do be careful now," and once or twice Daphne looked at her with a kind of dazzled incredulity.

But life went on placidly except for her gathering "awareness." She felt things and knew things that she herself had never experienced, and she felt them no longer in terms of phantoms or premonitions but on a subtler, more internal, more enveloping level. And she finally grasped the fact that she had become one of the Others. She had turned into her father, into Elizabeth, into Miss Malachi. She had turned into Jasper and Pompey and Mrs. Pope. They lived on within her, she had welcomed them back and their obsessions fluttered home to her like pigeons at dusk. It was restful to have Augusta and Daphne back home again but she knew deep inside that both Augusta and Daphne were illusions, they were merely the casual encroachments from an undeveloped sphere and the ones who had really come home again were neither Augusta nor Daphne but those fleeting intuitions that came in the summer-house at twilight.

One day Augusta said to her: "Come, Grace, now tell me the truth about it."

Grace murmured: "About what, dear?"

"Do I need to be specific? Listen, Grace, and try to be sensible. We all have our problems, there is nothing to be ashamed of and God knows there are plenty of skeletons in the family closet, but I think the time is coming when we really ought to do something."

Grace blushed. "What do you mean?"

"Call a doctor. That's what I mean."

Grace stared into the garden. It was May, the bees were buzzing and the Gloires de Dijon were out in their splendor.

She folded her hands and said quietly: "It's too early for the doctor, Augusta."

Augusta looked aghast. "Don't tell me that you're dreaming of . . ."

"It has nothing to do with dreams," said Grace with finality.

"I'll phone Doctor McClintock, shall I?"

"You'll do nothing of the sort," said Grace. She rose and kissed Augusta gently on the forehead. Then she crossed the veranda and stepped into the garden.

It was on the eleventh of June that the moment arrived. Augusta was in Belleville for her usual Thursday duplicate and Daphne had gone to Euphoria to see Miss Applebee's lantern slides. It was violently hot. Grace sat out on the veranda for a while. A spicy flavor, like curry powder, came drifting across the lawn.

Finally she got up from the rocking chair, plucked absently at one of the geraniums, entered the door and locked it behind her and stepped into the drawing-room. She glanced around hesitantly. Something in the room looked a little odd to her. It was as though some piece of furniture had been stealthily shifted.

She sat down at the piano in the fading light and started to play. It was *The Maiden and the Nightingale* from the *Goyescas* by Granados. She played it very softly and a bit more slowly than usual. And as she played the lingering stillness in the rest of the room seemed to materialize, to prick up its ears, to be listening among the shadows.

The notes died away. She sat in the dark, tense, motionless. All was still, the breath of the night flowed through the curtains like steam. Her head started to nod. She was feeling very drowsy. She closed her eyes for a moment and then rose from the stool and walked cautiously toward the window. It was dark. The sky had turned from a ruddy copper to a powerful blue—a blue so engulfing that it seemed that the Chesapeake had flooded the garden.

She closed the window, turned out the lights and crossed the hall into the library. The glowing pyramid of a lamplight floated above the writing table. The fluted inkwell and the marble dolphin shone brightly among the litter of papers. They had the air of kindly Penates guarding the peacefulness of the household. She paused by the chair and gave a flick to the terrestrial globe. The continents whirled noiselessly, then gradually slowed down again. She pressed her thumb to the globe. It was a game she had often played—where in the world had she landed? Barcelona? Or the Gobi desert? She leaned over: she was in the middle of the Atlantic: Tristan da Cunha.

She sat down on the leather couch and stared into space. She grew aware of an unusual density, a thickening oppression in the room. She leaned back with a little cry. There was a thrust of pain in her abdomen. She reached for the agate box, took out a cigarette and lit it.

All was still. Not a murmur. The grandfather clock had stopped ticking. The heat gradually thickened, it seemed to congeal into a brownish gelatin. She heard a very faint rustling, a delicate staccato among the vines. She closed her eyes: she wasn't sure whether it was the pattering of raindrops or some rythmical clicking deep in her body.

When she opened her eyes she saw with a shock that the lights were out. The blackness was so intense that it was like a new, throttling presence. Only the cigarette in her hand was glowing very faintly. She sat without moving. The pattering of raindrops had stopped.

Gradually the objects in the room took on their familiar shape again. The suggestion of a halo clung to the shiny brown globe and the pendulum in the clock glimmered faintly, like an eye.

At that moment the doorbell rang. It was like a scream from another world. Just a single high peel and then a deep, breathless stillness. She waited a minute. Then she crushed her cigarette, groped her way through the room and stepped out into the hallway.

Framed in the pane of the big front door she saw the silhouette of a man. It was blurred in the feeble light: the powerful shoulders were hunched like a monkey's. She put her hand on the bannisters. It was slippery with moisture.

"There. I'll have to be brave," she whispered. "I mustn't be frightened."

She crossed the hall, turned the key and quietly opened the door. There was no one, of course. The veranda was empty.

She nodded. "That's right. Just who I thought it was, I guess."

A half-moon had risen. The heat had lessened a little. The lawn lay smooth as a pond, everything looked peaceful and familiar. Her eyes were used to the dark and she could see the markings on the sun-dial and one of the mallets tossed carelessly across the lily-bed.

She limped down the driveway till she came to the gate. She paused, turned her head and looked back at the house. Then she opened the gate, feeling the wetness of the latch in her palm, and crossed the narrow road into the clover-smelling meadow. Her skirt grew drenched as she walked through the weeds. She could see every leaf and every wrinkle in the treetrunks. The woods grew gradually denser; once her heel caught on a log, so she slipped off her shoes and threw them casually into the underbrush. Once she halted. There was a sound like a mocking-bird calling. But then she realized that it wasn't a mocking-bird, it couldn't be a mocking-bird.

Finally she came to the Eagle's Rock. She hadn't been here for months. She was startled by the way the place was tangled and overgrown. But she still remembered the path, she remembered every cranny and soon she was crouching at the mouth of the Cave.

Part Nine

I

Dimitri rented a cottage for the winter on the Coast of the Sun. Two checks had arrived from Paris, one from Krauss and one from Giorgiu, and Consuelo's own little monthly allowance had also arrived, and once a week they could afford the little inn at Cascais, where they had a fried sole with almonds and the cold white wine from the hills.

Dimitri had become very solemn about his diary. It took on the air of a "spiritual and intellectual autobiography" and sometimes Consuelo woke up to a blaze of light in the middle of the night and saw him scribbling down some *aperçu* that had come to him in the darkness. She took up tempera again, remembering Miss Malachi's admonitions, and she sat on the fishermen's beach and painted the rows of old fishing boats with their mango-colored sails and toucan-eyed prows.

At night they'd go strolling down to the fish-auction in the market-place and there under the arc-light lay the fish all spread on the marble, the long silver fish that were shaped like stilettos, heaps of mackerel and slate-blue sole, gleaming swarms of sardines, red-finned fish ringed with diamonds and the slimy eels that lashed their powerful tails at them. The idiot boy Tão would run in and out of the stalls, scooping the fish out of their bowls and laying them out in tidy rows, and the fishing girls from Peniche sat on the edge of the fountain as they waited to fill their baskets and carry them up the hill. These fishing girls stank with the smell of ripe cod but when they strode up the stairs with their baskets on their heads they moved with a stately, half-savage elegance. Their skin was a velvety gold and their calves were as thick as an athlete's, their wicked eyes and ivory teeth gleamed brightly in their Moorish faces.

She fell in love with the land. The sloping sails on the horizon, the bony pastures up in the hills and the blood-red cliffs below Marina, the odorous alleys of Queluz festooned with fresh laundry and the ramparts of Leiria still fragrant with clover, the breathless stillness of Portinho da Arrabida where the water glowed like black marble, the black bulls of Santarem and the sloe-eyed novices of Mafra, the mile-long waves that came bellowing across the bay of Capranica and the spray of the breakers down at Boca da Inferno; and then the impenetrable mournfulness of the people, their veiled tragic torpor, the whole rot of century after century imbedded in their eyes, the whine of the *fado* echoing after dusk behind the wine shops and the stealth, the appalling patience of the beggars on the shore, the pariah dogs gnawing at a corpse on the crags of Guincho, the crazy old women howling in the graveyard at Alcobaça; all this began to blend into a deepening solicitude, as though the land were mutely expressing some desperate need for her love of it.

There was a lame old fisherman who used to sit with her on the beach. They called him Stinking Vasco. He walked barefooted, even in the wintertime, and the soles of his feet were

gnarled like an elephant's. He wore a tufted maroon cap and
striped green breeches, stiff with the filth of generations and all
in tatters. He'd go roaming along the beach, singing his mournful old songs, begging for *"uma copa da vinho"* and distributing
his wisdom. After a while she grew used to his juicy sibillants
and judicious nasals, she would nod and smile vaguely as he
uttered his maxims.

"Bad winds and bad marriages," he'd say, "blow from Spain."

Or he'd say: "Good and evil follow each other like beads on
a chain!"

Or else: "A woman is like a sea-bass, she slips through your
fingers unless she's hooked."

Or else: "We don't dream dreams, senhora, it's the dreams
that dream us . . ."

And for a month or two she was happy again. She walked
with Dimitri through the pine woods, he took her hand and they
stood without a word in the spicy darkness, hearing nothing but
the whisper of the needles and the throb of the sea. They sank
down on the earth and made love as they had always done, and
she felt that the zest of their first desire had been recaptured,
though it was tinged more than ever with a hint of urgency,
of premonition. There were moments when she was shrewd
enough to discern that by converting Dimitri to serenity she
would also drain him of intensity, of the violence that festered
in his temperament, and that if their love were no longer
threatened by physical alarms it would soon be threatened by
stagnation and staleness.

II

One windy evening, as she wandered along the beach on her
way from the market, Consuelo noticed a small black bundle

in the sand. She flicked it casually with the tip of her shoe; an edge of the wrapping tore open. There was a flourish of scroll-like lettering on the sea-soaked vellum. She picked up the parcel and peeled off the covering which was in layers like the skin of an onion. What she finally held between her fingers was a sheaf of five-pound notes, still soggy with the sea and lightly peppered with grains of sand.

She glanced about quickly. She was alone on the beach. Up on the esplanade a girl in a yellow smock was rolling a hoop. She stared out over the bay as though in search of illumination. Then she walked back to the house a bit more dreamily than usual, tossed the pack on the glass-topped table and said: "A gift from the sea, my lamb."

That night they dined at the casino on lobster and champagne. They danced a waltz and a rumba. Then they strolled into the gambling rooms. The grey pongee curtains swayed limply in the sea-air and the whine of the Brazilians rose from the Pavillon d'Amour. There was a ritualistic hush hovering over the roulette tables, perforated by the drone of the croupier and the rustling of plastic chips.

Dimitri strolled to the booth and changed forty pounds. "Luck," he whispered, "is a smell that I haven't smelled for over a year." He returned with a handful of chips and elbowed his way toward the table, where he sat down between a man with pince-nez and an elderly woman with carmelian ear-rings.

For a while she watched the croupier as he spun the wheel and flicked the ball. Then she glanced around the table. Dimitri looked calm, almost phlegmatic. He was quietly fondling his chips with an absent-minded air. She circled the table until she stood directly opposite him.

The man in the pince-nez placed two hundred-escudo chips on *pair*. The woman with the ear-rings placed fifty escudos on number eleven. *"Rien ne va plus!"* The ball whirled. It bounded crisply and landed in twenty. The chips were raked in; no one had gambled on twenty. Four apple-green counters were deftly manoeuvered toward the man in the pince-nez.

"Faites vos jeux, messieurs!" said the croupier. The woman in puce placed fifty on eleven. The swarthy young man placed two hundred on *manque*. The wheel started to purr. Dimitri's eyes were beginning to brighten. *"Rien ne va plus!"* It was eleven. Four more chips to the dark young Hindu, and the croupier counted out three turrets of chips for the lady in puce.

Dimitri reached forward, his hand was trembling a little. He placed fifty escudos on *pair,* then fifty more on *passe.* The wheel spun: the ball went bobbing, then dove neatly into thirty-two. Four fifty-escudos chips went gliding over the felt toward Dimitri.

Consuelo stood motionless. The scent of jasmine rose from the table; probably from the stout little blond in black lace who sat in front of her. She felt a pleasant magnetic glow rise from the long green table, as though it were a brazier filled with gently glowing coals.

Dimitri's eyes were taking on a concentrated glitter. He seemed to be whispering to himself; his lips kept moving. He reached forward, hesitated a moment, then placed two chips on number seven.

His jaw sagged a little as he watched the wheel spinning. *"Rien ne va plus!"* The little ball circled idly, then gathered speed; it piroutted, leapt daintily, and lit with a click in number seven.

Seven thousand escudos were steered noislessly in Dimitri's direction.

The place was unnaturally silent. The gamblers leaned over the table. Their sweat-beaded faces reminded her of a séance she had visited one night on the Quai d'Orsay. Dimitri sat very still; an unusual tranquillity hung over him. He seemed unaware of anything except the scurrying caprice of the little ball. Even the chips as he stacked them casually seemed a matter of indifference. A misty smile passed over his lips, like the smile of someone dreaming.

He gambled on *noir* and won; then he gambled on *passe* and lost. He gambled on *rouge* and won, then gambled on *impasse* and lost again. Then he carefully placed two hundred escudos on twenty-five. *"Rien ne va plus, monsieur!"* There was an instant of cold suspense. The ball seemed to hesitate, it turned and leered at Dimitri like a fish-eye. Then it spun around quietly and lit in its silver cubicle.

"Vingt-cing!" cried the croupier.

Dimitri half-closed his eyes as he gathered the mountain of azure chips. He looked suddenly remote, lost in a trance, almost ecstatic, but a small slavic gleam lurked deep in his eyes, a gleam of chaos.

She made a rapid calculation. One hundred and fifty thousand escudos. He had more than tripled the value of the five pound notes she had found in the sand. Yes, she thought, in a feverish haze, it was enough for a year of happiness; it would take them to Valparaiso, it would take them to Tahiti.

The woman in puce seemed deeply interested in Dimitri all of a sudden. "Wait," she whispered. "Put it on twenty! It's time for twenty! Twenty's coming!" The young Hindu looked at Dimitri with a gleam of hatred in which there was discernible also a flicker of adoration.

Consuelo raised her fingers and tried to catch Dimitri's eyes. But he didn't see her; or refused to see her. He took a thousand escudos and placed them on red. He won. He took two thousand more and placed them on black. He won again. He took five oval counters and gambled on black. Black it was. Ten thousand more on *pair,* and then another ten on *passe.* He kept winning. He leaned back on his chair. His lips were shining.

A circle of gamblers from the neighboring tables had gathered around him. They watched him fixedly, with the cold yet intimate glitter of connoisseurs, nodding occasionally, exchanging glances, jotting down figures on scraps of paper.

"Here, try twenty again," whispered the woman beside him, white with excitement. Her ear-rings quivered like wasps, tears clung to her blackened eyelashes.

A rush of fear rose up in Consuelo. Her exultation had vanished. There was a look of sublime aloofness, like that of a *saddhu*, in Dimitri's face. He was breathing very calmly. His hands had ceased trembling. But a cramp-like sensation was spreading in her chest, so intense that she clutched at her throat to stifle a cry.

He put a thousand on seventeen. *"Vingt-sept!"* cried the croupier. He put two thousand on seven. *"Onze!"* shouted the croupier. Then he put ten thousand on *pair* followed by another ten on *passe*. He lost both times. But of course he was still ahead, very comfortably. He still was smiling with that bland Asiatic aloofness. His hands stirred vaguely in front of his face, like a somnambulist's.

He put ten thousand on red, then on black, then on red again. He lost. He tried *manque* and then *passe*. Still he lost. He glanced about placidly, got up from his chair, walked toward the money-changing booth and took a bundle of notes from his pocket. He returned with a mass of chips and sat down with a feverish expression, a glint of suppressed violence tinged with something like stealth.

He carefully, after a pause, put ten thousand escudos on number eleven. He lost. Ten thousand more, still on eleven, and then twenty: he lost them all.

"'Try seven!" said the woman in puce.

Dimitri tried number eleven again.

"Sept!" sang the croupier, with a hint of a smile.

"Oh God," cried the woman, clutching his arm. "I told you, darling! I told you!"

He kept losing and losing. "Dimitri, please," called Consuelo. But a kind of trance had taken hold of him. He was staking larger and larger sums. Once he won; it was number two. He had bet on two and on twenty. A battalion of chips paraded silently in his direction. But five minutes later he had lost it again. He was sweating very heavily.

"There, it's your last chance," pleaded the woman, "try thirteen, darling, put everything on thirteen!"

Dimitri hesitated, then carefully placed the rest of his chips, some sixty thousand escudos worth, half on *pair* and, after a moment, the rest on number nine.

"*Rien ne va plus!*" The ball skidded; it darted and bounced. Then it fell with a hiss in thirteen. He had lost absolutely everything.

A visionary smile still clung to his lips as he rose from the table. He caught sight of Consuelo. His eyes darkened slightly.

"Come," she said. "We'd better be going."

He looked at her emptily. Then he nodded and followed her down the stairway.

III

The fourth of Freya's island was a rock in the Aegean, a large central rock with a ring of smaller rocks around it. The inn was a two-story building with castiron balconies looking down on a dusty square which adjoined the harbor. There were no trees on the island, only a few whispy shrubs, and the poverty on the island was even more intense than the Sicilian poverty. But it was a clean arid poverty, free of filth and oppression, and since the island was very tiny there was no feeling of squalor. Everything was clear and exposed, naked and barren under the sunlight. The rocks were washed smooth by the waves of the Aegean and a golden-blue light played over the sea-varnished beach. Vultures circled in the distance, waiting for something to die, and as soon as something died, a dog or maybe a donkey, they swung down and whittled away the flesh from the bones, so that the skeleton lay naked and clean in the blaze of sunlight. The bandy-legged fishing boys dragged their nets out of the sea and the fish lay squirming on the rose-tinted sand, and even the boys and the fish had that sea-purged look, smooth and bare and iridescent in the light of the Cyclades. There was a sadness on the island, the gloom of barrenness and isolation, but all the same she preferred it to those other three islands, the one with the grottos and the one with the broken columns and the one with the snow-capped peaks rising in the distance.

And for three or four weeks she felt very close to happiness. There was something in the air that smelled of permanence and timelessness and the crises in the distance lost their meaning and urgency. She had dinner at dusk under the vine-covered trellis and there was a crisp, clean taste to the squib and the peppered rice, there was a spiciness in the cheese and the glow of the sun was still in the grapes and she enjoyed the faint tang of resin in the wine.

It was the plainness, the very crudity of things that made her happy. Usually the sky was completely cloudless but when the clouds did appear they were clouds without menace, white and foamy and exhilarating. They looked like great sails moving across a sunlit sea, moving on toward some far-off happiness long dreamed of or still undreamed, and even the actual sea had a muted, expectant look in the presence of that grand and floating armada.

She sensed that in this happiness there was also a certain truthfulness, and that in the very crudity of her joy she managed to see things as they were. She looked deep into the unadorned texture of natural objects; she felt at one with the sea and rocks and in harmony with the people and animals, and even after a while with the barnacles and the seaweed. Her paintings were filled with the shapes of the seaweed and barnacles, with seashells and sea-fronds and finger-like corals, but the real thing in the paintings wasn't the shapes or the chiseled symmetries but the pure prismatic glow, the aridity of the ancient sunlight.

IV

Every day Demetrios the boatman came and rowed her across the harbor to a row of barren rocks that jutted out of the water. Demetrios was blind and he had always been blind, and one day she asked Petros how a boatman could be blind.

"He listens," said Petros, who served coffee under the trellis. "He keeps listening to the water and his listening is as good as seeing. He knows the sound of the water in each separate place and he can tell just where he is from the sound of the water. And even on windless days when the water is soundless there's a feel in the water and Demetrios can always recognize the feel of it."

There was something strangely vacant and attentive in Demetrios's face. Most of the time his eyes were closed but sometimes he opened them and there was a listening look in his cloudy gray eyeballs. Soon he was able to recognize the sound of Freya's footsteps, and when he heard them he hurried down to the boat and waited for her. She could see in his smile that he was delighted whenever she came, and there was something very touching in the way he always waited for her. He was a powerful young fellow, blunt and swarthy and strong as an ox, but his blindness had preserved a childlike look on his face.

He lingered close beside her while she sat in front of her easel. Usually she disliked having an audience but with Demetrios it didn't matter; he was blind, and the sound of his voice was extremely gentle and melodious.

"Tell me," he said, in his halting English, "what you're looking at. What is it, madam?"

"Very well," said Freya, holding her brush up in front of her. "Above me is the air, which goes endlessly on and on."

"And what does the air look like?"

"There's no look to it," said Freya. "Way in the distance it seems to melt into blue if the sun is shining, but the air close around us is quite invisible, as though it didn't exist."

"What is blue, please?" said Demetrios.

"Blue is a hollow, innocent color. The sea is blue if you see it from a distance. Some flowers are blue, such as cornflowers. Some of the houses are painted blue. The little girl standing on the shore is wearing a pale blue dress."

"And what other colors are there?"

"There is green, of course," said Freya. "Green is a fresh growing color, very peaceful and reassuring. Green is a mixture of the blueness in the air and yellowness in the light, and together they make a color which is calm like blue and alive like yellow. The sea is a greenish color if you look straight down at it. Leaves are green. Grass is green but there's not much grass on this island."

"And there's red, isn't there?" said Demetrios.

"Yes, there's red, of course," said Freya, "but it's hard to describe red, it's such a restless and angry color. If you cut yourself you must visualize the color that flows out of you. That is red. The color of blood. It's the color of the poppies up on the hillside."

Demetrios smiled. "It's just as I thought. I can't see the different colors, but when I touch different things I can recognize their color just by the feel of it. We have two cats in the house, one is black and one is yellow, and I can tell which it is just by the feel of the fur."

Freya nodded. "Yes," she said, "there's more to colors than just the look of them."

"Sometimes," said Demetrios, "I can even smell them if I try hard enough. If you hold a flower in front of my nose I can tell if it's white or blue. If I smell a woman's dress I can tell if it's crimson or purple. Sometimes it's puzzling because there are several different smells blending together but black things have one smell and red things another . . ."

Once he whispered to Freya: "Do you mind if I touch you, madam?"

He leaned forward and drew his fingers across her cheek and over her eyelids, and then he stroked her hair with his palm very lightly.

"Yes, your hair is a warmish color, like the horse of Pappachristides. Your skin is very cool. Do your eyes have a color, madam?"

"They are grayish," said Freya. "Neither one thing nor another."

"And what color is your dress?"

"White," said Freya, "with yellow flowers."

"Just as I thought," said Demetrios. "Cool and warm, both together. I can feel the coolness of the white and the warmness of the yellow. Tell me, madam . . ."

"Yes?" said Freya.

"Are you beautiful?"

Freya laughed. "Not in the least."

Demetrios lowered his head. "Maybe I'm lucky that I'm blind. I can see things the way I want them. I can see you as beautiful. If I could see with my eyes it might be a terrible disappointment. Maybe everything would look much less beautiful than I think . . ."

One evening Demetrios cautiously steered the boat into a cove where the water was sheltered by an overhanging rock. The water was calm and warm in the cove and the shadow of the rock darkened the water to a greenish black.

"May I say something, madam?"

"Yes," said Freya, "of course you may."

"I have a wish, madam."

"What is the wish?"

"You'll be angry!" said Demetrios.

"No," said Freya, "I won't be angry."

"You promise?"

"Certainly," said Freya.

"It's a little wish but an earnest one."

"What is it?"

"Just once!" said Demetrios.

"Well?" said Freya.

"May I kiss you, madam?"

Freya felt troubled, disconcerted. She had already guessed what Demetrios wished. She felt touched by a compassion for Demetrios, and she even felt drawn toward Demetrios's body, which was healthy and powerful, with the blood pulsing in his temples. But she felt an alarm at what might follow from this feeling of tenderness, and she also was afraid of hurting Demetrios.

"Certainly," she said, "you may kiss me, but the kiss must be innocent!"

Demetrios nodded. "It will be innocent. It's only the longing on my lips. They only want to feel what it's like to touch your cheek, madam."

He leaned forward and placed his left hand carefully on the oarlock, craned his neck and kissed her very delicately on the cheek. Then he smiled and opened his eyes and nodded appraisingly. "Yes," he said. "It's just as I thought," and he rowed her back into the harbor.

A month went by and Freya thought, "I am happy, I am utterly happy, I keep saying to myself that I'm happy, but something is wrong. What is wrong? Underneath the happiness there's something that is missing. Is happiness just a word, a meaningless word, like all the others? Or does one look for something more as soon as one is happy? Is there something in happiness that makes it want to destroy itself? Is there something insufficient in the very nature of happiness? Something more . . . Yes, but what? To accomplish something, to believe in something, to suffer for something—is that what one looks for? Yes, there's something more that I'm looking for. Some day I'll know what it is. Some day . . . and still, this happiness is so glowing, how can I bear to give it up? How can I bear to live without it? What else can take its place?"

After a month she started to notice that not everything on the island was clean and sun-purged. There were dark little shadows; there were crannies of ugliness. One day a pregnant bitch crawled out of a cellar window and fell clumsily on the pavement, like an over-ripe egg-plant. She lay motionless in the heat, bloated and bleeding, teeth bared savagely, and then the flies started to gather and the vultures began to circle.

And one morning Freya was sitting in the little square, drinking coffee, waiting to stroll down to the water where Demetrios was waiting for her. A youth in a white embroidered shirt entered the square. He was leading an emaciated black horse by the bridle. Something terrible had happened to the horse, it thrust its head about with a look of panic and its belly was taut and weirdly distended. And as she watched a wound burst open in the horse's belly and a great bleeding cataract of intestines flowed out. The horse's hind legs gave way and it sank into the dust, panting violently. An officer stepped out of the door and, at a signal from the youth, raised his pistol and shot it twice into the horse's brain. Suddenly the churchbells started to clang in a crazy wild way and Freya rose and walked quietly down to the water.

Two days later she said to Demetrios: "I'll be leaving tomorrow."

"Why do you leave?"

"I'm going to Athens. I have some things to do in Athens."

"There is something else," said Demetrios softly.

Freya looked at Demetrios. She trailed her fingers in the sea, over which a cloud was beginning to gather.

"You are bored," said Demetrios.

"No, not bored," answered Freya.

"Angry, a little," said Demetrios.

"No," said Freya. "I am never angry."

That same night after supper she strolled down from the hotel and followed the shore along the beach to the promontory. Only a few white-washed houses lay scattered along the promontory, and one of them was the house of Demetrios, where he lived with his wife and daughters. She started to walk toward Demetrios's cottage, there was a farewell gift that she wanted to give him, but then the wind shot over the Aegean and a sudden rain raced over the water. She could see it peppering the water down below in the harbor, and then it hurried across the rocks and started to whip at her face. A patch of clear sky still hung over the island where the dome of the church rose from the top of the hill. The dome looked like a long white finger pointing toward the hole in the clouds, through which a few last stars were still shining.

She saw a dark hooded shape hurrying across the stony pasture. It halted for a moment behind a stable and then went scurrying along the beach. The rain grew more violent. A gust of spray whirled over the rocks. She felt the drops on her face and tasted the salt on her lips. A claw of wind gripped her by the shoulders and swung her around violently, so that her back was abruptly turned to the sea. A bony woman in a black knitted cloak was standing in front of her; her cloak flapped in the wind like the wings of a chicken.

A branch of lightning snapped through the sky and in the momentary brightness she saw the gleam of a long silver blade in the woman's hand.

"Who are you?" said Freya.

"I'm Demetrios's wife!" screamed the woman.

"What do you want?"

"You know what I want! Snake! Viper! You'll see what I want!"

She jumped forward and struck at Freya with a kind of fluttering clumsiness, like a buzzard delivering a blow with its beak.

Freya felt the coolness rip through her cheek, so smooth that she hardly noticed it until the blood poured over her chin and the salt of the spray started to sting.

She watched Demetrios's wife run back to the cottage through the rain and then she turned and walked to the harbor, clutching at her face with her blood-soaked hands.

V

Coils of drizzle and mist came welling in from the Lido. The beds were dank and the bars were empty and the restaurants were desolate. There were days when the Piazza was knee-deep in water and a musty smell, like mouldy shoe-leather, filled the basilica.

"A terrible city," said Mrs. Nightingale. "They talk of the blue Tiepolo skies. But here we are: I smell nothing but fish, I hear nothing but water dripping, I see nothing but dirty rainwater and wet, sour faces."

Now and then as they sat at Florian's, feeling the wind seep through the crevices, Mrs. Nightingale opened her bag and took out a travel brochure.

"I must tell you about Iviza. Iviza is very reasonable. One can live in a tiny bungalow for three dollars a day, which includes a girl to do the cooking as well as the food and the wine, nothing sumptuous I suppose but a leg of lamb or a smallish chicken and of course those marvelous ensaimadas for breakfast."

"Who told you?" said Barbara.

"A charming boy named Miguel. He was sitting at Quadri's yesterday. Not handsome exactly but poetic, imaginative. He lives in Iviza with an elderly Peruvian pianist. He makes it sound very cozy. I am dying to see Iviza."

But they lingered on at the Danieli all of January and February, in spite of the clammy dampness and the rolling mists from the lagoons. On the first of March Barbara rented an apartment in the Palazzo Betti, which faced the Grand Canal just beyond the Campo San Angelo. The living room was lined with a faded beige brocade; the dining room had a sculptured ceiling and a row of mirrored panels. In her bedroom stood a seventeenth century cabinet from Naples, with twisted pillars of tortoiseshell crowned with small golden capitals and at the end of a perspective was painted a chiaroscuro of a ruined castle, with a shipwreck among the rocks and a volcano smoking in the distance.

"It's a little larger than what we need, I should think," said Mrs. Nightingale.

"I don't intend," retorted Barbara, "to suffer from claustrophobia."

"Have you heard from that lawyer yet?" said her mother. "What's his name—Pasquale?"

"I doubt," said Barbara snappishly, "that you need to fret about our finances."

Occasionally they spoke about the family, but with a curious, ironical aloofness.

"There is a letter from Consuelo. She's in Portugal," said Barbara casually.

"They eat nothing but fish in Portugal. I hope she is circumspect," said her mother.

"And Freya's been visiting one of those desolate Greek islands."

"Her taste for archaeology," said Mrs. Nightingale, "seems quite insatiable."

"All is calm in Blue Hills."

"The calm of a morgue," growled Mrs. Nightingale.

"And Grace seems quite contented."

"Grace's home is the Great Invisible!"

"And Peter's still in Paris. Painting busily," concluded Barbara.

"Darling Peter! Elusive Peter! Sad little Peter!" sighed Mrs. Nightingale.

March went by. They played bridge in the afternoons with the Castellotti's and at night they went to the films or to a concert at the Fenice.

"But why Venice?" said Mrs. Nightingale. "What possessed us to come to Venice?"

"All year long you've been talking of nothing but Venice," said Barbara.

"But not in the winter! Think of Fez! Think of Marrakech!" said Mrs. Nightingale.

"I don't believe that tropical food would agree with your liver," said Barbara.

But even in Venice the food seemed a little too oily, and after dinner as she sat by the fire with a glass of Strega in her hand Mrs. Nightingale said: "I really must go on a diet."

"I'll speak to Rosina," said Barbara.

"I feel unwell," said Mrs. Nightingale.

"It's the *mousse au chocolat*."

"I wish it were," said Mrs. Nightingale. "No, I'm afraid it lies deeper. It's the way the world is going. I feel lost in this world of cannibals and maniacs . . ." She fixed her heavily mascarared eyes with sudden intensity on Barbara. "Do you know what I sometimes feel? I'm being buried alive! Yes! Gasping and choking! Buried alive in this shriveling body! When people talk about growing old, the calm and the poise and the resignation —well, I laugh! I just laugh! I could laugh till my heart splits open!"

VI

April came, the weather grew balmy, the café tables were set in the piazza. Charming excursion trips were arranged; picnics on the Brenta, dinners in Torcello. The floating blueness of the Venetian sky shone through curly white clouds. Fragments of gold danced in the sunlight—gilded lions on gilded flag poles, gilded saints with gilded dragons, flakes of gold embedded in glass, the dazzle of gold in the great mosaics. The magenta-striped awnings swayed in the brackish breezes and a faint whiff of honeysuckle was wafted from the Lido. The leaden gloom of the Adriatic winter changed overnight into a wine-colored, pirouetting gayety.

But oddly enough, instead of relief after the weeks of miserable weather, Barbara felt an accelerating restlessness which bordered on panic. The persecution mania which had always nestled in the depths of her character began to feed and fatten like an enormous tapeworm. Her memories of Rome grew tainted with ugly suspicions. Everything associated with Rome took on a sinister ambiguity. She detected a hidden malice in the letters from Aunt Gina. Even in the most haphazard episodes, such as the loss of her cigarette case, she saw the manipulations of an all-seeing enemy. And even Orazio himself, who grew increasingly vivid in her mind, seemed to be peering from the beyond with a mixture of pity and reproachfulness.

And as for Sandro, his very image was touched with something diabolical. She kept a few little notes from him tucked in her bag and whenever she looked at his handwriting she started to shake like a cripple. Sometimes she had to stretch every nerve not to cry hysterically and then she knew with a sickening hopelessness that she had never stopped loving him. It was only that this love, once so fleshly and irresponsible, had gradually developed a hideous deformity and was linked in her mind with a series of obsessive photographs, some of them exquisite, some of them vicious, all of them tinged with the hues of nightmare.

She took to wandering about in the twisted byways of the city. An hour or two in the morning, including a coffee at Florian's, and another hour in the evening after the bridge game at the Castellotti's. She stepped into secluded, ill-lit churches where a Tintoretto might be lurking; she roamed through half-hidden *campi* where swarthy beauties peeped through the blinds.

These aimless strolls had a reassuring effect on her nerves. The endless current of anonymous faces acted as a kind of narcotic. No one knew her; no one cared about her; no one was waiting for her; no one was watching her. Her mind grew pleasantly drugged. The images of Rome gradually receded. The glitter of dark brown eyes and the hum of laughing voices flowed over her nerves in a cool, caressive rhythm. Sometimes she stopped in the Campo San Luca for an iced *negrone* but after five or ten minutes a beckoning restlessness took hold of her again and she hurried off into the warm whispering whirlpool.

Certain faces grew familiar after a fortnight or two. There was the girl who sold fruits in a little alcove off the Merceria. The violet scars of a burn covered the whole left side of her face; on the right she had a virginal Botticelli-like loveliness. There was a boy in his teens who worked the machine in one of the espresso bars: a titian-haired lad with eyes of a cat-like emerald who blushed and lowered his gaze whenever she entered the café.

There were days when the world seemed perfectly normal again, when the weight of obsession lifted and the streets looked calm and impersonal. But then suddenly, at the sound of a voice at the hairdressers perhaps, the calm would crumble and a sickening flutter would start in her heart again and the terrors would seethe like a swarm of hornets.

At these moments she felt a choking and uncontrollable need, like the need of a man dying of thirst in a desert. A need for freshness, for movement, for ablution and transparency; something to purge the rotten tissues of old emotions out of her soul. She felt a swelling in her brain like a pus-filled bubo: an accumulation of waste and refuse, festering grievances and guilts, lost desires, stale ambitions, lingering jealousies and dark remorses, all needing to be flushed away into oblivion.

One warm evening she went for her stroll a little later than usual. She was intending to buy some stockings as well as a bottle of French perfume. She took her usual way toward the Piazza and entered the long colonnade, where the light brightened the flagstones in great golden scallops. She bought the Paris *Herald-Tribune,* sat down in front of Lavena's, ordered a double Scotch and soda and looked idly across the Piazza. The campanile was still wearing a fire-tinted cap but the rest of the buildings were sinking into shadow. A group of Germans sauntered past with their cameras dangling. Two tweedy spinsters sat down at the neighboring table and ordered tonic water. She had a lurking impression that she had seen them before. One of them looked at her with a sloping, rather militant air, then turned and spoke softly to her spectacled companion.

Barbara rose and walked aimlessly back to the arcade. She turned at Quadri's, went through an archway and paused on the bridge. The black prow of a gondola came gliding around the corner. The gondolier looked up and grinned at her slyly. He was an ape-faced fellow in a blue-striped jersey. The passenger was a man in a dove-gray coat and a blue beret. His eyes were fixed on a balcony directly above the bridge but as he passed he turned his head and shot an electrical look at Barbara.

She stood motionless for several minutes after the gondola had vanished. The water lapped at the reddish walls. It caught the glow of a blazing shop-window. A thin trail of cloud slid through the crevice overhead. She ran her finger along her throat, glanced listlessly back at the archway, then walked down the steps and entered the maze of darkening alleyways.

VII

She kept walking. Night fell. The lights were lit in the narrow shops. She followed *calle* after *calle,* vaguely looking for the Piazza but then forgetting about the Piazza, forgetting about the stockings, forgetting about the perfume. She heard the whistle of a vaporetto, which was followed by a tolling of bells; she heard the fluttering of pigeons, or what sounded like pigeons. But every time she turned the corner it wasn't the Piazza after all, it was the same monotonous vista of dingy walls and dim-lit windows. Identical façades loomed in front of her. She crossed bridges she had crossed ten minutes earlier. She saw the same loaves of bread and crystal bowls in the same little shop-windows. A pair of red leather beach slippers dangled in front of her; the brooding eyes of a soprano stared from a row of record albums. An old cripple was selling pencils in front of a dry-cleaning establishment and the smell of steam drifted through the doorway, stale and repulsive.

She grew aware of a pain in her heel. She paused for a moment in front of a butcher shop. The slabs of white-streaked flesh had a dangerously wilted appearance, as though their sickly mauve were the after-effect of a deadly poison. She hurried on. A little child called in a desperate falsetto: "Signora!" She wheeled around. But it was somebody else who was being called, apparently: a stoutish woman in a flowered dress with a Pekinese in her arms. A sulphurous odor leaked out from a public urinal. A boy scampered past, bouncing a blue rubber ball. The bells tolled again, this time directly above her. She glanced up. The stars were shining. The clock over a door said nine o'clock.

Nine o'clock. She had left the house at a quarter to six. Something was wrong. Somebody was making a ghastly blunder. Nine o'clock; and then she remembered the date at Harry's Bar at eight. The Castellotti's had asked her to dinner to meet the Viennese conductor, Herr von Waldrath. No. Ridiculous. There was no such person as Herr von Waldrath. There was nobody waiting for her at Harry's. There was nobody waiting for her anywhere. Except, of course . . . No, that too must have been an optical illusion, like everything else. She felt dizzy. She almost fell when a yellow cat darted in front of her.

She crossed the *calle* and stepped into the neon-lit bar behind the cinema. She sat down and ordered another Scotch; then she groped for her cigarettes. In the back of the room two men in open shirts were playing cards. A whiff of sweating bodies seeped through the smell of coffee and *grappa*. The barman whistled a few listless chords of *Marinaiello*. Then he ran a wet rag over the black glass bar. He was a bald little man with a lachrymose expression. Yes; definitely; he looked familiar. Somewhere or other, on a rainy night . . . Fondling the bottles on a shelf . . . No. Nonsense. Impossible.

She finished her drink and crushed the cigarette. Then she paid the waiter and hurried into the street again.

At that moment the atmosphere grew as sharp as a needle. A man was standing under a dark rectangular archway beside a church. A fleck of shadow fell over his face; he seemed to be wearing a mask. He looked at Barbara, raised his hand, glanced at his wrist-watch and nodded quickly. Someone else stepped up behind him, a tapering man in a blue beret. He gave a small gray envelope to the man with the wrist-watch, who slipped it into his pocket and vanished around the corner.

She spun about and ran into a narrow unlit alley behind the church. An acrid flavor rose in her gullet, like the taste of glue. She waited for several minutes in the shade of a doorway, then darted across the *campiello*, turned sharply to the left and found herself on the edge of a canal which was bordered by a row of square gray columns. In front of her shone the arch of a bridge, which was reflected in the unruffled water. A light went on in one of the windows overlooking the bridge. A woman stepped on the balcony and looked out into the night. She was wearing a low-cut dress of crimson silk striped with black; the light from the room beyond shone on her naked white shoulders. A man in a polka-dotted bathrobe stepped up behind her, kissed her gently on the neck and drew her back into the room. There was a sound of muffled laughter, followed by a half-hysterical squeal. The curtains were drawn abruptly; all was silent again.

A small black plummet slid through the water: a rat was crossing the canal. It sprang up on the *fondamenta* directly in front of her, glared at her viciously, and shot into a crack in the bottom of the wall.

The rush of nausea was so violent that she felt herself reeling. The feathery tickling in her stomach rose up in a sickening spasm. She sank to her knees on the clammy paving-stones and leaned over the water and spewed forth an acidulous vile-tasting paste. She watched the green row of bubbles drifting down the canal, leaving behind a wavering stench of pickled crayfish and whisky.

A feeling of lucidity gradually returned to her as she knelt there in the darkness. Yes, it all was perfectly obvious. She had made a slight blunder. Somewhere or other she had lost the way. She had taken the wrong turning. But where exactly? And when? Back at the bridge behind Quadri's? Or was it earlier than that? Was it yesterday, or maybe a week ago? Was it back in Rome, possibly, one sultry day on the Via Giulia? Or even before that? So long ago that she couldn't remember? Somewhere or other in a maze of shadows, in a twilit forest, on the edge of a bay? Yes, definitely, somewhere or other a tiny error had been made, an error so fleeting that it could never be identified but so crucial, so all-enveloping that she had never been able to find the way again. What was it? Was it predestined? Was it irrevocable? Or was there hope, still?

Someone was crossing the bridge and walking slowly in her direction. The night was clear but she had the impression of a silhouette emerging from the mist, a figure clouded in vapor and gradually materializing in the light from the street-lamp. It was a slender young man in a dark-striped suit and black suède shoes. He had blue-black hair, a little oily-looking and much too much of it. He might have been an artist, there was a suggestion of the aesthete in his long-nosed profile; but the sideburns, the leer, the strutting gait, the swaggering costume, these suggested something else, something vulgar and predatory.

He came to a halt and looked down at her with a half-teasing, half-obsequious gleam in his eyes.

"Pardon me, signora. I think you've lost something." He dangled a glove in front of her daintily, with his little finger cocked playfully in the air. It was a long black glove, rather frayed and old-fashioned looking, with a ruffle of dirty white lace along the edge.

Barbara glanced at it and shook her head. "It's not mine," she said hoarsely.

"Isn't it? Are you sure? I could have sworn I saw you drop it."

"I've never seen it before," said Barbara.

"I'm sorry," said the stranger. "Very silly of me." He looked down at her thoughtfully and was about to say something else. But then he thought better of it. He folded his arms and stood motionless. Yes. She was sure of it now. It was the man she had seen in the archway.

She said softly: "What do you want?"

The stranger smiled. "Forgive me, signora. Or shall I call you Principessa? You will probably think it unpardonably rude of me, but the fact is that I've been watching you for a considerable period. You don't remember me, do you? Perhaps, if I refresh your memory a bit . . . In Rome, in Frascati, yes, even in Paris and St. Moritz. Never mind. Mere details. Let's come to the core of the matter. You've been wondering just where you made your original *faux pas*. An idle question but a natural one. Perhaps one shouldn't use the word *faux pas*. You erred but it wasn't an error that could have been prevented or should have been prevented. It wasn't what you did. Not in the least. It wasn't even what you didn't do."

"What was it, then?" said Barbara.

"It was the worm in your heart," said the stranger.

"What do you mean?" said Barbara tensely. There was a pleading note in her voice. She was still kneeling on the pavement, with one hand resting on a flagstone and the other clutching instinctively at her handbag.

"You saw the surface, only the surface. You cared about nothing but the surface. You had the capacity for insight and that's the pity and the tragedy of it, but you insisted on surfaces, you concentrated on surfaces, you knew that the depths were there but you refused to recognize them and even when the moment of passion arrived—yes, I admit that it wasn't worthy of you, it wasn't quite up to your delicate sensibilities—but it did arrive and even then you insisted on surfaces, you rejected the depths, you rejected the humiliation and the sacrifice. And what happened?"

Barbara stared at him meekly. Her eyes were watering. "Yes? What happened?"

"You rejected the terrors of real experience. You perferred your so-called security. You preferred those other terrors, the subtler and more insidious terrors."

"Which terrors?"

"The terrors," said the stranger, "of not being what you were meant to be. The terrors of living in a perpetual self-deluding limbo. Not out of ignorance. Nor even bad luck. You were always lucky, you were always clever enough. Not out of timidity even. You were always brave in your little way. But out of vanity. Yes, out of vanity! What might have been remorse, what might have been a struggle of conscience or even a genuine searching of a soul—you finally reduced it all to petulance. *Superbia et vanitas!* What a horrible thing it is, signora, to hurl away one precious life, one's brief and irreplaceable moment of existence! And why? Out of vanity! It's an appalling thing, signora."

Barbara was beginning to shiver in the chilly dampness that rose from the water. "How," she whispered, with trembling jaws, "do you know all these things?"

"Do you remember," said the stranger, "the lost cigarette case?"

"Yes, but what . . ."

"Do you remember the shattered wine-glass?" continued the stranger.

"I don't see that there's any . . ."

"And that note you wrote to Sandro. Rather revealing, wasn't it?"

"I never sent it!" said Barbara. "I tore it up! I threw it away!"

"And do you remember that little episode of the rat-poison, by any chance?"

"Goodness! I hope you don't imagine that . . ."

"And the medicine you gave Orazio? Those greenish powders? Was *that* an accident?"

"Oh God," cried Barbara, "it *was* an accident! You know that it was an accident!"

"Nothing," said the stranger, "is an accident. There is no such thing as an accident. Everything you do, however trivial, springs from something that went before. Yes, I was watching you, signora. You almost caught me once or twice. You noticed the doorknob turning, didn't you? You noticed the silhouette in the hallway. You heard the whispering behind the leaves, you saw the footprints by the fountain."

"Who are you?" screamed Barbara.

"You know perfectly well who I am," said the stranger.

A faint fog came floating over the glassy darkness of the canal. A man was crossing the bridge very slowly and haltingly. He was followed by a thick-set woman, and then another woman and two men. They moved like somnambulists, groping their way through the thickening mist. They walked down the *fondamenta* and came to a halt beside the stranger and gazed at Barbara with a mingling of curiosity and compassion. Wisps of fog still lingered about their faces but one by one she began to recognize them. The tall, stooping gentleman was wearing a blue beret. The stoutish lady was carrying a Pekinese dog in her arms. The young woman she recognized instantly by the huge blue scar on the left of her face. Next to her stood the little espresso boy with the cat-green eyes, and at the end of the row, half-lost in the darkness, was a corpulent man with a bald white head.

"Who are these people?" said Barbara, still crouching there. "What are they doing here? What do they want of me?"

"Don't you recognize them?" said the stranger. "They're all friends. Or enemies, if you'd rather. They've been watching you, just as I have. They've been trying to help you. But you refused to be helped. Human beings, that's all they are. Nothing illustrious, nothing elegant. They loved you, some of them wisely and some of them stupidly, but in their different ways they loved you. They wanted to speak to you, to touch you. They wanted to be a part of you. But they failed, of course, poor creatures. They were doomed to failure."

The five visitors—wraiths, somnambulists, phantasmagoria, or whatever they were—turned slowly and started back on their way to the bridge. But as they turned and the yellowish radiance of the street-lamp fell on their faces, Barbara noticed something strange. Without visibly changing, without discarding their original identity, their features took on a new and half-hidden significance, like that of a palimpsest. Their faces were masks transfigured by a deeper identity. She recognized the ice-gray eyes of the elderly man in the beret and the sensual pouting mouth of the espresso boy; the desperate gayety of the fruit-girl and the lonely wistfulness of the little bartender, and even the haunted tragi-comical adventurousness of the lady with the Pekinese. It was the impression that frequently came in her dreams: of disguises half-concealing an unmistakable identity and making that identity all the more piercing and all the more passionate. They continued on their way. Their faces dipped into the shadows. She watched them wandering over the bridge and disappear in the darkness.

"Wait!" she cried. "Where are they going?"

But the stranger too had vanished.

VIII

The bells started clanging again. It was midnight. The street was deserted. She walked aimlessly toward an area of lights in the distance and suddenly found herself in the Merceria, where a few late stragglers were wandering home from the Piazza.

She felt herself walking with an almost supernatural lightness. Her feet hardly seemed to be touching the pavement. The pain in her heel had gone away and the throbbing in her eyeballs had disappeared. Everything around her had an unfamiliar brilliancy, as though seen in the blaze of a flood-light.

All of her memories were suddenly unreal, and the entire past was as though she had never experienced it. Her whole character had come to an end, a knife had cut the thread of its continuity and what was left was no longer herself, no longer an active personality, no longer a flow of hopes and feelings but just an anguish of waiting with nothing left to be waiting for, and nobody even left to feel the anguish.

A tiny black church stood at a bend in the Merceria. The door was open and she stepped through the leather-lined curtains and knelt in the semicircular chapel to the left of the altar. The smell of burning tallow hung in the cold wet gloom.

"Oh God," she whispered, clasping her hands and unclasping them again, "if you really do exist, forgive me that I was never aware of you! Forgive me that I never even tried to be aware of you! Forgive me that I never needed to be aware of you! Forgive me all this emptiness and ugliness which is overflowing in me! Help me out of this nightmare! Help me to be quiet! Help me to forget myself! Help me to make life bearable! Help me to be real! Help me to be human!"

An elderly hunchback in a pale blue cap was rolling a cart through the empty Piazza. It was beginning to rain; the huge gray stones were speckled with drops. She hurried on through the arcade toward the Napoleonic wing at the end of the Piazza. Under the columns beside the mosaic shop stood a powerfully built young man in a blue-striped jersey. He smiled at her with his monkey-like face as she passed.

"Signora!" he whispered. "Gondola, gondola, signora!"

She paused, nodded her head and followed him down to the gondola.

IX

Ever since that night at the casino a disturbing change had come over Dimitri. He had grown lethargical and listless. He stopped working on his diary. He stopped walking with her in the pine woods. He seemed lost in a perpetual day-dream.

And she too had gone through a bewildering alteration. She sometimes felt as though she were shedding her own familiar skin, the brownish, humdrum covering she had grown over the years, and were emerging into a new, half-reptilian personality. Her Baudelaire lay untouched. She had given up Camoëns. She stopped writing letters. Her box of temperas was gathering dust. She no longer sat on the beach listening to Vasco's mellow apothegms.

Instead she lay on the couch leafing through copies of *Punch* or else simply ruminating, waiting for something to happen. She went prowling in Cascais, stopping at the tavern for a glass of wine, listening to the women singing their *fados,* watching the soldiers along the quay, staring at the sails in the darkening distance, waiting and waiting, continually waiting, with no idea for what she was waiting and with no idea how long she could wait, only knowing that she would have to go on waiting a little longer.

And sometimes to her horror she suspected that her love for Dimitri was withering. Just as his own emotional needs seemed to have grown monogamous and sessile, she herself was growing tense and dissatisfied and restless. His very presence oppressed her. Even his tenderness bored her. She was irrated with his pangs of conscience, his self-probings and self-accusations. And what was more, he was growing fat. He no longer shaved regularly. He grew slovenly. His caresses grew more and more bizarre, and at the same time there were signs of gathering impotence in him.

So it was with a glow of relief, lightly shadowed with guilt, that she left the pink cottage and strolled to Cascais. She found pleasure in the silky looks that followed her in the street. She liked the purring closeness of those cat-like bodies. She felt the beckoning lustre of Fernando's flesh as he poured out the wine for her, she even relished the lewd little whisperings of the soldiers as she passed. Once or twice, as she glanced at some phallic young corporal, she thought with a little shock, "Good Lord, what is happening to me?"

The wind and the rain were over. It was May. They were penniless. She had written to Barbara; no answer had arrived yet. The only luxury still left to them was the little tours in their rusty Citroën, fleeting visits to Batalha and Mafra and Setubal.

One day they drove to Sintra. Down on the coast the sun was shining but the hills were shrouded in a thin, clinging mist. The camellias were wet with dew. The blue-tiled palace was dripping with moisture and drops fell from the cheeks of the plaster cherubs. Way in the distance they could see the waves of the sea like the scales of a monster.

They sat under a fig-tree and watched the tide of lilac shadow move slowly along the valley into the Tagus. A narrow stream of light, like a river of wine, was emptying over the beach of Estoril. But everything was seen through a film of mountain mist, all that brightness and color seemed remote and unreal.

"Strange, isn't it?" said Dimitri. "Life is short, we live only once, in fact it's a fantastic stroke of luck we were born at all. Two tiny spermatozoa surviving out of hundreds of billions, and here we are, sitting in Sintra under a fig-tree, drinking brandy. We ought to be feeling nothing but a delirium of joy and gratitude. And what happens? We brood. We see darkness all around. We luxuriate in melancholia. Ridiculous, isn't it?"

"Maybe we brood, said Consuelo, "just because we're so lucky and we know that our luck can't last forever. We're terrified of the future. We're aghast at our own gray hairs. We can't stand the thought of our luck running out on us!"

"We're afraid of dying," said Dimitri. "Is that what you mean?"

"Oh, is it?" cried Consuelo in a queer bleating voice. "Maybe it is! Maybe we're just afraid of dying, that's all! But maybe it's something else. Maybe it's something worse than dying. I can stand the thoughts of death, after all it's only a moment, it's only a cessation of things, there's nothing ugly about dying. But the rot that comes before—that's what I'm scared of, Dimitri. The waste and the blur, the emptiness, the feeling of never haveing been alive, the horrible suspicion that our lives might have been rich and full of meaning! And instead—nothing but waiting, nothing but fog and decay! Yes, Dimitri, that's what I'm scared of—not death but emptiness!"

Dimitri lifted his ox-like head and stared at her tensely. He nodded. "Yes, I know. I know what you're driving at. You feel you've wasted your life with me. We're poor and shabby and lonely. There's nothing to show for it. Yes, I know. Don't interrupt me. I know what's been happening. I've seen you sneaking down to the village and hanging around the wine-shops! I've seen you flirting with that dirty little rooster Fernando! Well, I'm sick of it, I tell you! You can go, do you hear me?" His voice rose to a howl. He banged his fist on the table. "I'm bored! I'm disgusted! I wish you'd leave me alone! That mousy little mind of yours dabbling with Schopenhauer and Hegel! And that bitchy little body looking for nothing but a fresh young penis! I'm disgusted and bored with it! You belong in a brothel!"

Consuelo sat quietly with her hands in her lap. The glasses shook on the metal table. The inn-yard was empty. There was only the cat dozing on a wine-barrel and the squeak of a cart slowly climbing the hillside.

Dimitri's eyes were fixed on space. He looked broken and old, ugly. The pouches under his eyes were blue with unhappiness. Suddenly she noticed great tears rolling down his unshaven cheeks. He reached out his hand, then clumsily fell on his knees in front of her.

"Oh God, Consuelo, my darling, forgive me for what I am! I'm a wreck! I'm a débâcle! I'm a fool and a weakling! For years I've been fooling myself into thinking that I'm a hero. I've posed as a fiery martyr, a bleeding victim, a dedicated idealist. And God knows it's all been a farce, just a bloody little farce, just a drawn-out charade to hide the miserable truth. Do you want the truth? I'm a weakling. I'm weak and I'm tired. I'm done for. All I want is to lie in your arms and forget the rest of the world . . ."

Consuelo put her hand on his enormous brown head. She drew it gently toward her and kissed him on the brow. "Get up, Dimitri. It's late," she said. Then she took his hand and whispered, "Yes, I love you. I'll always love you, there it is, it can't be helped . . ."

X

In June the monotonous south wind started to blow. The heat had a swollen, exasperating feel to it. It kept blowing and blowing; the palms rattled their branches. Little carpets of sand were flung over the esplanade. Even the light, that miraculous Portuguese transparency, was blurred with a veil of peppery dust.

The eleventh of June was Dimitri's birthday, and that same day a check arrived from Barbara. Consuelo went down to the wine-shop and bought a bottle of champagne. It was a hot, gusty day; not a cloud in the sky. The sun was still bright as they rode through the pine woods.

Toward sunset they arrived at the beach of Guincho. The sand stung their feet as they crossed the empty dunes. There was no sign of life except for the gulls that clung to the cliffs. Even the wind had suddenly died. The smell of heather filled the air. On the horizon still lingered three Nazarene fishing-boats, their yellow and black sails pinned to the water like sulphur butter-flies.

They spread their blanket over the sand and filled their glasses with champagne. They lay staring at the stars as they peeped through the dust. Night fell. The scream of the sea-gulls died over the water and the only sound left was the slow, deep rhythm of the breakers.

"It's so still, so wonderfully calm," said Dimitri, laying his head in her lap. "One would think that all's well in the loveliest of worlds, almost, wouldn't one?"

"By the way," said Consuelo. She reached into her bag. "There's a letter from Paris. It was waiting at the Atlantico."

"From Krauss, I suppose," said Dimitri.

"More than likely," said Consuelo.

Dimitri opened the letter and held it in front of him. It had grown too dark to read it; he slipped it into his pocket. Then he emptied his glass and laid his head in her lap again.

"The stars," he said. "Look at them! They're swarming like bees."

"You're full of whimsical thoughts tonight, aren't you?" said Consuelo.

She turned her head quickly. There were footsteps crossing the sand. A lean, grotesque figure came limping through the darkness. He spread his arms like a scarecrow. It was Stinking Vasco, the lame old fisherman.

"Good evening, Vasco!"

"Good evening, *senhora*. You're having a picnic?"

"Sit down, Vasco. Have some wine. Sing us a song, Vasco, why don't you?"

Vasco's features grew animated with the delight of human company. He wrinkled his nose as he emptied the glass. "Queer, this wine. It's as though the sea-sprites had gotten hold of it!"

He frowned and licked his beard. Then he crouched on the sand beside them. His yellowish eyes grew blurred with the strain of recollection. Then gradually, like a spectre afloat in the darkness, she grew aware of his thin, eerie voice beginning to sing.

"Maria da Silva
Lived in the village of Nazaré,
Her love was Duarte
The tamer of bulls.

"She stood in the darkness
And watched for Duarte
To wander on his way
From Maria da Cunha.

"His footsteps came tinkling
Like a ripple of goldpieces
As he came down the stairs
By the church of São Paolo.

"She stood by the shore,
Her knife shone like starlight
And she cried 'Ah, Duarte,
The world is too dark for us!'

"Like a snake his blood
In the surf lay writhing
And Maria da Silva
Sank to her knees.

"O Mother of God
Forgive us in blindness
Who darken with dread
The dazzle of happiness!"

"Is that all?" said Consuelo.

"Yes, that's all," muttered Vasco.

"Why did she kill him?"

"Oh," said Vasco, "it was all just a blunder. Poor Maria was wild with jealousy. She thought that Duarte had betrayed her. She was wrong. He still loved her. But she killed him in a frenzy of jealousy. And that's the sadness of the story. Not that Maria suffered or Duarte died, but that it was all just a silly misunderstanding!"

He fixed his bleak majestical gaze on her. "Blunders, just blunders. They'll bring the world to its ruin. Not human wickedness but human stupidity." He tugged at his beard. "I'm seventy-seven! You should have seen me in the old days. Big storms we used to have then, waves that towered as high as Sintra! Even the fish were bigger in the old days. Everything

was bigger and wilder. We used to go boar-hunting down in
the woods of Alentejo and up north, way up in Minho, we'd
go and kill wolves. Look at my teeth. White as a gull's! My
body's still full of fire. It's still healthy except for what a woman
did to me once in Guimaraës. She filled me with poison and it's
never left me. When I'm dead the wild grass will grow thick
over my head and people will say, 'He was a desperate old
fellow, that crazy Vasco!' "

Dimitri lay on the blanket and closed his eyes. Stinking Vasco
went limping away in the darkness. The sea had calmed down.
The only light to be seen was the beam from the lighthouse on
Cabo da Roca.

She sat quietly on the sand, watching the dance of the sea.
Then she drew off her clothes and stepped into the warm black
water.

XI

Beyond the flurry on the edge of the beach the sea was calm
and sleek. A flicker of panic shot through her as she plunged
into the water. A pang of terror it was at first, the grip of the
dark was like the fur of a beast. But then she knew it was really
joy, a great wild surging of animal joy.

Little beads of phosphorescence hung on the slow-moving
ripples. They sparkled and danced in little parabolas, like fire-
flies. Down to the right loomed the squat black igloo of Cabo da
Roca; she saw the gushing of spume where the waves fell crashing over the rocks.

She turned on her back and lay floating with the tide. The
stars looked like a shower of white-hot coals pouring through
space. But then they came to a sudden halt, they soared back

into their terrible remoteness again and the earth looked empty and forlorn, devastated. It was thrilling to go gliding like this through the furry blackness, with a million eyes watching her and the water whispering in her ear, and the things she had always been afraid of were reduced to a chimera. Nothing was real but the grip of the sea, nothing was frightening and nothing was evil, nothing could ever disturb her again, nothing human had power over her, and she experienced a sense of freedom such as never had seemed possible; a deep and exquisite harmoniousness, as though her flesh were being blended with all that uncontrollable blackness and blaze.

She felt chilly; the water had suddenly turned colder. She rolled over and started to swim back to the shore again. But the swimming grew difficult. The waves were angry and choppy. She looked up and saw that she had passed the edge of the cape. The beach of Guincho was only a pale thread of sand. She started to swim faster. But the shore kept receding. She was caught in the grip of the outgoing tide.

She felt herself carried out into the sea with an eerie swiftness. The crash of the breakers was looming on her right now. She was panting. Her arms had stiffened. She stopped struggling for several minutes and lay back in the water to catch her breath.

And strangely enough, instead of terror she felt something quite different. The water was growing warm again. She had floated beyond the current. She was out in the calm black spread of the sea. She was gathering her strength. The feeling of brittleness had left her. The sea was malleable and yielding, tender almost. She could keep on floating forever, she thought, just staring at the stars. No, not forever, she then realized. A delicate weariness crept over her flesh. It enveloped her body like fine threads of wire. Ten minutes more? Maybe twenty? Yes? And then? What would happen?

But then she knew, with a rush of joy that was like a delirium, that it didn't matter. Twenty minutes; twenty hours; twenty years. How could it matter? The only thing that could matter and the only thing that had ever mattered was this glow of joy, this passionate harmoniousness which was like an oasis in the middle of a desert; long sought for and long imagined, and now attained by a kind of miracle.

As she glanced toward the shore she saw on her left the wand of light that was probing the water from the top of Cabo da Roca. To the south rose a rat-shaped promontory; Cascais. Directly in front lay the bay of Guincho. But it was so far away now that the whiteness of the sand was as thin as a thread.

She cried softly, "Dimitri!"

It occurred to her that she had forgotten something, something urgent she wanted to say to him. Something new that she had discovered. But what it was she had completely forgotten.

She saw a light skirting the beach, then coming gradually to a halt. It turned. The glow of the headlights passed over the water. Yes, what was it she had discovered? What was it she had forgotten? The gleam of the headlights had died and only the ray from the lighthouse still fingered the sea. Then she saw, crawling like a jewel from the snout of Cascais, the glow of an ocean liner bound for America.

At that moment, bursting from the cliffs, she heard the sound of a gun. Or was it a gun? The echo lingered a while, then died.

And then a wave swept suddenly over her. A fist of water shot into her lungs. She flapped her arms and clutched at a wave and gave a thin, strangled scream. The stars whirled crazily for an instant; a fiery claw scraped at her temples; and she felt herself sinking into a bottomless stillness.

Part Ten

I

There was a man named Trombetta who was an elderly crony of Quilico's, and he had an antique shop in the forest near Fontainebleau. One evening they were having dinner on the Rue du Dragon and Trombetta suddenly said: "Why don't we try to make a fortune? We could certainly make a fortune if we all worked together. With my experience and Peter's charm and that slyness of Quilico's we could make a lot of money if we really put our minds to it!"

So Peter and Quilico moved out to the woods of Fontainebleau and started to work in the back of Trombetta's shop. At first it seemed to Peter that their work was perfectly legitimate. They worked in the studio all morning and walked in the woods in the afternoon and in the evening they played chess or cracked jokes over a glass of Kirsch. Most of the things in the shop weren't especially valuable but occasionally there was something that brought a nice profit. There were gilded wall barometers and Louis-Philippe lamps, Régence lavabos out of pewter and porcelain parrots perched on rocks. There was a Saxe porcelain ink-pot with a nosegay of flowers; there was a cut-glass sarcophagus resting on a set of bronze lion's paws. There were Faïence jardinières and apothecary jars with gilded bands and an array of old chocolate pots and barrel-shaped canteens. There were also a few paintings, maybe a Napoleonic battle scene or a group of cavaliers having a picnic beside a fountain.

Most of the things were perfectly genuine even if not of the highest quality, and it seemed only natural when Trombetta added a touch or two, boring worm holes in a chair or applying a mellowing amber lacquer. He was an expert in "restorations" and often a brand new piece of furniture, astutely treated with drills and chisels as well as acids and varnishes, and maybe reupholstered with a piece of tattered old velvet, would emerge as a convincing and highly priced antique.

Soon the shop grew more prosperous. Expensive cars drove up to the door and stout Brazilians and swarthy Egyptians invested in the more expensive items, such as a Louis Quinze fauteuil in russet "Utrecht" velvet or a charming little pastoral by Théodore Rousseau. Peter enjoyed watching Quilico as he worked on his "imitations," which he regarded as prankish whimsies, though he was rather startled by the prices they fetched. Quilico was especially clever in his hazy Corot landscapes, which usually had a cow standing in a copse of misty willows. He was also quite successful with his Delacroix odalisques and his plumed Algerian warriors sitting on wild-eyed chestnut horses. He was careful to use old pigments and dusty old canvasses, so that in a sense the antiquity was perfectly genuine, and he scrupulously studied his models from a grease-stained volume of photographs. After the painting was dry he cracked the paint by delicately pounding it; he sprinkled dirt in the crevices and "weathered" the surface with bits of sand-paper and finally covered the canvas with a coat of peppered shellac.

"Why do you bother with these things? Is it just for the money?" asked Peter.

"Not in the least," answered Quilico. "Oh yes, the money will come in handy, but what I'm after is a triumph, a very special kind of triumph. To deceive the whole world, not only the millionaires from America but the connoisseurs, the curators, the art historians of the future! What a victory! And the ultimate beauty is that no one will be aware of the victory. To paint like Ingres may be admirable, if you happen to admire Ingres, but to paint a genuine Ingres, that is nothing short of a miracle!"

"But why," said Peter, "do you bother, if you really despise all these people?"

"Exactly! Because I despise them! It's my own private vengeance. Nobody else will ever appreciate it but I'll snicker in my coffin. My own paintings were a failure, nobody bought them, nobody admired them, I was rotting away in poverty until I suddenly became a genius—a genius at fraud, which is a perfectly genuine form of genius. The world is a fraud, society is a fraud, the museums are frauds and the collectors are frauds, and even the money they pay for their miserable art is a fraud. So why shouldn't I play my own little role in the giant fraud? I'm the only one that plays his role with a perfect fraudulent integrity!"

They were walking in the woods after a lavish luncheon in Barbizon. Quilico had recently been making a lot of money with his forgeries but he still insisted on wearing his greasy scarves and dirty pullovers, and his only luxury was an occasional banquet at a two-star restaurant, to which he treated Peter with an air of grandiose generosity. The sun was shining, the birds were chirping, the lilacs blossomed behind the nunnery, and the sound of the brook was like the sound of children's laughter.

"Is nothing wicked, in your opinion?"

"Inner falsehood," said Quilico, "is wicked."

"To deceive others is not wicked?"

"Not when the others are false already." Quilico stroked his black mustache with a virtuous, reproachful air. The light from the foliage shone on his vixenish little face. "There's a certain integrity and even beauty in these paintings of mine. They are false but they glory in their falseness so that their falseness becomes sincerity. They don't strive for originality, they merely strive to be perfect forgeries, and there's something rather splendid in such humility, don't you think?"

"Is it humble to pretend you're Delacroix?"

"I'm not pretending that I'm Delacroix. Not to you nor myself, not to Trombetta and not to God. I am paying homage to Delacroix, the most devoted and slave-like homage, and the only thing I'm attacking is the fraudulence around me!"

Quilico's specialty was the nineteenth century. He did a splendid Daumier which they sold to an American museum for eight thousand dollars. He tried his hand at Courbet and he did a plausible Manet and a Maharajah who lived in Cannes bought an obscene water-color by Rodin. He soon branched out into modern painting, which was much less laborious, and his Vlamincks and Utrillos were sold to a gallery on Madison Avenue. Finally he decided to embark on more ambitious ventures and he started on a Poussin *Rape of Persephone*.

"I'll retire to Tahiti if I ever sell it," he said, opening a champagne bottle. "And then maybe I can work on a masterpiece of my own. Like Gauguin!"

II

One morning a pale blue limousine drove up to the house and an elderly gentleman stepped into the shop, followed by a chauffeur wearing a fez. The elderly man wore a camel's hair coat and a pair of slanting sun-glasses and his thick grayish hair was carefully combed in little waves. He inspected the antique furniture, which included a Louis Quatorze poudreuse, a Louis Quinze gaming table, and a Louis Seize commode. He also surveyed the paintings, which included a sketch by Boucher as well as a charming Marie Laurencin, both of them done in Quilico's most elegant manner.

"Have you any clocks?" said the gentleman. "I'm a clock-collector, as it happens."

The only clock in the shop was a clock of Meissen china; a Temple of Love crowned with Juno and a peacock.

"How much is it?" said the gentleman, smiling affably at Peter.

"A hundred thousand francs. Distinctly a bargain," said Peter.

"It certainly is," said the gentleman, nodding. "You seem to know about these matters."

"Not much," said Peter, blushing. "But a little. Inevitably."

The stranger's name was Mr. Styne, Mr. Alastair Styne, and he lived in a villa on the Riviera. Just a week after his visit a letter arrived from Eze, amiably inquiring whether Peter would care for employment as a "private secretary," which would include compiling a catalogue of first editions and *objets d'art* as well as tending to the correspondence with various book-dealers and auction-houses. The salary would be modest, only eighty thousand a month, but room and board would be included as well as some items of wardrobe.

"It's a pity," said Quilico. "Just when you were getting the hang of things."

"You're a fool," said Trombetta. "Moving in with a raving pederast."

But Peter had had enough of Trombetta's chicanery and Quilico's cynicism and he packed his little bag and took the second class to Cagnes.

The Villa Velma stood on a rock overlooking the valley below Eze. The mimosas were in flower and so were the peach trees on the hillside. Fat oil-jars on the balustrade were trailing manes of russet blossoms. Mr. Styne had his lunch under a trellis beside the pool, watching the chauffeur Mohammed and the Negro gardener Desiré do their swan-dives against a backdrop of bougainvillea. He usually wore an Algerian burnous or a Japanese kimono and the scent of lily-of-the-valley lingered about his person. The Chinese butler, whose name was Ling, poured the wine from a decanter and placed a small cutlet on the Nymphenburg plate.

"I don't suppose you'll believe me, Peter," said Mr. Styne, wiping his chin, "but I saw Marcella Sembrich in *Traviata* in Dresden. I saw Frieda Hempel in *Les Huguenots* in Covent Garden and I heard dear old Melba sing the mad scene from *Hamlet.* Those were the days. There was no one who could sing the Bell Song like Tetrazzini! I once presented a gardenia to Galli-Gurci in her dressing room. I'm seventy-seven, those marvelous injections have cut my age by thirty years, but I can assure you that I'm grateful that I was born in the nineteenth century!"

He kept his clocks in a row of cabinets at the end of the drawing room, except for the Louis Quatorze *buhl* clock which stood on the mantlepiece. There were Russian clocks and Bavarian clocks, clocks from Padua and Copenhagen. There was a Dutch clock with a silver dial surrounded by a garland of roses. There was a Venetian clock which played a minuet by Boccherini on the hour. There was a lacquered clock from Lisbon with seashells and sea-horses blown in gold over the surface of the case and surrounded by anchors.

"How," said Peter, "do you happen to be so fond of clocks, Mr. Styne?"

"They are the symbols," said Mr. Styne, "of my private victory over time. I'm a part of the past but I've survived remarkably well, don't you think? It's partly those Swiss injections and its partly my mode of living, which is thoroughly disciplined in spite of the evidences to the contrary. But most of all it's my philosophy. I believe in timelessness, like the orientals. Ask Ling. He believes in timelessness. Even Mohammed believes in timelessness. Only Desiré, who is a rascal and a pagan, is scared of time!"

Sometimes after dinner they would sit in the library, which was paneled in eighteenth-century boiserie. One wall was filled with books done in elaborate leather bindings. There were bindings by Godillot and Trautz-Bauzonnet and Maylander, and there were bindings engraved with the arms of Madame de Montespan and Maria Teresa. Another wall was filled with precious first editions of the seventeenth century. There were the *Fables* of La Fontaine and the *Maximes* of La Rochefoucauld, as well as *La Princesse de Clèves* and *Le Discours de la Méthode*. The most precious of all was Buffon's *Histoire Naturelle des Oiseaux,* which filled ten big volumes with beautiful hand-colored engravings. The third wall, which faced the fireplace, was devoted to poetry. Mr. Styne was a poetry *aficionado,* as he himself put it, and his collection was a monument to the outmoded, the faded, the discredited. There were obscure pamphlets by Rosetti and autographed rarities by Swinburne, but most of the space was given the poets of the Nineties and the early "Georgians." There were bibelots by Austin Dobson and Lionel Johnson; there were "sheaves of verse" by Lascelles Abercrombie and James Elroy Flecker. Occasionally Mr. Styne took out a volume and read aloud, his creaky voice caressing the lilting villanelles and triolets.

In the summer they dined on the terrace by the light of Moroccan oil-lamps and Mr. Styne's conversation swerved in the direction of carnal oddities. The entire history of art and literature, according to Mr. Styne, was under the sway of homosexuality, which he referred to as the "Athenian attitude" or the "Mohammedan mentality," or just plain "chinoiserie." There was no need to dwell on the examples of Oscar Wilde or

Marcel Proust. Not only Socrates and Plato as well as Leonardo and Michelangelo, not only Rimbaud and Whitman and Tchaikovsky were included in his list, but even relatively unsuspected candidates such as Goethe and Beethoven, not to mention Shakespeare and Tennyson and even Dickens and Thackeray, whose domestic crises Mr. Styne regarded as "symptoms," and whose works were obviously teeming with references to male beauty. Every man had a streak of the "outré" in his system, and the more he tried to deny it the more it enslaved him, said Mr. Styne. Don Giovanni was merely an invert doubly inverted, he insisted, and he presented a distinguished array of athletes and warriors to prove his theory. He was convinced that the majority of men spent their lives in camouflaging their tendencies, smoking pipes, playing football, wearing crew-cuts and visiting brothels, all of them infallible symptoms of more sinister inclinations which they tried to hide under exaggerated postures of masculinity. Even the boy delivering the groceries was under suspicion if he wore blue jeans, and the postman, who was an amateur boxer, was obviously "one of the brotherhood."

"People keep running down the sins of the flesh," said Mr. Styne, "but how about the sins of the spirit? They're the ones that bring misery! The envy and malice in one little village cause more unhappiness than the entire history of fornication, in whatever shape or form. People are obsessed with the thought of sex because they've never had enough of it. They're indignant because they're envious. It's all hypocrisy, just rampant hypocrisy. Nobody's soul was ever damaged by a harmless bit of hanky-panky!"

Once he murmured to Peter: "Tell me, Pierino, what are your habits?"

"Habits?" said Peter. "What do you mean, sir?"

"Tastes. Proclivities," purred Mr. Styne.

"I'm afraid they're very dull, sir. Very commonplace," said Peter.

"What a pity. You could go far in the world of the ethereals," said Mr. Styne.

Any misgivings Peter had felt were finally assuaged at the Villa Velma. Those little pangs of the past—his love for Cleophas, his love for Malcolm—had nothing at all in common with this orchidaceous atmosphere. There was certainly something childlike and submerged in his sexuality: his adoration of the seven sisters had always been wistfully spectatorial. But now that he caught the full aroma of what Mr. Styne called "the Florentine penchant," he knew that his own inadequacy, his shyness, his sexlessness, were not the products of inversion but of something subtler and still more personal.

As time went by Mr. Styne developed a fondness for Peter, in spite of Peter's indifference to Mr. Styne's philosophical outlook. They drove to Monaco to look at the aquarium and to Grasse to look at the perfume factory. They drove to Nice for the Battle of Flowers and to Cannes for the tennis matches.

"I'm going to turn you into a gentleman," said Mr. Styne with complacency. "It is démodé to be a gentleman but life is easier if you behave like a gentleman. People treat you with respect even if they secretly resent you. It's always useful to have good manners and know how to dress, my dear fellow."

Sometimes he said: "You're a splendid character, my boy. I shall remember you in my will."

Or: "I'm planning to leave you my Sèvres. You seem to appreciate it."

Or, rather wistfully: "I have no heirs. Would you like my clocks when I die?"

And there were moments when Peter detected a liquid blackness in his eyes, a flicker of terror, a hint of awareness of the looming emptiness on the horizon. His face had grown smoother and more baby-like with age and all his appetites were still intact, the gastronomical as well as the sexual. He still loved living, he loved the flowers and the sunlight and the beautiful people but in his eyes there was a tell-tale hint of something else, an inner panic that quivered like a cobra in front of a mongoose.

Sometimes Peter drove to Villefranche with the chauffeur Mohammed and they'd spend the day fishing from a boat which they hired in the harbor.

"It's funny," said Peter, "but you never seem to catch anything, Mohammed."

"I don't care," said Mohammed. "Does it matter if I catch anything?"

"Then why do you fish, if it doesn't matter?"

"I like fishing," said Mohammed.

"Oh," said Peter.

"You see," said Mohammed, "I have no luck, I was born unlucky. I've never caught a fish and I'll probably never catch one but sitting and waiting is good for the soul. I hope. I pray. My spirit flowers while I wait for the fish."

III

Peter discovered one morning that he had had his fill of the Villa Velma. The day always came when he had his fill of a given place. He had found Rome suddenly repulsive and he had found the Apennines unbearably sad. He found Paris depressingly brittle and he grew sick of the chicanery in Fontainebleau. And so it happened that he finally grew appalled by the Villa Velma. Not so much by the hot-house plushiness and the sexual innuendos as by the vacuum underneath, which sometimes bordered on lunacy. He soon felt, as he eventually did everywhere, that he didn't belong there. He didn't feel lonely exactly; but merely aloof and hopelessly alien.

There were times when this aloofness in him was almost like a sickness. He felt incapable of human intimacy. He felt caged in his isolation. But what was it, he kept wondering, that was really at the root of his separateness? He had never laid eyes on his father: that was a part of it perhaps. His mother had sent him away when he was a child and that was probably a part of it. He was frail and pale and queer-looking and maybe that was a part of it. He had lived with seven sisters and been enchanted, and that was surely a part of it. He kept looking for love but his love lay scattered among the enchantresses. He kept looking for a home in a world where homes no longer existed. He kept looking for ancestors but his family and his ancestry were lost in the mists. He kept looking for certainties but the world was steeped in ambiguities. There were times when he felt convinced that he was different from all other men: an ash-blond little gnome encased in a globe of impenetrable secrecy, perpetually watching and waiting, but doomed to perpetual solitude. And there were times when he even suspected that he really didn't exist at all but was merely an invisible watcher: a memory; an omen; an apprehension.

One day as he sat by the pool while the rest of the household was still asleep he saw a bird settling on the bough of one of the mimosas. It was a bird he had never seen: a brilliant orange striped with black. It had a long reddish beak and a tuft of white on top of its head. There was something about the bird which inexplicably moved him. Its queerness; its loneliness; its passionate delight in its very queerness and loneliness. It cocked its head at Peter, spread its wings in a dazzling sunburst, then flew over the trees and vanished from sight.

And once again, the following morning, he packed his bags (he had two of them now) and arranged for his visa and boarded the express train in Nice.

Two days later he stepped out into that cobwebbed ecclesiastical city which his granny used to talk about in the summery dusk at Cleghorn's Inlet. He immediately sensed something odd in the atmosphere. He passed a church. The two great doors were flung open at that moment and he could see the silvered saints shining dimly in the candlelight. A young officer in a pale gray uniform walked past with ice-blue eyes; a spotted bitch with swollen teats raced by with a bone between her teeth. The rain started to fall. A foggy rain, blue as evening, and the domes of the ancient church rose in the sky like great fists.

He left his bags at the wretched little "modernized" hotel, bought a map, glanced through the phone-book and started off through the labyrinth of alleys. Three names were on his list: Tadeusz Kosowski, Watchmaker, Ulica Krucza II; Irma Kosowska, Lessons in French, Ulica Wiejska 27; and Sonia Kosowska, Artificial Flowers and Funeral Wreaths, Nowy Swiat 42. He carefully studied the street signs, then crossed a cobbled square and entered a winding street that smelled of coal-dust and wood-shavings.

He entered the tiny watch shop. For a moment it seemed quite empty. Then he noticed a girl with two white braids sitting by the window.

He said gently in his halting Polish: "Could I speak to Pan Kosowski?"

She stared at him suspiciously. Then she crossed the room and peeped through a curtain. Finally she said: "Who are you?"

"My name is Kosowsky. I've come from America."

The girl's eyes hardened slightly. "We have no relatives in America."

"Perhaps, if I can talk to him . . ."

"He is sick. He is very sick."

"I am sorry. Maybe tomorrow . . ."

"No," said the girl. "Not tomorrow."

For a minute she stood silently, staring tensely through the darkness, and then she whispered: "Very well. He is sick but maybe he'll talk to you."

He followed her through the curtain into a stuffy little bed chamber. This room likewise looked empty, the bed was empty, no one was visible, but then he noticed something stirring in the armchair in the corner.

"Yes? What now?" squeaked the man.

"It's an American. His name is Kosowski."

"He's lying!" shouted the man.

"Maybe he is," said the girl reluctantly.

"Step closer. I want to look at him."

Peter walked toward the shape in the armchair, which was sheathed in a long gray dressing-gown spattered with stains and torn at the elbows. The face was like a ferret's: white and furry, crafty and merciless.

"You're an American?"

"Yes," said Peter.

"Go back," said the man. "And tell them the truth!"

"What truth?" said Peter uneasily.

"The only truth!" screamed the man. He shook his fist at the ceiling. "It's ugly and stinking! Go back and tell them!"

Peter waited a moment.

"Go! Go!" shrieked the sick old man. "There's nothing more! That's all there is! Lies and cruelty! Vomit and excrement! That's all there is! Go back and tell them!"

Peter stepped out of the shop and followed the street past St. Stanislaus and finally he came to a narrow house with pots of geranium in all the windows. In one of the pots was stuck a sign: "Irma Kosowska. French and Italian."

He rang the bell. A voice cried out: "Don't bother, darling! The door's wide open!"

The room was draped with rather cheap-looking oriental tapestries. An inlaid Turkish table stood in front of a cushion-littered couch. On the table stood a tea-pot and a dried chrysanthemum stuck in a vase. On the couch, half-reclining, was a heavily mascaraed elderly woman.

She grinned coyly at Peter. "Well, sweetheart? What's the news?"

"Forgive me for bothering you," said Peter.

"No bother at all! Just make yourself comfortable."

"It's not for lessons, I'm afraid," said Peter.

The woman laughed. "Who's talking about lessons? Jesus and Mary! To hell with lessons! If it's lessons you want you can go to the whorehouse!"

"My name is Kosowsky," said Peter politely.

"Well, what of it?" said the woman. "You want it free, just because of a name? How do I know you aren't lying?"

"I've come from America," ventured Peter.

"Don't put on airs," said the woman contemptuously. "I'm tired of hearing about America. America! America! What's so wonderful about America?"

"I thought that maybe . . ."

The woman sat up and pounded the tea-table furiously. "You can go to the devil, do you hear me? You're not so handsome as all that! To hell with your thoughts! To hell with your name! To hell with your silly simpering America!"

The rain had stopped falling when he stepped into the street again. A dampish breeze blew up from the river. He crossed the bridge and skirted the park, which was merely a gravelled square with an equestrian statue in the middle of it.

He paused and glanced about. The whole city looked infected. The shutters were closed; there was no traffic; the rain-streaked shop-windows were almost empty. The few pedestrians hurried past with stealthy, averted faces. It looked like a city in the grip of a pestilence.

But even so, in spite of the gloom and the drizzle and furtiveness, he felt a tension in the air. Something was lurking around the corner. A cadaverous piebald mare was dragging a cart down the street. The cart was empty; the driver had his hat pulled down over his face. An old woman hobbled past carrying a cat all covered with scabs. A factory whistle blew. A piano was tinkling behind a curtain.

At the end of the park was a broad gray building marked

42. A row of oblong signs hung from the wall next to the entrance. One of the signs, gold on black, said: "Sonia Kosowska—Floral Ornaments."

A middle-aged woman cautiously opened the door. She was vast, elephantine: the fattest woman he had ever seen. She wore a red velvet dress stained with sweat under the armpits. Her flesh bulged and billowed, every gesture set it atremble; her eyes were nothing but slits in a grotesquely puckered mask. On the table stood a decanter with a half empty glass and a plate covered with bones, crusts of bread, crumbs of cheese. The whole room was filled with flowers—bouquets of roses and wreaths of heliotrope, made of paper and wax and bits of wire and cheap satin. The smell of the artificial flowers filled the room—the smell of glue and dyed fabric, suffused with a certain intimate, quince-like pungency.

"Well," said the woman, "what do you want?" She spoke in a hoarse, mannish tone. Her hair was clipped like a man's. A cigarette drooped from her mouth.

"My name is Kosowsky . . ."

Her chin shot forward.

"I've come from America . . ."

She stared at him glassily.

"Well, you see," said Peter mildly, "I've been looking for my ancestors and I couldn't help wondering, all in all, in view of the name . . ."

The woman stared at him tensely through her Chinese-looking slits. There was a glint of appraisal, a rat-like flicker of recognition. She coughed hoarsely; a ripple passed over her bosom like a breeze over a sail.

"Oh, God," she muttered. "What a brute he was! What a fiend! With a heart of stone! We got married in Katowice and then we moved down to Poznan. He suddenly left me just like that and ran off to America. I had a baby but I couldn't stand the sight of her. I sent her off into the country. I couldn't help it. It wasn't my fault. It's a disease, that's what it is! It's a com-

pulsion, a lunacy! I tried to control it but what was the use?
He despised me! Oh, he was handsome, he was lovely as Apollo
but he was a devil! He was a fiend with two horns, he was a
stone-hearted monster!"

She stood motionless in front of Peter like some great forsaken monolith, absolutely motionless except for the flurries
that passed over that velvet vastness. There was a mahogany
mirror behind her and he could see her back reflected in the
mirror, with a fly crawling slowly along the nape of her neck.

Dusk fell as she spoke. The room darkened gradually. Her
features grew blurred; she turned into an enormous red Buddha.

"I still remember, it was autumn, we were riding out into the
country, two fine horses, as black as ebony and the leaves all
red on the maples. Ancestors, eh? You're looking for ancestors?
Let me tell you about those ancestors! He stripped me naked
under the trees, I still remember the whole foul business, the
leaves crackling beneath us and the crickets chirping in the
meadow. I started to cry, I was in pain, I felt he was ripping
me to pieces! It was like a great white snake writhing through
the middle of my body! And would you believe it, I hated him!
I hated the smell of that hairy scoundrel! I loathed and detested
him! I wanted to scratch out his eyes! And then that nakedness,
that filthy nakedness! I felt that my skin had been torn away,
I was turned inside out like a plum ripped wide open. I
wouldn't speak to him for a week. But then it happened, I
can't explain it, this awful longing, this desperation. You can
call it love if you want but it wasn't love, I tell you, it was more
like hatred! It was hatred all mixed up with a sickening bleeding
misery. I kept thinking of what he looked like, those teeth
clenched with frenzy, and the hair all over his belly and that
hideous thing digging into me! I could think of nothing else,
I went out of my mind with the memory of it. And that's what
they call love! Well, I spit on it, do you hear? It's nothing but
misery, just madness and misery!"

IV

It was a bright golden day, birds were twittering in the goose-berry bushes and the fields were all shining, with the dew still clinging to the buttercups. The bus stopped at a crossing and the driver cocked his thumb. "Two kilometres, maybe three. There's a big red church right in the middle of it."

Peter took out his bags and started to walk down the side road where the cart-wheels had dug ruts like gaping wounds in the thick red mud. He walked past a wheat-field which was rippling in the morning sunlight and then followed some pas-tureland which ended in a copse of baby birch-trees. Way in the distance he could see the walls of a big old manor-house. But the driveway to the house was shaggy with weeds and dappled with bluebells. An old man in a leather jacket came strolling past with a rifle; a bird that looked like an owl was slung from the belt of his jacket. There was something about the place— maybe it was the smell of the rain-soaked earth or maybe the clouds floating so peacefully over the birch-trees—there was something that stirred some old, unidentifiable memory.

The road turned abruptly and the village rose out of the valley: a jumble of dirt-splashed cottages with an onion spire jutting from the center. Two white oxen were pulling a wagon through the dung-matted street. Two nuns were following the wagon. They lowered their eyes as they walked past Peter.

Finally he arrived at a squat gray house at the edge of the market-place. A sign over the door said: "Stanislas Kosowski. Coffin-Maker."

A thin, blond woman with pale blue eyes opened the door and stared at him solemly.

"Is your father at home?"

"My father is dead," she said, expressionless.

"My name is Kosowsky," said Peter.

The woman looked at him blankly.

"My father was Thomas Kosowsky."

"*My* father," said the woman, "was Tomasz Kosowski."

Peter said: "You're my sister."

Her face froze. "I am *not* your sister!"

"Nearly my sister, then. My stepsister . . ."

A great tear rolled down her cheek.

"Come in," she whispered. "I'll take you to grandfather. We're all alone now, just the two of us . . ."

The old man sat in the workshop, staring out of the window. He turned his head when the stranger entered and nodded ceremoniously. The sunlight shone on the side of his face, leaving the other side in shadow, so that one of his eyes glittered brightly and the other was hidden in darkness. He was a handsome old man with long white hair that hung to his shoulders. A network of fine purple veins covered his cheeks.

He listened intently with folded hands while Peter told him his story. He nodded. "Yes," he said, "there's a definite resemblance, no question about it. The eyes, mostly. I see it in the eyes. He was hefty, a regular stallion, and you're skinny just like Maria, but that's often the way it happens. A thick-blooded father with thin-blooded children." He leaned back and fixed his one glittering eye on Peter. "America. Hm. Well, there it is. It's a modern world we all live in. When I was a child I believed in fairies. But times have changed. There are no more fairies. You're a modern sort of fellow, I can see it in the cut of your pants. You only believe in what you see and in what seems reasonable and makes sense to you. I'm old, much too old, I still believe in the Hand of God. I've never been to America. I still believe in fairies and witches. Time's short, I'm much too old. Soon I'll be leaving this crazy world. Step up, boy, step up. Kiss your miserable old grandfather!"

And so it was. That's how it happened. Simple and casual, like every ending. For three weeks Peter lived peacefully in the house of his grandfather, sketching in the forest every morning, helping Maria with the cooking, feeding the cat and the magpie, watering the asparagus, walking in the meadows.

Old Kosowski would light his pipe and sit on the doorstep in the evening.

"Well, you see, one can't help developing a certain attitude to people. I'm a coffin-maker. It's only natural that I think of people as corpses. When they walk down the street I already see them as corpses. I size them up. I think of their measurements, the price they can pay, the wood I'll use, the color of the lining, the brass fittings, yes, I even grow a little bit impatient . . . There, help yourself to the coffee, it's a regular luxury nowadays . . . One develops one's own philosophy, that's what I was talking about, isn't it? Life is waiting for death, that's all, and maybe one is aware of it and maybe one isn't but there it is, one's waiting for death and that's the one thing that's true of everybody. We've got this new society here but of course it's all a hoax, they pretend things are different but things will never be different. Death is the one big thing that finally happens to us, not making love or making money. People make love and make money just to keep the whole thing going, just to breed more candidates for the coffin and to keep the coffin-makers busy. Maybe they're aware of it and maybe they aren't but there it is, you can't deny it!"

He was proud of his beautiful coffins, which he said were the best in Poland. He was very fastidious about the wood, which he chose with great astuteness. And he was equally fastidious about the linings, taffeta for some, brocade for others, and occasionally merely muslin or a high grade quality of cotton.

"Business is bad," he said glumly. "People are living much too long now. Too few young people and too many old. What's the point of it? It makes for gloominess . . ."

He looked disconsolately at the ceiling. "I've always had

one great ambition. To produce a masterpiece, one last chef d'oeuvre, a kind of swan-song, you might say. The loveliest coffin in the world. A coffin that will make people's eyes pop. Rosewood and ebony, beautifully inlaid, the finest Italian silk, brass fittings from Paris, Bavarian zinc, the whole works. But what's the use? There's nobody left who deserves such a coffin. And who'd appreciate it, except the worms? That's the tragedy with coffins . . . All that beautiful craftmanship stuck in the earth and nobody to appreciate it!"

After supper Peter went strolling in the fields with Maria. She must have been thirty but she was as lean and trim as a boy. Her breasts were as flat as a child's and her eyes were like a child's. She wasn't exactly an idiot, it was more like a lingering vacancy. Something or other had failed to develop. What should have happened had never happened to her.

Once she said, "Yes, I remember! I know who you are now. I was walking down by the stream, it was Easter Sunday and the sun was shining . . ."

"Yes? What happened?"

"I crossed the bridge and a little frog was sitting on a pebble beside the stream. He looked up with his sad little eyes and he started to speak to me. 'Darling,' he whispered, 'weep for me, weep for me!' 'Why should I weep for you?' I said. 'One little tear, just one little tear, please!' So I wept for the poor old frog, and as I wept he grew transformed, he changed into a tall young man with ash-blond hair and rosy cheeks."

"Yes? And then?"

"But that's the point of it! The man was you!" said Maria excitedly. "His eyes were your eyes! His voice was your voice! Yes, I swear it!"

"And what happened?"

Maria looked puzzled. She frowned; she was trying to remember. But then she shrugged her shoulders and said, "Isn't it funny? I can't remember!"

And they wandered back home through the stillness of the evening.

But the stillness of the place was deeper than the stillness of mere peace. It was like the stillness of a hiatus, the ghostly calm of a limbo. As he walked through the fields in the morning or through the market place in the evening he grew aware of something glassy in the air, a trance, a petrification. Instead of finding a place where he had roots and a people to whom he belonged he found his loneliness more insuperable and sickening than ever. As he watched his thin, pale stepsister sitting beside the stove or his gaunt, one-eyed grandfather out in the workshop it was like looking across a chasm deeper than time, as deep as death almost. He no longer was able to paint; the brush fell from the canvas. He was no longer able to think or to care about anything. One day a spotted deer stood in the middle of the path and looked at him. Maybe it was the look in the eyes of the deer that suddenly did it, that suddenly changed it all. "Hurry! Hurry!" the eyes were saying. "So little time, so much to do still!" And finally it dawned on him that his whole obsession with loneliness and restlessness was really a mask for something else, an elaborate camouflage for a deeper intensity.

The following morning he packed his bags and said goodbye to the old coffin-maker, who was sitting beside the chicken-coop, whittling away at a little crucifix.

"Goodbye, grandfather."

"Goodbye, my boy. Kiss me on the cheek. Here's a present for you. It isn't much, and if you were older I'd give you a lovely brass-lined coffin but you're young, you sneer at coffins, you only believe in what you see!"

Down by the gate to the manor-house he saw Maria standing under a poplar tree. Her hair had been neatly braided and she was wearing a white lace dress, with a ribbon around her waist and a golden chain around her neck. She looked like a girl dressed up for Communion except that she was a grown-up woman, flat-chested and a trifle feeble-minded but with eyes as pure as an angel's.

"Goodbye, brother."

"Goodbye, sister."

He kissed her tenderly on the cheek.

"I wish I could come along," she said. "It's so sad and so empty here!"

On top of the hill he looked back toward the village, which already was hidden behind the birches. Maria was still standing by the crumbling gate of the old manor-house. He raised his arm and waved at her but she stood there motionless; white and thin and lonely and unreal, like an apparition.

v

"It won't be easy," said the thin man, whose name was Echevarria.

"Yes, I know," said Freya quietly. "I don't expect it to be easy."

"And it won't be especially pleasant."

"I don't expect it to be pleasant."

"Tell me. Why do you want to go? You're absolutely sure that you want to go?"

"Because," said Freya, "I want to change myself. Outwardly I've changed enough already. You can see the change in my face and I accept the change without regrets. I never was beautiful and I never tried to be beautiful, and now I'm ugly and there it is. All it did, this sudden ugliness, was to make me want to change myself inside."

"You are both honest," said the man, "and brave. But this change. What kind of change?"

"It all," said Freya, staring into the sherry glass, in which her twisted face shone like a mask, "it all has something to do with islands. I always believed in the possibility of happiness, a strong and invulnerable happiness, and to keep believing in happiness I needed to look for another island. It was quite unconscious, I assure you. I was fascinated by islands. I kept dreaming of islands. I saw islands as the answer to everything."

"And your paintings?" said Echevarria. "Did they answer your love for islands?"

"Each of my paintings," said Freya, "was a tiny island in its way."

"And now?"

"I am horrified by islands. I'll never set foot on another island. Don't misunderstand me. It isn't anything that happened on one of the islands, it's rather what didn't happen. I'm frightened of islands and their terrible emptiness, and I'm sick of my paintings and their island-like emptiness."

The Spaniard nodded. "So it is. We grow frightened sooner or later. No so much of what we did or what we felt or what we were but of what we didn't do and didn't feel and didn't become. We grow frightened of our own reflections, with their corpse-like grin of unfulfillment."

The crowds were milling through the dusk. Their footsteps sounded like rustling leaves and their gossiping voices sounded like the rustling of fallen leaves. Freya and the Spaniard sat under the awning of a little café near the end of the Rambla and the people glanced at them uneasily as they passed the table. They paused imperceptibly and then quickly looked away again, as though there were something forbidden or ill-omened about the place, or about the particular table, or about the man who was sitting at the table.

"And you?" said Freya.

"Oh yes," said the man. "I quite forgot. I'm still alive, I still exist but there are times when it slips my mind that I'm still existing. You speak of your ugliness but your ugliness is nothing to my own, I promise you. Your ugliness is an outward accident but mine is an inner necessity. You were born to be happy and I was born to be miserable. You were born for the sunlight of a paradisical island, but you discovered after a point that the paradise could be an inferno. I was born for God knows what. Saintliness, grandeur, self-sacrifice! That's what I thought. But the grandeur and saintliness turned mysteriously into acid, and the point is that one can't fulfill oneself merely by performing a beautiful role. One can seem to become the role and people may think that one has become it, but it's only for a while and then the role shrivels away and one is left like a grinning effigy, an empty horror dangling in emptiness."

"Yes," said Freya. "A scarecrow."

"Time is short," said the Spaniard softly. "The birds are wheeling on the horizon. Another twenty or thirty years. A mere instant in the churning of the galaxies. It seems incredible, I can hardly believe that it is the destiny of the race to kill itself. But something will certainly happen. The slate will be wiped clean. Nobody will care about a Beethoven sonata or a soliloquy from *Hamlet*. Small white crustaceans, no bigger than a pinpoint, will climb over the rocks. A new consciousness will evolve. There will be another chance. Another beginning."

"Well," said Freya, "you are a pessimist and I am an optimist and that's the difference. It's not in what we believe but how we feel in believing it. I'll go with you to the Xingu and we'll do what we need to do. It won't be particularly pleasant but at least it won't be an island and you're perfectly right, Pablo, I'm not easily frightened. I am not afraid of the snakes or the insects. Or even the sicknesses."

The Spaniard smiled. "Snakes. Insects." His haggard face grew distorted but his eyes were delicately illuminated and sweetened by the smile. He got up and said, "Tomorrow then. At nine. I'll see you in the customs house." He walked hurriedly down the Rambla, grotesquely tall, like a man on stilts, and she watched him until he vanished around the corner of the Grand Victoria.

VI

Peter put down the letter and walked slowly toward the window. The sun was shining on the long gray façade on the opposite shore. A funeral procession was crossing the bridge and after the column of cars came a few straggling pedestrians, all in black, eyes fixed on the pavement. A whistle blew. A dingy house-boat passed slowly under the bridge and the smoke from the stack flowed like a garland over the bridge. A few heads were raised and then discreetly lowered again. The boat chugged downstream in the direction of the Grand Palais and the funeral procession disappeared under the foliage in front of the Louvre.

He walked back and glanced at the letter which was lying on the table. A bee came buzzing through the window and settled on the envelope.

And quite suddenly it was as though this sequence—the funeral and the boat and the little bee—had opened a door inside him, like a key turning a lock. He felt neither excited nor exultant; merely dazed with a gentle shock in recognition of the thing that was there, that had always been there, waiting to be recognized. He sat down and picked up the letter and read it a second time, more carefully. And after the daze of the shock was over and the recognition had been accepted, what he felt was a violent and almost uncontrollable surge of longing, as though for years this same longing had been lurking in a shadowy crevice and had suddenly shot forth with all the impact of an illumination, deepened by years, sharpened by waiting, and all the more dazzling because of the shadows that had hidden it.

He left a telegram with the goat-faced concierge and hurried into the travel office around the corner. It was all uncannily simple and easy and obvious. He spent the following morning on a farewell visit to the Louvre and that same evening at dusk he boarded the steamer in Marseilles.

It was a Portuguese freighter called the *Fatima*. His cabin was close to the engine-room, a stinking alcove rather than a cabin, with the fetid air reeking over him like a ripple of oil. It rained as they passed Gilbraltar but then the weather grew brilliant. They passed Madeira and the feel of the tropics slid through the air. The days were balmy and beautiful but the nights were a nightmare; he lay dripping with sweat, listening to the wheezing and thumping of the machinery. He heard the giant screw throbbing and the scuffling and shuddering of the waves, and when he opened the cabin door he heard the creaking of hammocks and the muttering of the sleepers. Now and again there would be a crash of something falling in the darkness or the sound of a chain rumbling ponderously against the metal. So he crept to the upper deck, stumbling past the ropes and the iron windlasses, and spent the night in a deck-chair under the starlight.

The heat grew sharper and the nights grew deeper and at night under the stars the ship looked strangely abandoned, like a kind of ghost ship. She moved aimlessly across the water, which after ten days at sea seemed endless in its immensity and sinister in its calm. Under the calm lurked an invisible savagery and bloodshed, and when Peter stood on the deck and watched the wake coiling below him he felt the spell, the dangerous enchantment of all that immensity. He felt that he was moving toward some far-off enigma and that the wake, bright with phosphorus, was pointing toward something which was lost forever.

The Dutchman De Korb came and stood beside Peter.

"Yes," he said, "in America you have this wonderful optimism, this faith in the future, in future wealth and future glory and the elimination of evil, and in Europe we have this pessimism, this clinging awareness of death and darkness, but the queer thing I've noticed is that it's the Americans who grow afraid. With all their optimism and faith they are the ones who grow afraid. It's those cynical Europeans who build a wall against darkness, and it's the Americans who grow panicky when they see the beast prowling on the horizon . . ."

De Korb was immensely fat and of a phosphorescent pallor. He had spent his whole life in places like Java and Surinam but the sun of the tropics had never touched his flesh. He never stepped into the sunlight, he was terrified of sunlight, he slept the whole day long and prowled about during the night. He wore even at night a huge raffia hat and a dripping silk shirt and shoes of perforated suède. The sweat looked like quicksilver as it rolled from his painted cheeks and in his fatness there was a hint of anguish, a flutter of monomania.

The days floated past with a menacing slowness. They entered the Caribbean and the smell of coffee seeped through the atmosphere. The boat swayed in the azure water, so blue and serene that in the distance it was indistinguishable from the blue of the sky.

A part of the crew on the *Fatima* was Chinese, from Macao. They'd squat in the shade of the deck eating rice with their chopsticks and one of them, a boy named Li, would dance about with a parrot on his shoulder, swaying to the music of a battered phonograph while his friends clapped their hands. In the shade lay three oxen and a pair of white-dappled ponies and the smell of hay and ox-dung hung over the deck. Now and again the *Fatima* slid into the crystal waters of a harbor, a foul, forsaken vessel among the yachts and holiday steamers. Little boats drifted past filled with naked black boys who grinned contemptuously and waved their hands at the filthy old freighter. On the wharf the spectacled vendors sold things of tin and mahogany and porcelain, urns and rattles and talismans, chains of beads and bottles of scent, and some of the girls had their hair colored a deep and brilliant scarlet, with silver ear-rings dangling all the way down to their elbows.

And the heat grew still sharper and the nights still more brilliant and one night old De Korb loomed through the shadows and stood by Peter. Something eerie had happened to the Dutchman. His immensity was sagging hideously, it hung from his bones like a great white sack. His face had turned into a kind of shrunken balloon which was grinning feverishly under the tall Chinese hat.

"I don't understand it at all," he whispered, staring desperately at Peter. "I am baffled, entirely baffled, I can't comprehend it at all. Do you know what I dreamed last night? A herd of elephants. That's all. Just elephants. They were crossing a valley. They came to the end of the valley. The moon was shining on their tusks. It seemed like the end of the world in all its nightmarish loneliness, those big gray beasts with their wise little eyes and the wind in the bushes. What did it mean? Will you tell me? Why do I feel so entirely baffled?"

He clutched at the railing, limp with delirium. "Yes, I remember it now, it's all quite clear to me. We were walking in the woods one morning. I saw a rabbit and I shot and killed it . . . Wait! Don't go. What's that I hear? Drums beating? Or somebody singing? . . . People, people! God forgive them! The treachery and meanness, the insane stupidity! And why? What's the point of it? Why can't they learn to be sensible? . . . There. Yes. Well, I've forgotten. No use worrying about it any longer. Still, it's a pity, a burning pity. Meanness, meanness, nothing but meanness!"

The following evening toward sunset two young sailors brought up a bundle which they carefully placed in the shade of the upper deck. It was a long shapeless bundle wrapped in a tattered brown canvas. They placed it on a plank. A priest stood by; they lowered their eyes. After the prayer and the Amen the plank was raised and slowly tilted until the corpse slid into the sea with a glittering splash.

VII

The trip up the river lasted eleven days and a half. The water changed from oyster to emerald to obsidian. For the first two days the delta had spread out like a giant turtle, glazed and windless in the murderous heat, sprinkled with drab faceless islands. In the distance a spire of smoke would rise from a dingy fishing village whose corrugated roofs shone through the leaves like yellow scales. The inertia of the bay seeped even into the colors—the sky lost its blueness, the vines were peppered with parasites, the distant boats dangled like spiders in that huge gray stagnation.

Then for a week they sailed upstream through the monotony of swamp and jungle. Often the scene looked so exactly like an earlier one that the senses grew tangled and the *Guimaraës* seemed to be retracing its path through time as well as space. Morpho butterflies skimmed over the treetops like broken chips of sky and the catopsilias blew over the marshes like a cloud of orange petals. Even the villages were all alike, haphazard clusters of slanting huts, and the villagers had the same, vacuous solemnity of opium-eaters.

The river deepened; the water darkened. Unidentifiable shadows stirred in the thicket and the tangle of green was splashed with violet, flame, canary. Long-necked birds stalked through the lilies and chromium fish flashed in the shallows. The monotony of the trees sharpened into a procession of vegetable fantasies. Even the flowers that hung from the vines took on a crazy eroticism—coral vulvae and purple scrota lay mirrored in the stillwaters. Claws and intestines flung from the boat vanished like lightning in invisible jaws. A beetle as large as a rat clung to the pillow one morning.

In the evening of the eleventh day they came to the village called Sessimbra. A towering man that looked like a mantis stood on the edge of the wooden pier. He wore an absinthe-colored shirt and a pair of lemon-striped slacks.

"I am Dr. Echevarria."

Peter shook his enormous hand.

"Miss Nightingale is away. Unfortunately."

Peter stared. "Away? Where?"

"She has gone to Tomar." There was a tightening of the eye-lids, hardly perceptible. "There's been trouble in Tomar. An unusual outbreak, certainly not cholera but some of the symptoms are a little like cholera. I was against it but she insisted. Who can tell? She may be right. Two of the boys went along. Maybe she's right. You can't be sure."

"Tomar?"

"It's hardly a village. More like a scattering of tiny camping sites. I've never been there myself. Dr. Pereira has told me about it . . ."

They strolled up the path toward the hospital, which stood in the middle of a clearing. It was a shabby white-washed struc-ture: a central section which contained the wards, flanked by a clinic, a dispensary and an operating room. Two of the assist-ants, both Brazilians, were playing chess in the dispensary, which smelled faintly of iodine and hydrochloric acid.

Peter peeped into the adjoining ward, which was nearly empty. In one bed lay a boy whose arm had been ripped by a crocodile and in another lay a man in the throes of delirium.

"And what," said Peter an hour later, as they sat with their glasses on the veranda, "do you think was at the bottom of it? Merely a scar? Or something deeper?"

"How can we tell," said Echevarria, "what is really at the bottom of our decisions? Just once in every life a man or a woman comes to the crossroads, and maybe they are aware of it and maybe they aren't, maybe they feel the gravity of it and maybe they don't, but the decision must be made and the decision is irrevocable and even no decision at all is a kind of terrible last decision. She made her decision and she was perfectly aware of the gravity of it. The scar was purely an accident. There was a hunger. A call."

"And those islands . . ."

"Oh, those islands! They were symbols, nothing but symbols. She wanted to reduce the chaos into dimensions that she could handle. Her paintings too. They were bits of chaos woven into patterns that she could handle. But the time finally came when she saw the futility of islands. The only way to handle the chaos is by ignoring the chaos and the only way to save oneself is by drowning oneself in self-forgetfulness."

"And now?"

"Well, she is happy, if you want to call it happiness. Our happiness when we're young is very different from our happiness when we're older. There was happiness in her eyes. It was unmistakable. She had the power of innate happiness and when the original happiness was broken she found another kind of happiness. You may think I'm exaggerating, I don't like this kind of word, but in her own special way she had the purity of a saint."

"Do you think I will find her?"

"Oh," said the doctor, "you will probably find her. Look." He leaned over the map and drew his finger along the river. "You turn into the Rio Rosso and then you follow the fourteenth tributary and from this spot, which they call Figueira, you cross the hills to Tomar. Aipuri will go with you. Yes, you probably will find her." He leaned back and spread his huge, knotted hand over the table. "As I say, I see no point in it. It is merely to satisfy a need in you. Not even curiosity. Not even solicitude. Merely an obsession. Pure romanticism. Oh yes, you will probably find her, there's nothing sinister in the Rio Rosso and don't misunderstand me, I applaud your motives, I applaud your loyalty. But you'll find very soon that the land is bigger than the obsession and it's possible, just barely possible that you will suffer a disappointment!"

Night fell. It was as quick and complete as the fall of a curtain. In less than three minutes the scales of fire died over the Xingu and the tangle of leaves dissolved into a massive black screen. The stars began to blaze. The insects started to scream. The woman drew the netting and set the oil-lamps on the table.

VIII

The Indian boy Aipuri came to his room soon after dawn and with Aipuri he went down to the yellow house by the pier and had his passport elaborately inscribed by the local authorities. Then he walked up the path hand in hand with Aipuri and bought a coriara from the shriveled little man who ran the local post office. And after he had paid for the coriara, which was a dug-out with a sail and a paddle, he went to the store with Aipuri and bought the provisions. Six hard-boiled eggs, some cakes of casabe, ten tins of meat and a bottle of quinine as well as a jar of water-purifying tablets: to this were added a machete, some beaded bracelets and tiny mirrors and a cucumber-shaped calabash which served as a water bottle. The Spanish doctor also gave him a mosquito net and some articles of clothing—khaki shorts, rubber sneakers and a white pongee helmet. For the coriara he paid forty-eight dollars and the provisions cost him another nineteen dollars. He kept fifty dollars for emergencies and gave Aipuri ten dollars and the rest of his dollars he left with the Spaniard Echevarria. The following morning at dawn he said goodbye to Echevarria and headed upstream in the cocoa-colored dug-out.

The wind was cool in the morning but toward noon it grew suffocating. They slept in the shade and woke up two hours later. The scenery changed from a tropical dazzle to a flame-edged delicacy. They paddled upstream until they came to a broadening of the river and Aipuri pointed to the left and said softly: "Rio Rosso."

The water changed from mahogany to a rosy-streaked green; the jungle gave way to a land of fern-sprinkled glades. The inlets were covered with rugs of flowering water-cress and python-shaped lianas hung from the feathery gray branches. There were no signs of humanity but there were movements among the leaves which suggested the shifting of a curtain, the delicate stirring of an eavesdropper.

Once they noticed a long canoe moving silently in the distance but it vanished abruptly under the overhanging foliage. They passed tributary after tributary. Peter kept count of them: there were seven. Gradually the river grew narrow and the banks turned into a quagmire. Slime-coated roots spread their claws from the grottoes of greenery. The light softened and Aipuri whispered: "Now time for make camp, senhor." He carefully guided the dug-out to a sandy island in the middle of the river. The island was free of growth except for a fringe of mud-soaked lilies and he spread the sail on the sand some fifty feet from the edge of the water. He thrust the net-poles into the sand and quickly draped the mosquito net; then he opened a meat-tin and laid out their dinner. And though the décor was bleak and the menu disconsolate they ate greedily and cheerfully and the Indian murmured: "You lovely man, senhor."

"How old are you, Aipuri?"

"Seventy, senhor. Older than turtle!"

"I don't believe you, Aipuri."

Aipuri looked hurt. "Maybe sixty."

"You're younger than sixty!"

"Maybe fifty . . ."

"You're younger than fifty, I'm sure, Aipuri."

"Nobody know, senhor," said Aipuri. "Me born on Madre de Dios and nobody remember it how or when, senhor. Aipuri older than lizard and only his body still young, senhor."

Aipuri's voice was melodious and mocking, like the voice of a little bird, but there was a melancholy in back of it which was like the mournfulness in his eyes. He might have been sixteen or seventeen; his limbs were supple and hairless but his eyes, both gay and defeated, were the eyes of a very old woman.

Scarcely a minute after sunset the mosquitoes came out in a torrent. The men slipped under the net and lay down on the canvas sail. Aipuri during the day wore only a loin-cloth on his body and at night he took the loin-cloth and hung it on top of the netting pole.

"Keep off ghosts, senhor," he murmured with a decorous expression.

Peter glanced at the sweaty ribbon a little bit sceptically.

Aipuri grinned; he pointed casually to his dark skinned genitalia. "Smell of seed," he said slyly. "River ghost no like seed. Much seed in Aipuri keep off two-face crocodile!"

The net was black with mosquitoes but after a while the moon came out and the insects darted away and the roar of the jungle crashed through the wilderness.

IX

Soon after daybreak three days later they finally came to the fourteenth tributary. Tall hills rose in the distance, ruddy and cone-shaped, like great wigwams. The place was called Figueira but there was no sign of life: a broken pier half-covered with reeds and the charred remains of a customs hut. They fastened the coriara with a chain and tied the provisions in a knapsack and Aipuri led the way with the machete in his hand. The moment they entered the thicket they felt the heat welling over them. It was a thick clammy heat, not like the blaze that fell on the river but stagnant and fetid, as though it were crawling out of the marshes. There were traces of a path but they had to watch for the scars of the hatchet; a network of vines was already woven across the corridor.

The path dipped into a hollow. A gaseous stink filled the air. The lianas shrouded the place in an adder-blue twilight. The mud oozed over their ankles and squirmed up to their knees and they waded across the quagmire through a fog of mosquitoes. Big black sacks seething with maggots hung from the boughs overhead. Soon their thighs and even their armpits were speckled with leeches. When they reached the edge of the swamp they were reeling with misery. They squatted under the trees and scraped off the leeches with a razor blade.

The path started to climb. The heat grew less hideous. A faint eastern breeze flowed from the direction of the mountains. They paused for a rest and then started uphill again and quite suddenly there was a strange transformation in the atmosphere. The path turned. A shower of pollen fell from the barricade of ferns. Great birds sat perched on the boughs like crimson lyres or bronze helmets. The air was alive with thousands of candle-shaped blossoms and the strangest of all were the butterflies, which swirled through the light like a shower of confetti, a confetti not of paper but of blue lamé and gold brocade.

They sat down under a fern and ate their eggs and casabe. Through a gap in the trees they could see into the valley. Aipuri pointed to a thimble-shaped knoll at the end of the valley. He whispered "Tomar" and rested his head on Peter's shoulder.

"Much anger in Tomar. Mountain ghost no like Tomar . . ."

From the bottom of the valley they could see the huts of Tomar: thatched domes set on stilts in a large dusky semicircle. They followed a wrinkled stream to a palm-shaded waterfall and here an assembly of Indians stood waiting beside a precipice. At first there were only a few but as Peter came closer he could see the feathery *tonores* gathering cautiously in the thicket. A smell of charred meat hung unpleasantly in the air; a ribbon of smoke rose from the huts in the distance.

Aipuri spoke to the chief, a bow-legged dignitary with the face of a tortoise. His oily hair was dyed purple; his teeth were as black as ebony. He leaned forward and ran his fingertips across Aipuri's temples. Then he nodded: the rest of the villagers stepped cautiously closer. They were naked except for the long wooden chains which hung from their shoulders, decorated with snake-bones and feathers and polished green shells. One of them, a powerfuly built fellow who kept standing beside the chieftain, wore a large dappled headdress made from the skin of a jaguar. Most of the men were heavily scarred; some were bleeding from open sores; some were hobbling on canes; one was crawling like a wounded animal. Only the man with the headdress looked healthy and stalwart. The rest looked decayed, hollow-cheeked, flushed with fever. The women were almost invisible, clinging in a cluster among the shadows, but they too looked emaciated and dead-eyed and comatose.

They listened carefully to Aipuri, interpreting his dialect to one another and glancing occasionally at Peter, who sat on a trunk in the shade of a palm-tree. They spoke more and more shrilly; their eyes flashed; they growled and gesticulated. The man with the headdress stepped forward. He spoke angrily to Aipuri and a man with a club-foot started to dance in front of the chieftain.

Aipuri returned, looking tense and dejected.

"What are they saying, Aipuri?"

"Bad things, senhor," said Aipuri.

"What about the lady? Where is the lady?"

"They no speak about lady."

Peter stared at Aipuri. "What has happened to the lady?"

"Bad things, senhor," said Aipuri. He looked guiltily at Peter. "Much anger in Tomar. Much fear of Ancuru."

"Ancuru?"

Aipuri looked agitated. He touched Peter on the forearm. "Come, senhor! Back to Sessimbra! Tomar full of badness! . . ."

Peter opened the knapsack and took out the bracelets. "Here," he said, "give them to the chieftain. Tell him we are friendly, please, Aipuri."

Aipuri took the bracelets and knelt down in front of the chieftain.

He returned, looking miserable. "Much fear of bad mountain-ghost!"

Peter opened the sack again and took out the mirrors. "Give them to the chieftain, please, Aipuri. Tell him we are looking for the medicine lady."

Aipuri crossed the clearing and spread the mirrors in front of the chieftain. But the chieftain raised his hands and turned his face toward the mountains. The man with the club-foot snatched a serpent out of a jar and wrapped it around his neck and started dancing in front of the chieftain. The man with the headress walked gravely toward Peter and took him by the arm and led him gently into the village. They crossed the clearing, followed by a procession of purple-haired elders. The stench of rot and suppuration mixed with the odor of burning straw. A drum started throbbing; a woman let out a wail. The procession moved silently through the length of the village and came to a halt at the end of the path, where a heap of ruins lay smoldering; wisps of smoke leaked from a heap of burned thatch and charred rafters. The chieftain came to a halt. He clapped his hands ceremoniously. An old man stepped out of the column and crossed his arms over his chest. The Indians turned their heads and fixed their eyes on the white man while the man with the club-foot knelt in the dust between two bushes. He carefully raised a mat which had been spread over a prostrate body and the man with the headress led Peter toward the body. It was charred beyond recognition and grotesquely distorted; impossible to tell whether it was a man or a woman. The clothes were shriveled to ashes and all the hair had been burned away. The whole corpse was nothing but a mass of enormous black blisters.

The drumbeats started again. The man with the headdress took Peter's elbow and the procession marched solemnly back through the village.

X

They sang. Their piping voices wove monotonously through the firelight and after a while it seemed that the voices were merely an echo of the firelight; they were ribbons of flame that hung floating over the embers. *"Pala unini quari. Esse tabi. Pala unini tabi . . ."* Now and again one of the elders came tottering across the clearing and held out the melon for the prisoners to sip from. It was a thick rosy liquor which tasted like asparagus. The man with the club-foot sprinkled a powder over the fire and the flames turned from scarlet to a fierce metallic blue. They kept singing and singing while the women wailed in the background. The man with the headdress stepped into the center of the circle. His eyes shone like a madman's and his hips started to writhe and he cried: *"Saba sali! Anaquari! Saba salari!"* They kept sipping from the melon and their heads nodded tipsily and the wailing of the women died away in the darkness. The flames sank and died. Silence spread through the village. The drunken bodies lay scattered among the ash-powdered urns. Time passed —maybe an hour. The sense of time had deserted him. He slept and awoke and then slept and awoke again. There was a shuffling of naked footsteps. Then silence once more. A voice whispered suddenly: *"Paraga, senhor! Paraga!"* He felt the rope gently loosening as the knife carved through the knot and Aipuri lowered his head and murmured: "Quick, quick! No more dead now . . ."

They crawled through the dew-drenched thicket toward the shade of the precipice. The mist of early dawn moved like a dream through the empty valley.

XI

The sun was rising when they finally caught sight of the tributary. It lay shining way below them, twisting through the trees like an anaconda. They followed the route which Aipuri had hacked two days earlier and which already was invaded by the raging tongues of vegetation. They both were thirsty and horribly hungry; the meat and the casabe had been confiscated and all that was left was the little bottle of quinine capsules. The heat had grown poisonous. It was more than heat; it was a frenzy, a pestilence. It stung like a swarm of ants. It had arms like an octopus. Sweat poured from their bodies as they lurched through the swamps. Aipuri's eyes were violently bloodshot. He was shivering with fever.

Finally they reached the banks of Figueira and stepped out on the broken pier. The coriara still was there, carefully hidden among the reeds. Aipuri cleared out a place in the shade of an *amapu* tree and spread out a layer of the thick rubbery leaves.

Peter dipped his hands in the river and sprinkled his face with the lukewarm water. Then he sank back into the warm loving arms of Aipuri.

He fell asleep instantly. Fantastic images passed through his mind—a twilit harbor surrounded by temples, a bearded satyr playing a lyre. The sun shifted. He was awakened by a spear of light that struck his forehead. A delicate, persistent clicking rose from the ground close beside him. He glanced down: thousands of termites were nibbling away at his tattered clothes. He rolled over and crouched in the shade and shook the insects from his body. A sickening pain shot down his spine. He crawled to the edge of the water and dipped his head in the plum-blue river. A haggard face stared back at him feverishly: the chin was covered with beard, the matted hair was a mop of curls, the eyes looked desperate and savage, like a starving animal's. His clothes were nothing but a blood-stained tangle of rags. His shoes were ripped into shreds; a moss-green rash covered his body.

Aipuri stepped from the bushes and knelt down beside Peter.

"Eat, senhor. Eat! Eat please!"

He held out a handful of long white worms from which a yellowish liquid was oozing. Peter retched with disgust but Aipuri said gently: "Eat, senhor. Look bad but much luck for soul, sweet senhor . . ."

Peter kept his eyes closed while Aipuri fed him the worms. As he bit he felt their skins burst like grapes under his teeth and the soft inner flesh squirt up at his palate. The taste was as smooth as cream, with a faint flavor of cocoanut. Revulsion gave way to an uncontrollable rush of appetite and he clutched Aipuri's wrist and hurriedly wolfed down the rest of them.

Aipuri nodded and smiled. "Now full of good moon-ghost . . ." They lay down and slept soundly until the stars shone over the river.

Epilogue

The light of the flame danced on the walls; it hovered gently on the fluted inkwell. It cast its glow on the marble dolphin and floated casually across the globe, where the vast stretch of Asia glimmered faintly like the skin of a lion.

"What went wrong?" said Augusta.

"Nothing went wrong," said Peter thoughtfully. "That's the way it all happened and that's the way that destiny wanted it."

"Destiny! And what is destiny?"

"What is hidden," said Peter, "is destiny. What we think of as the reality of life is only a veil hiding the reality. And the thing that is hidden under the veil—that is destiny."

"Words, words," said Augusta. "We keep looking for reality but the more we juggle with words the more twisted it becomes.

We can't capture the reality with words. We can only feel it in our blood. We can't capture the truth. Either the truth is in us or it isn't.''

"What is truth?" said Peter. "Is there such a thing as truth when it comes to people?"

"It is only in people," said Augusta, "that truth exists. There's only one kind of truth and that is purity of heart. All other kinds of truth, all the truths that are printed in numbers, they're just stratagems, just acrobatics. Truth has no meaning when it comes to infinity."

Peter glanced at her face. She had aged, her hair was graying, and the unhappiness in her eyes had deepened into a rocky tenacity. For the first time he realized that Augusta was very beautiful: not beautiful as a woman is beautiful but like a landscape or the ocean.

"And still," said Augusta, staring at the fire, "I keep wondering what went wrong. Say what you wish, something went wrong. And it wasn't just destiny."

"It was a sickness," said Peter. "There was a sickness in the atmosphere. God knows where, God knows why. There was a sickness but we didn't recognise it."

"Oh," said Augusta, shrugging her shoulders, "I came to recognise it in the end, all right. I finally grasped what it was. It was sloth. It was half-heartedness. When we live with half of our soul and love with half of our heart and create with half of our energies and believe with half of our spirit—that is evil, that's what evil is, that's when we defile all that is best in us. Whatever we do with our whole soul, that is good, that is salvation. And what we do with only a part of ourselves, that is ugly and brings corruption."

"We made blunders," said Peter, "all of us. We couldn't help it. There was nothing to guide us."

"It's never the blunders," said Augusta, "that hurt us in the end. Whatever we did, with all the blunders and follies and miscalculations, and God knows there were plenty of follies and miscalculations, at least we finally shook off the ugliness of un-fulfillment. We entered the quagmire. We cleaned our hearts by befouling our bodies."

"Is it the only way?" said Peter.

"So it seems," said Augusta.

"Is it the way things were intended?"

"So it seems, almost," said Augusta.

They could hear Mrs. Bontecue setting the table in the dining-room and Daphne calling softly to the spaniel out in the garden. The breeze rattled the shutters and the ivy slapped at the panes, and the sounds all blended together into a single delicate insistency, which was the insistency of mortal life still continuing, and of all the strange separateness of things still continuing.

"And all that hurrying about . . ."

"Yes," said Augusta, "all that hurrying."

"Was it flight or pursuit?"

"They are the same in the end," said Augusta. "The lion pursues the lamb because he is fleeing from death and the lamb flees from the lion because he is still pursuing life. Was Daphne pursuing or fleeing? Was Consuelo pursuing or fleeing? and Freya? What was she pursuing, do you suppose? And Barbara? What was she fleeing?"

"Maybe it was love that Freya was pursuing and maybe it was love that Barbara was fleeing."

"And then everything was turned around. They exchanged their roles. And that's the mystery of it."

"Queer, isn't it?" said Peter. "Do you know what Grace said to me? She said that all seven of you were really the same person. And that what happened to one of you really happened to all seven of you, and so in the end you all shared in the same experiences."

"Grace was the only one," said Augusta, "that never fled or pursued. She sat back and accepted. The truth was in her from the beginning."

"Truths, phantoms," said Peter. "How can we ever tell the difference? Sometimes it's the truth we keep looking for and eventually the truth becomes a phantom, and sometimes it's a phantom we look for and eventually the phantom becomes the truth. Barbara's truths turned into phantoms; I could see it in her face. And Freya's beautiful phantoms finally turned into truths."

"And Grace's truths *were* her phantoms," said Augusta, nodding her head. "When we found her in that cave I knew that for her it had been a fulfillment and it wasn't sad or dreadful but merely inevitable."

"Grace was the first one that I loved," said Peter.

"You loved all of us, didn't you?" said Augusta.

"Yes," said Peter. "One by one."

"Even the ones who didn't deserve it."

"You all deserved it. Much more than I felt it."

"Words, words," said Augusta.

"Even the words are ghosts," said Peter, holding his palms in front of the flames. He turned from the fire and looked at Augusta with sudden intensity.

"Tell me, Augusta, what do you think? What do you hope for after death?" His voice grew softer. "Tell me the truth. Are you frightened of dying?"

Augusta closed her eyes and folded her hands in her lap. "I feel old, terribly old. I feel as old as the Appalachians. I've thought about these things, I've been thinking and thinking, but I realise that there'll never be an answer to such thoughts and the things are much too big for any of our thinking. Sometimes I feel that I'm immortal, but then I know that it's only a word. Immortality is merely an endless prolongation of time and time, just like space, is only a terrestrial hallucination. In eternity and infinity, which are the only true reality, neither time nor space exist and immortality is meaningless. Time and space are only things that exist for the living, and when we die we finally enter eternity and infinity. And it's hard for us to grasp, it's almost impossible for us to grasp, the thought of dying forever is so hideously painful, but one thing I'm sure of and that is that death will bring an end to everything that any of us can possibly imagine. But something else I'm equally sure of, I can't conceive of things otherwise, and that is that we all will enter eternity when we die. And in a way, though we'll never grasp it, we'll become a part of the true reality and the illusions of identity will shrivel away, like the shell from an egg. And in the end, though I've never believed in any God that people have told me about, I know that when I die and finally enter eternity I'll become a part of God and I'll find my true existence."

"Yes," said Peter. "But in the meantime we're still alive. We're still separate."

Augusta smiled; her face melted. "We're still alive. We love and suffer."